Forthcoming titles from Strong Books by
JERRY LABRIOLA

MURDERS AT BRENT INSTITUTE
STOLEN IDENTITY

MURDERS AT HOLLINGS GENERAL

MURDERS AT HOLLINGS GENERAL

BY
JERRY LABRIOLA

STRONG BOOKS

Strong Books
P. O. Box 715
Avon, CT 06001-0715

Copyright © 2000 by Jerry Labriola

First Printing

ISBN 1-928782-00-0

Library of Congress Catalog Card Number 99-70735

Published in the United States of America by Strong Books, an imprint of Publishing Directions, LLC

The characters, events, institutions, and organizations in this book are wholly fictional or are used fictitiously. Any apparent resemblance to any person alive or dead, to any actual events, and to any actual institutions or organizations, is entirely coincidental.

Cover photo: Boden/Ledingham/Masterfile

Printed in the United States of America

To my wife, Lois,
whose encouragement and
insightful suggestions helped this story unfold

ACKNOWLEDGEMENTS

This book would not have become a reality without the talents of editor Roberta J. Buland, cover designer Deena Quilty and layout designer Ellen Gregory. A special salute to my daughter, Sue, to Al Grella, and to the Goshen Writers' Group who served as sounding boards and offered quality advice. Kudos to Publishing Directions, LLC and their imprint, Strong Books, for their constructive input, and to Madeleine L'Engle for her support. Finally, hearty thanks to those others who reviewed the full manuscript and kindly provided the testimonials included herein.

Jerry Labriola

1

Dr. David Brooks remembered the man behind the surgical mask as shorter and left-handed.

"Strange," he whispered, turning to Dr. William Castleman, the young Director of Emergency Medicine, "back in the Navy, he was a *little* man. They used to give him a stool to stand on when he operated."

"Maybe it was years of military food," Castleman said, straightening his starched white jacket. "Gave him a growth spurt."

"Sure, and made him ambidextrous." David had removed his blue blazer and placed it across his knees, half again higher than Castleman's.

They sat together in the center of the first row overlooking Suite 7, the surgical amphitheater of Connecticut's venerable Hollings General Teaching Hospital, on a viewing balcony crowded with doctors, nurses, medical students, administrators and news reporters. Frozen forward, eyes homed in on the operating surgeon, their breathing stalled for a collective silence. Before them, bright lights reflected off an otherwise invisible glass partition. On the wall, a clock's second hand cogwheeled to precisely three-thirty. The balcony smelled scrubbed and antiseptic.

David asked himself whether he remembered wrong.

Poised to the left of the operating table, its occupant intubated and asleep, the surgeon drummed his latex fingers on the patient's chest awaiting a scalpel to be snapped into his right hand. An anesthesiologist guarded the head of the table while three other physicians were positioned to the right of the body, including the hospital's Chief of Surgery and the Associate Chief. Six nurses bustled among the instruments, lights and monitors. An electrocardiographic tracing showed the rhythmical complexes of the patient's heart.

A rotund nurse broke from the pack and like a hydroplane, glided off to the side. A wisp of chalky hair strayed from her constrictive cap. She eyed the operative field and spoke into a microphone attached to her surgical gown. "Ladies and gentlemen, I'm Virginia Baldwin, the Nursing Supervisor of our Surgical Department. We're indeed honored to have Dr. Raphael Cortez here with us today. He's about to make his initial abdominal incision and the pancreatic transplantation will begin. I'd like to inform you—especially those of you from the media—that the patient is Mr. Charles Bugles, the Board Chairman of this hospital. I mention it because somehow I think it's fitting that he should be the first to receive an organ through the transplantation program here at Hollings General. I'll come back to you every so often during the procedure, but I'll leave the microphone on. It's pretty sensitive and you may pick up instructive interplay here. Dr. Cortez, please feel free to explain anything—anything at all. I'm sure our students would be very appreciative." From a speaker above the viewing balcony, her words resonated against the drone of the patient's monitored heartbeat.

Castleman stretched up and cupped his hand around David's ear. "Doesn't a doctor like Cortez deserve prime time—like eight in the morning? Why three-thirty?"

David cupped back, "He may be famous, but he's just a visiting dignitary. Remember, it's his first case here. Anyway, who would they bump? Friedman? Scully? Matthews?" He tweaked his floppy mustache which was as wide as his bow tie. "There'd be mutiny," he added, flashing his thin linear smile, not the curved one—happy and pronounced—when only central incisors would show, their companions retracting out of sight, his skin florid.

"You kept in touch with the guy?" Castleman asked.

"Only with Christmas cards."

"Have you seen him since he arrived?"

David considered before answering. "No, I haven't had a chance yet. I understand the Credentials Committee acted on him. I don't think anyone's met him except them—and maybe they just looked at his photo."

The surgeon made the initial transverse incision with a flair. Nurse Baldwin announced, "Here we go."

Castleman leaned closer to David. "Did he do any transplants when you were in the Navy?"

"Not really—except on animals. But, he was always experimenting. Then after I left, he started with pancreas trials while everybody else around the country was doing hearts and lungs and kidneys. I guess you'd say he's a pioneer in pancreatic replacements."

David pushed down on his feet, leveraging his six-five frame for a better view of the surgery forty feet away. He saw the surgeon's eyes flit over the abdominal cavity, toward his assistants and back. They tugged on retractors and applied internal sutures while a nurse dabbed the surgeon's forehead.

Two minutes into the operation, the Chief screamed, "No, not there, Doctor!" Blood spurted against the palm of his gloved hand. "What are you *doing*? Where are you *cutting*?"

The anesthesiologist said calmly, "Pressure dropping—eighty over forty."

The Chief said, "Christ, let me get in there!" He ran around to the left of the table and tried to muscle aside the operating surgeon.

"Get back to your position, Doctor! You may be Chief, but I'm in charge of this case. Open the blood drip to full. Get four more units ready."

David jumped up and pressed his hands and face against the glass partition. He saw blood well up in the patient's abdomen and heard the beep become thready. Then, there was a continuous hum, the kind that had torn through his stomach too many times before. Castleman bit his knuckle.

"More sponges!" the Associate Chief shouted.

"Ligate above. Ligate above!"

"I can't see. Suction. Suction, damn it! How can I ligate if I can't see?"

"Then feel. Son-of-a-bitch, feel!"

"Can't get a pressure!" the anesthesiologist cried. "Forget the drip—pump the blood in. And push in a pressor."

Five seconds later, David stared at a straight line on the heart monitor. "Oh, my God!" he said and felt his own blood drain from his face as he regarded Castleman.

"And I arranged for Bugles' surgery myself. Cortez. He's supposed to be the best in the world at this thing." He spoke as if wounded by his own words.

David looked back down. Personnel poured in from adjoining rooms. Faces contorted. The suite swelled into chaos. Babble vibrated from the overhead speaker.

"Get more suction going—hurry up!"

"Pressors—pressors—and more blood!"

"Move over, move over!"

"Hundred per cent oxygen!"

"Trendelenberg—get him in Trendelenberg position!"

"He's in it, damn it!"

"Run the blood in—run it in, c'mon!"

One doctor injected medication into the patient's heart. Others packed sponges tightly around tubes straining to suction from the operative site.

David wondered aloud: "Did he cut through the aorta?" He answered his own question. "But, there'd be blood on the ceiling. No, maybe a renal artery. Or more." The heart tracing remained flat.

David searched the room for the lead surgeon. He had vanished.

"I'm going down through the lockers. Bill, you go straight down. See if we can head off Cortez."

David scrambled from the row of wide-eyed, muted onlookers and had to duck as he bolted out a back door, down a flight of steps and into the afternoon quiet of the surgeons' dressing area, on his way to the operating suites on the second floor. He stumbled among the rows of lockers, pushing the pace beyond the usual for this behemoth who now felt more cut out for sleuthing than medicine, instantly obliged to trace a murderer instead of a runaway teenager. Deep in the green interstices, David stopped abruptly when he came upon a small man draped over the bench before an open locker. He was in street clothes and motionless.

David turned the body over and recoiled at the sight of a pearl dagger handle protruding at an upward angle from the man's left chest.

He felt for a carotid pulse; there was none. He pulled away the victim's limp arm which had fallen over his face.

"What ... the ... hell. It's ... Raphael Cortez! Then who ... ?" Suddenly, David wasn't sure he wanted to graduate to this level of criminal investigation.

"Code 3 in OR, Code 3 in OR," the public address system blared. David felt his shirt clinging to his shoulders.

He examined the man's hands. No defensive cuts. He saw no blood around the dagger, yet noted a small pool on the floor below the body and a few spatterings on the bench. David recalled no injury on Cortez's backside but above the belt buckle, he spotted a linear entry wound. He lifted the shirt and found no surrounding discoloration suggesting to him that the dagger's hilt had not been pushed against the skin. Stabbed just enough to paralyze before the final plunge, he thought.

He leaned over to inspect the dagger. Third left interspace, precisely over the heart.

"Who's this? Are you okay?" Castleman shouted from behind.

David stiffened to full height. "Good Christ, man, how about some warning?"

"Oh, sorry. Who is this?"

A forehead taller than his colleague, David tapped downward on his chin. "Sorry myself. This here, I'm afraid, is Cortez. The guy upstairs was an imposter. Any sign of him?"

"None. How could that happen?" Castleman squeezed each word to a higher pitch.

David preferred his own question: "What about Bugles? Never came around, I assume."

"Never. He exsanguinated. What the hell's going on, anyway? If Dr. Imposter wanted to kill Bugles, why go to that extreme? Why not a bullet in the parking lot? And then later, using a dagger? Or a stiletto, or what-ever-the-hell that is."

"Same thing, although this is a big jobbie."

Castleman bent forward and circled his head around the dagger.

"And don't say, 'then later,'" David said.

"How's that?"

"Then later implies after, and this was no after. This was before." He nodded toward the body. "He was the first to go."

"It sounds like you're about to get involved in this one, my friend."

"That I am," David said, distantly.

"Well, now you can stop complaining about your fill of simple runaways and missing persons."

David made a quick notation in a notepad. "Bill," he said, "why don't you notify Administration. And better include Security. I'm sure they know about the botched surgery, but tell them about Cortez. I'm calling Kathy."

Castleman walked to a wall phone as David rushed down to a small corner office. He sat at a desk and scribbled a few more notes in the pad before placing a call to Kathy Dupre, his past high school sweetheart, present contact at the Hollings Police Department and future Mrs. Brooks. He heard the phone ring only once.

"Homicide. Detective Dupre here."

"It's me. You won't believe this. You're sitting down, right?"

"David, between some of your weird neighborhood visits and some of my weird homicide business, I've heard it all. Remember the book we're going to write— *Housecalls and Homicides*? Yeah, sure. Maybe every so often we should devote a night to writing instead of … but that's a different story. What's up?"

"Just a couple murders."

David could hear Kathy thinking. Finally, she asked, "Where are you?"

"Here, in the hospital."

"Murders—in the hospital?"

"You got it. One's a stabbing. The other—poor guy— got his belly hacked up. Bled out."

"His belly?"

"Right in front of us. In the pit."

"David, what are you talking about?"

"The board chairman, Charlie Bugles, was having pancreatic surgery. Remember the Dr. Cortez I told you about—the guy I met in the Navy? Well, he's right around the corner from me. Dead. Fancy dagger stiff in his heart. The surgeon was an imposter. He did his dirty deed, under lights and all—in the amphitheater—then took off. We all saw it. You or somebody better get over here."

David hung up the phone, hoping Kathy would be assigned to the case, not that he had ever been disregarded by others in the Department. In fact, he enjoyed a unique relationship with them. They called on him when time was at a premium and stressed the advantages of his amateur status, like conducting searches without warrants, or entrapping without legal worries. In return, they documented his cases for future licensure. It had all started during his Navy days. Naval Investigative Service. What better choice for undercover operations than a medical officer, he had been told. After discharge, he pursued medicine and part-time sleuthing, and no one doubted his commitment to both.

At Cortez's locker, he found Castleman staring at the body.

"Security's on their way."

"So are the police," David said. "I'd better do my preliminary snooping."

"It sounds like an official ritual."

"Not official at all." He cocked his head. "Come to think of it, if I ever get licensed, there go my snoops."

"Look, David, I'm probably in the way here so I'll head back to the ER. Hope I can concentrate. Call me if you need me. Good luck ... and, jeez, what a hospital."

"Thanks Bill, and don't be surprised if some administrative types show up there in shock."

Once alone, David winced when he crouched down on his bad knee to examine the dagger site at close range. He shifted knees. Tendonitis had been kicking up, the price of vigor against younger competitors in percussive karate. Why keep going back to Bruno's? He visualized the matted studio. It even hurts to climb the damn stairs there.

Teacher lines broadened at his temples as he studied the weapon's entry angle and its handle. Why was it

pearly? Too pretty for commandos. It had to be ceremonial, then. He lined up its length against the width of his
four-inch palm. It was exactly the same. He mouthed a
calculation. Handles are usually forty per cent, meaning
the blade in there is six inches. This here's a ten-inch dagger. Some big sucker!

David put the back of his hand to the side of Cortez's
face. It was warm. The body appeared waxy-blue and its
lips and nailbeds were pale. He pressed on the skin and it
blanched. He verified Cortez had been killed within the
hour.

Stabilizing his flexed knee with his forearm, he lifted
himself up and stepped back, inspecting the pool of blood
beneath the bench. A tiny interruption in the pool's border registered in a double take, and he cast his gaze over
the floor toward the exit at the end of the aisle. He sidestepped to his right, peering down at a string of large,
irregular blood stains: one ... two ... maybe three.

David walked out the door and into a stairwell. He
inspected each step as he descended and found no other
traces of blood until he saw two spots on a landing and a
single, lighter one halfway down the remaining flight.

On the first floor landing, the left door opened into
a passageway leading to the pathology labs while off to
the right was an exit to an exterior alleyway. The route
from the lab up to Surgery was the one routinely taken by
pathologists for frozen section examinations during surgical procedures. How many times had he traveled that
way?

David peeked into the lab and, scanning its central
corridor, detected no blood trail from that vantage point.
He paused, then decided to call on his old mentor, Dr.

Ted Tanarkle, the hospital's Chief Pathologist. Head down, he strolled past the Emergency Medical System's unused dispatch window and, finding no further stains to that point, hurried past the Autopsy Room and into the sprawl of interconnecting laboratories: Cytology, Hematology, Bacteriology, Chemistry. He fixed a smile on his face and sensed his technician friends had questions on theirs.

Rounding the far turn, he arrived at Tanarkle's secretary's desk which was tucked in a corner and surrounded by cases of yellow pathology journals under glass. She had just put down the phone.

"Dr. Brooks. I haven't seen you for weeks," Marsha Gittings said, patting both sides of her hair, straw-colored and mounded like a haystack. Fiftyish, lofty and buxom, David believed she sacrificed breathing freedom for glandular elevation.

"Hello, Marsha. Ted in?" David picked up a miniature skeleton from atop a case and blew away its dust.

"No, he's gone for the day but he'll be back in the morning. Can I help you with anything, or shall I have him call you?"

"No, that's okay. I'll drop by tomorrow."

He replaced the skeleton and was about to leave.

"David, wait," Marsha said. "What's going on?"

"With?"

"The murders." She kneaded the back of her neck. "It's scary."

"You know about them already?"

"Are you kidding? The whole hospital knows."

"I don't *know* what's going on yet, Marsh."

"Are you handling any of it?"

"Yes."

"Good. Ted will be happy about that."

David retraced his steps to the landing and felt bothered by the secretary. Murders in a hospital! And I'm bothered because she seems matter-of-fact? But how about me? Or, is even an investigator supposed to wear alarm on his sleeve?

Careful to use his elbow and not a hand, he pushed on the emergency bar of the other door there and received the full blast of a January squall whipped into the alley along with its snow, like in a wind tunnel. He welcomed the refreshing taste of some flakes and, brushing away the rest, released the door which snapped shut.

He leaned against the wall and ran his finger over his bottom lip. Did the murderer take his gown and scrub suit and gloves with him, or what? Did he exit deliberately past Cortez? He must have. But why? It's not the quickest way out.

David headed back through the lockers, pausing to inspect the floor between Cortez's body and Suite 7. He saw no blood and stopped short of entering the suite door, fearing distraction by the few people he heard conversing inside.

His finger returned to his lips. The son-of-a-bitch must have paused to look at Cortez—the pool is under the bench. So … the blood must have gotten on his toe, on his shoe's surgical slip-ons. But why stop to look at a guy you already killed, especially when you're in a hurry? And the blood can't be from Bugles because there's no trail from there to here. Could the murderer have killed Bugles before he gave the chiv to Cortez? That doesn't figure. He was taking Cortez's place, remember? You couldn't have him and Cortez scrubbing at the same time.

He tried to visualize a shoe covered with green cloth that was smeared with blood in varying degrees of clotting.

He slapped his forehead and rushed to the bottom of the stairs again and looked closely at both doors there. The bottom edge of the left one—the one to Pathology—bore a slight pink stain.

When David arrived at Suite 7, security guards swarmed about the halls surrounding it. He shook hands with one of the men he recognized.

"Just a quick look-see, that okay, Hank?"

"Sure, doc, but don't step in any blood."

He walked in. The room was empty except for the purplish corpse of Board Chairman Bugles which still lay in the tilted Trendelenberg position. The skin was waxy, almost translucent and the eyes were flat. David looked around, imagining all the stainless steel had lost its sheen, so blasphemed as a backdrop to murder. It was one thing for a surgical procedure to go sour; it was quite another for the nobility of such a place to be violated, for the trust of the consigned to be so severed.

He saw tubes dangling loose from the anesthesia and suction apparatus. Syringes, surgical instruments and blood-caked towels were scattered over the floor. Stools and a cautery machine lay toppled against a wall as if the room had been ransacked.

At the operating table, stationary retractors were still in place exposing the upper two-thirds of Bugles' abdominal cavity. David peered inside, scrutinizing the now malarranged vicera and supporting structures. He had seen his share of corpses before, but this was a carcass, a melange of crimsons, lusterless and brick-dry, and of deflated intestines tucked behind gauze strips. They probably suctioned away all the blood he had. The more he bled, the less they could see. So the more they suctioned. He examined the retro-spaces at both flanks where kidneys, now prune-like, had been shorn of their protective tents. And look there: both renals cut. Up here: liver lacerated end to end. On the other side: spleen sliced in two. David balled his hands into tight fists. There's the scalpel. One final swipe from quadrant to quadrant, and the bastard dropped his weapon before he bolted.

He had seen enough. Leaving, he heard voices coming from the hallway. He recognized Kathy Dupre's.

"We got here as quickly as we could. The traveling's terrible," Kathy said.

David resisted the urge to iron out the pout of her lips with his own, to pat her short wet hair which had kept its waves. He had often reminded her she was too petite and luminescent for a cop. A blue London Fog was tucked over a purse that hung down from her shoulder. She wore his favorite black suit and, this time, displayed a badge on her hip pocket as he had often requested. "Keeps the bird dogs at bay," he had once said. "Especially when your stockings match the suit. And hair, come to think of it." He imagined the feel of her unpowdered skin, the brush against her high cheekbone below a hint of eyeshadow.

"David, I'd like you to meet my new supervisor, Detective Chief Nick Medicore. He's moved here from the West Coast."

David clicked him in as drab as Kathy was striking. "How do you do, Chief?" he said. "Welcome to Connecticut, your mirror image on the East Coast."

"Except for the weather, but thanks. How do you

stand this stuff, Dr. Brooks? It's bad for my bowling ball." He pointed to his head.

"We don't, and it's David." He reached down to shake Nick's outstretched hand while engaging his eyes. The Chief was the first to disengage.

"Medicore?" David said. "This should be right up your alley."

"Some people call me Mediocre," Nick replied with a crooked grin.

The Chief carried a gray overcoat and wore a white turtleneck under a checkered jacket, and there was a badge over the swelling near his breast pocket. His nose was redder than his red face, and he was smooth-shaven with cheeks that bore venous markings like tertiary roads on a highway map. David wondered why he hadn't grown a beard.

"And you know Walter Sparks, our criminalist?" Kathy said.

"Yes, of course. Good to see you again, Sparky ... I guess."

David nodded to the others who had arrived: Alton Foster, the hospital's administrator with two of his associates; the medical examiner and his deputy; and four uniformed police officers. He motioned Foster aside and put an arm on his shoulder. "I'm sorry this happened here, Alton. Hope I can speak with you about it in the next day or two."

"Yes, yes. God, this is so terrible," Foster said, his voice cracking. His hair, normally plastered for hurricanes, was disheveled.

David signaled Kathy and she joined them. "What happened to the Emergency Response Team?" he asked.

"This is it, now. It's been streamlined."

"No Evidence Officer?"

"You're looking at him ... I mean, her."

Nick walked over. "So how's your seven-eighths professional sleuthing coming along?" he asked. "Kathy's been telling me about you. You're really building up the credits."

"Not nearly seven-eighths, I'm afraid, but I'm working at it." David was not sure about the man and hoped his elbowroom would not be narrowed. "Have you seen the other body, yet?"

"No, but we'd better look there first," Kathy answered. "Then, Sparky, you can do your dusting and stills and whatever. Where's the other one, David?"

"In the locker room, down the hall."

David felt the vibration of the digital phone attached to his belt. "Wait up," he said. He checked its display face. "It's Belle from the Hole."

"His nurse/secretary," Kathy said, looking at Nick. "She operates out of a cubbyhole they gave him downstairs in the basement. He's never dared call it an office."

"A hole with no rent," David said, punching in numbers. Contact was immediate.

"Everyone's looking for you," Belle said at the other end.

"Who's everyone?"

"The world. But mainly the media. They already know you're investigating the murders. Isn't voice mail working on that pocket doohickey of yours? I've been trying to get you."

"Preoccupied, my sweet. It's out about the murders?"

"Out? Since I know, then everyone must know. When

are you going to let me in on what happened? You okay?"

"Frazzled, but yes. I'll go into it when I see you. Jasper's house call still on?"

"Yes, definitely. His office called four times already."

"I'm on my way. Look, Belle, I'll go alone this time."

"That's all right with me, but there go the books and here comes more insurance rigmarole. I still say you should carry some forms with you."

"Come off it, Belle, what do I know about what line they should sign?" David signed off and placed the miniature unit back into its leather case on his belt.

Nick creased his forehead. "House call? I thought they were obsolete."

"And if I don't make it soon, Dr. Jasper will be furious. Probably is, in fact. Unless he's heard about the commotion here."

"You're making a house call on a doctor?"

"No, not *on* him. *For* him. That's what I do now. I'll explain later. Bye. See you in about an hour." He wheeled around and groaned, clutching his knee. "Tough to get old," he said.

"C'mon," Nick replied, "you're young enough to be my son."

"If you diapered him when you were still in—let's see—high school senior year?" Kathy said.

"Close enough," Nick said. "And, tell me, Dr. Brooks, shouldn't those house calls be your first priority?"

David took it as a statement, not a question, and he pretended not to hear. As he limped by Sparky, he said, "I can phone you later if you're not still here?"

"Sure."

David paused, expecting a tag to the response, but there was none. He thought briefly about hanging around to see if he could learn anything from the police procedurals but, instead, pressed a door activator and breezed through the surgical booking and administrative wing, waving to several doctors and nurses before reaching the outer stairwell. He was certain the hues and cries from a small reception room were those of corralled news reporters. On the third floor, he crossed a ramp to the parking garage. The hospital had not yet reclaimed his private spot even though he had resigned from full-time employment there a year ago.

He exited to the garage and walked down a slight incline lined with cars parked at right angles on both sides. He paid little attention to a car revving up at the next higher level.

Suddenly, he heard a roar and screech and knew the car was bearing down in his direction. No time to look back. He locked his knees and, ignoring a twinge of pain, dove between two parked cars, somersaulting onto his haunches.

He smelled rubber as he twisted around to glance down the incline. But the car had rounded the lower corner and disappeared.

What the hell! David's first impulse was to give chase, but it was too late for that. He stayed down for a moment, embracing both knees, and although stunned, managed to give thanks that Belle had not come along for the house call. As his breathing normalized, he also gave thanks to all fight-or-flight stress reactions and to the exalted levels they could take one's body. Has there ever been a choreographed mini-second somersault?

He pulled himself up on a fender, dusted his trousers and, wobbly as a decelerating bicycle, headed for his car.

So, these are the stakes. Welcome to murder investigations, pal.

CE LINE DO NOT CROSS POLICE LINE DO NO

2

CROS

David weaved his black SL500 Mercedes convertible along the backroads of his Connecticut birthplace, thoughts thrashing through his mind, having conceded that the light but swirly snow had nullified his option of lowering the top—even though he believed he was a better fit when exercising that option.

His stature was a genetic mutation, he theorized—quantum leap from diminutive parents. They had operated a small corner store—Brooks Grocery—for thirty-five years before reluctantly folding six months earlier, another casualty of the supermarket blitzkrieg. Along the way, they had budgeted for their only child's college and medical school tuitions at Yale.

David wouldn't activate the heater until the engine had warmed up. Usually when he arrived where he was going. He wore a blue tweed jacket and charcoal trousers. No hat, no overcoat. Just his trademark black scarf and gloves. From December to March, he added t-shirts, his only other winter concession. He eschewed clip-on bow ties in favor of the real McCoy. He appeared top-heavy, with an upper-body contour of a less towering man, perhaps a boxer. Empty-hipped, his trouser legs broke clear to his toes, a sight not lost on most observers. He would offer a dismissive wave. "Helps warm the tops of feet, you know."

It was an effort but he forestalled a consideration of his brush with death. What's there to consider anyway? The killer used a dagger and then a scalpel. Why not a car?

Pondering what he would eventually say to Nick Medicore about the origin of his house call practice, he wondered how much detail he should offer. The bottom line was that he had soured on both private, office-based practice and full-time hospital practice. It was a question of freedom. Freedom from staggering stacks of paperwork, from the annoyances of dealing with insurance companies and Health Maintenance Organizations, and from other elements in the burgeoning Managed Care approach to medicine. Meanwhile, he had become increasingly intrigued by police detective work. He had, in fact, always considered himself a medical detective, deriving more pleasure from making a diagnosis than from treating a disease. Yet, he didn't want to abandon patient care altogether. The solution, then, in avoiding the issues that irked him and in fulfilling his investigative and patient contact interests would be to restrict his practice to afternoon house calls for other doctors and to reserve mornings for sleuthing. David preferred the word, "snooping."

He had been given a brief medical history about Megan Kelly, the patient he would soon examine and knew that a youngster with diabetes was as brittle as they come—that he might find her about to lapse into coma, or about to convulse from too much insulin, or anything else in between. But for the last half-mile to the Kelly apartment, he overrode the medical scenarios he had waded through many times before.

Sure you want sleuthing at this level? Why not? My hospital. My friends—gone. Friends? Cortez maybe. But Bugles? Now, one less Christmas card and no more aftershave stenches. And what's with what's-his-name, Medicore? Just feeling people out?

He told himself he wouldn't miss those mornings in the halls when he was between clinical meetings and the old industrialist strutted around, wearing his Board chairmanship on his sleeve, intolerable but for his money. That was Bugles. Nonetheless, he had been murdered now along with one of Surgery's pioneers.

David aggravated over the two deaths. He had never been so close to major crime before. Never heard the frantic cries of doctors who knew better, in a killing whose M.O. was unspeakable. Never seen a pearly dagger in the chest of a distinguished colleague. Never tasted fumes while brushed by a speeding tire.

But the surgery was brutal murder. A knifing in a sanctum sanctorum. And he was almost number three. Accept the challenge? Bring it on.

David had called on ten-year-old Megan once before, when he had found her on the verge of insulin shock because she had played a vigorous soccer game but had not reduced her insulin dose beforehand. So, he had no trouble finding the third floor flat behind Hollings' newest strip mall. Small black bag in hand, he climbed the exposed stairs in back, glancing down at a macadam play yard, its icy surface ruptured by frost heaves, like mole work on a spring lawn.

Mrs. Kelly stood at the open door, wringing her hands. "I saw you through the window, Dr. Brooks. Megan's very sick."

"Let's have a look, Mrs. Kelly," he said, handing her his scarf and gloves.

They walked through a kitchen with an uneven floor and by a table whose mustard oilcloth matched the paint chips David noticed beneath a windowsill. A crucifix hung over the door to the child's bedroom.

Megan struggled to push herself up in bed. "Hi ... doc ... tor," she said breathlessly. Her words brought on a coughing fit. When she settled down, David noted her shallow, rapid respirations. Her mother went to the window and raised the shade.

"Just lie back down, Megan," David said. "That's it, easy does it."

As he leaned over the child and placed his hands on both sides of her neck, he detected the fruity smell of acetone. She felt hot and dry. Her black hair was knotted, her eyes sunken. She scraped her tongue over her lips.

"You checking her urine, Mrs. Kelly?"

"Every day. I checked it four times today."

"What are they showing? Both readings are up, right?"

"Yes, Doctor." She consulted a small piece of cardboard which she pulled from the pocket of her housecoat. "The sugar is four plus," she said, "and acetone reads strong positive. It's been like that for three days." Megan's chest heaved during another coughing paroxysm.

David examined her from head to toe, then returned to her chest. He put his stethoscope aside and said, "There's the problem, Mrs. Kelly. Has she been coughing long?"

"All week. She can't seem to shake it."

"Well, she has bronchitis and that's upsetting the control of the diabetes. Here's how we should handle it." David scribbled prescriptions for an antibiotic and an expectorant, advised setting up a vaporizer, instructed the mother to triple the child's fluid intake, and explained how and when to increase Megin's insulin dosages.

Winking at Megan, he said, "I know you feel rotten but you're going to do just fine." He motioned Mrs. Kelly to the hallway.

"Now, get the prescriptions filled right away—you know Hatcher's down the corner will deliver—and if she's no better by morning, call Dr. Jasper. Between now and then, if you get worried, call me, okay?"

She nodded and said, "Could you wait one more minute?" She disappeared into a back room and returned waving an insurance form.

He thrust out both hands defensively. "No, no, those things scare me. I'll have Belle at my office contact you." He left, not at all certain he would give Belle a record of the visit.

David raced to his home on the eastern edge of Hollings, a city of 100,000 people—big for Connecticut. Several decaying but proud manufacturing plants clasped hands along the valley river, holdouts to the exodus south, to warmer climates and cheaper human resources. Industrial parks with their prefabricated look-alikes occupied higher ground while yet above them, unpretentious residential houses stocked both hills, each a template for the other. The city's shape and color changed with the seasons, a croissant in foliaged autumn, a warship in the grimy sludge of winter.

He intended to freshen up before returning to the hospital, to splash his face with cold water at the bathroom sink, again ignoring the mirror and the reflection of his chin. Another mutation. The cleft there was a shaving trouble spot, a breeding ground for nicks and cuts among inaccessible stubble, always the trigger for morning obscenities and vows to bury the gap in a goatee some day.

David noticed the snow falling more heavily through the dark now, sucked against his windshield like bits of confetti. On the car phone, he called in his report to Dr. Jasper's office—that he had found the child in stable condition but upped her insulin dose in the face of a respiratory infection. He glanced at the dashboard clock which registered five-twenty. "Ah, shoot!" He had missed the start of his karate class. From five to six on Tuesdays, David helped Grand Master Bruno Bateman conduct a class for beginners, and on Thursdays, he polished his own skills during controlled combat with other black belts. He punched in the studio number. Agnes, the receptionist, answered.

"Gorgeous? Tell the boss I'm sorry but I'm tied up tonight."

"He understands, David, and he's already started the class. We caught the news on TV. I couldn't believe my ears—murders like that in a hospital. Guess you'll be preoccupied."

"To say the least, but I'll try to make Thursday—unless things get worse." His last phrase had sneaked out, and he hoped Agnes wouldn't ask him to explain.

"I'll tell Bruno you called, and you be careful, okay?"

Before David and Kathy had cemented their relationship, he and Agnes had shared a drink or two, and more than a few all-nighters. Sometimes he reminded her that she taught him moves which were not exactly martial arts.

"I'll be careful. See you Thursday, I hope."

David hung up the phone and resumed his silent monologue.

How did the killer know he was involved— if it was the killer who ran him down? Had he been seen in the amphitheater? Surgery? The lab? And he had to know where the parking space was—or, if not, he had to go look for it. In either case, he most likely knew there was still one there.

David dodged answers that came at him like flashes from a strobe. He settled on a few and also concluded he would not inform the others of the ambush; they might somehow limit his movements.

He ran through a list of possible suspects as well. At the top was Dr. Ted Tanarkle, the pathologist. The blood led to his department. He was off for the day. But, killing like that? Why, for God's sake? And taking a swipe at his good buddy?

Oak Lane. 10 Oak Lane. He sideslipped into the driveway of his yellow, four-room ranch which was cloned in a cul-de-sac. From out back, heavy oak trees hung over it, trees which David had often spoken to. He would level with Kathy about his silent conversations and, although certain she had rolled her eyes whenever she turned away, he couldn't recall that she had ever challenged his sanity.

Inside, after his sink ritual, he slipped on a shoulder rig containing a semiautomatic Beretta Minx .22 and gathered up his attaché case. On the ten-minute ride back to the hospital, he told himself that most likely no one had ever seen him open the leather case, and he liked that. Not much visible in it except an Undercover .38 Special wrapped in terry cloth and some extra rounds of ammo. Hidden behind a retractable panel beneath its lid, however, were a whistle, a small cylinder of Mace and a Scout knife. He also liked the fact that the case announced he was in his detective mode, often parodying, "Some wear two hats; I carry two bags." He would smile. "Two guns, too." He had a name for his case: Friday. Nothing to do with Joe Friday or Girl Friday, just the day he bought it.

A quarter mile from the hospital, a formidable complex crammed into the eastern hillside, David's eyes caught its commanding clock tower on the horizon, a reflex he was certain all visitors shared. Six-fifteen. This wasn't the first time he admired the hundred-year-old structure, a landmark continuation of the elevator shaft still in use for the administrative section of the building complex. Half again as tall, it sported silent clocks on three sides, shaded by a copper cupola; and, in David's mind, it pierced the sky like a foundation pile in reverse. Architecturally, it was the only feature of the hospital he liked, tested and timeless amidst a mishmash of wings and additions, red brick against greys and tans and glass.

Inside, he discovered that Suite 7, the locker room and both hallways on either side had been cordoned off. Also, the stairs to Pathology. Kathy and Nick stood talking to a police officer.

"Aha, there you are," she said, "we're starved."

"You're through?" David asked.

"Yep."

"At both scenes?"

"Sparky's not done but we are. He just started with Cortez. Let's go eat. Is the cafeteria still open?"

"Better be. Sure, let's go; I can do my thing later. I'd like to see the legitimate surgeons at the operation before they go off gallivanting or something. Hope they're still around."

"Are you kidding?" Nick said. "We detained everybody within earshot, like good police are supposed to. We already interrogated the doctors. They're in the caf right now. They wanted to go home but we told them to wait for you."

"You mean you're running interference for me?"

Nick nudged Kathy with his shoulder. "She said I'd better or she'd make my life miserable."

"Who's the supervisor here?" David asked, his smile improvised.

"I just arrived, so she is until I get the lay of the land. Eventually, I get brutal."

They sat in a corner of the cafeteria, their meals on trays before them. Elongated planters defined rows of tables. They deaden the noise, David had once been told. Here and there, young men coated in white and collared with stethoscopes either gobbled down food or fiddled with their pagers. Nurses in multicolored uniforms picked at salads. Recognizing the Chief of Surgery who sat with his associate several tables away, David spread out his fingers to gesture he would visit them in twenty minutes. They ate in silence, avoiding each other's look. Even from a distance, David could see splotches of black blood on the scrub suits beneath their unbuttoned lab coats.

He addressed Nick. "Shall we compare notes?"

"Compare with Kathy," Nick answered, winking.

"I'm observing."

Kathy, who had dug into a sandwich, looked up at Nick and said, "You know, you're one heck of a boss." David gathered she was finally able to insert the comment she hesitated making earlier.

"Like I said, give me time, I'll get worse."

David pitched in: "I find that hard to believe." He waited for a response and, hearing none, said, "I haven't found much except the obvious. You saw the stains, I take it?"

"They tracked to Pathology," Kathy said.

"Or through Pathology."

"There are stains on the other side of Pathology?"

"What I mean is," David said, "the killer may have gone through the department. That is, he didn't stop there. No, I don't think there's any blood on the other side."

"'Think'? Did you check?" Kathy asked.

"Well … no."

There was an awkward silence before David said, "See, I'm learning."

Kathy said gently, "We found no stains there." She buttered a roll. "Did you see the Chairman's body up close?"

"Unfortunately, yes, and it's hard to believe Mr. Killer did what he did. Right under our noses, too. He sure had— block your ears, Kath—balls." He watched her for a moment and then added, "You should be blushing."

"David, my darling, after years with you, I'm beyond that."

"You sure you didn't stop blushing before you met me?"

Kathy crimped her mouth in annoyance.

Nick said, "Now what do you see in a guy like that?"

"Oh," Kathy replied, "blond hair, blue eyes, gorgeous physique—but who's bragging? I don't know about that mustache though—it might have to go after the wedding this summer. That, and the little house."

"Samson's strength was in his hair, you know. I'm not Samson, but I am David."

"Don't shave it off," Kathy countered. They chuckled.

"And I like my small house," David said.

"Un huh."

They had dated on and off in college and then veered apart not only vocationally but romantically. It was a decision of David's choosing, colored by a fierce determination to train hard for a medical career, unencumbered by any serious personal relationships. They continued to exchange more than Christmas greetings but, by the time he was discharged from the Navy, Kathy had been married and widowed. Her husband and fellow police academy graduate had been shot and killed in a drug raid. And though he shared her grief, in the decade since her husband's death, David came to believe fate had gradually emboldened his love for her. Over half that interval, he had become a one-woman man. Plus now they worked together in police investigations.

Near the end of his meal, Nick removed his glasses and gesticulated with them as he spoke. "Dr. Brooks, in twenty-four years of detective work, I never came across an M.O. like this, so we can't round up the usual suspects. Besides, it's most likely an inside job, don't you think?"

"It seems that way, but we'll see."

"Do you know of anyone in this hospital who would kill so dramatically?" Nick continued. "Especially the surgery bit. He seemed to be making a point, not to mention thumbing his nose."

"Or revealing a machismo complex," David said. "There are lots of guys here with that. But driven to murder? I can't say that."

"Now, here's where you can top *us*, David," Kathy said. "Those were slices through those organs? Liver and—what—the spleen?"

"That's part of what killed him. Blood loss from there plus the arteries to the kidneys were cut clean. So he bled to death."

"Hold it, you guys," Nick said, "I'm having calve's liver here, remember?" He stared at his plate, then pushed it aside. "Think I've had enough. I'm going back for some coffee. You want some?" They both nodded.

David answered more of Kathy's anatomy questions and when Nick returned, he said, "Dr. Brooks, I've been wondering—how can you fit in criminal investigations with your practice?"

"What practice? That's gone, finis. I didn't like it so it didn't last long—maybe four years."

"I still don't understand the house calls."

"I make them full time. For other doctors. Well, not exactly full time—afternoons. But it's all I do. Except for today, and that's only because I had recommended Cortez."

"And except for karate, guns, communing with nature, the theater," Kathy said. There was a touch of resignation to her voice.

"Wait a minute, you go with me to the theater. And

you probably know more about handling a gun than I do."

"Maybe, but I don't collect them. You should see his basement, Nick."

"Almost every gun there was given over to me by Dad."

She stirred her coffee and said, "I've never thought of it this way before, David, but, you know, you're a series of contradictions."

"Meaning?"

"It's nothing really earth shattering: you drive a Mercedes but you've got a tiny house up in splinter village. There's karate but you like opera. My heavens, you read mythology! What else? Oh, the gun collection but you adore animals. And how about the business of talking to your trees?"

"Kathy, don't! What *is* this? We've got dead bodies here and you're talking mythology?"

Kathy reached across the table, grabbed his hand, rose up and kissed it. "Don't be hurt. It's part of what I love about you." She sat back in her chair but still stroked his hand with the tips of her fingers.

"You two want me to leave?" Nick asked.

"Sorry, Nick," Kathy said. She drew back her hands and explored David's face. "You look tired," she said, "and when you're tired, you get effusive. Why not give him the whole spiel?"

"You mean effuse it to him? And I'm not tired."

"Effuse the spiel?" Nick said. They giggled like teenagers over a raunchy joke. David sensed most heads turning their way.

He shrugged and whispered, "We'd better cool it, folks." They shifted in their chairs. Kathy swept away some crumbs.

"Okay, Nick," David said, "the background, quick and simple. After the Navy, I tried private practice but it wasn't for me. They were looking for a full-time doctor here, working on the administrative side of things in conjunction with Dr. Tanarkle. So I signed on."

"The pathologist?" Nick interrupted.

"The pathologist. Terrific guy. He taught me a lot—especially forensics. Shipped cases to me or recommended me because he knew I was interested."

"And he's now a suspect."

"Now a suspect. God, I pray it doesn't pan out." David crossed his fingers in the air. "Anyway, despite Ted, the challenge was never there and I *did* miss patient contact, so I quit after being assured by enough of my colleagues that they'd use me for house calls. I latched onto Belle who works out of the Hole in the morning and sets up my afternoon schedule. We usually have lunch here and then she comes with me on the calls. Handles the paper work plus all the other details. And here I am—been at it for a year, now. So far, so good, and I have more time for snooping ... ah, sleuthing ... and those other things Kathy blasted."

"I didn't blast them."

"I mean, referred to." This time, David reached for Kathy's hand and said, "So she's doing what she likes, I'm doing what I like, we're racing each other to forty and we're getting hitched in six months."

"Married. And you're the one who said 'blasted.'"

"Married and hitched."

"You're so into control."

Nick ran his hand over his scalp. "Now, just to firm

up this investigation," he said. "Of the three of us, I'm needed the least for day-to-day operations, so you two take over. But keep me posted. You know, the press, city hall. They're all watching."

Kathy glanced at David and said, "And between the two of us, I need your help more than you need mine, so you sort of take over. Keep me posted, too, and just remember, I love you, honey, but let's not blow it."

David, surprised but reassured, pressed on a rare twitch in his toe and said casually, "Don't I always keep you informed?" He believed the comment didn't fit and added, "It's bigger than what I've been doing."

"Well, you wanted more experience," Kathy responded. "You certainly know your way around the hospital. And it's not that you won't have forensic support from our department."

David felt obliged to indicate he'd check with them on a regular basis.

"That's important," Nick said. "We're really accountable to city government. And you're private. Besides, I've learned fast that we have a cut-every-year budget and we're short-handed. The entire police detective division is running on a shoestring. Crime scene search units are way understaffed, as you saw. Our homicide squad's been cut in half so Kathy here has twice as much to do." He counted on his fingers. "Electronic Unit, Polygraph Section, Forgery Squad—forget it. Sparky does it all. Precinct squads? We're lucky to have any at all; some have been moved to Narcotics and some to Sex Crimes. So you see, Dr. Brooks, we're simply enlisting your assistance at a time when things are piling up. You can be the point man, but it has to appear as though Kathy and I are.

It shouldn't be a problem."

"I understand." David did, but he also judged it to be a half-baked endorsement. Homicides? Never sifted through them before. Nick knows it. Certainly Kathy knows it. So even if our investigations run parallel, they've given me *some* slack. They've talked this over plenty. Obvious. But, as Nick said, they've got other things, plus they're hurting. Me? Give it full attention, maybe take some afternoons off, beat them to the punch. Yeah, that's it. Problem is though, beating the killer to the punch.

"Publicly, it will seem like a natural," Nick continued. "An M.D. sleuth whose stomping grounds are where the crimes were committed. And, if this is what you want, have a go at it, and you're lucky, you know, because we've, like, come to you. Back in San Diego, we had guys knocking down our doors to get a little business."

Yeah, they talked it over all right. That's how Kathy would put it: "Tell him he's lucky, Nick."

Kathy said, "I'm confident you're ready to handle it. Just remember it's not just another 10-65."

"Why does everybody in law enforcement always bring up Missing Persons with me?"

"Because that's what you always complain about. And, really, that's about all you've handled till now."

"Not so. I never told you I had a 10-91H when you were at that convention a couple months back."

Kathy stifled a laugh poorly. "A stray horse?"

"Sure, rode him back to the farm, too."

"You would."

"Why wouldn't I?"

"Because you never rode a horse."

"I have now." They got up to leave.

"And incidentally, Kath, speaking of horses, if you were one, you'd probably be a Shetland." David held his arm at a right-angle over her head. "Have you cleared five feet yet?"

"I'm way past that."

"What? Half an inch?"

"No, a full inch," she replied with an exaggerated nod. She stomped her foot in the process.

David reminded them he would walk over to see the Surgical Chief and his associate. He shook Nick's hand and kissed Kathy lightly on the lips. "Thank you both."

"So long, cowboy," she replied.

David joined the two surgeons halfway across the room. They stood when he arrived, and he felt the air crackle with tension. The Associate's face was scarlet. David continued his handshake with the Chief as he spoke: "Ned, Steve, thanks for waiting. Sorry—must have been agony witnessing that butchering."

"I feel awful about it," the Chief said. "Two murders like that, and what's it do to our new program?"

"I know. Look, I won't keep you long. Okay for just two questions?"

"Take all the time you need, David."

"Well, first and foremost, how'd that creep end up taking Cortez's place?"

"We blew it," the Chief said. "I thought Steve here would be meeting with him before the procedure and he guessed I would."

"Not 'guessed,'" the Associate snapped. "You told me you would. I can still hear your words."

The Chief scowled. "We'll talk about that later. Anyway ... "

David broke in as if to minimize their bones of contention. "Did either of you recognize who the imposter was?"

"We never saw his face," the Chief answered. "He came in wearing a surgical mask. Later, I took it upon myself to ask the same thing of the nurses and technicians. They saw him only masked. Even beforehand, while he scrubbed. I checked at the desk; nobody saw him come in. And, I'm kicking myself for not arriving sooner, but, as I said, I assumed Steve would be here. The guy never said a word during the surgery ... if that's what you call it ... never asked for an instrument, just reached out. You know how it works, the scrub tech automatically snaps them into your hand."

The Chief exhaled as if blowing out a match. He continued: "Earlier, when I said, 'Good afternoon, Dr. Cortez,' he just nodded. But, I figured, hell, he's the dignitary. He's the one getting our organ transplant program off the ground. Don't interfere with his concentration. And, David, as I look back, his eyes were so eerie. They never stopped moving around. They were everywhere. How anything had a chance to register with him, I don't know."

"Tell me, did he seem to know what he was doing?"

"To the point when all hell broke loose, I suppose he did. But, you know the usual procedure, David. After his initial incision, I entered the peritoneum for him, just like a resident would. He never got to the pancreas, but he sure knew where the renals were."

"And the liver and spleen," the Associate said.

"And the liver and spleen. Everything happened so damn fast. It was like his punctuation mark," the Chief said. "You saw what he did?"

"Yes."

David rose. "I said I'd bother you with only a couple questions, and that's all the information I need for now." He looked at his watch. "It's after seven and you two must be bushed. Thanks for waiting—I'll be in touch. And, oh, by the way, how did the transplant brouhaha settle out with Bowie County across town?"

"Some friendly sister hospital. It never did settle out. They made it quite clear that if they didn't get a piece of the action, they'd refer their cases out-of-state."

3

CE LINE DO NO CROSS POLICE LINE DO NO CROS

When David got back to 10 Oak Lane, his favorite tree had offered silent support to his rhetorical question, "Not a bad spot for a single guy, right?" Inside, he tossed his case, Friday, on the sofa, ignored a blinking answering machine and circled around the four rooms which were laid out in an unimaginative square. He and Kathy had combined to dub the front living room: "Lush and Plush"; the den: "The Nest"; the rear kitchen: "Lean and Mean"; and the bedroom: "No Comment." A one-car garage was attached to the den.

Like a new buyer, he inspected each of three rooms and its contents before moving to the next: soft Drexel pieces before the living room's fireplace; the table-dominated kitchen surrounded by blue counter-tops and canary yellow appliances; the den with computer, martial arts trophies, miniature deer figurines and collection of opera CD's. There, piles and rows of books engulfed his computer corner: *Bulfinch's Mythology, Police Procedural, Body Trauma, Scene of the Crime, Complete Crime Reference Book*, and Dr. Henry Lee's *Manual of Forensic Science*.

Kathy's words, "the little house," rang in his ears. Little, but cozy. Maybe too dimly lit, even sloppy. She should sleep over more often.

There were nine phone messages from state newspapers. He decided not to answer any and vowed not to help sell newspapers, then or ever, having soured on the print media long ago. Something to do with misquotes and inaccurate reporting. He went to his computer in the pine-paneled den, one of two rooms separated from the main street by a thirty-foot-deep yard. He entered:

Tuesday, January 13.

MURDERS

> Chas. Bugles—hacked in O.R.
> Raphael Cortez—stabbed in surgeons' locker room.
> Witnessed Bugles' killing from observatory balcony.
> Both most likely killed by same person.
> Killer knows some anatomy and ? surgery.
> Blood trail leads to Tanarkle's dept. ? suspect.
> Ambushed in parking garage.
> Kathy and new supervisor assigned from Homicide. Gave me blank check incl. forensic support.
> Bowie County pissed we got Certificate of Need for transplant program.

David stopped short to listen to a car idling out front. He heard a thud against the house. He ducked. Again, the screech of tires. In one motion, he hit the floor and withdrew the Minx which was still holstered to his shoulder.

Scrambling to his feet, he dashed to the back of the house, his breath stalled in his throat. An eternal five minutes brought no explosion so he eased back through the den to the front door. He widened a crack slowly, looking from side to side, the grip of his pistol pressed against his chin. Slipping out, he maneuvered behind a foundation shrub to the base of his bay window where he spotted an egg-like object embedded in the superficial snow cover. He rolled it over with the barrel of the Minx, covered it with a handkerchief and picked it up. It was a rock bound by two crossed adhesive strips. In the light streaming from the window, he rotated the rock in his beefy hands as he read the precise lettering on one of the strips:

LET COPS HANDLE THIS

David felt a heat surge at his temples. Bullshit to you, buddy. He looked at the window and wanted to throw the rock through it himself. He ran to the street. Vague remnants of tire tracks had been obliterated by the persistent snow.

Inside, he put the rock in a plastic bag, placed it in Friday and marched with it to the basement. He stood thinking in the center of a room circumscribed by gun cabinets, their metallic odor unchecked by glass doors. All sizes. All heights. All filled. There was a cabinet for weapons according to manufacturer: Colt, Ruger, Smith and Wesson, Charter Arms, Dan Wesson. According to calibers: .25, .32, .38, .45. Cabinets for pistols, for revolvers, for rifles and carbines and machine guns and shotguns. One was engorged with spare parts and ammunition.

On a table near the Ruger cabinet, David opened Friday and replaced the .38 Special with a Super Blackhawk .44 Magnum.

CE LINE DO NO 4 CROSS POLICE LINE DO NO CROS

The following morning, Wednesday, David glanced at the tower clock as he rounded the entrance to the doctors' parking lot. It was eight forty-five.

He chanced that Virginia Baldwin, the Surgical Nursing Supervisor, was in her office. David had a thing against calling ahead, anywhere, unless it involved traveling great distances. When reminded by whomever—family, friends, colleagues, teachers—of the virtue of courtesy or, at least, of good time management, he would respond, "Courtesy's in my family's genes. So, big deal, a generation was skipped." It had some bizarre connection with nature. Unannounced keeps everything natural. No pretense. No makeup. Nothing staged. Of course, they don't have to receive me. It's their choice, not mine. But then they're the discourteous ones, right?

It might not have been entirely germane, but, somehow, he used house calls as an illustration. That's why I like to make them. The patient and the family are in their natural setting. I get to see how they live. That might help in my counsel even though I'm nobody's primary care physician.

Nurse Baldwin was in. She sat at a desk besieged by papers, folders and schedules. She looked less massive without surgical cap and gown. Glasses were perched low on a thin nose, unsuited for a puffy face, as if she had forgotten to take a diuretic pill.

"I'll tell you, David, I never want to see another day like that again. Never."

"Amen. You were up close. Can you remember how tall he was?"

"Well … not your size, that's for sure. Average, I'd say, maybe five-ten or so."

"That certainly narrows the field."

She thinned her lips.

"Sorry Ginny, just thinking out loud. Was there anything distinguishing about him?"

"Only that he was so quiet. I remember thinking how different that was. Usually, the big shots who come through here can't stop talking, you know."

"You make up the daily schedules, right?"

"Right."

"There were no other cases at three-thirty?"

"Not starting then. The G.I.s and neurosurgicals started early but were over by then. We had a couple hips but they were over, too. E.N.T., some vein stuff—they were on at two-thirty and were still going."

"So, most likely no one else was in the locker room just before three-thirty?"

"Most likely."

"Ginny, thanks—see you."

"Wait. Are there any suspects?"

"Not yet, but I think I've ruled out a couple."

"Oh, who?"

"You and me. By the way, have the police talked to you yet?"

"Last night—not today. They cut it short, though. I was too upset."

David sauntered through the administrative offices of the O.R. wing, speaking briefly with nurses, unit clerks and orderlies. He wrote their names on a pad. Next to each he added a zero.

He had more to do at the hospital but decided to make a quick run to the Hollings Police Department. He wanted to deliver the taped rock to Sparky for analysis and perhaps have the results by noon.

Ten minutes later, David pulled into the department's parking lot and climbed the steps of a new prefabricated entranceway, harsh against walls of blanched brick and pitted mortar. He tucked Friday under his arm like the guardian of a kryptonite sample. He greeted friends at the dispatch window and was buzzed into a maze of hallways and interconnecting rooms. Steam radiators banged, and the floor creaked beneath half partitions and shiny modular furniture as employees traipsed about their filing cabinets and worked their computers. David proceeded directly to the Lilliputian crime lab, past benches of microscopes, chemical bottles, latent fingerprint equipment and the brothy smell of petri dishes. He entered the criminalist's corner office without knocking.

Sparky sat at a king-size desk inspecting a piece of cloth. He wore plastic gloves. Various wire baskets, magnifying tools and paper stacks seemed arranged for a neatness contest. A lamp dangled on a cord from the ceiling above the dead center of the desk. The lamp's green metal shade matched Sparky's visor.

The criminalist was a forty-some-odd throwback to a Western Union clerk in a 1940's B movie: slicked down black hair parted in the middle, wire-framed glasses, gartered shirt sleeves.

David snapped Sparky's suspenders and said, "Morning, my friend, I have a little something for you."

"Hey, David. I thought you'd be phoning me." Sparky popped up briefly to shake hands.

"Hope you're not too busy." David took off his scarf and gloves and placed them over the back of a chair.

"It's no problem. I'm always too busy."

David opened Friday, draped a handkerchief over the taped rock and deposited it on the desk.

"This was tossed toward my window last night. Lousy shot. Can you run it through the usual checks? I can call this afternoon if that gives you enough time."

"Late afternoon should be fine." Sparky read the message and shook his head. "Did you see the guy?"

"Nope. And there were no tracks in the snow—just acceleration gauges. Sure as hell sounded like ... " David caught himself. Don't want to mention the garage incident, right? Almost blew it, pal. He launched into his next sentence without missing a beat. Sparky seemed preoccupied with the rock, anyway.

"Look, Spark, if I ask you for another favor and you can't do it, would you have to mention to anyone that I asked you for it?"

The criminalist removed his visor and, leaning back, said, "I never breach confidences. How can I help?"

"Don't tell Kathy or Nick about the rock, okay?"

"I suppose, but why not?"

"My first murders, my first ultimatum—you know—

I don't want them tightening the reins."

"I won't say a word, but don't be silly. If you want the truth, we're so damned busy around here, they think you're a godsend. Really. I've heard them say it."

"Thanks, that's what I needed to hear." He sat on the edge of the desk. "Now, about Bugles and Cortez ..." Sparky didn't let him finish.

"David, I dusted and sprayed and dipped and fumed. I couldn't bring out any prints other than their own except probably the locker room attendent's. His—I assume his—are all over most of the lockers. I'm checking it out. But nothing on the dagger. Or on Cortez's skin, so far. I had to act fast on trying to lift there. I used x-rays and I've got a call in to the Tokyo Police Department to see where we go from here. They've perfected the technique. The blood—I'll have all that by the time you call about the rock. I've got to warn you, though, David, prints rarely come through from rock or stone. Brick, for that matter. And incidentally, I found a couple blood smudges on the shelf in the locker." He looked at the clock on the wall. "I'll know whose by noon."

"Good. And the dagger?" David moved away, hands on hips.

"I've never seen one like it. The blade's ten inches. Steel. I'm still checking on the handle and, sorry, I can't release it to you but here are some photocopies plus a few stills from both scenes." He pulled out a batch of photographs from a drawer and handed them to David who put them in Friday without examination.

"What about the trajectory of the stab wound? From above, right?"

"The chest wound—correct. The abdominal one—

you saw that?"

"Yes."

"It was shoved in most likely underhanded, just to stun the guy."

"I figured." David put on his scarf and gloves and expressed his thanks. "I'll call you later today, then," he said.

"I should have it all put together."

"Great. And one last thing, Spark. If a guy puts a piece of tape on a rock from, say two o'clock to eight o'clock, and then crosses it with another piece from ten to four, what would you conclude if the second piece was the top piece?"

The criminalist frowned. "Sorry, David, I don't quite follow. What are you getting at?"

"Just this. It seems to me that's what would happen if someone right-handed put the tape on. But for a left-hander, that top strip—the one from ten to four—would be on the bottom. See, look here." David picked up the rock and pointed to the top strip. "See, ten to four. This bastard could be left-handed, wouldn't you say?"

The criminalist put his visor back on as if it imparted greater lucidity. He examined the rock, twisting it around with one hand while making crosses in the air with his other. Finally, he said, "By golly, I think you're right. I've never had evidence like this before, but I think you're onto something. Of course we've had things tossed through windows—mostly bricks—but never with messages on adhesive tape. Usually on paper secured with rubber bands. Sometimes twine. Come to think of it, maybe the way rubber bands are put on could tell us the same thing."

"It could. Just work backwards ... I guess." David added the last two words to soften any perception of up-staging. For good measure, he called on humor: "I won't charge you for any of this, you know."

"Wait'll you get *my* bill." They both smiled.

"But seriously," David said, "even though what I said about the tape strips could be possible, wouldn't you agree this right-handed-left-handed stuff isn't foolproof?"

"No."

"No, it's foolproof or, no, it isn't foolproof?"

"Sorry. Yes, it's not foolproof."

David left the crime lab and thought of visiting with Kathy and Nick several suites away but was anxious to question Ted Tanarkle in Pathology and the hospital's administrator, Alton Foster. Buoyed by Sparky's assurance that he was considered a member of the investigating team—if not, *the* team, he thought—he swaggered from the building more aware of his surroundings. Looking around and recalling the crime lab, he imagined Methuselah trying to catch up to Bill Gates.

As he approached the pathologist's office back at the hospital, David spotted a familiar figure down the hall. The director of the Emergency Medical System was struggling with a bulky carton at the door aside the old dispatch window.

"Vic," he hollered, "hold on, I'll give you a hand." He quickened his step and helped unwedge the carton from the door, guiding it to the floor." He felt his knee complain.

"Thanks, David. Haven't seen you in a long time. What are you up to these days?"

Victor Spritz. Smooth-faced, fashioned hair, shorter

than David by a hand, and older by a decade. Roots unknown. Etched smile. Coppery hair. Angles at the wrists. Elbows exaggerated laterally. A twenty-year veteran at Hollings and a loner, he headed up the city's Emergency Medical System which was administered from the hospital. Despite Spritz's medical care orientation, David believed he had the personality of a hornet in a Mason jar.

"Oh, not much. Still making house calls and sleuthing on the side, but I'm thinking of reversing that."

"Because of the murders?"

"Because of the murders."

Spritz shook his head. "How God-awful."

David peeked behind Spritz into the EMS office. He saw chairs stacked on tables, books piled on the floor, papers strewn about. The room beyond an archway appeared undisturbed, a space he'd heard Spritz call his "Ambulance Without Wheels" with its spare stretchers and benches of masks, aspirators, oxygen tanks, splints and canisters. "What's going on?" he asked.

"I'm moving out." It was uncharacteristic of Spritz to wear a blue denim shirt and tattered jeans while in the hospital. Rarely was he in coat and tie, but usually, as a hands-on director, he sported the customary uniform of the EMS paramedics in Hollings: dark blue trousers, white shirt—open at the collar—with insignia on the sleeve and name pin over the left breast.

"Moving out? Why?"

"Haven't you heard? I lost the contract. As of the first of the month, I'm terminated. Out of here."

David understood the awarding of the EMS contract had been a yearly problem not only for both city hospitals but also for rival companies. He, himself, had once lobbied for Spritz among the joint oversite committee members of both hospitals.

"I'm sorry to hear that." He put his arm around Spritz's shoulders which stiffened. David was momentarily lost for words. He managed, "So what happens to your fleet?" The ambulances were maintained in a bank of garages two streets away. EMS crews occupied quarters upstairs at the same site.

Spritz unetched his smile. "It's not mine. The fuckin' hospital owns it. Except for the defibrillator van—that stays with me. Shit, who do you think started the cardiac defib program around here? I probably shocked more hearts into normal rhythm than anyone in the city's history."

"Who's on the committee these days?"

"Foster—that chairman wimp; Coughlin, across town; the prick next door ... " He motioned toward Tanarkle's office. "And Bugles—at least he was." Spritz's eyes had turned to pinpoints of fire.

David deliberated. Our administrator, their Chief of Staff. Sounds logical. But why our pathologist? What's he doing on the committee?

"Well, no sense crying over you-know-what," Spritz said. He checked his watch. On his right wrist, David noticed. "I've got to get going. Sure hope you make your catch." He returned to his outer office and began packing another carton.

David watched for a moment and wondered whether most southpaws wore their watches on their right wrist. "See you around, Vic," he said.

In Dr. Ted Tanarkle's reception room, he stared at the secretary's wrists without saying a word.

"David, you're back."

He tried to finish his thoughts without delaying a response. Everyone wearing watches on right wrists? What difference does it make anyway—wasn't the imposter a male? Christ, what are you supposed to do—go through life checking people's wrists?

"David?"

"Marsh, I'm coming right out and asking you a direct question."

"Sure, but ..."

"Are you right-handed or left?"

"Right. Why?"

"Curious, that's all." He stood at her desk and looked vacantly at the diplomas, citations and group pictures on the wall behind her. "Then why wear your watch on your right wrist?"

Marsha looked puzzled but spread out her left hand. "See, just to balance these."

"Nice rings," he said. There were four of them. He ground his teeth.

"David, are you all right?"

"What? Yeah, I'm all right. Just mulling over some things. Is Ted in?"

"Yes, but he's on the phone with Dr. Coughlin. He called him on some slides. I'll go put a note on his desk." She opened Tanarkle's office door. "Oh, you're off. Dr. Brook's here to see you."

"I'll see him." David heard the words run together, closer then usual—and feebler. Dr. Theodore J. Tanarkle had been Holling's chief pathologist for over three decades. Best known visually for an engaging gap between his two upper front teeth and professionally for his clinical acumen without ever seeing the patient, staff doctors would feed him signs and symptoms which invariably initiated, "Have you thought of"? He had married late, to a woman a generation younger. Soft-spoken, his sentences were, nonetheless, blurted not spoken, as if he had to get rid of them.

David thanked Marsha and walked in. It was one of those offices that swallowed you up, that made its nine-by-twelve Oriental carpet look puny, its ceiling-to-floor bookstacks of no great account.

He saw Tanarkle standing, arms locked on his desk, his head a tomato covered with dew. When he straightened, David measured his height by noting he could see directly over the head of the pathologist.

Dr. Tanarkle sat clumsily and, running his hands through the last vestiges of hair at his temples, said, "The son-of-a-bitch threatened me!"

"Coughlin? What did he say?"

"That the patient on the table yesterday should have been me, but that he'd settle one way or another."

David knew the background: fiery Dr. Everett Coughlin, the mover and shaker pathologist at Bowie Hospital; Ted Tanarkle, his counterpart at Hollings; the bitter battles over which hospital should be granted state certification for the city's first organ transplantation program; the late Charles Bugles and his dollar-splendored petitions at the state capitol.

"Keep it cool, Ted, you know Coughlin."

"Yes, that's the problem. He still can't accept the transplant decision." Tanarkle shook open a neatly folded handkerchief and wiped his brow and the back of his neck with his right hand. "And another thing, David—stranger than hell. He wanted to know if you're still on the case."

"Did he say it like that? *Still* on the case or just *case?*"

Tanarkle stroked his forehead. "You know, I can't remember. He meant the murders. Is it important how he said it?"

"It could be. What was your answer?"

"I simply said, 'As far as I know.' Jesus, my head is hot. Do I look like a beet?"

"No, a tomato. A tomato in a gray lab coat."

Tanarkle seemed to loosen up.

"Ted, I realize you're miffed and probably in hypertensive crisis, but do you mind if I ask you a question or two?"

"Ahh … no, that's fine."

"I could come back later."

"No, go ahead, it's okay."

From a table submerged in medical journals, manuscipts, trays of specimen slides and boxes of projection slides, David pulled out and sat on the only chair not itself submerged. He opened his notepad.

"For starters, do you know of anyone who might want to knock off Bugles?"

"Charlie? Plenty of guys. He got things done over twenty years, I guess, but you've got to admit, he was a detestable sort. Even when you were here with me, you must have seen how he barged in and threw his weight around."

"You willing to name some names?"

"Sure. Coughlin hated his guts probably more than mine. Marsha out there couldn't stand him. Foster upstairs—even some of his associate administrators. By the way, you know that Charlie put Foster into that job, don't you?"

"No, but I'm not surprised."

"Sure. And he manipulated every one of his strings. Foster resented it. Probably would have been long gone except for his wife. Nora likes it around here for some reason."

"How about you?"

"Me what? Killing Charlie Bugles? Depends on what you mean. Did I want to kill him sometimes? Absolutely. Could I or did I? No."

"Are you or the medical examiner doing the post?"

"I am, at one o'clock. He asked me if I would and I agreed."

"Cortez, too?"

"After Bugles."

"Mind if I drop by?"

"No, be my guest."

"Hold on a sec." David backtracked on what he had written thus far and made a few notations in the margins. "Okay, now, about the blood. There were stains on the floor leading from Cortez's body to the lab here. At least to the alley door entrance. Matter of fact, there was one at the bottom of that door. Any idea why?"

Tanarkle sat mute, his face a mannequin's.

"Please understand, Ted, I'm not implying anything. But the blood did trail here, and I think you'd agree you'd ask the same question if our roles were reversed."

"Yes, yes, of course. I know of the trail, but I guess it was just shocking to have it mentioned in the form of a question like that." He sighed. "And, no, I have no idea why."

"Good enough. Well, not good, but … well … let's let it go at that."

"I wish I could be more helpful, David."

"You're doing fine. And finally—you and I go back a long way and you don't have to answer this if you don't want to ..."

"No, no, go ahead."

"Why weren't you in yesterday?"

"I was the guest speaker at Grand Rounds at Boston Childrens'. I'm often away like that. Medical expert. You know: anyone from out-of-state."

David drilled the last period into his notepad and got up. "Many thanks, Ted."

"See you after lunch. And, David ..." He extended a hand. "Good luck."

David shook the hand. "Thanks, my friend. Hang in there." Rounding the table, he glanced at a slide box labeled, "Grand Rounds: N.Y.C. 12-17-97." Next to it was a box labeled: "Grand Rounds: Boston." There was no date.

At the doorway, David paused, about to turn back to ask about the label. But he figured he'd be checking on the alibi later in the morning.

5

Ten-thirty. It was too late for coffee with the morning gang, but David decided to head for the cafeteria anyway. Better to be alone for a moment. Friday in tote, he strode his stride, now barreling along smoothly, now ducking at imaginary ceilings. The hospital quiet implored on property signs was pierced by the operators' curt, flat pages that sounded like Space Center announcements. In the hallways, he passed the usual inhabitants: doctors writing while they flitted by; nurses in pairs; technicians with lab trays of vacutubes and tourniquets. David recognized them all, but no one stopped to chat. It was as if they knew he was on a mission. And, their greetings were … well … different. Was it their polite nod? Did each feel suspect?

He fixed a coffee. The cashier said, "It's enough to give you the willies."

"What does?"

"C'mon, doc, them murders. You got the black case there. You got the weapon in it, right?"

"No, Sophie, no weapon, only my lunch." David gave her a dollar and didn't wait for change.

He grabbed a table off to the side and sat facing the wall, stirring his coffee in slow sync with the personalities drifting through his mind: Spritz, Tanarkle, even Marsha. And what of Coughlin across town? Venom, big time. Enough to go around for more than one murder.

Motive-wise, he had begun to combine the murders into one. Cortez had to go in order to kill Bugles in the outrageous fashion the murderer selected. But, why that way in the first place? David still hadn't taken a sip.

He returned to thoughts of Spritz and Tarnarkle and the necessity of questioning friends. Questions with an inference. But wait till the real stingers come—like, "Where were you at such-and-such a time?" It should get easier, right? Separation of friendship and criminal justice, pal.

He took his first sip of coffee and left. Ninety-five cents to stir, a nickle to drink.

Next, Foster. He took an elevator to the sixth floor and crossed over to the administrative wing.

"You know him," Foster's secretary, Doris, said, "he's all over the place. Especially the surgical wing. He's always there, it seems. Never in the cafeteria, though—I don't know why. He's brown-bagged it ever since I've been here."

Doris was one employee David had never dated. Fair, fat and forty—good candidate for gallstones, he mused.

She looked at the clock on the mahogany wall. "He should be back at eleven-thirty, Dr. Brooks."

David's phone tickled his hip.

"Are you in the building?" Belle asked.

"Yeah, I'm heading down. What's up?"

"Two things. First, I'm not sure whether to book calls. You're tied up for awhile, right?"

"Not completely. We'll talk about it. I'll be right there." He was about to replace the phone. "Wait," she said. "David, I just received the craziest call. This guy says, 'Is your boss still on the case?' He sounded so creepy."

"What did you say?"

"I didn't know what to say but I blurted out something like, 'I'm sorry, this is Dr. Brooks' medical office,' and he hung up."

"Did you recognize the voice."

"No. It was deep and kinda muffled."

"Definitely male?"

"Yes, unless she had a bad cold."

"See you in a minute."

The Hole was located off a corridor on the basement level next to an equipment room, not far from the old elevator. It was a tiny space with a door and had ratty walls, a ratty ceiling and a ratty cement floor. Hugging the top of the corridor, flaking cream pipes came at the door from both sides and snaked through its header to fan out above three furniture pieces and a cabinet inside. The pipes which David swore were sheathed in unreported asbestos, ran through two cellar-like windows on the outer wall, apparently into a rear corridor. He often wondered what in hell he was doing in such a rattrap. Some favor Foster's doing me. Rent-free, but sure as shooting, he's claiming a tax credit.

Once in a while, David could smell medicinal and detergent crosscurrents from the pharmacy and laundry on opposite ends of the corridor. And just as often, as he dashed from the Hole, he would freeze in his tracks to avert the daily caravan of laundry carts.

Belle sat on a tubular steel chair at a green metal desk. She appeared more flustered than she had sounded on the phone.

"Whew," she said, "that never happened during your missing persons cases."

"What never happened?"

"That voice."

"Forget it. He knows goddam well I'm still on the case."

"Then why call?"

"Intimidation, my Belle, intimidation. Goes with the territory." David felt a brief rush of pride at his sudden expertise in crisis management.

"So you're definitely in this thing? It's what you want?" Belle asked.

"It's what I want."

"I'm worried about you."

"I've had an interesting life."

"David, cut that out!"

An Emergency Room nurse for years, Annabelle Burns Osowicki agreed to be "borrowed" by David until "you get your newfangled practice off the ground." She had divorced after a year of marriage and lived with her eleven-year-old daughter. David had sworn her to secrecy about all phases of the investigation.

He had had his pick of the hospital's eligible women and often picked Belle until Kathy resurfaced for good. He never received a signal from Belle that she felt abandoned, probably because their talk had never reached a serious pitch. He guessed she had once kept her figure for him, but now, on the cusp of menopause, had begun to let straighten what was once curved and let curve what was once straight. Yet her hair still flamed, her smile was just as engaging, and she could still turn a head or two.

"Sorry. Look, this guy's not after me. There's something else bugging him. All this stuff about running me down and cryptic messages and now a follow-up phone call—is just bullshit. He's grandstanding. Or, better still: he knows I'm an amateur, and I wouldn't be surprised if he's doing this to send a message to the police."

"What kind of message?"

"That he's concerned about yours truly more than about them. He's sort of vouching for me. And if I'm that worrisome to the killer, the pros are more apt to relax and let me handle things."

Belle gave him the same look of admiration he had seen many times before. But not in the middle of a killing game.

"You know," she said, "you never explained why the cops are letting you take over, except for Kathy."

David sat on the other chair. "They say they're overworked. That's bull, too. They probably are—at least Kathy looks tired all the time—but that's not the reason. I think the real reason is that this isn't an ordinary case. Most murders don't happen on an operating room table, in full view of the whole damn hospital, for Christ's sake! So it's not your run-of-the-mill killing and isn't about to be cracked overnight. Next, what happens is they slowly begin to lose interest and allow themselves to get bogged down in their other garbage. They know all this. And now they have me."

"For sure," she said softly.

"Picture it, Belle: a gumshoe on the inside who can devote all his time to this one case. Knows the medical ropes. Is practically Kathy's husband. It's perfect for them and perfect for me."

"For you?"

"Yeah, I have their backup, all their forensic support. All I have to do is call. Plus, I'm in the big leagues now."

"Just don't strike out."

"Hey, very good."

David played with a small scar near the cleft in his chin. He called it his decision scar. "Okay," he said, "I've decided to cut into my schedule—maybe by half. Not yours, of course. You still run this ... this hole. Take messages, explain my temporary ... yeah, that's it ... my temporary unavailability."

"I figured."

"Think the other docs will be upset?"

Belle snickered. "They—they hate making housecalls. So there'll just be less made for awhile and more patients will wind up in the E.R. Even you sent them in, remember?"

"No, I didn't."

"I know; I was there."

"Well, that was only if my office was like a zoo."

"Their offices aren't like zoos?"

"Well ... "

"David, let's put it this way. They'll take whatever they can get whenever they can get it, so yes, they'll be mad at first but then they'll welcome you back with open arms."

"Good," he said, brightening. "Now, how many house calls for today?"

"Four, starting at one-thirty."

"Only four. How come?"

"I told you I wasn't sure about booking. So I got selective. Are you complaining?"

"No, not at all." He fingered his scar again.

"Now I think we'd better check on Ted Tanarkle's alibi. If I'm going to do this at all, I'm going to do it right. Give Boston Childrens' a call and make up some cockamamie story but find out if he was their speaker at Medical Grand Rounds yesterday. If so, ask from when to when."

"Done."

"And then, starting today, I'll keep making the house calls alone. You'll have enough to do fending off the angry jackals." He got up fast and reached over to kiss her forehead. "Thanks, doll, I'm off to see the boss. Incidentally, I'll be looking in on Bugles' autopsy at one."

"Don't forget your first call at one-thirty."

At the door, David heard the rush of laundry carts. He turned and said, "You're a pain in the ass."

The administrator of Hollings General for fifteen years, Alton Foster had protruding thin lips, a sallow complexion and a waddling gait. He reminded David of a bespectacled duck. A six-foot tall bespectacled duck. And the fact Foster liked yellow shirts—no matter the suit— did little to erase the similarity. But he was no duck. More like a hyperactive rooster—the Road Runner—scooting around the hospital each day, observing and offering advice. Meddling, according to some department heads. Not at all the wimp Victor Spritz had labeled him. He had been enticed to come to Hollings by the then new Board Chairman and now brutally divested Charles Bugles. Although Foster's bottom-line wizardry had turned steadily increasing profits for Hollings, most observers considered his capstone achievement to be the fledgling organ transplant program. It took four years of hearings, lobbying and connivance to obtain a medical Certificate of Need, the state's validation of the program. And four years of exploiting Bugles' political connections.

"I still can't get over it, David," Foster said. He sat at his desk surrounded by rolls of architectural plans, opening a brown paper bag. The room—expansive, sterile and uninviting—appeared as though its complement of furnishings had never arrived. It contained a basic contemporary desk, swivel chair and blue pastel filing cabinet. Ten paces away was an arrangement of two black leather chairs astride a coffee table sporting the latest editions of *Forbes*, *Business Week* and the *Journal of the American Hospital Association*. Its hardwood floor was glossy and slippery, and haphazardly placed scatter rugs looked like welcome mats for stoops. The walls were composed of built-in cabinets sweeping down to a narrow counter which strangled the room on four sides. David saw no books anywhere and would have wagered the cabinets were empty. The air smelled of furniture polish and fish.

"Why in hell Nora packed two tunas, I have no idea. You want a sandwich?"

"No thanks," David replied. "I'll eat later but you go ahead. I'll get right to the point. I'm helping out the police in their investigation." He was instituting a different approach, one he was more comfortable with in dealing with friends, one that carried with it the stamp of legal authority.

Foster acted as if the words hadn't been processed.

"It's bad enough to lose a friend," he said, "but what a setback for us. For the whole hospital family. For the whole community. And for them." He pointed at photographs of major benefactors that paraded on the countertops encircling the room. "Did you catch the papers? They crucified us. And on top of that, the accreditation people have already phoned me. They're calling yesterday's surgery a 'Sentinel Event,' and are threatening to close the hospital. They want us to reexamine all our protocols and procedures and to start emergency educational classes for everyone who works here. That was no Sentinel Event, for heaven's sake. That's not malpractice; that's murder by an imposter."

Offhand, David didn't know how to interpret the comments—he was never certain about most of Foster's comments—but, instinctively, he rolled his eyes, glad that Foster was busy peeling away a plastic wrap and hadn't noticed. His right hand was in command, David observed. He also observed an exit door off the rear wall.

"I didn't know that Cortez fellow," Foster said. "Sad. But, I've been insisting for years that our privileges for visiting professors should be tightened." He sighed and added, derisively, "But, oh no, the medical staff says that would be insulting. Too demeaning. As it is, these prima donnas can zip in, zip out, no one has to talk with them, check them out. Shit, it's a miracle a Good Humor man hasn't wandered in and treated a patient."

"Alton, listen." David flipped open his notepad and sat on a black leather sofa facing Foster. "Can you think of anyone wanting to do Charlie in like that?"

Foster bit into a sandwich. "Charlie was a fine man. His heart and soul were in this institution. Whoever was responsible really didn't know him." David didn't write anything down or bother to rephrase the question. He knew Foster was pulling a Sarah Bernhardt for it was common knowledge that, despite his brassiness, he had been Bugles' patsy, and Foster resented it. An hour earlier, Tanarkle had no hesitancy in saying as much.

"Now, just for the record," David said, "but, besides, I know they'll want me to ask—can you tell me where you were during the—ah—surgery?"

"Right here."

David cast a furtive glance toward the back door and made an entry in his notepad.

He continued: "One thing I've never been able to figure out. Coughlin across town—did it make any difference to him that EMS ran from here? I would have expected him to want it there at Bowie."

Foster placed the sandwich on its wrapper and met David's stare. "It's a loser, David. Not all cities do it like us. In some places, EMS ambulances are dispatched from a municipal building. But long ago, our hospitals together agreed to help out. Oh, we're reimbursed by the state but not nearly the full amount. And, in a spirit of coopera-tion—for public consumption, of course—the agreement calls for EMS cases to be taken to alternating hospitals unless the patient has a definite preference or time is of the essence. You know, like a car accident a block away from here—they wouldn't run a patient clear over to Bowie. So, both hospitals pretty much break even on the cases but we have to pay Spritz ourselves. Clever, that Coughlin."

"Why agree to a deal like that?"

"Public relations, I guess, but primarily to be considered a full-service provider. Every little bit counts, you know, when you're trying to start up a transplant center."

"But why fire Spritz?"

"Money again. Between you and me, David, I like Vic. On the erratic side, maybe, but professionally he never gave us any trouble. So even though Anderson EMS is a bit less expensive, I voted to retain Spritz. The other three voted to switch to Anderson."

"Did Spritz know the vote?"

"Of course. I had to break the news to him and I told him the truth—that personally, I supported him."

There was a knock on the door and Foster's secretary stepped inside.

"Excuse me, but I thought you ought to know before I went to lunch: Dr. Coughlin just called. He went on and on about consultations or commitments or something through Friday morning—I believe he used the word incommunicado—and that, if he didn't make Mr. Bugles' funeral in time, he'd make your house afterwards. He insisted I not put him through to you but to relay the message."

"Thanks, Doris." She left as Foster checked off a name from a list he had withdrawn from a desk drawer. Shaking his head, he said, "That's how the guy communicates with me—by message. It's a good thing we have others at the Joint Conference Committee meetings. But, fuck him."

David had never heard him use the phrase.

Foster continued, "If you hadn't dropped by, I'd have called. I contacted Bugles' family, such as it is: two sons. That wasn't easy. Which reminds me—there could be a lawsuit here. Brother! Anyway, in case you haven't heard, there are no calling hours and the funeral is on Friday morning. Afterward, we're having some people over to the house. I hope you and Kathy can join us."

"Yes, of course, we'll be there."

David got up to leave and Foster waddled behind him to the door. "By the way," he said, "one more housekeeping detail. We checked with Credentials to get Dr. Cortez's address in Chile. We've been in touch with the family. The medical examiner's finished with the body and after the autopsy, we're shipping it down there."

David thanked him for the meeting and stopped at the secretary's desk to ask for Cortez's address. He would wire flowers later. He felt put through a wringer but it had missed the sweat he wore under his collar. Housekeeping details?

Back at the Hole, he slouched into a chair and let his arms drop to the floor. He felt ensnared in more ways than one.

"What's wrong?" Belle said. "You're a bundle of sighs."

"I couldn't wait to get out of there."

"Where?"

"The cabinet room of our eminent administrator. The housekeeper." He sat up. "I'm telling you, Belle, the more I pry, the more I realize we've got a swamp of grudges around here. And I thought I knew the landscape pretty well. Uh-uh."

"You sure you want to go through with all this?"

"The prying and prowling? The snoops? More than ever. So if I complain now and then, disregard it."

The phone rang and Belle picked up. As she traded barbs with a receptionist, David abbreviated a few thoughts in his notepad and punched in Sparky's number on his cellular.

"Sparky? David. Too soon to call?"

"Not at all. I got the blood confirmations a while ago."

"And?"

"Just as we suspected. The stains on the floor were Bugles' and the one on the lab door was Cortez's."

"The locker shelf?"

"One spot was Bugles'. The smudge was all Cortez. And I couldn't lift a print anywhere—nothing on the locker or stool or walls except the attendant's. His were all over the place. I had him drop by for prints and they match."

"Maybe I should question him."

"I wouldn't bother. Mousy old guy, about five feet tall, all hunched over. Hope you don't mind, but I asked him if he saw anything unusual yesterday. He answered in the negative but said he leaves at two everyday. He mostly cleans and opens lockers for the morning docs who misplace their keys."

"Did your contact in Tokyo call back?"

"Yes. I went over the x-rays with him and he's certain there were no prints from Cortez's skin. But, David, listen to this. I described the pearl-handled dagger to him. He said if the pearl is real, the dagger could be an original from centuries ago when the samurai of his country had a foothold. They were very militaristic and he said they always carried swords and many of them, daggers. They carried them in pairs because they believed a single dagger gave protection but matched daggers also gave mystical powers. And he talked about Japan's great history of pearl production. So that fits."

"And if he's right, there's another dagger around somewhere?"

"Sounds like it."

David was taking notes and asked for a moment to catch up. Then, "What about the rock?"

"It's common sedimentary found anywhere around here. No prints. The writing on the tape came from a lead pencil, probably number two."

"It's ordinary adhesive tape, right?"

"Right. Nylon. From any doctor's office or hospital."

"So nothing spectacular there. What about the printing? Could you tell if he was right or left-handed by the way he printed?"

"Not at all. And I don't think the way the strips were laid really pinpoints it either. I got to thinking about it, in fact tried both ways. I'd say it favored a lefty a tiny speck—but no more than that, in my opinion."

"I tend to agree but if I were totally certain, I'd stop checking wrists. Maybe I will anyway."

"What?"

"Nothing important. Sparky, I want to thank ..."

"One last thing. Two, really. About the tape. Stuck beneath one of the strips was a thin strand of fiber. It checked out to be cotton."

"Any dye?"

"No."

"Can you save it for me, or, at least, if I can hit upon where it came from, can you see if there's a match?"

"Sure, but once again, it's always difficult to say positively."

"What's the other thing?"

"Well, I don't know if it means anything. The tape is old."

"Old?"

"Yes, frayed, faded—you know, yellow."

"Come to think of it, I remember that," David said. "You think it's important?"

"I'm not sure."

"We'll see. Anyway, Spark, good job. And, thanks a lot. I'll be in touch." David returned the phone to the case on his belt. Suddenly, he dwelled on daggers, museums and pawn shops.

Belle had finished her phone conversation. "Lots to dissect?" she asked.

"What? Oh, yeah, there is. Did you get ahold of Boston Childrens'?"

"Yes, Tanarkle was there all right. They thought he was great. Inspiring. Grand Rounds were held from nine to eleven. No one seems to know whether he stayed for lunch."

"That means he could have made it back in time."

Belle squinted and he waited for her to comment. "I find it hard to imagine his giving an inspiring presentation, then racing back here and committing those hideous things," she said.

"You took the words right out of my mouth," he said. "Now, next. Can you go back to having lunch with that gossip crew of yours from the E.R.?"

"Sure, and they're not gossipers. They just happen to know the pulse of the hospital."

"Okay, have it your way: keep it medical. And keep your ears peeled. See what you can find out."

"They're always peeled."

"I mean, even try to lead the conversation. But be subtle. Think along the line of, 'Do any of you have any dirt on Spritz or Tanarkle or Foster'?"

"Oh, that's real subtle."

"I don't mean come right out and ask them. If they're talking about those guys, milk it along. Belle, you're a pain in the ass." He knew she smiled inside.

"You already said that today. Are they your suspects?"

"And Coughlin." David's voice took on a deeper texture. "Of course, everyone's a suspect until proven otherwise."

"Well, I'll be darned," she said, fondling an amber locket that hung from her neck.

"What?"

"You're becoming a pro."

6

Dating back to his medical school days and continuing on through his tenure in the Department of Pathology, David hated the sights, sounds and smells of a postmortem examination. He called them "flesh-in-the-raw" smells. But, particularly the sounds were awful. He could never harness the jolt to his body by the screech of rotary saw on skull bone or the splash of water hose on body parts, its sound shriller than the dousing of his front lawn on a dog day in August. The saw and hose seemed so out of place there, giving him as they did, the feel from chalk high-pitched on a blackboard.

At twelve-fifty, he set foot in the autopsy room and expected to watch Ted Tanarkle do the post on Charlie Bugles for only the time required to form an impression of the pathologist's demeanor. Besides, he had just yesterday witnessed the slaughter and later scrutinized the havoc in Bugles' belly.

David deliberately arrived early to catch Tanarkle's initial reaction to the "Y" incision across the chest from shoulder to shoulder and down the front of the abdomen to the pubis. The pathologist would extend the vertical slit across the abdominal incision made earlier by the imposter in the operating room, and David believed it would be at that point that Tanarkle's facial expression would be the most revealing.

He leaned against a wall feeling like a traitor to his longtime friend and mentor, awaiting his arrival, intent, therefore, not in collecting pathological evidence, but in detecting a flinch, a subtle twitch, an incriminating comment. David let his eyes drift over the varied shapes of stainless steel he'd seen many times before: the mobile cart for transporting bodies to the morgue; the autopsy table with holes to allow water and fluids to drain; the small-parts dissection table with its own set of drain holes; the tank for delivering water to the tables; the scale to weigh each organ—another misplaced item, he thought.

The room was warm, so warm that he believed he would not have been surprised to see vapor lifting from the cold steel surfaces and from the cold, naked body. Sun poured from a thin bank of windows at ceiling height, dissolving onto the walls, rendering them creamy, the body more wax-like.

He removed the phone from his hip to call the Hole, hoping Belle had returned from lunch.

"You're back early," he whispered.

"Hospital food's good for dieting. No, I didn't learn anything yet from my crew, and why are you whispering?"

"The post should start any minute. Do me a favor, will you?" David looked at his watch. "Unless I call you back, buzz me at exactly five after, and when I answer, hang up."

"Why, pray tell?"

"So I can leave."

"Why be there in the first place?"

"So Ted will think I'm conscientious." David clicked off.

At two minutes before one, Tanarkle entered the room alone through a swinging door. He wore a green scrub suit and brown rubber apron.

"Hello, David. You're right on time." David nodded.

The pathologist clipped a tiny microphone to the neckline of his shirt and squeezed his hands into a pair of latex surgical gloves. He opened a metal-bound chart and flipped through its first few pages as he moved to the foot of the body. He checked the number on a tag tied to the big toe against a line on the chart. Then he dictated: "This postmortem examination is performed at the request of Dr. T. Y. Tippett, Medical Examiner of the city of Hollings. Deceased is Charles J. Bugles, Accession Number 1569-777. Hospital Chart Number 100745. The body is that of a well-developed, well-nourished white male who appears his stated age of 65. His head is bald; his eyebrows and pubic hair appear gray-white. Height and weight listed are 70 inches and 182 pounds."

Holding the chart in one hand, he ran his other over the body's face, neck, arms and legs. "Skin is generally greenish-red; neck and jaws slack; rigor mortis resolving in extremities. There is a tattoo of a bird's head on the lateral surface of his right upper arm …" He put the chart aside and, rummaging through a steel jar, pulled out a small Stanley retractable ruler and held it against the arm. "… measuring 5-by-6 centimeters."

The autopsy room was excluded from the hospital's paging system and Tanarkle's words echoed in the silence.

David stood on the other side of the body, his eyes riveted on the pathologist's face.

"Externally, there is an obvious trans-abdominal incision between the xiphoid and umbilicus, measuring ... 19 centimeters. There are no other skin lesions."

So far, nothing, David said to himself. Tanarkle's voice was firm, his face expressionless.

He swept a scalpel deftly from the right shoulder to the lower part of the sternum and repeated the process on the left side. Next, he cut straight down in the midline, over the trans-abdominal incision to the symphysis pubis. Then, he retraced the incisions for a deeper cut.

The grainy sound ignited David's nerve endings, and he was relieved by the phone vibration at his beltline. He didn't want to hear the separation of ribs and cartilage which was soon to follow.

He spoke softly into a dead phone: "I'll be right there."

David thought himself foolish for not having activated the audible ring because Tanarkle had no way of knowing he was being summoned. Yet, David excused himself with no apology. He had learned little from the pathologist's stoic demeanor and ritualistic conduct.

But maybe, he rationalized, in learning nothing, he learned something.

David decided to skip lunch at the cafeteria, instead opting for a fast-food takeout on the way to his first house call. Top down on his Mercedes, black scarf starched in the wind, he munched as he drove along well-plowed streets. A Pavarotti aria blared from his tape deck as high C's and the aroma of French fries escaped into the dry but brisk afternoon. He liked the burn of the wind on his leathery face. On one long stretch, he was unable to shake a tailgater and, more than once, tucked in a shoulder to feel the reassuring rock that was his Beretta Minx. He split his eyes between highway and mirror until the car turned out of sight.

The first visit was to a male patient of thirty-two who over-complained about a sore back. He had first felt it after fixing a flat tire. After his thorough orthopedic and neurological assessment revealed no pathology, David resorted to misdirection.

"You know," he said, "I used to complain about the screams and loud laughter of children playing—until I said to myself I'm lucky I can hear them."

"I don't get it," the patient said.

"Your problem is only a pulled muscle, and think of it this way, Danny, my boy. You're lucky you can walk." David outlined a treatment regimen as Danny looked on sheepishly.

It took David two hours to complete the other three calls and to phone reports to doctors' offices.

At the Hole, he gave Belle four three-by-four cards, one for each patient he had examined. He had scribbled date, name, diagnosis and treatment on each card. There were no exotic diagnoses that day.

"These would really stand up in court, you know," she said, sarcastically.

"Screw the courts," he fired back. He remembered Foster's earlier word choice but toned it down. Even so, he added, "Scratch that comment. If a court of law required more information, I could easily elaborate."

"But, you have nothing in writing."

"It's up here," David responded, tapping twice on his forehead. "Besides, I've handed you index cards for a whole year. Why gripe now?"

"They used to be five-by-eights and they were filled."

"I've honed my craft."

Once home, David nursed the first half of a Manhattan until he figured Kathy had arrived at her condo across town, unless she had worked overtime. He was about to try her when the phone rang.

"Where are you?" he asked Kathy.

"Home."

"You're on time. Thought you guys were busy?"

"We are, but I'm bushed."

"Funny, I was about to call. Too bushed to spend the night? The house needs straightening out."

"Sure it does. That's why I called. The answer is yes. Do you think this mutual serendipity means anything?"

"If I had to guess, it means our hormones are lined up in formation."

"When I get there, will I find out for sure?"

"Affirmative. I have a five-minute plan."

"Five minutes? What can you do in five minutes?"

"Tease away your clothes."

"I'll be right over."

David drained the rest of his drink and, while he waited, he lit the fireplace, a task whose results he enjoyed but whose execution he dreaded. The flames finally took hold as he heard a car pull into his driveway. He added another log and, looking out the window, saw Kathy framed by two icicles, trudging through snow, trying to find the front path. A garment bag was slung over her shoulder and she carried a small overnighter.

Inside, she said, "You really ought to do some shoveling."

"Can't, bad knee." David took the bags and placed them on a chair.

"Then have some kid do it for you."

"Can't."

"Why not?"

"They charge."

She was about to reply when he picked her up with his left arm and covered her mouth with his right hand, whereupon he lowered the uppermost two fingers and replaced them with his lips, but only for a moment. He relaxed his hold and allowed her thin frame to slither down his body.

"We'd better go straighten out your bed," she breathed as she ran her tongue over moist, plum lips.

"It doesn't need straightening."

"It will in half an hour," she said, her voice now throaty.

On the way to the bedroom, she stopped abruptly. "Wait!"

"What's the trouble?"

"Your knee."

David led her by the hand and said, "I'll grit my teeth."

An hour later in the kitchen, he poured Kathy her usual Chardonnay. She wore one of his shirts, a potato sack that reached her knees. She tugged on white athletic socks she had selected from his dresser drawer.

"What next?" she asked.

"Eat. Check the freezer. There's probably something there for two."

She did and there was.

In a minute, Kathy was at the stove. Off to the side, David sat at the table, pretending to read a magazine. He studied her face, heart-shaped with skin like China silk, trying to dislodge the thought that she was a cop. She cast an occasional blue-eyed glance his way while he reprised the cologned fragrance and the movement of buoyant breasts against his skin.

"What are you doing?" she asked.

"Wondering how such a wisp can do police work."

"I avoid trouble. Plus I get hulks like you to do my dirty work."

David pinched the blond stubble on his chin. "That reminds me," he said. "I've got some dirty work for *you*. But let's wait till we start eating."

"You sound famished," she said.

"Not any more." His eyes ranged freely up and down her body.

"David!" she said with feigned annoyance.

He sprung to her side and said, "You called?"

She pulled down on his shoulder in an unsuccessful attempt to lift up to his ear. He hardly heard her words: "Get out two forks."

They sat on a blanket before the fireplace, prepared to picnic on hamburgers, salad and soggy potato chips. Kathy said, "I never realized the color of your hair and mustache were different."

"They are?"

"In the firelight they are. The mustache is darker. Smile."

"What?"

"Smile. Let me see your teeth."

He flashed a row of teeth, perfectly aligned save for a single lateral incisor. "I feel like a horse that's up for sale," he said. "Why not spread my mouth so you can get a look at my molars?"

Kathy giggled. "Well, yesterday you called me a Shetland." She lifted his upper lip. "They're a little off-white. The fire must shade things differently."

"Kathleen?"

"Huh?"

"Do me a favor?"

"What?"

"Eat."

Over time, David added logs and stoked, and added logs again. The fire dwindled and raged, its finicky glow playing off the walls and off Kathy's face in a manner he hadn't ever noticed before.

She was first to finish eating but remained stretched out on her side, her head braced against a hand. "So what did you accomplish today?" she said.

"Medically, only a few house calls. I've decided to ease up for the time being. And I went to Bugles' post, or at least the start of it. Learned nothing I didn't already know."

David played with her knee. "But I got my main interviews out of the way—Foster, Tanarkle, Spritz. Foster's a phony tightwad. I still don't know how I wangled that so-called office from him."

"David, darling. Think about it. You make house calls for doctors who are kept happy because they have the time to see more patients in their offices. Therefore, more

patients might get admitted to Foster's hospital. There-fore, Foster's happy—and he wants to keep you happy."
"I suppose you're right. Anyway, Spritz is a dingbat and Tanarkle? Well, you know how I feel about Ted. I owe him—wish that stupid blood didn't lead to the lab."
"Stay objective, David."
"I know." He swallowed the last of the food. "I spent a lot of time with Sparky—he's really with it. Tomorrow, we'll see if Coughlin cooperates. You can get off for Bugles' funeral?"
"Yes."
"Okay, good. Afterwards, there's a little get-together at Foster's house. What a laugh—he's got to keep an image. Maybe you can scout around."
"Sure, but what's your take on the guys you questioned so far?"
They had been lying on their sides. He straightened to a crossed-legged position. "Kath," he said, punctuating the air with his fork, "any one of them could have done it. They all had the motive and the opportunity and the means, that's for sure. And that had to be a payback crime. Lots of bones to pick around there. Forget Cortez—he was just in the way. Someone wanted to commit as preposterous a murder as he could think of. Why? Well, first, he's nuts. And, second, he wanted not only to eliminate Bugles, but also to do something else at the same time."
"Like what?"
"I'm not sure, but possibly like ruining the hospital's reputation."
"He'd go to that extreme?"
"As I said, he's off his rocker but that's a very deter-

mined thing he did. And if the reputation angle is part of it, I hate to imagine what could still happen around here. My read is those guys would think spit's a nice aftershave for each other."

Kathy changed to a sitting position. "You mentioned dirty work," she said.

"Well, it ties in. Let's wait for now, but if someone needs shadowing, can you arrange it for me? I know you're short-handed, but ... "

"No problem. We can always scrape up a body from somewhere."

"And, another thing," David said. "You think these hospital people find trouble with my wearing two hats?"

"Do they answer your questions?"

"Yeah, but I recoil inside."

"So? Look, if you ask and they answer, why sweat it? Personally, I think you can get more out of them than we could." She took hold of his hands. "And also, David, one thing Nick and I won't do, I promise. We won't ever press you for minutiae. 'Nit-reporting', we call it. That smothers an investigator. He and I both know. We've had it done to us. You plow ahead—just give us broad up-dates. If you think we can help—like that shadowing—give me the word."

"What's with Nick?"

"Him? He's testing your commitment. It'll work out."

"No further questions, your honor," he said. He dabbed his lips with a napkin which he then made into a ball and hurled across the room before wrestling her to the floor. They retired early.

7

In several years of solving cases as an amateur detective, David had tracked stolen goods, runaway teens, missing records, embezzlers—but never a matching, pearl-handled dagger, particularly a facsimile of those the samurai wielded centuries ago, or, perhaps an original. He was prepared to devote the whole day, Thursday, to some serious legwork before attending his martial arts class at five.

At ten in the morning, he accessed the Internet and contacted three resources he estimated might be helpful: Defense/Link of the Department of Defense, the National Technical Information Service, and the Smithsonian Institute. Neither their web sites nor the software he downloaded gave any indication they might provide a clue in locating a Japanese dagger. Next, he phoned an Information Broker he had dealt with before. The broker said he couldn't begin that type of case for three weeks, but David couldn't wait that long.

So, after scowling at the computer, he set out on a clandestine search he was sure had no precedent in the greater Hollings area, and a quickened pace belied his confusion over where to turn first. He simply wanted to accomplish as much as he could before predicted gale winds struck.

He chose, first, the library. Whether it was because he knew every librarian and clerk there or because a dagger had been described by the media recently, David decided to fend for himself between index files and bookstacks. He learned about daggers used by British commandos during World War II, about M6 bayonets, and about the bowie knives of the Civil War. He perused a book about military weapons of Far Eastern nations, and read an article—more slowly—that stated daggers are used chiefly for self-defense or sudden attack, but some have served purely ceremonial or decorative purposes. Finally, he came across a passage entitled, *Japan's Men-At-Arms,* and read it twice:

"The material symbol of the martial spirit of the times was the warrior's principal weapons, his sword and his daggers. In later years the privilege of carrying these deadly instruments came to be reserved for the knightly samurai, but during the Kamakura period, some men of lower birth also had them and used them to carve their way to glory. They were not, however, weapons only; to the samurai especially, a sword and a pair of pearl-handled daggers were the central objects of an elaborate cult of honor."

David toyed with the idea of abbreviating his legwork for the day because he had already succeeded in discovering more than he expected, namely that his research had validated what Sparky had said about the dagger pair. And that probably, not possibly, the twin to a murder weapon was concealed somewhere in the vicinity.

Yet, he wanted to make a second and final stop. He drove to the city's north end, past tenement blocks and a Mobil station, and he parked across the street from a one-story storefront with three golden balls fastened to a bracket. A tarnished matching sign read, HARRY RAZBIT, PAWNBROKER. David had grown up with the owner's son and had seen the father occasionally but never professionally.

He climbed out of his car and looked right and left on the desolate side street, the wind feeling and sounding as if worse were to come. A red and white "OPEN" sign hung from twine on the inside of the centrally placed door. Before entering, David perused the displays through the windows on either side.

He saw silver and gold timepieces; brightly spangled rings and bracelets; vases, urns, place settings and silverware; cameras, stereos and tape recorders. There were desk sets and trophies; and a baseball glove and football helmet and fishing rod. Perched on the uppermost shelf were a trombone, a cornet, several guitars and even a tuba that appeared too big to lift, much less blow through.

David wondered about the plight of the legitimate people who would surrender such items: the budding tailback without a helmet, the hero without trophies, the musician without a guitar or tuba. He also thought about the penny-ante rewards of lawbreakers who lied their way around Mr. Razbit. In the face of widespread availability of credit cards, Razbit's continued to survive because of the honesty of its proprietor.

David walked through the sound of a jingle into a

blown-up replica of the window displays. Essence of vanilla could not hide the must of half a century. Behind a glass counter crammed with jewelry, an Albert Einstein look-alike emerged from the back door. Open-mouthed, he pointed at David and said, "Well, I'll be! David Brooks. I mean Doctor David Brooks. And, I understand, a detective for good measure. I haven't seen you since you and Harry were in high school."

The reedy, little man raised on his toes, pretending to see over David's head. "What have they been feeding you, my son?"

"Hello, Mr. Razbit. Good to see you again. How's Harry, Junior?"

"He's fine. He's a doctor, too, you know. Up in Albany."

The old man wore a faded tan sweater whose shoulders dangled down his front. His hands bore plexuses of veins the size of his fingers, and David guessed he could slip his thumb under the man's leather watch strap.

"I must write him some day. But I've come here to show you …"

"This is about that terrible killing over at the hospital, isn't it? Couldn't it have been an accident?"

"There was also a knifing in the surgeon's locker room."

"Oh, right, yes, right. I guess you can't fall on a knife."

"No sir, not very well. And that's why I'm here."

David placed Friday on the counter and removed the photograph of the pearl-handled dagger from it. "Have you, by any chance, seen something like this recently?"

David observed Razbit's face and concluded he'd

like to meet him in a poker game some day.

"A dagger," the pawnbroker announced. "That's a dagger, right?"

"Right."

Razbit's eyes took on a hunted look. "Yes, David, I'd have to say yes."

David, confident, pressed on. "Can you tell me about it?"

"I read about the pearl handle of the dagger in the newspapers, but I'm bound by the ethics of my business. I'm like the poor man's banker, you know, and respectable bankers follow the ethics of the banking industry."

David believed the pawnbroker was stalling and chose a word to preempt an anticipated oration. "So?" he said.

"So I can't give you names."

"But, can you say a dagger like the one in the photo crossed your hands recently?"

"Yes."

"A dagger or a pair of daggers?"

Razbit looked helpless. "A pair."

"A pair was bought?"

"Yes."

"You can't give names?"

"No." David knew a fake name had been used, anyway. He gave the old-timer his most piercing stare.

"Can you at least describe the person who bought the pair?"

Razbit rearranged a collection of lockets on the counter.

"She had dark hair—wore dark glasses—had a bandana on—was all bundled up. That's all I can remember."

"That's all?"

Razbit now looked captured. "Maybe one other thing."

"Which is?"

"She had a husky voice."

"Was she tall? Short?"

"Everyone looks tall to me."

David decided he'd pumped as much information out of his school chum's father as he could. He assured him the interview never took place, asked him to be remembered to his wife and walked out the door.

At five, David cursed as he climbed three flights to Bruno's Martial Arts Studio. *How about an elevator, for Christ's sake? But I suppose we black belts aren't supposed to have trick knees.*

He pushed open the door at the top of the stairs and waited to hear its laminated glass panel shake, as it always had for nine years. Imprinted in black at each corner of the glass were, in turn, CHINESE—JAPANESE—KOREAN—AMERICAN. In the center was:

MARTIAL ARTS
Bruno Bateman, Grand Master

Inside, it was as if David had crossed a bridge to a land far removed from turmoil, stress or even tedium on given days. One would think it was merely because of the concentration of fending off serious injury in percussive *tae kwan do* combat: kicking, elbows flying, slashing with hands and feet. But it was more than that. His senses were piqued again: the smell of sweat, the talcum taste, the clash of expiratory grunts, the give of the shiaijo mat under his bare feet.

David had become somewhat of a master himself in

bujutsu, a form of Japanese martial arts that stresses combat and willingness to face death as a matter of honor. He had never been required to take it that far since he began the study as a teenager, but he respected the spiritual concepts on which it is based: Zen Buddhism and Shinto. And it was through the pursuit of those teachings that he grew to understand Japanese culture in general.

He peeked in at Bruno who was in a side room and had already begun his class for beginners. He alternated it nightly with a class for intermediates. The middle-aged Grand Master was as tall as David but thinner. Ruddy complexioned, he had cheekbones that appeared inverted and greying hair gathered in a ponytail. When not in combat, his movements were economical, and he kept his hands pressed to his sides like lethal paddles. Even his smile took a full sentence to form—but a period to dissolve.

"Sorry I missed Tuesday," David said.

"Understandable," Bruno responded, one eye on David, the other on a student he had in a partial hold. "See you next week?"

"I sure hope so, but if things get hairier, I might have to skip again."

"First things first, and I wish you success."

In deference to his knee, David had recently given thought to limiting his workouts to non-percussive *aikido*—merely to throwing or locking, and neutralizing his opponent without striking. He couldn't abandon, however, the gusto of what had become second nature to him: the give and take of the inherently lethal; in his mind, the only bona fide karate. Moreover, the pain would come later.

He was one of a handful of members who had been issued lockers. On Thursday nights, he changed into a pajamalike costume of white cotton jacket and pants and a black belt. On Tuesdays, he wore simple gray sweats. This time was no different from other Thursday nights: mats all filled, friendly chatter between yowls, exchanging opponents around the room, his savoring the ambiance of a full hour. He took a shower. There had been nothing unusual up there.

Outside, a fierce, biting wind whipped a drizzle to the side. Newspapers blew around David's legs while, nearby, a Stop and Shop bag was tangled in a tree. Only after winter classes did David have a stocking cap handy to join his scarf and gloves because he had been told in physiology class that thirty per cent of body heat was lost from the head. And that it was probably more if one's pores were open. David had always gone along with the thirty per cent, but he had difficulty picturing pores opening and closing. So suppose they're open now—what difference does it make under two tons of hair? Nonetheless, he took the cap from his pocket and put it on.

He hopscotched over puddles to the parking lot across the street, rehearsing what moves he would use should anyone accost him. About to slide into his car, he noticed a small scrap of paper under a windshield wiper blade. He pried the paper loose and was about to roll it into a wad when, under the stanchion light, he was drawn to two lines smeared in black ink:

SOON AGAIN

MY FRIEND

David pulled out his Beretta Minx .22 and shielded it in the hollow under his left arm as he turned in a circle, casting his gaze at trees and shrubs and along rows of parked cars. Inadvertently, he dropped the scrap of paper. He returned the gun to his shoulder rig and, before speeding off, searched the macadam around him, finally concluding the paper was lost in a gust of wind.

He felt the force of the wind against the side of his car and tightened his grip on the wheel. The trip home was slow and he had time to convince himself he would level with Kathy for a change. David figured this new message could refer to anyone but, for the first time, he included his own life in the deadly scheme that might unfold.

Once home, he called Kathy and told her about the wiper message, only to be admonished that he should have a uniformed police officer nearby at all times. David swore and nixed the idea.

8

CE LINE DO N◯T CROSS POLICE LINE DO N◯T CROS

On Friday morning, the funeral service for Charles J. Bugles was brief. It was also poorly attended, the collection of mourners as sparse as his remains. He had been cremated. Through the thrum of rain on slate at St. Matthew's Episcopal Church, David heard not a sob. He wondered whether the organ was on the blink, and then he strained to see if the two black-clad figures alone in the front pew resembled Bugles, but their heads remained stock-still ahead.

The minister recited a brief generic eulogy, the gist of which David thought he had heard before. He decided to leave early, hoping there were more people at the reception. He hated funerals and everything associated with them and was glad there had been no wake.

As he negotiated the turns on a hill overlooking Alton and Nora Foster's estate, David saw cars lined like dominoes on both sides of the circular driveway. At the main gate, he obeyed the homemade sign, its arrow's ink dripping in the rain, and drove along a path beyond the Tudor house, past hedges of arborvitae and a traditional bread oven enclosed by topiary loaves. He swerved into a tight slot and, patting his left shoulder, dismissed the idea of bringing Friday along. He squeezed out of the car and slid through an ice-ridged field toward the house. David had been there twice before and remembered cursing the salary Foster commanded but, since then, had learned of the gilt-edged securities inherited by his wife. In the foyer, a silver-haired gentleman in an ascot helped with coats. David handed him his scarf and gloves as if, coatlike, they had concealed the black double-breasted suit and straight necktie he wore uneasily. He stepped into a sunken living room and raised an eyebrow whose slant questioned why a piano player had chosen *Summertime*—at a funeral reception in midwinter. Abstracts in gaudy frames cluttered each wall. The guests, noisy in their late morning excuse for Bloody Marys, mingled like politicians working a crowd. David shook his head at some who leaned back, their shoulders shaking as they laughed. A bartender in a red blazer cracked jokes.

He knew most of the guests who were packed in there: board members, department heads and their spouses, several private physicians, a few nurses dressed for work, administrative types, area industrialists. And one secretary he recognized: Marsha from Pathology. He spotted Kathy balancing two drinks an arm's length away from her slate turtleneck dress. She dodged her way toward him and, extending a glass, said, "Here, I saw you come in. Sorry I couldn't make it to the church after all. Something came up."

"You weren't alone," he said, taking a sip and looking around. "Quite a reception. See anything interesting?"

"Just that Foster, Tanarkle and Spritz are avoiding each other. At least I think it's Spritz from your description. Reddish hair, always smiling—kinda fake?"

"That's him."

"Tanarkle brought his wife. She's all gussied up. Giant hoop earrings. Quite a knockout. Is Spritz married?"

"Are you kidding?"

"Oh."

Above the gathering, David could make out Betty Tanarkle talking with Foster and tossing her head about in rich laughter. David couldn't resist thinking his pathologist friend had married a bon vivant whose main goal was to cha-cha through life. He wandered over.

"Well, David, glad you could make it," Foster said.

"Nice party, unfortunate reason."

"Really?" Foster said. He paused for a response which he didn't get.

"You know Betty Tanarkle, here."

"Yes, of course," David said. "Good to see you again. How's Ted holding up?"

"As well as could be expected, thank you, David." Her over-painted lips hardly moved as she spoke. "It's quite a strain, you know. Ted and Charlie go way back."

David was referring to something else but didn't pursue it. She misinterpreted, he thought, or maybe it was a lame attempt at deflection.

Betty was taller than her husband or Foster, more so in cranberry platforms. Even David believed the androgynous look of blonde hair clashed with her black bollero and full skirt. And even *he* felt embarrassed by her neckline, confining his eyes to one brief sweep.

"Excuse me," he said, moving aside, "there's Everett

Coughlin. I think he's about to leave. See you in a bit."

He reached Bowie's pathologist and key booster at the front door. "Dr. Coughlin, wait."

"Oh, hello, David." He removed his brown beret and twirled it in his hands. An older muttonous man, Coughlin appeared as vinegar-lipped as David had always pictured. If the old coot tried to smile, his face wouldn't cooperate, David opined under his breath.

"I just figured out why Bugles was cremated," Coughlin said. "Not because he thought a normal burial was a wasteful use of land as his sons over there claim." He waited to be prompted.

"Why, then?"

"Because he wanted his ashes rubbed in everyone's face." Coughlin said impassively.

"You didn't take to him much, did you?"

"Take to him? I suppose it's proper to say it's too bad he's gone, but I must admit, I hated being in a room with him. He contaminated the air around me."

David didn't remove the notepad from his pocket for fear Coughlin would clam up.

"I hear your hospital's referring its transplant cases out-of-state," David said.

"That—is—correct. Wouldn't you?" Coughlin said. His marinated face took on a dark, fierce look.

"I'm glad I don't have to make those decisions." On a roll, David decided not to let up. "How about Hollings— you're still sore, right?"

"Sore? I'd say gangrene has set in."

"I'm sorry to hear that."

"Too bad I have to put it that way, but it's the way I feel. They have no conscience."

"You still giving lectures there?"

"Yes, until they kick me away. I have one tomorrow, in fact. At nine—why not try to make it. I've entitled it, *DNA. What Next?*"

"That's right up my alley. I'll be there. You game for a few questions afterward."

"I'm always game for questions after I speak."

"About anything?"

Coughlin's nostrils distended. "About anything," he said. He put on his hat and stormed out the door. There had been no handshakes.

David believed he had felt the vibrations from a volcano but chose not to dwell on it. He had not learned anything new except for the Saturday morning lecture and the depth of Coughlin's animus.

He returned to the living room and put his unfinished drink down at the back of a table filled with sardine canapes, salted nuts, assorted cheeses and minced chicken paté. Eying Nora Foster leaving the piano player, he headed her way, chewing on a single nut. First thank her, then her husband, then mosey by the Bugles men. *The Way We Were* hung in the air.

"Nora, thanks for the invite. I preferred your other parties, but it was nice of you to do this."

"Thank you for stopping by." She held out both hands with a flourish. David shook one. "Horrible, ghastly killings," she said in a cavernous voice. "They've made it so difficult for everyone connected with the hospital, especially for Alton."

He thought the incongruity between Nora Foster's anorexic face and her spherical body had increased since he saw her last. Her black hair was thin, her heavy makeup jagged as if she had applied it in the dark. She wore glasses framed in mottled brown. A brown caftan was sashed at the waist. How did she have enough to make the knot? In their brief encounter, he saw her twice feel for the knot and tighten it. See, even she wonders. They nodded and, as they exchanged picture smiles, he noticed speckles of dandruff on her shoulders.

He small-talked as he picked his way among hospital friends until he found himself standing before the only two guests who were sitting. They were the two black-clad figures he had seen at the funeral. He stared at them and they stood. Neither reached David's stratosphere, although the thinner one appeared to be six-feet tall, the other, a couple of inches shorter and chunky.

"You must be Charlie's son," David said after introducing himself and grasping the outstretched hand of the shorter and younger looking of the two. He realized he had also shaken the sleeve of the man's jacket. He pegged one son's age at thirty, the other's at forty-five or so.

"Yep, I'm Robert. This here's my brother Bernie." Bernie's hand felt like a wilted dandelion.

David thought Robert looked familiar. "Where do I know you from?" he asked.

"Bruno's karate classes. I took them for two years. I saw you there sometimes."

"Of course, now I remember. That was awhile ago. Did you end up with a belt?"

"Mine's brown." Robert sounded disinterested.

Intermediate, David thought.

Robert's eyes appeared moist and red. He blew his nose. "I'm glad Mom doesn't know how my Dad died," he said to the floor, shoulders collapsed.

"Oh?" David said, turning to look at Bernie.

"Mother passed away ten years ago," Bernie stated. David was struck by how much Robert resembled his father: droopy lids, omelet eyes, mottled, dark complexion. And, except for a bold nose, his face was as flat as a painter's canvas. A linear port-wine stain wrapped around the angle of his right jaw. In contrast, one could make a case that Bernie's features were a softened version of his brother's and father's. David couldn't label his bearing. Regal? Mysterious? It was something he did with his eyelids—turning his blue eyes inanimate—like bottle caps. But, his left earring clashed with the bearing. David rubbed his decision scar.

"I give you both my condolences," he said, mustering a measure of sincerity.

"Thank you," they said in unison.

They sat in a circle of three straight chairs and spoke about the "obscenity" of Charlie's murder and about his having been "a self-made man." David, while preoccupied with the better fit of Bernie's tuxedo, suddenly snapped to attention when he saw him check his watch.

"That's about it," Bernie said. He got up and disappeared in the crowd only to return twenty seconds later to add, "Glad to have met you, Doctor. I'll be in touch, Robert."

What's going on with right wrists these days? David tried to act inconspicuous as he got up and looked around the room to determine that as many people held their glasses in their left hands as in their right.

Focusing again on Robert, David said, "He's in quite a hurry, I see."

"Who, Bernie? Oh, yeah, he has a flight to catch.

One of them business trips."

"What's his business."

"He went to school to be an engineer but now I think he's ... he's a little bit of everything. You know, trading. Yeah, he's into trading." He flashed a tobacco-stained smile.

"What's he trade."

"He tells me he trades everything."

"Where's he flying to?"

"Tokyo. Got some kinda plant there. He's part owner, you know."

David sat again and edged closer to Robert. "And what's your line of work?" he asked.

"Me? I'm in the box factory. Packaging." He rocked in his chair and whined, "They know me as Charlie's son or Bernie's brother."

"Robert," David said, pausing, "look, this may be the wrong time to bring this up, but I'm assisting in the investigation of your dad's death. I understand he lived alone."

"Yep, like my brother said, Mom died. I was in high school."

"Would it be possible for me to visit his place? Just to browse around. It could give me a clue or a lead." David knew a search warrant could be obtained if he needed one. He lowered his eyes and flipped open his notepad hoping it might underline the importance of his request. He could feel Robert's silent once-over.

"My dad said he liked you, Dr. Brooks. And he told me about you being a doctor and a private eye and everything like that."

David stalled as long as he could before looking up.

He thought it best to proceed with another question. "He lived at the Highland Estates, right?"

"He was even there when it started. Maybe … I'm gonna say … twenty years now."

"You have a key?"

"Sure. So does Bernie."

"Well?"

"Dr. Brooks, if it'll help in finding the son-of-a-bitchin' butcher what killed him, sure, you can go there."

"I'd feel better if you came with me, Robert. When do you get off from work Monday?"

"Three-thirty. That's when I punch out."

"Good, I'll call you. You live in Hollings?"

"Yep, my apartment's on Chestnut street. Over there near the hospital. Dad owns—uh—owned the building." Robert's eyes refilled.

"I'll call you at four. Then I can pick you up."

David gave the son one final expression of sympathy before seeking out Alton Foster.

"Alton, thanks. Is there anything I can do?" David asked.

"Like what?" Foster said, smiling.

"I don't know. Like parking cars or putting rock salt on the ice out there." David didn't wait to see Foster's expression. He spotted Kathy and signaled he was leaving, then thought better of not conversing with her. Sidling over, he said, "I've had enough of this charade. I'll call you."

"Learn anything?" Kathy said.

"I'll call you. And, oh, I have a question."

"What's that?"

He lowered his voice. "In this huge collection of humanity, guess who loves you?"

He zigzagged through the gathering, bounded up the step to the foyer, asked the guy with the ascot for his scarf and gloves, and then felt like he was doing a Bernie Bugles when he returned to Foster.

"Incidentally, Alton," he said, looking around, "wasn't Victor Spritz here?"

"Yes, but he didn't stay long," Foster replied.

Once alone on the front stoop, just this side of a chilling rain, David filled four pages of his notepad with notations and sketches.

The next morning, the tower clock registered eight-fifty. David got out of his car and hurried to the cafeteria to pick up coffee and a doughnut.

At the cash register, he heard the page operator scream, "Dr. Brooks, stat! Dr. Brooks, stat!" David had heard plenty of pages before, but they never quivered with such emotion.

"Paging me?" he said aloud.

He bolted to the nearest wall phone. "Dr. Brooks, here."

"They want you at the parking gate."

"Who's 'they'?"

"Security police. Said it's something serious. They saw you drive in earlier."

"Thanks, Helen." He was about to hang up the receiver. "Wait," he said, "which gate?"

"Doctors' parking lot."

David heaved his breakfast into a trash container, and, Friday in hand, burst through the cloakroom and out into a gloomy drizzle. Shallow mounds of snow rimmed the lot. Ahead, stern faces huddled around a late model white Cadillac parked directly opposite the card machine at the toll gate. Its arm was in the up position.

A security guard met him halfway. "We opened the door to see if we could help the guy, Doc, but it was no use. We probably got our prints all over. Looks like a single bullet through the temple. The police are on their way."

At the driver's side of the car, several resident physicians and nurses separated for David. He noted the window in the opened door was down. He saw a man slumped over the passenger seat, his face twisted back and to the left. David leveraged himself on the headrest and leaned forward to get a better look. It was Dr. Everett Coughlin.

9

David straightened when he heard sirens getting closer. He reached over and palpated unsuccessfully for a carotid pulse, careful to avoid the sliver of crimson that crusted Coughlin's jaw above. Turning, his left foot slipped to the side and, after catching himself, he bent to verify that the corner of a shiny object wedged between the front wheel and a clump of snow was worth identifying. It was a laminated plastic entry card bearing Couglin's name and the designation, "Courtesy Staff."

Face hardened and flushed, David clasped his hands behind his back and walked to the passenger side. He peered through the wet front window as he put on his gloves, and he carefully opened the door. The body's head and neck were now more clearly visible. There was a small round wound above the left ear but no tattooing, soot smudge or burn. A slender ribbon of blood was caked down the ear. He didn't disturb the head to examine it for an exit wound.

Three police cruisers, flashing lights cutting through the raw grey morning, funneled to a screeching stop along with a small van and several nondescript cars. Kathy, Nick, Sparky, a technician, the medical examiner, two deputies and a handful of uniformed police officers piled out. One officer ran back to the parking lot entrance to cordon it off with yellow tape. Others ran tape from both corners of the nearby hospital wing to trees deep in the woods on the opposite side. Another sealed off the entrance from the hospital itself. David rubbed his nose, wondering how doctors would retrieve their cars to leave. Worry about that later. He also wondered if the crime scene unit kept its vehicles idling, waiting for such calls to come in.

"It didn't take you long," he said to Kathy.

"Luckily, we were having a special Saturday morning briefing. Dropped everything. What do we have?" She raised the collar of her blue trench coat against the drizzle, now turning coarse.

"Coughlin."

"Coughlin? Dead?"

"Very."

"They said 'shooting.'"

"I just got here myself, but looks like he took it in the temple."

Kathy raised her voice as she looked around. "Anyone hear a shot?" No one answered.

"Probably used a suppressor, anyway," she said.

As Kathy joined Nick who was leaning over the body from the passenger side, David drifted off into the elevated wooded area opposite the gate, surmising the killer had sniped from a dense cover there rather than from the bluish shell of a budding psychiatric building on a higher landing fifty yards away. For six months, crews had worked the equipment in forty-hour weeks but the diesels and jackhammers were silent on weekends.

He examined for footprints and, damning the rain for melting the snow among the bushes, felt his knee buckle as he threaded his way up the ice-crusted slope. On a small ridge behind an oak, he spotted a rubber object sprouting through some wet leaves and used a handkerchief to pick it up; it was a rubber nipple from a baby bottle. Two feet away, he found a single cartridge casing resting against a heap of cartons, planks and mortar discarded from the construction site. He placed them into separate envelopes which he took from his breast pocket. David returned to the oak tree and inspected the bushes on either side of it. He stood there for a moment, proud of collecting evidence but frustrated by the turn of events. Another murder to foul things up. Coughlin didn't do the first job? Is this a diversion killing or the second in a payback plan? Spritz? Or some enemy we haven't met, yet. Two murderers? Coughlin threatened Tanarkle pretty good. And, what about the police. This botches *that* up: there goes my leeway.

He walked left to a gentler slope and returned to the car. He tried to disguise the look of anguish he felt in his face. "I had a premonition," he said to Nick.

"That Coughlin would be killed?"

"No, that he'd be the one who would kill again."

Nick flashed a superior grin. "Well," he said, "at least you got the character right."

The statement didn't resonate well with David and he sensed Kathy noticed. She motioned him aside. "You all right?" she said. "You seem wounded. Forget it, that's just his brand of humor."

"Ha-ha, laugh a minute," David said. "But, that's not it. That over there—I guess it's kinda ... you know ...

jolted my confidence." He curled his lip in disgust as he nodded toward Coughlin's body. "Well, it shouldn't. It should just double everyone's responsibility, that's all."

She moved closer to him and whispered, "David, you've done all the right things. It's not your fault the guy killed again—plus ... "

"Yeah, I know," he replied, stepping on her words. He thought he'd finally licked his habit of cutting people off in conversation. "Look, you all carry on. I'm going to walk it off for awhile. I'll be back."

He started to turn but then reached into his pocket and handed Kathy the envelopes. "Here's your suppressor," he said. "It's pretty crude. Plus a spent casing." He pointed toward the bank of woods. "I found them up there by the big tree."

David slouched off like a kicked dog and headed for the Hole. He'd had setbacks in the past and walks like this, all brief but therapeutic. So, by the time he reached Belle's desk, he had decided on at least the preamble to a necessary new resolve. He left a note on her desk for Monday morning:

> "Belle—you've read the papers or we've already talked if you called me. Don't book any more house calls. We'll play it week by week. D."

He returned to the others, coming first upon Sparky who was overseeing the technician taking photographs. "Here we go again, Spark," David said. "Same as before— I can check with you later?"

"Absolutely. I'll be around all weekend, I'm afraid."

David felt a strong hand on his shoulder. It was

Foster's. "David, this is lunacy! You realize we're ruined? Why couldn't he have been shot in his own goddamned parking lot?"

"Nothing like healthy sorrow," David said but—reconsidering—winked. He saw Nick talking to a group of security men and jotting down notes in his own notepad. Kathy was half inside the back of the car inspecting the floor with a flashlight.

David spoke to her, his voice carrying an edge of resignation. "Kath, I've seen enough for now and Sparky said it'll be okay for me to check with him later. We're still on for tonight, right?"

She emerged and, after scanning his face, shook the beam of light on it. She turned off the light and inched closer to whisper, "C'mon, darling, snap out of it. This is what happens if we have a killer out there with a planned agenda. And, yes, I'll be over after I finish here and freshen up. We can cover what we have so far and I can watch you you-know-what."

"What?"

"Tie one on. Right?"

David didn't react.

"Right?" she repeated, sticking the flashlight against his solar plexus and twisting it.

David doubled over in mock distress and, forcing a smile, said, "If you insist."

That afternoon, David stepped onto his small front porch to check the weather. The rain had stopped but the aroma was damp and the air was so heavy on his arms, it felt like sleeves.

Twenty minutes later, he climbed out of the shower

as the phone rang. It was Belle.

"David," she said, her voice raised a notch, "I know about Coughlin. It's all over the news. But before that, you've got to hear this. It can't wait till Monday. At first I thought it could but the more I thought of it—you know I wouldn't call unless it was important and so I figured ..."

"All right, already! Calm down. What have you got?"

"You know my old lunch girls at the hospital—the E.R. gang?"

"Yes."

"One of them just called. Cindy. I don't know how she found out, but if she says something's true, it's true. Alton Foster and Betty Tanarkle have had something going for months, if not years. Can you believe it?"

"She said that?"

"Yes. And she's pretty certain Ted knows about it."

"Well, I'll be a son-of-a ... how about Nora? Does she know?"

"Cindy can't be sure."

David thought out loud into the phone. "Why that old duck. No wonder he never wanted to leave here. Taking all that crap from Bugles."

"What's she see in him, anyway?" Belle asked.

"Power? Some physical quirk? People are funny." He deliberated, oblivious to Belle's next question until she repeated it.

"You still there?" she said.

"Yeah, I'm—uh—I'm still here. This blows my mind. This absolutely blows my mind."

"It couldn't possibly tie in with the murders, could it?"

"I don't know." David shook his head. "Unless we

say Foster's our man—and that's remote to begin with—and that he knocked off Bugles because he knew about the relationship, and Coughlin because of their rivalry." He spoke as if he were addressing himself. "Those are pretty big leaps."

"Do you think there'll be more?"

The question jerked David off his line of thought.

"You mean murders?" He knew what she meant.

"Yes."

While David speculated, he heard breathing at the other end and was conscious of his own. "Give me your opinion," he said. "If you hadn't just heard about Foster and Betty, would you still ask the question?"

"Probably yes. It's been on my mind. There's a wacko around here, that's for sure."

"And my gut tells me Time is our enemy. That's my answer, Belle."

Before hanging up, he mentioned the note he had left on her desk, indicated that on Monday they would touch base on the particulars of Coughlin's murder, and asked to be kept current on the Foster/Tanarkle liaison.

It was five-thirty. David had tossed off a drink and anticipated Kathy's arrival. Another glass in hand, he stepped eagerly to the computer, names flashing in his mind, applying to each the customary trilogy of "Motive—Opportunity—Means." He opened the "MURDERS" file dated Tuesday, January 13, reviewed its contents, and then sat back to sort out which new kernels to enter this time.

He knew he had "snapped out of it," as Kathy had implored, because he could smell the cologne from his face and feel the sweatshirt against his skin. Either that or it's the Manhattan, he told himself, although he was reluctant to be included among those he had heard could think more clearly after a drink or two. He typed:

Saturday, January 17

MURDERS, continued—

Everett Coughlin—sniper bullet at parking gate. No witnesses. Single shot to temple. Killer had to know time of lecture. Casing found in woods.
Who wanted him dead?
Victor Spritz:? still on mission bec. loss of EMS contract.
Ted Tanarkle: Coughlin threatened him royally.
New wrinkle: Betty Tanarkle romantically linked to Foster. Ted knows.
Have feeling killings not over. Better guard Foster.
Spritz and Tanarkle both have motives.
Keep Bernie Bugles in mind—not sure why, yet.
Pawnshop dealer sold pair of daggers to ? woman in disguise.
Concerned about my credibility but will plow ahead—unless gendarmes crowd me out.

David heard a key in the door. Kathy strolled in and removed a redingote.

"It's nice out, now," she said.

He rose slowly from his chair, admiring her lavender skintight pants as she pulled out a hanger from the hall closet. He was at her side before the coat was hung.

David pulled her close and, running his hand over her backside and tugging on the pants, said, "And what's with these, may I ask?"

"I figured you needed it. Complaining?"

"Complain? No, oh no. You look great, you smell great, and, here, let me check." He kissed her firmly on the lips and smacked his own. "And you taste great."

Kathy slapped him on the shoulder and said, "What am I, a dinner entree?" She rubbed the lipstick from his lips with the corner of a tissue. He kissed her as before, only longer.

Breathless, she said, "What's that all about?" She rubbed his lips again.

"We wouldn't want to waste a whole tissue, would we?" he said, leaving for the cramped kitchen to pour her a glass of wine. Only when she was at home with him did he look through narrow doorways and realize he could see a slice of every room. Yet, there was something erotically symbolic in the constriction of those four spaces, adding, he imagined, to the intimacy he and Kathy shared. He hoped a larger spread later in their marriage would not signify the ho-hum he had heard so much about.

She sat in an easy chair, one leg tucked under. He retreated to the sofa and stretched his legs over the coffee table. He wished he had remembered to light a fire.

"The mayor called," she said.

David swallowed hard. "I suppose he wanted to know what in hell's going on."

"That and what are we doing about it."

"And?"

"And I told him someone's on the loose probably carrying out a vendetta, and that we're working on it as hard as we can."

"He let it go at that?"

"Sort of. He said people around town were getting impatient."

"Impatient? After only four days?"

"That's what I told him. He got real apologetic—said he was only doing his job."

"Did he ask about me?"

"No, but I mentioned you were assisting in the investigation. He said 'good'—that he'd heard about you. See, you even have political support, David, so chill out. Another murder's no reflection on you personally—or any others if they happen."

"Any others? God, help us."

"As long as we're doing what has to be done—either you or us."

"What's that mean?"

"We collaborate—no different from before. We have the legal responsibilities but you, de facto, run the show—still." Kathy got up and joined David on the sofa. "Do you hear that?" she said, tweaking his cheek, "Still."

He shrunk back and shot her a conspiratorial wink. "Do you know what would relieve me even more? If, in the future, you informed people we're doing things in parallel."

"I can live with that," she said.

"How about Nick?"

"How about him?"

"Can he live with that, or does he prefer I step aside?"

"Now you're being ridiculous. You misunderstood that remark this morning," she said. "We *need* your help.

And, what's more, he likes you more than you think."

"Be still my heart." David had been taking a sip a sentence. He pinched the back of his hand and looked up to catch Kathy's critical squint.

"Now what are you up to?" she asked.

"I can feel it fine, so I need another Manhattan."

"You're incredible. But here, fill mine, too."

David returned from the kitchen, balancing two dripping glasses. He sniffed Kathy's Chardonnay like a connoisseur and said, "Not bad at all," and handed it to her. He took a long draw of his, assumed a judicial expression and said, "Also not bad." He spilled some of his drink on his trousers as he sunk into the couch.

"Now then," he said, "you want to hear the corker of all corkers?"

"Sure, one more drink and I won't mind anything. We should have been munching, too."

Kathy's reaction to the revelation from Belle was, "You mean Betty Tanarkle is Foster's paramour?"

"You got it."

"But what's she … ?"

"I know: what's she see in him? That's the going question."

They had their usual discussion about whether to eat in or out and settled on grilled ham and cheese sandwiches which David triumphantly prepared. Afterward, he said, "Instead of reviewing what's happened to date, look here—see what I've summarized." He led her to the computer in the den and they read the screen together.

"That says it all," Kathy commented. They moved into the kitchen and he saw her linger by the sink of used dishes and promised himself he would keep more current from that point on. At the table, she took one of two chairs and, while David stood flipping through pages of his notepad, she said, "Your 'better guard Foster' statement? I agree with that."

"You also agree that Spritz or Tanarkle could be after him?"

"You bet. Money and sex. Never fails. But I have a question." She rose abruptly. "Maybe two." She went over to the computer and scanned the screen which David had not cleared. "Yes, two."

"Shoot."

"Why would Tanarkle kill Bugles?"

"I'm not sure, except when I worked in Pathology they bounced off each other like bumper cars."

"And Bernie Bugles? I didn't get a chance to speak to him at the reception yesterday. Why's he listed?"

David sat and took his time to answer. He wrote BERNIE on his pad and underlined it three times. Then he circled it. He said slowly, "I don't know. But, then again, there aren't any explanations for intuition."

"Okay, so we watch over Foster," Kathy said. "No problem. I'll dig up a hard man."

"A hard man?"

"A bodyguard."

"Oh. But I think it should be discreet."

"I'll have him keep his distance. Should we let Foster in on it?"

"No. He'd probably scream bloody murder. He'd say if anyone found out, it might reflect badly on the hospital and the staff and all the fine people of the community and blah, blah, blah. Translation? The bottom line."

"Got it."

"Let's be clear on this, Kath. I've decided to do the guarding, myself."

"You?"

"Yeah, I think it'll be less obvious."

"You're calling the shots," she said, with a peremptory gesture.

"Now, another thing. I'm calling Sparky tomorrow. He goes in Sundays, I assume."

Kathy emptied her coffee cup and played with its handle for a moment. "Darling," she said, "do me a favor. You look tired. Take tomorrow off. Start Monday refreshed. Call him then. I'm sure he'll call you sooner if he finds anything startling."

"But Coughlin's autopsy. I *should* call Ted. Funny, contacting a suspect who may be doing the post."

"Maybe an assistant will do it. But that can wait, too. What are they going to find? It's pretty obvious. There was no exit wound so the man has a bullet in his head. So Tanarkle has the bullet plus the casing you found up on the mound and, hopefully, he can pinpoint the weapon. It's got to be a rifle shot from eighty feet away—we did the measuring after you left. I'm telling you, it can wait till Monday."

David gave her a bewildered glance and said, "Tell you what. I'll do just what you say if you forget what I once asked you to do. Or did I? Wait a minute." He rubbed his decision scar. "I'd decided to beg off asking old friends the tough questions, like 'where were you when the murder took place'?"

Kathy returned the bewildered glance. "You lost me."

"I intended to ask you to do that—more as an authority, not as close as friends—you know. Did I ever discuss it with you?"

"Not that I can remember."

"Well, forget it anyway. This thing has ballooned and I'm in it for the duration, come hell or high water. And, if that's the case and it is, I'm asking any questions that need asking—of anyone—repeat—anyone who needs to be questioned."

Kathy stood and approached him from behind. She rocked on her embrace and said, "So *there*." Hand in hand, they walked into the bedroom.

It was the only room which reflected a flair and an attention to coordination which Kathy insisted on: terra cotta bedspread, mint green chaise lounge in jacquard fabric, celadon drapes with matching lampshades, and a blanket chest at the foot of the bed.

She pulled a quilt up tight around her while David slid off his Beretta Minx rig and placed it on the dresser next to Friday. He rolled in next to her and turned off the light. She flopped her arm over his body and, nearing sleep, whispered, "I'm so proud of you."

Suddenly, he leaped out of bed. Kathy sprung up. "What's wrong?"

"I forgot something in the basement. Be right back."

Three minutes later, he made room on the dresser for a left ankle rig containing a Smith and Wesson snubby.

Long after Kathy had fallen asleep, David lay awake, his mind a pinball machine. He was glad, however, that he hadn't "tied one on" as Kathy had foreseen, because he might not now appreciate that, psychologically at least, he had gotten his second wind and that he was prepared for Monday morning.

10

It was a long and arduous night and at breakfast, David's eyes had not lost their heaviness. Sunlight muscled its way through the kitchen's grainy curtains.

"You look like the wrath of God," Kathy said.

"Thanks. And, speaking of that, you going to church this morning?"

"Yes, I'm picking mom up at ten. Then, after I bring her back, I'll go home from there."

"Do you think *He*'ll mind if I don't attend today?"

"Yes, *She* will."

"Oh, brother."

Their meal was simple: orange juice, toast and two coffees for each.

"You're relaxing today, correct?" Kathy said. She wore one of his red plaid shirts.

"Except for one thing."

"David, you promised." She put her hands on her hips and regarded him sternly.

"This doesn't count. I make a request. Hopefully, someone else does the work." He got up, paced a moment, then changed his mind. He sat to massage his bad knee. "Bernie Bugles—remember him?"

"Of course. Charlie's son. You put him in your computer."

"He said, or rather his kid brother said, he had to catch a flight to Japan directly from the reception at Foster's. I'd like to check on whether or not he went, and also on where he lives. He's not in the phone book."

"Consider it done. We have cousins who have broad responsibilities. I'll call from here before I leave."

"Your relatives?"

She chuckled. "No, not my relatives. 'Cousins' in police jargon means 'stoolies'—'belchers'—you know, 'informants.' Some of our elite do more than inform though, and they take pride in it."

"Like what?"

"Information like what you need plus general background checks."

"Perfect. You'll set it up then?"

"Sure, I'll do it now."

Kathy leafed through a small leather book she pulled from her purse. She picked out a number, placed the call and spoke with a man named Archie, explaining the lowdown they wanted.

"Within twenty-four hours, Arch? Good. Buzz me."

She turned to David. "That's that. Now, you'll take the rest of the day off?"

"Yeah, yeah. I sure hope the murderer does."

He mostly napped the daylight hours away.

At nine o'clock Monday morning, David made his way to the hospital's Hole, cutting corners sharply, conscious of the drag of Friday at his wrist and the press of a snubby against his ankle. He was puzzled by the flood of pages over the public address system.

After discussing Coughlin's shooting death with Belle, he phoned the page operator and learned that several emergency meetings were being organized for that afternoon, all focusing on "the hospital murder crisis."

"Who's meeting?" David asked.

"Who isn't? The Medical Staff Executive Committee, the hospital's Board of Trustees, the Hollings Nurses' Union representatives. They're concerned, Dr. Brooks, real concerned."

Next David called the Medical Staff Office to check on the sign-in sheet for the lecture Everett Coughlin never had a chance to give. He asked whether Ted Tanarkle was there.

"No," the secretary said. "At least, he didn't sign the sheet."

"How about Victor Spritz? He ever go to those things? He never did when I was around."

"Victor at EMS?"

"He was."

"Oh yes, that's right. But that's who you mean—the ambulance guy?"

"Yes."

"As far as I know, he's never attended one. Let me run down the ... Spritz, Spritz, Spritz ... no, his name's not here."

"How about Alton Foster?"

"On a Saturday? Are you kidding?"

"Jill, thanks. We'll do lunch sometime."

"Sure, David, lunch in the caf. I can't wait."

He hung up the phone and asked Belle for a ruler. He could feel her stare when he drew lines in his notepad, twisting it around, erasing now and then, drawing more lines. After scribbling a word or two in the boxes he'd created, he pantomimed a magician's reaction to a rabbit's appearance and held the pose.

"Do I dare ask?" Belle said.

"Belle, I'm well-rested, my mind is clear, people are counting on me, and, damn it, I'm going to be organized and neat."

She considered her nails cursorily and said, "You want a blue ribbon?"

"Very funny."

Now for Sparky. He should have been called yesterday regardless of what Kathy said.

"Spark? David, here. You in the middle of something or can we talk?"

"You must be psychic. Only two minutes ago I got off the phone with my Tokyo friend. Real good guy— said he might wake me up after midnight sometime, just to even the score. I called to get his input on the bullet Dr. Tanarkle found in Coughlin's skull, and I described the casing. He wanted the bullet's groove and land count. Didn't take him long, David, and his feeling matched my own. It's a good bet the murder weapon was a Japanese Sniper Rifle Type 97 chambered in 6.5 mm. It's an offshoot of the old Type 38 with Mauser design points. This one is shorter and has provisions for a telescopic sight."

Thoughts scooted through David's mind. Telescopic sight? Understandable. But, Mauser design points? That's okay, he's the pro. Besides, the clincher will be the rifle, itself, if we ever find it. His last and most fleeting thought was of Bernie Bugles boarding a Japan Airlines plane.

"Good work, Sparky. I assume there were no prints

on the casing or the nipple?"

"None."

"How about that—using a nipple?" David said.

"How about that? Of course, nothing really silences, and I suppose it's as good a suppressor as anything. You can get it at any drugstore."

"Or from the hospital nursery."

"There, for sure."

"Nothing unusual from the car?"

"Nothing."

David was uneasy taking up the criminalist's time on a Monday morning. "One last question and I'll let you go. Did you check the killer's possible vantage point at all?"

"'Probable,' I'd say. Yes, I did."

"Eighty feet away?"

"Eighty feet, right."

"Did you notice anything different about the branches on either side of the big tree there?"

"No."

"Yeah, on the bushes hugging the tree. On the right side from the back, a few twigs were broken. But, not on the left. Seems to me, if Mr. Sniper is right-handed and he took a position behind the tree, he'd aim his rifle from the side where the twigs were snapped. Maybe he even leaned the thing against the tree, but I couldn't find any bark abrasions."

"Makes perfect sense," Sparky said. "If he wanted to aim a rifle and shield himself behind the tree at the same time, a right-hander would inadvertently damage the right-sided bush, as he faced the car. You sure you're not gunning for my job?"

"No way. Me in a visor cap in that lab all day long?"

"You'd have to raise the lamp a foot or two."

They exchanged robust laughs before David said thanks and that he'd be in touch.

He made more notations between the lines in his notepad. Picking up Friday and pausing at the door he said, "Belle, I'll be in the house for awhile if you need me. I'm heading for Spritz's office and then Tanarkle's."

Within seconds, he changed his mind, deciding to visit the newborn nursery. He got off the elevator on the third floor and waved to a nurse acquaintance on Pediatrics, down the hall on the right. The nursery was to his left. He had been there many times before for one reason or another, but this was the first time he understood why one gained entrance only after passing through twin sets of swinging doors. He met a cacophony of cries of such severity that, after responding to a nurse's greeting, he added, "Is it like this all the time?"

"Like what?"

"The noise."

"What noise?"

"Boy, I'll tell you, if I ran the show around here, you'd all get raises."

"What are *they*?"

The nursery had no nurses' station and the two of them stood at one end of a narrow, forty-foot long anteroom surrounded by pink and blue walls and white equipment: tables, baby scales, incubators, spare bassinets.

"Jean, mind if I look around?" David asked.

"No, go ahead. Is everything all right?"

"Oh, sure, just checking on something."

The closer David got to the other end, the stronger

the sweet fragrance of powder, the more fragmented but piercing the noise. It was like an army of infants in a vocal competition.

At the end of the counter immediately before the far archway, David spotted what he was looking for: several open trays of rubber nipples, each one individually wrapped in plastic. No doubt about it—if you time it right, you can help yourself to one of these with no problem.

David made like he was interested in the next room, popping his head in and nodding to the nurses and aides working there: feeding, back-patting, tucking in, suctioning.

He did an about-face, approached Jean and, even though he knew the answer, asked, "Has anyone come in and taken one of those nipples down there? Anyone you wouldn't expect?"

"No, not that I know of."

"The other gals didn't say anything like that?"

"No, not to me."

"Even from the other shifts?"

"No. You sure there's no problem, Dr. Brooks?"

"No, no problem. Curious, that's all."

"About a baby nipple?"

"Yeah, even a strange thing like that. Jean, thanks for your help."

Back on the elevator, David fancied the entire Nursery staff and half the hospital already knew he was making inquiries about baby nipples. On the first floor, he ambled down the corridor in the direction of the Pathology wing, thinking of which questions to ask Spritz first, and then Tanarkle.

On Spritz's office door next to the EMS dispatch

window, he saw a beat-up piece of cardboard covering the EMS emblem above his name. On the cardboard were the neatly penciled words: "EMS BY HOLLINGS." David's eyes narrowed speculatively. He tried the door; it was locked. He looked both ways before ripping off the sign and laying it flat in Friday.

With his cellular phone, he contacted the page operator. "Helen? Dr. Brooks. You know if Victor Spritz is around?"

"He's not. He called—Thursday, I think—let's see, it's posted here—yes, Thursday. And he won't be back till tomorrow."

"Who's running EMS?"

"His assistant, Jack Ryan. He's at home. You want his number?"

"No, never mind. Thanks."

David leaned against the wall and stroked his decision scar. He phoned Sparky who said he'd be available after lunch, then hurried through the laboratory rooms where the pungent stench of chemicals bit his nostrils harder than usual.

Ted Tanarkle's secretary, Marsha, was not at her desk. David paced a minute or two, rapped on the inner door and entered. He found the pathologist dictating the results of an autopsy into a tape recorder: "There was evidence of widespread effusion in the right pleural space along with petechiae and a major infarct in the adjacent parenchyma. David! Have a seat."

"Coughlin had an infarct?" David asked, pointing to the recorder.

"No, this was another one I did over the weekend. I already dictated his but before we get to that, I have something to say." Tanarkle threw his pen across his desk. "David, I did not kill Everett Coughlin or anyone else, I swear to you! Why would I? I know I'm a suspect because of those stupid bloodstains, but you know me. How could I?"

David, taken aback by the starkness of his former mentor's comments, remembered Kathy's advice: "Don't let it get subjective."

"I don't really think you could, but I've got to ask the questions." His last phrase was uttered advisedly because he wanted to imply he was going by the book.

"That's okay, as long as you have some trust in me. We go back a long way."

"That we do." David cleared his throat. "I only have a couple things to ask about. First, Coughlin's post findings."

"Yes, yes, the post." Tanarkle swiveled his chair around and selected a folder from a cabinet behind him. He perused its contents for a few seconds. "There was nothing out of the ordinary except for the gunshot wound to the head. Straightforward entry site, left temple, above and between the eye and ear. No exit wound. The bullet danced around in there and did considerable damage. I found it lodged in the cribriform plate. Sparky's already been by. The rest of Coughlin's body was commensurate with his age."

David was writing rapidly when Tanarkle added, "You don't have to take notes. I'll make you a copy of the report before you leave."

"Good—thanks. Next, the lecture Coughlin never gave. You didn't attend?"

"No. For as long as I can remember, he never attended mine and I never attended his."

"Two pathologists within two miles of each other. Too bad."

"I agree, but unfortunately that's the way it worked out."

"But you always exchanged slides and otherwise consulted with each other? At least you did when I was here."

"Yes, we did. Sort of a necessary evil for both of us, I guess. It helped in the litigious climate we live in these days, and it was convenient. You see, it wasn't that we didn't respect each other's professional skills."

"Jumping to another topic, Ted. Where were you at the time of the shooting, a little before nine, Saturday morning?" See, that wasn't so hard after all.

"Home."

"Mind if I call Betty to verify that? I have to do this, Ted."

"Yes, I understand. You can call, but Betty wasn't there. She and some friends left for the mall in Center City at eight-thirty."

David kicked himself for not asking first whether Betty was home around nine. "No, I won't bother, then."

Silent, Tanarkle took his autopsy report to a copier in an adjacent alcove as if to signify his hope that the interrogation was over.

"That's it for now," David said, folding back his pad and inserting the pathology report within its pages. He shook the pathologist's hand firmly and said, "Hang in there, my friend."

"I'm trying. Got a lot on my plate right now, but I'm trying."

David saw the opening but chose not to broach a new subject—like the infidelity of Ted's wife— and left with a vague sense of pity.

At an unoccupied desk in a corner of the Microbiology Lab, he sat and, after bringing his notes up-to-date, reflected on what had just transpired. Christ. Forget the pity. Who knows if Ted was really at home when Coughlin was zapped? And, David, my man, you didn't learn any more in there than you knew ten minutes ago, except that the bullet ended up in a goddamned cribriform plate!

He felt his phone buzz at his waist. "It's me," Kathy said. "Apparently Mr. Bernie Bugles is a slippery guy."

"You heard from the, ah, hard man?"

"Yes. There was a flight from JFK to Tokyo at three-fifty Friday afternoon, but Bernie wasn't on it. So he either missed it or he was lying. And if he was, why would he be so elaborate—knowing the time and all?"

"Unless he'd taken it before and didn't have to research it," David said.

"Well that jibes with his background info."

"Which is?"

"After college, he spent five years working in Japan in and around Tokyo. Let's see, I have it all written down here. He's forty-five, divorced, has the one sibling, Robert, and apparently didn't get along well with Charlie who's really his stepfather. Mother died ten years ago."

"What's he do for a living?"

"Archie's still trying to find out what he's doing now. Apparently, not much. He got a Ph.D. from the University of Chicago, then went right to Japan to work for a company specializing in prosthetic medical devices. He spent most of his time with their artificial heart valve division—had a hand in spearheading major improvements. They must have thought highly of him because he became their main representative in the field—demonstrating the devices at the leading medical centers in the Far East. Even scrubbed on open heart procedures to assist in inserting them."

David jotted down a few key points. "Where's he live?"

"New York City—West Side. I've got his address."

"Maybe I'd better pay him a visit."

"Good, I'll go with you," Kathy said. "We can combine business with pleasure. Haven't been to the Big Apple in years. Maybe we could take in a show? An opera—there you go—an opera. Right up your alley."

"Aren't you being a bit cavalier at a time like this?"

The silence at the other end prompted David to remove the receiver from his ear and look at it. Finally, Kathy said sternly, "No, I don't think so. David, look, you're winding everything into a tight ball, including yourself. Stretch it out. Pace yourself. Work your tail off, but live a life, too. You'll work better."

"You don't understand."

"Yes, I do understand. You're trying to do too much at once—and that's based only on what I *know* you're doing."

"All this because you want to see a New York show?"

He heard Kathy groan into, "Oh, for heaven's sake!"

David forced a laugh. "Maybe you've got a point." He became conscious of his fluttering eyelids. "But I just can't get away from thinking I'm in a race."

"Against who?"

"Time."

They agreed to spend part of an afternoon at Lincoln Center, at a time David would select to grill Bernie Bugles. But that would be later on, for what had started out as an emergency undertaking, now slipped in his list of priorities, undoubtedly because his mindset didn't include musical diversions. He left the desk, mulling over what Kathy had said about the tight ball, and over what the top priorities should be.

There is, for example, the matter of tracking down the other Japanese dagger, if another exists at all, although Mr. Razbit says it does. And what about locating the Japanese rifle used to kill Coughlin? Suddenly, we have two murders with an Asian connection, and if Bernie's our killer and his Tokyo experience twenty years ago qualifies, we have three. Then again, maybe his experience is more current than that. And, where the hell is Victor Spritz?

After lunch, David drove to the crime lab with the cardboard sign he had torn from Spritz's office door. "Do you still have the strips of tape I gave you?" he asked Sparky. "You know, from the rock." He removed the sign from Friday and dropped it on the desk.

"I see what you're driving at," Sparky said. "Yes, I keep everything. Excuse me." He opened the bivalve doors on a side wall and pulled out one of several old shoe boxes piled on the top shelf. It was labeled, "Hollings Hospital: 1/99."

Sparky placed the rock on the sign and said of the block letters, "They seem to match all right—to my eyes, anyway."

"Mine, too," David said. "Son-of-a-bitch!"

"Wait, now, we're not pros at this. I've seen mistakes made."

"So? Let's get a handwriting expert. Do we have one around here?"

"Certainly. Darn good one, too. She's on call. But I want to warn you, David. They're good at excluding a sample, but swearing to a definite match can be ticklish. If they can't be sure, they do like pathologists do with slides: they send samples around to colleagues they respect to get a consensus. That could take a week or more."

"We don't have that much time. Hold off for now."

Back at the Hole, David was perusing his notes when his cellular buzzed. "David, I got more for you," Kathy said.

"From Archie?"

"No, from our Assault Unit. Foster's been arrested."

"Arrested? For what?"

"Trying to punch a news reporter."

"I can't believe it! Where?"

"In his office. Guess he thought the reporter could soften the impact of the killings on the hospital's reputation. The report states Foster was told by the kid—he's been with the paper about a month—'All crimes occur in society and a hospital is part of society.' Foster was apparently impressed with that, so he invites him up. Only when he gets there, the reporter starts talking about how brutal the crimes were, and about the hospital's lack of security; and doesn't he, as administrator, worry that people will be too frightened to choose Hollings for their care now?"

"Jesus!"

"That's when he tries to slug him."

"Where's Foster now?"

"Not in jail. They released him on his own recognizance. He went home."

"Well, I'm not calling him. Stupid jerk. They should have jailed him. Then I wouldn't have to be a frigging nursemaid."

But he thought he should at least check with the reporter. "Do you have the kid's name? And which paper?"

"Adam Slaughton at the *Herald*." She gave him the phone number and extension.

"Talk to you later," David said. He punched numbers into the phone; a spiritless voice answered.

"This is Adam Slaughton."

"Adam, Dr. David Brooks here. I'm associated with Hollings General Hospital and I've been asked to help in the investigation of the untoward deaths here."

"Yes, I know. I've tried to reach you several times for a comment or two but I kept getting your machine." The tone of the reporter's voice never varied. "Is that why you're calling?"

"No, I'm calling to ask about what happened with Alton Foster today—if you feel you can talk about it."

"I've already written the story on it, so why not? I started what I thought was a straightforward interview and when I got to a certain question, he went ballistic."

"What was the question?"

"Something like, 'I hear you and Mr. Bugles didn't get along.' He screams, 'That's not true!' and then throws this roundhouse punch that even my grandmother could dodge. I could have clobbered him but I thought better of it."

"So you pressed charges."

"Correct." It was the first word released from a monotone. "If I hadn't, no telling what the guy might have said to the police. I told my editor about it and he said I should file an official complaint which I did. We had to preempt anything Foster might have concocted."

"I see," David said. He squared himself in his chair. "By the way, how big are you?"

"Excuse me."

"Are you short—tall—heavy—thin?"

"Frankly, I don't know why I'm answering this, but I'm about six-one; maybe 210. Why? What difference does that make?"

"Curious, that's all. Thank you for the details. You've been a great help."

"You're welcome. Can you tell me now—you have any solid leads?"

David had wrapped his scarf around his neck with one hand. He cradled the phone on his shoulder and said, "No, not at all. But, tell you what, Adam. When a lead becomes so solid that the perpetrator is obvious, I'll give you my only interview."

He replaced the phone and felt good about laying the word "perpetrator" on a news reporter.

11

It was dark and cold when David and Robert Bugles arrived at Highland Estates, an upscale condominium complex ten minutes from Hollings General. Set into a knoll not far from the gated entrance, Charlie Bugles' unlighted unit appeared swallowed by slabs of ledge as David followed Robert up gradually circling steps of compressed bark. Only an iron handrail gave David any sense of direction.

Inside, Robert turned on the lights from a central switch and said, "Here we are. I'll go watch T.V. You do what you have to do, Dr. Brooks." He unwrapped a candy bar.

"I won't take long. If nothing catches my eye, we'll be out of here in five or ten minutes."

Robert disappeared into the next room and David stood in the foyer for a moment. He could see segments of four rooms from there and was surprised at how compact the unit was. Not much bigger than his. Kathy wouldn't like it.

As he wandered from room to room—kitchen, living room, dining room—he smelled the dampness of a cave he once played in as a boy and, at the television's initial blare, he recoiled the same as he had from the piercing cry of bats he had never gotten used to.

He didn't spend much time in those rooms—he didn't want to—but headed straight for a small rear one that he thought might be a study. Its walls were coated with plaques and citations, and David was tempted to remove his shoes before stepping onto its Oriental carpeting. The room was dominated by shades of red—lamps, leather chairs, cherry desk and tables—and its tidiness would have done justice to a home furnishings ad.

He wasn't sure what he was looking for, but nothing seemed out of the ordinary. Then, after pivoting to leave, he did a double take, his gaze returning to a photograph perched on a coral filing cabinet. It looked like a blown-up original. David picked it up and read a notation on the back: "Blue mosque—Istanbul."

Idly, he opened the top drawer of the cabinet. The first folder was labeled "Hospital—Foster." He thumbed through it, stopping at a letterhead from Philadelphia General Hospital. He eased it out of the folder. It was dated, "June 15, 1978," and signed, "Marcus Oblink, M.D., Chief, Department of Surgery." It was addressed to "Mr. Charles Bugles, Chairman, Hollings Hospital Corporation." The letter's essence was contained in the last paragraph. It stated that Dr. Alton Foster, having not performed satisfactorily, was dismissed from its surgical training program after two years of residency.

The information struck David like a battering ram. His fingers crimped the sides of the letter as he made his way to Bugles' desk and dropped heavily into the chair.

He reread the letter, then rested his chin in his hand as he massaged his decision scar.

Foster, a doctor? Booted out of surgical training? He shook his head as if ridding his brain from infectious data. *That's* why he hangs around operating rooms! A fit for Bugles' murderer? You bet. And he's about to be guarded? David sat at the desk for a time, visualizing the murder scene, imagining Foster behind the mask. Opportunity was there. Motives were several. Means? Surgically trained.

But he had trouble reconciling the Foster he knew with the brutality of the crime. And what about the hospital—Foster's own hospital, his bottom line hospital? Or the funeral reception?

David reached two uneasy conclusions: he would not yet confront Foster with what he had just learned for fear of raising his guard. And, for the time being, he would not inform Kathy because she might not agree with the first conclusion.

Burdened, he thought about slipping the letter into Friday but instead replaced it in the filing cabinet. From a cluster of photos on the desk he did, however, pirate one of Robert and Bernie. It won't be missed.

Now, the desk. While here, the desk. David had always believed if he had a choice of desk drawers to inspect, it would be the lower right double one. That's where he kept anything of moderate importance in his own desk. Extreme importance? His safe deposit box at the bank. Time to check for moderate importance.

Inside the drawer, he found a metal box; it was unlocked. It contained an out-of-date passport and a ledger book. The passport was issued in 1984. The name listed was, "C. H. Bugalash." The place of birth was, "Istanbul, Turkey." The photograph was that of a younger Charlie Bugles.

Bugalash? Istanbul? David pored over the ledger which contained entries dating from 1978. Hand printed on the first page only was the heading, "DATE SHIPMENT RECEIVED." He estimated there were ten to twelve dates a year, filling pages of columns, from the seventies to the present.

David knew the Middle East was the world's primary heroin source, particularly Turkey. He imagined the shipments referred to drugs. But, then again, they could be carpets, for Christ's sake. Drug dealer or rug dealer?

If knowledge of Foster's past had jolted him, this blew his mind. Moderate importance? Christ! What's in his safe deposit box, the drugs themselves?

David decided he didn't want to search any further— or couldn't—because processing beyond the forming mosaic, he felt, would have yielded little. Until more tiles were in place, he would keep the past activities of one C.H. Bugalash as close to the vest as those of Dr. Alton Foster.

On the way home, David broke a long silence. "You seen your brother lately?"

"Nope. He's in Tokyo," Robert answered, pushing himself back in the seat.

"For how long?"

"Who knows? He never tells me nothin'."

David's last thought before dropping Robert off was about the following day's vigil for an administrator whose credibility he now questioned. Phony vigil? Phony administrator? Must protect the flanks. He reasoned that if

Foster's surgical training cast him into a murderer, then all bets were off, and guarding him could be a camouflage for surveillance. And if he were innocent, the original bet still stood.

Her Chevy Cavalier a safe distance behind, Kathy had tailed David and Robert to the Highland Estates and, after the men had entered Bugles' unit, she decided to circle around the complex. She had done her share of shadowing in a twelve-year police career, but for the first time—secretly following David—she felt ill at ease, and she concluded that such a feeling had produced her deep chills. She turned up the heater.

On her return, she spotted a familiar car ahead, three units shy of Bugles' unit. She eased in behind the car and recognized it as Nick's. Kathy stormed out her door and, approaching the driver's side of his car, saw Nick resting a revolver on his lap. He lowered the window and appeared vexed.

"What are you doing here?" Kathy asked, her eyes narrowing.

"I could ask you the same question." He shoved the revolver into his waistband.

Kathy knew her voice would become shriller. "What did you do, follow me out?"

"What's that supposed to mean? For your information, I was following him out." Nick pointed toward David's Mercedes. "Could I help it if your car happened to be between us?"

Kathy realized she could have sunk his argument but decided to jump to a more pressing thought and shot back, "Well, I'm perfectly capable of checking on this alone."

"Hold on now!" Nick's voice was not shriller, but louder. "I give the orders, right? Did I say for you to follow the guy?" He turned on the ignition, gunning the accelerator.

Kathy peered down her nose and said slowly, "Boy, it didn't take you long, did it?"

"Meaning?"

"Meaning to get brutal. Last week you said you'd wait till you got the lay of the land."

Nick stuck his head partially out the window and said, "I've gotten it." He squared his body forward and stared blankly through the windshield. Kathy pinned him in place with her own stare.

Finally, he turned toward her as if in pain and declared, "So we both know he came here. Now what's that tell us?"

"That the guy, as you call him, is doing his job."

Nick appeared to begin a different sentence, settling with, "I suppose he is. Let me know later what he found here. He'll tell you, but not me—that's for sure."

"If he tells me at all."

"Why the doubt?"

"Because I'm not about to ask him," Kathy replied, firmly. "It has to come from him, or we'll scare him off."

"Nonsense."

"Look, you want him helping, or not?" Kathy motioned with her hands.

After a long pause, Nick said, "I'm not sure … see you tomorrow." He pulled away.

She wasn't certain of what to make of Nick's comments except that he had abruptly moved from colleague to supervisor. She also wasn't entirely certain why she had followed David but, as the pro, wanted to begin the process of spot monitoring someone who was not only the love of her life but also her protégé.

As she motored home, Kathy puzzled over two questions: What was the real reason Nick had chosen to tag along? And could she continue monitoring David? She had no answer for the first and a reasonably definite one for the second: most likely, she would abandon spot checks on David. She hated the feeling.

The following morning, Tuesday, Foster exclaimed to David, "It's utterly absurd!" They sat in Foster's office shortly after nine. "There's no reason for anyone to kill me and what if people here—and in the community—and down at the newspaper office—hear I'm being guarded? The CEO of the hospital needs a guard outside his office. Really! Do you realize what that would do to our census? As it is, it's practically in a free fall."

"You have no choice in the matter, Alton. And if you make another fuss, the press will have a field day. I'm sure they did a number on you this morning and, by the way, I won't even comment on your actions. You'll have to settle that problem yourself."

"I'm not worried. That creep made inflammatory statements and should be driven out of the business."

David slipped out of a caramel tweed jacket, unknotted his bow tie and rolled up his sleeves. "You handle it," he said, "but can I ask you something?"

"What's that?"

"Haven't you ever thrown a straight haymaker? Why a roundhouse?"

Foster made a fist and fired it in a half circle. "I was

off balance when I let it go," he said.

David instructed him to keep his back door ajar because that would be the most direct route "for me to intervene."

"In what? You mean an attempt on my life? Bah!" Foster fanned the air in a show of disgust. "So, what am I supposed to do if a goblin appears?"

"Yell. I'll be in the Bugles Room," David said, referring to the boardroom off the back corridor, directly opposite Foster's office. It was named in honor of the late chairman who, twelve years before, had underwritten new carpeting and furniture, including a six-figure teak table.

"There's nothing to read in there, I suppose."

"Grab a few magazines in the reception room. Really, David, is all this necessary?"

"Just go with it, okay?" David left through the front door and addressing the secretary, said, "May I? I'll bring them back later," as he scooped up two magazines and continued out beyond the elevator and around to the rear corridor. In view of the findings at Bugles' condo, David sensed Foster would "go with it" with about as much gusto as he had in guarding him. But he wasn't sure either about Foster's cooperation or about the significance of the findings.

In the boardroom, he sat at the sprawling table before a wall of gold drapes, Friday on his lap, feet fastened to the floor. He knees scraped the table.

He had propped open the door with a serving table and, yet, no sounds were added to the silence around him. After thirty minutes of such quiet that it nullified any sense of immediacy, he decided he was not cut out for sentry duty. And, besides, Foster knows he's being guarded now, so why not have Kathy send a cop at noon. On second thought, that's stupid, too. This guy's a prime suspect, not a potential victim. Hunches, move over. He untied and retied his size twelve shoe.

Then he turned rigid upon hearing the rapid-fire voice of Ted Tanarkle coming from the direction of the office.

"I've made my decision," the pathologist said coldly.

"But why?" Foster asked.

"There's no need to talk about it."

"You can't tell me why?" Foster continued.

Straining, David made out a final exchange.

Tanarkle: "Good day."

Foster: "Ted, listen to me."

David sat motionless, trying quickly to decide whether to walk in on Foster or run around to the front and "casually" bump into Tanarkle. He rose quietly and concealed himself against the doorjamb to listen, but he detected no further conversation.

Suddenly from the left, he heard a reverberating, decrescendo scream. David knifed past the serving table toward Foster's door. It was closed and locked. He struggled with the knob for only a moment and then bolted left, around two corners. He stopped short when he came upon Foster, his hands clutching the sides of his head. The administrator stood slouched, facing the elevator. David whipped him aside with one arm. He saw a gaping door with no car.

David braced himself against the wall and, arching his head forward into the black shaft, looked down and thought he could make out the outline of a body, spread-eagled and still. He glanced at Foster.

"I started to follow him out. Then the … the bloody

scream! God, it was so …" Foster didn't complete the sentence. "And I saw that door closing just as I got here," he added, pointing to the adjacent exit.

David checked the metal dial above the elevator. Its hand pointed to "G." He exploded into the stairwell and, more than once resisting the impulse to grab his knee, puffed his way to the basement. There, the elevator door moved to and fro, rattling against a chair on its side, a wedge that kept the door from closing, the car from rising.

David snatched up the chair and, in the car, pushed the "Hold" button. Standing on the chair to reach the emergency ceiling panel, he twisted the latches and pulled the panel down, exposing Tanarkle's head, neck and shoulders.

"Ted! Ted! Can you hear me?" he cried. He groped for a carotid pulse, but all he felt was what he knew was a final shudder.

He heard Foster's rapid breathing behind him. "Is he … ?" Foster said in a loud whisper.

"I'm afraid so. Poor guy. What a way to go."

"I knew it would happen sooner or later."

"What's that supposed to mean?" David said, as if the comment had shattered his moment of grief.

"An accident. This old contraption should have been torn out years ago. Damn the board! Damn the history!"

"It's hydraulic?"

"Unfortunately, yes. And a strain for six floors. It always was."

"Where's the control room?"

"Around there," Foster said, nodding to the left.

"You have a key to the door?" David asked as they

walked past the corner.

"Not with me but in my office." Foster's forehead was dotted with sweat.

"Wait!" David shouted. "What the ... it's been jimmied!"

David bent over and squeezed into the sooty compartment. Its smell reminded him of the times he stood under his car, watching an oil change. Steadying himself on a slippery, squishy floor and brushing cobwebs aside, he yanked on the cord to an overhead light and found he was standing in a pool of inky oil.

David's eyes flitted back and forth across the ram cylinder, the pump and the oil storage tank, finding it hard to process the entire scene in one swallow. He finally settled on an oil line and squatted to get a better look. It was disconnected at the tank end where he saw oil in a thin ooze. Off to the side, he noted that the synchronizer for the car door and hoistways on individual floors had been tampered with.

He was about to stoop out when he spotted a piece of adhesive tape on the pump housing. Printed in neat, block letters was: "SEE?"

That was a last straw. David reeled back, numbed by death and mockery at the base of the clock tower he so revered.

12

Having notified hospital security and Kathy of Ted Tanarkle's fatal plunge, David paced about the Hole awaiting the arrival of the usual investigative unit. Earlier, he had suggested to a shaken Foster that he retreat to his office—that he would be contacted shortly.

Now what? Has Victor Spritz neared his goal of eliminating the entire EMS oversight committee: Bugles, Coughlin, and now, Tanarkle? That leaves Alton Foster.

Like in a dream, he heard Belle's questions echoing in the background. And further behind, the panicky voice of the page operator. But David was in an impenetrable zone, seized by an obsession that he was in over his head. In over his head and down in the Hole, a two-bit command post whose dank smell told him he was below ground. And now there was to be an investigation of another fiendish crime, this time sixty feet away. They're getting closer.

He shuddered. It's happening. It's what you wanted, isn't it, baptism under fire? Fire? You mean a goddamned raging inferno. It could make you hard-boiled. So shape up, David, and be hard-boiled!

Kathy came in. She rose on her tiptoes to kiss his cheek. He felt placated by the aroma of her presence.

"Here we go again," she said.

"Are the same people here?"

"Same people."

"Mind if I listen in," Belle said, "so I know what's going on?"

David stared at her for a moment. "Belle—sorry—Ted Tanarkle's been killed. He either fell or was pushed down the elevator shaft." He pictured the control room and corrected himself: "Pushed."

"Oh, no!" Belle exclaimed. She exhaled loudly. "Where? Which elevator?"

"Around the corner."

David gave Kathy the details of the past half-hour, concluding with what he discovered in the control room. He saw Belle dabbing the corners of her eyes, something he was certain she hadn't done after she learned of the other murders.

"The bastard got into the machine room over there and rigged the controls so that when Ted pushed the button upstairs, the door there opened but the car stayed down here. You know, I just can't imagine an observant guy like him not noticing the floor dial, or even worse, walking into an open space. Either he was distracted or pushed."

"Ugh," Kathy grunted.

"Okay if I don't join you and the team next door?" David said. "Foster's upstairs and I want to clear some things before they settle out."

"We'll go up afterward," Kathy said.

"And then, I'm looking for Spritz. He's turned into

a loner—a frigging disappeared loner. If you run into him, call me, will you?"

Kathy nodded. "David." She beckoned him aside. "Nick says we have to step up our involvement. Says we've got a damn serial killer on our hands."

"Big revelation."

"You know what he means. People can be on our butts more than on yours."

David checked to see if Belle was watching before scooping up the unaware detective. "You can be on my butt any time you want," he whispered.

Kathy pulled away. "David! This is serious. Even the hospital unions called. And now, after this, everyone and his uncle will demand the impossible. Like bring in the killer in an hour."

"Sorry." And he was, after rationalizing he had permitted himself a moment of therapeutic giddiness. "But, shouldn't that be 'his or her uncle or aunt'?" David asked with a straight face.

Kathy peered down her nose and gave him a dismissive gesture.

Although David couldn't resist the quip, he scolded himself for compounding inappropriate and indelicate behavior. Idiot! He was your friend and mentor.

Before leaving, he handed Kathy an envelope containing the adhesive strip from the control room. "Could you give this to Sparky? Calling card. I'll explain later. Thanks."

David paraded the length of the building to the front elevators, rode to the sixth floor and doubled back to Foster's office suite. Now there's police officialdom to contend with. So we bump into each other. But maybe not; it's not as if they haven't been working the cases from the git-go. Okay, then, last one across the finish line's a rotten egg!

Foster's secretary was not there so he assumed she was on a coffee break—it was ten a.m. He barged into the administrator's office and found him standing at his desk, sorting through some letters which he fumbled to the floor.

For the first time since Bugles' murder, David realized Foster had switched from sport jackets and slacks to more formal suits. This morning, he was in shirtsleeves and open vest. His coat lay slung on a table between a lamp and several overturned portraits.

"I didn't mean to frighten you, Alton."

"Who's frightened?" Foster said, stooping for the letters. "This institution is merely crumbling around us."

David sat stiffly on a chair before the desk, directly in line with threads of sunlight pouring through a venetian blind.

"Here, let me get that," Foster said.

"No problem," David said, moving the chair. "A few stripes of light on a black day. Black Day at Hollings General."

"Sounds like a murder mystery."

"Then how's *Murders at Hollings General?*"

"Jesus! Murder! What did we do to deserve this?" Foster said. He sat behind his desk and stared vacantly into space.

David took out his pad. "Alton, I have some questions." He didn't wait for a response. "When Ted came here, what did he want?"

"He handed me his resignation."

David's head snapped up. "His—his resignation?"

"That's right. I have no idea why. I tried to talk him out of it but he wouldn't listen. He left in kind of a huff."

"Yes, I know," David said, laying a finger across his lips. "I could hear some of the conversation. And then you followed him out?"

"Yes, but not immediately. I waited a second or two, hoping he'd come back."

"I see. And the door. Your back door there. Why was it locked?"

"Locked? But, I left it open for you."

"I tried it, Alton. It was locked."

"Well, I don't know. It must have blown shut. It does that sometimes. I should have made sure it was kept unlocked. I don't think I did, come to think of it."

David didn't stop writing as he asked the next question. "Now, when you got to the elevator, you said you saw the exit door closing."

"Yes, I'm absolutely certain someone had just gone through it. But I didn't have the presence of mind to look. David, I was so shook by the whole thing. It happened so fast."

"And you didn't see Ted fall, right?"

"Right."

"You're sure?"

Foster's face darkened. "Yes, I'm sure. Are you suggesting … ?"

"I'm not suggesting anything," David shot back, aware he'd stepped on words again. But he didn't care.

"I got there and it was too late. What more can I tell you?" Foster said.

"Fine. That's your story and I've got it written here."

"David, for Pete's sake!"

"One last quickie, Alton. Did Ted drop in on you or had he called ahead?"

"He called ahead."

"How far ahead?"

"Oh, maybe half an hour. What's that got to do with anything?"

"Curious, that's all."

David read over his last few lines and got up to leave. "That's it for now. I think you may have to go through the same thing with the police. Don't take it personally but you were the last person to see Ted alive."

Foster tensed his jaw. "Me or the guy who went out the door."

"Yeah, that's true," David said. "Him or you. By the way, have you seen Victor Spritz anywhere?"

"No, and he's not in his office. I already checked. His second banana is running the EMS scene and I'm worried about that, too. He's not very reliable."

"I'm afraid there's more to worry about than EMS ambulance dispatches," David said, closing his notepad. "As important as they are."

In the moments between Foster's office and his secretary's desk, David thought: Screw it, this is hardball. Hard-boiled in hardball. So? Let him take the Hole away from me—if he's not on death row.

The secretary had returned. David said, "The scream I'm sure you heard ... "

This time, *his* words were stepped on. "Dr. Brooks, I hope I never hear anything like that again. Never, for the rest of my life."

"I understand, but can you remember whether the scream came before or after Mr. Foster passed you?"

The secretary pointed to spots in the air before her. "After. Yes, after."

"And, how long had you been at your desk?"

"I usually arrive at about quarter-to-nine."

"From the time you arrived until the tragedy occurred, did you have occasion to see Mr. Foster, other than when he passed you?"

"No."

"Or talk to him on the intercom?"

"No."

"Does he ever leave out the back door without letting you know?"

"Oh, please. More often than not."

David was about to pursue the issue when his cellular phone vibrated. It was Belle.

"Guess who's just been admitted to ICU—came in through the E.R."

"Christ, what now? Who?"

"The Bugles kid."

"Robert? What happened?"

"Somebody knocked him around, apparently. He's in pretty bad shape."

David waved off Foster's secretary who had pointed to the coffee maker. "Is he conscious, do you know?"

"The E.R. says just barely."

"I'm going over. Then I'd better join the gang downstairs. I can't believe all this."

He thanked Foster's secretary with a thrust of Friday in her direction and hurried to the Surgical Intensive Care Unit.

He entered the central control station, a long exposed area separated from the corridor by a workbench laden with stacks of manuals and requisition slip trays and strewn with metal-covered patient charts. Behind the bench, a nurse sat before a counter attached to the full length of the monitoring wall. Making notations, she scanned the rows of EKG tracings and vital sign windows, once nodding to a specific panel to indicate to another nurse that its corresponding room needed checking.

David hadn't visited ICU since his full-time days, and he thought that the ambient technology was louder than he remembered—the buzzes, the rings, the snaps; and that the odors were more prickly—the antiseptics, the detergents, the hydrocarbons. Once again, he imagined he smelled ether there but knew ether was no longer used.

He greeted the staff huddled around a portable chart rack as one of four green-clad residents led a case discussion among students in short white jackets whose side pockets bulged with small manuals, tourniquets and lab slips. An older gentleman in grey slacks and green blazer leaned against the wall. David recognized him as an attending surgeon and the session as the obligatory and hallowed "rounds."

"How's the Bugles boy?" he whispered to the head nurse.

"Just came in from Imaging, Dr. Brooks. They said his MRI's okay. He's a little groggy but knows where he is. He's down in 520. Madeleine Curry's with him. She's 'on float' and we grabbed her."

"Thanks, Annie. Good to see you again."

David proceeded quietly down an endless corridor, past rooms with curtains open or half-drawn or fully drawn; past patients artificially ventilated; patients invaded by drainage tubing; patients immobilized for fractured extremities, their legs and arms yielding to weights and pulleys and strange angles; cocooned skulls; moans and groans and sobs.

Room 520 was the next to last. David paused at the doorway.

"Hi, Madeleine, fancy meeting you here," he said softly. "The last I heard, you were a fixture on Men's Surge." She was blonde, full-figured, too sultry for her profession, and known for her scorching eye contacts.

"David! What have you been doing with yourself? Oh, wait, I take that back. It's house calls and that other love of yours, right?" She arose slowly from a chair, carefully closed the patient's chart and sashayed toward the door. One would have expected Madeleine, a little bird of a woman, to have been given to quicker movements. She raised up and David kissed her forehead, and, for a moment, her perfumed fragrance brought him back to the sizzle of the old days.

"Only the other love—and I assume you mean detective work," David stressed.

"What else would I … oh, I see, and then there's Kathy. Well that's a given, isn't it?" Her one-shouldered shrug connoted indifference tinged with contempt.

David squelched a frown, yet believed there was no subtext to the question. He left it unanswered.

Another of David's old flames, Madeleine had been one of his youngest and had made no bones about her displeasure at being cut off once Kathy reentered the picture. He still believed her sassiness enhanced her sex appeal but he felt now, more than before, that both were anathema to a hospital setting, particularly an intensive care unit. Besides, there were more pressing matters at hand, so he allowed the corners of his lips to turn up in a conciliatory smile.

David approached Robert who lay propped in bed between a sitting and supine position. His eyes were closed, the left a beefy lump, its lashes partly inverted. Dried blood caked his forehead and nostrils, and a padded bandage covered his left temple and ear.

"Robert, it's me, Dr. Brooks." David reached down to enclose Robert's crossed hands in one of his own, leaving it there.

Robert's right eye struggled open as the left side of his face creased and contorted upward.

"Don't try to open the other eye," David said. "You're going to be all right but you've got to rest it off."

Robert inched his head in David's direction and, prying his lips apart, mumbled, "Hello, Dr. Brooks."

"Who did this to you, Robert?"

Robert's eye appeared to blink uncontrollably. "My brother." He coughed and swallowed hard. "He got ... mad. He, he ... got ... mad."

"Why?"

"I let you in ... dad's place." Robert's eye clamped shut and tears seeped over his cheeks. Madeleine plucked a Kleenex from the box on the nightstand and dried the tears.

"That's enough," David said, gently squeezing Robert's hands. "You rest, now." As an afterthought, he added in a lower voice, "Too bad you weren't better trained to defend yourself." He immediately regretted the statement, or at least making it at the wrong time. But he wasn't sure Robert even heard it.

David backed up a few steps before turning to leave. Although it had crossed his mind, he judged it best not to inquire about Madeleine's personal life for fear of resurrecting talk of their schism years before.

On the way to the elevator shaft in the basement, he puzzled over the attack and its ramifications. Questions came at him like ticker tape. What does Bernie know? Foster's medical training? The shipments? Whatever from wherever. Istanbul? Is Bernie in on it? And, didn't Robert say his brother was in Tokyo? What's going on *there*?

David found the usual crew milling around the elevator and control room area. Sparky flitted about taking photographs. The hospital's security force of a half-dozen was there, and uniformed officers stood mute and soldierly at each end of the hall. A sheet covered Tanarkle's corpse.

Kathy and Nick emerged from the control room and David motioned them aside.

"Foster's all yours," he said, "and did you hear about Robert Bugles' beating?"

"When did it happen?" Nick asked in a matter-of-fact tone, drowning out Kathy's gasp.

"This morning. I just saw him in ICU. He's got some superficial contusions and abrasions. They'll probably keep him overnight as a precaution, but he should be all right." David thought Nick looked somber.

"Who did it?" Kathy asked. "Were you able to talk to him?"

"Yeah, and he said it was his brother, Bernie. We should bring him in. He was supposed to be in Tokyo but apparently he's around."

"He's always supposed to be in Tokyo," Nick said.

The comment convinced David that Nick was more involved in the murder investigations than had been let on.

"And while we're at it," David said, "anyone know where Spritz is? He's got to be questioned, too." He didn't want to stare at Nick, instead alternating his gaze between him and Kathy, disguising his greater interest in the reaction of the Chief Detective.

Nick hurriedly left to talk to one of the security guards.

David turned to Kathy. "Something eating him?" he asked.

"It's not you, David, if that's what you're thinking. He's just feeling the pinch. Four murders here in one week. City Hall's on his back. Don't forget he's new to these parts and he's responsible."

"I guess you're right." David put his hands on his hips and looked up and down the hall, and up above the elevator shaft to a point he estimated would coincide with the clock outside. "Four murders here in one week" rung in his ears.

"I hate to sound bossy, Kath, but we've really got to locate those two guys."

She was about to speak when he stepped on her words, adding, "You said I'd have logistic support."

"And you will," Kathy said in a placatory manner. She took a step closer. "Darling," she said, "I know you're feeling the pinch, too, but it'll work out. We'll all keep doing what we've got to do. We've checked Spritz's home and his office, and we talked to his backup and the page operators. No one's seen hide nor hair of him. So we put out an APB."

"And Bernie?" David said, "you have his address in Manhattan, right? Could we send one of your men down?"

"It's already been decided to do better than that."

"Meaning?"

"Nick wants to stake it out himself."

David knew his face turned to stone and his smile smarted as he responded, "Good, and maybe an APB on Bernie, too."

"You got it," Kathy said.

It took a moment for the stiffness to reach the back of David's neck. "Well," he said, "carry on. Let's contact each other if there's anything to report. Belle wants me at the Hole." It was an excuse to leave.

The Hole was just around the corner and David dragged out getting there to debate the questions that had peaked. Son-of-a-bitch! So, he's stepping things up? That's fine—two can play. Time for his decision scar. First off: Spritz. He's an employee here, right? Where's his file? Most likely in Foster's office. Unannounced is best, remember? No brainer, then. Break into his office later … whoa, how indelicate! *Visit* his office after hours. If nothing's there—simple—go right to Spritz's home. It worked at Bugles' place, right? In spades.

For a moment, he considered the alternative of simply asking Foster about Spritz's background but decided he didn't want to tip his hand because he hadn't ruled out any scenario, including collusion.

The minute David walked in, Belle held out the phone. "It's for you," she said. Her words sounded sticky. She pressed the phone against her hip and waved her pencil for him to come to the desk. She wrote on a scratch pad, "That same voice!"

"Yes, Dr. Brooks here," he said firmly as he took Belle's chair.

In falsetto, the voice said, "Time for us to get together."

"Say that again," David said.

"I think it's time for us to get together."

"Who is this?"

"That's not important right now. What is important is the news I have for you." Is he reading from a script?

David looked at his watch and scribbled the time on a piece of paper. "What news?"

"Uh-uh. In person."

"You're kidding."

"I mean business, Dr. Brooks."

"Is this about a medical problem?"

"Come now, Dr. Brooks. Don't act stupid. It's about the biggest medical problem the hospital's ever had, and you know it."

David's mind shifted into high gear. "Okay then, Mr.—Mr. Voice. I'll wait for you here at the hospital. I have a little room in the basement near … "

"Recycling Center at six tonight. Come alone."

David heard the click, yet said, "Wait." He hung up the receiver for a split second and then contacted the page operator.

"Helen," he said, "it's me. That call that just came through—did you recognize the voice?"

"Her? No, never heard it before."

"Did she ask for me, or did she give you my extension number?"

"Two-twenty-two: your extension. Everything okay?"

"Yeah, fine. Thanks." David tossed the receiver toward its cradle but missed. He picked it up and replaced it deliberately as he collected his thoughts.

"That bastard is no 'she,'" he said to Belle. "That's Victor Spritz, sure as I'm sitting here. Oh, sorry—here's your chair back."

"No, thanks, I'm too nervous to sit." She locked two fingers into her other hand.

He got up and swung around to the front edge of the desk. Half-sitting there, his eyes were still square to Belle's. "What do *you* think?"

She looked bewildered. "Sounded like a fake female … yes … definitely a fake female … God, that's spooky. But what makes you think it's Spritz."

"The cadence. And he knows my extension. But mostly the cadence."

"And he's coming here?"

"No, he said tonight at the Recycling Center."

"There? You going?" Belle gave her own answer. "David, don't. It sounds too dangerous."

"It sounds like a sucker request, Belle, but here's how I figure it. Let's assume he's the killer. Now, he's either sending me on a wild goose chase to take me away from something or someone, or … ."

"Like who?"

David ran his hand down behind his ear. "Like Kathy. He knows I'm with her most evenings. Now she'd be exposed."

"To what?"

"I hate to imagine. But, the other possibility—and this from my psychology brain—is that he'll be around there somewhere, to see if I show up."

"He'll take a shot at you, David."

"I don't think so. He's no fool. What's to keep me from bringing backup—I mean circles and circles of backup. If he takes a shot and even misses … ."

"Or doesn't," Belle said without missing a beat.

David raised his index finger and paused as if he had lost his train of thought.

"What I mean is—whether he missed me or not, they'd be all over him in a flash. While he's waiting, if he spots backup, what could he do? He has no leverage. There's no one kidnapped he could kill. So, my guess is he'll be well-hidden, out of shooting range, maybe with binoculars to see if I show."

"I don't get it. Why go through all that trouble?"

"As I said, psychology. Sort of a control thing. And speaking of that, sooner or later I was going to see El Shrinko Sam Corliss to check out some hunches about our killer. Now I can include this. Call and see if he can fit me in after lunch today."

"Call in advance? That's not like you."

"No, but those sofa jobs run an hour or more. I'm not about to wait around."

Belle finally sat and began twisting a paper clip. "David," she said, "why go just because he asked you to? You're asking for trouble and what's there to gain?"

"I know, I know. But look at it this way: does he expect me to back off?"

"Who cares?"

"It's important to psychopaths and don't tell me we're not dealing with one here. So, in going, I'm getting into his mind, sending back my own message."

"Which is?"

"That *I* mean business, too."

Before leaving for the cafeteria, David called Kathy intending to inform her of the phone call. She stated she was going to her mother's for dinner—straight from work. He convinced her to await his arrival there, hopefully at about six-thirty. "I haven't seen your mother in some time." He ended up not mentioning the phone call after all—and his likely visit to the outskirts of town.

Belle had arranged a midafternoon appointment with Dr. Samuel Corliss, Chairman of the hospital's Center for Behavioral Health.

David entered his office in Rosen Hall at precisely three. The small waiting room contained three soft chairs placed equidistant to one another around a triangular table. He avoided them, choosing instead to inspect posters of Paris highlights on each wall, moving quietly so as not to disturb an elderly woman sleeping in one of the chairs. There was no one in the reception area behind a window in one wall until Dr. Corliss, himself, appeared and slid open the glass panel.

"Why, hello!" he said, extending his hand over the counter and shaking David's as if he had returned from a war.

"Hi, Sam, how's it going? Keeping the phobias in check?"

Dr. Corliss laughed. "Come on in, David, come on in," he said.

"But what about … ?" David nodded toward the woman.

"Violet? She'll be fine. Always comes an hour too early. I let her keep the compulsion."

Inside, the office was as simple as the waiting room and not much larger: basic leather couch, two recliners, maple desk and high-back chair. Its ivory sidewalls were sprinkled with diplomas, certificates and photographs of class reunions. Paintings of Sigmund Freud and Karl Menninger dominated the wall behind the desk, framing Dr. Corliss as he sat. David sunk in a recliner before the desk, but he kept it upright, feet on the floor, knees higher than his hips.

The psychiatrist looked the part: white beard, pince-nez, frumpy ashen suit that coordinated well with the fluff around his ears. Wrinkles terraced his forehead. A star key medallion dangled from his neck and David, conjecturing it was used as a metronome in hypnosis, determined he would cry foul if he saw it move.

He was still conscious of men's heights: what's going on? Did Foster only hire department chiefs as tall as he is?

"Sam, I'm not sure what Belle said but I'm not here for myself—although the way things are going, the day might come."

"All she did was set up the appointment."

"I'll get right to the point, then. We've had four killings here now ..."

"Four? No. Let's see—Bugles and there's what's-his-name, Everett Coughlin, from Yonderville across town." He waved contemptuously.

"And Ted Tanarkle."

"Ted? Oh, no! When?"

"This morning. You hadn't heard?"

"No. Poor Ted. What a grand guy."

"Sam, you've been tied up reading too many of your

journals. You've got to cut back. Nothing changes in Psychiatry anyway." David corrected himself inwardly: except maybe you, Sam. You seem different.

"Ted Tanarkle?" Corliss appeared transported to the past. He repeated the name, shook his head like a stunned prizefighter clearing away cobwebs and said, "No, actually it's not my journals. It's my caseload. I've been cooped up here since seven this morning and even missed lunch. I'll let you in on something, David." Dr. Corliss pointed to a stack of patient records on a side table, looked both ways and measured his words: "People are getting crazier—and there are more of them."

David snorted. "Well, we have a case in point here. There's a real loony tunes running around this hospital."

"How did it happen? With Ted, I mean."

"He was on the sixth floor and, moments later, was found lying on top of the car at the bottom of the back elevator shaft. Someone rigged the mechanism."

"Down the shaft? Oh, my! It couldn't have been an accident?"

"Conceivably, but think about it, Sam—the mechanism was rigged. Plus the killer left a message." David revealed the contents of the smeared paper on his windshield the week before and of the tape in the control room. "Now," he added, leaning forward, "and this is why I'm here. What's your read on the kind of person doing this? Hardly your run-of-the-mill miscreant, right?" Hell, David thought, why not "shrink-speak"?

"Hardly. Take the way Charlie Bugles was slaughtered." The psychiatrist spoke deliberately. "Now you tell me about this elevator shaft thing—that took a lot of precision, I would guess. Why didn't our Mr. X just use a gun? He must have had a mental lapse in shooting Coughlin, and that's characteristic of this personality type—inconsistency. Next, we add the notes. That's also characteristic: 'Look world, look what I'm about to do,' or 'Look what I've done.' He not only kills, but gets a kick out of announcing it in advance or applauding himself afterward. The murder is not sufficient, even if there's real motive. He's compelled to add an unreal touch of the dramatic—an exclamation point, if you will."

David slid to the edge of the recliner. "He knows exactly what he's doing, then?"

"Yes, indeed. In my opinion, these aren't simply random killings. The guy's got motive and diffuse hostility. It's not well-organized like a specific gripe against a specific person or thing. It's diffuse. It's rage. And that's the worst combination: a person with a diffuse hostility who's presented with a motive he can't handle in predictable ways. He feels persecuted and goes bonkers."

David realized he was receiving insights from a man who drew on many years of experience in the behavioral field, insights that coincided with his own tenuous ideas. That's the way it was for him lately: uncertain, everything a battle in his own mind. David needed reinforcement. But also structure. He was getting both from Dr. Corliss.

"Sam, can I ask you about a specific person?"

"You mean some famous cases? The Boston Strangler? Son of Sam? Jack, the Ripper? None of them fits this profile, incidentally."

"No. I mean Victor Spritz."

"Victor Spritz? He's a suspect?"

"I'd have to answer yes, but I'm not sure. You know

him as well as I do. What can you say?" David leaned closer. "Better still, has he ever consulted you?"

Dr. Corliss stood and walked to a filing cabinet, draping a thick wrist over its top. "Everything in here is confidential, David. It would be a breach of medical ethics and my conscience, too, to reveal if a person is or is not a patient of mine, whether we discuss the case or not. You see, merely saying so-and-so was a patient gives him a label. A psychiatric label. And I happen to believe that an extension of that ethical canon—if we can call it that—is that it's unconscionable even to say someone has never consulted me. So the way we get around it is— if you're asking whether Spritz has ever seen me professionally, I can say there's no record of him in here." He patted the file cabinet.

"Sam, you're beautiful! Okay, let me ask, then— could he fit the mold you described?"

"Without a doubt." The psychiatrist fingered his medallion as David checked for movement. "I've seen Spritz at his worst and, frankly, he scares me. He's either easily triggered into rage reactions or he's got T.E.D."

"T.E.D.?"

"Transient Explosive Disorder. Either way, he should be on medication. I'd love to see his EEG."

Dr. Corliss returned to his chair and, drumming his fingers on the desk, said, "But do you know what? There are plenty of others tottering on that same edge—working right here in this hospital."

"Care to name a few?"

"Now, now. Ethics. Remember—ethics."

For the most part, David had received the information he sought. And as he departed from the psychiatrist's office, he realized what it was that appeared changed in the wizened psychiatrist. He no longer acted like a disgruntled loser as he had the year before in the election for Chief of Staff at Hollings General.

13

After the visit to Rosen Hall, David motored home primarily to upload three days of information into his computer. Typing haltingly, he came to understand such entries were another mechanism for structure, a means of distilling chaos while cleansing his mind.

Tuesday, January 20

MURDERS, continued—

Ted Tanarkle—bottom of elevator shaft.
Mayor and hospital committees acting up.
Bernie never took flight to Tokyo.
Sparky: Coughlin's murder weapon Japanese rifle.
Kathy: Says I'm still running show. But, what's
    Nick up to?
Foster had major surgical training.
Bernie punched out brother Robert.
Dr. Corliss said Spritz easily disturbed. I say he's
    not alone around here.

At five-forty-five, he left for the fifteen-minute drive to the other end of the city. Running north to south within a chain-link fence, the Regional Recycling Center was a strip of land sunk in the middle of a crater, not unlike the rectangular bottom of a wicker basket. A dirt road encircled the Center while, laterally, bushy terrain rose to the level of elm tops which were based alongside the road below. The high ground formed a rim which sloped on all sides to main streets leading to the city proper. Below and from opposite sides of the elevation, two blacktops shot to the rim only to become, on the other side, dirt themselves.

A block from the foot of the elevation, David stopped his car under a streetlight while he kept the motor running. He opened Friday, pulled out his Blackhawk Magnum and laid it on the seat between his thighs. He shrugged his left shoulder to feel the Minx .22, then reached down and patted his ankle snubby.

Halfway up the hill, he turned off the headlights and shifted to a lower gear for a slower, less noisy accent. A single lamp on a pole flooded the enclosure from the south side, and as his car bent down over the east rim, David saw the shadow of a hoisting crane spilling against the left bank, a giant crustacean perched on the latticed pattern of the fence.

Light fog drifted in the silent, sharp air and David pounced on his Blackhawk when he heard the guttural meows of cats in a standoff. Easy now. He returned his hand to the wheel and eased the car forward, head still, eyes sweeping to and fro. He stopped abruptly when, over the dimly lit rows of barrels and dumpsters and through the links on the other side, he spotted the shape of a car.

David was about to flash his lights. Wait! Who says he's in the car? He wanted to slouch down but the Mercedes wasn't built for his frame. He thus hunched his back and buried his head in his shoulders, turtle-like. Whipping out the Minx and grabbing the Blackhawk, he switched them in his hands and kept them close to his chest as he waited.

The other car's lights blinked. David returned the blink, put down only the Minx and took his foot off the brakes. His car reached level land and, instead of gradually accelerating, he swerved to the left and gunned around to reach the far end in less than a moment, screeching to a halt opposite the driver's side of a late model sedan. He felt the floodlight in his eyes and, in one motion, pointed the Magnum at a darkened figure as he tightened his finger on the trigger, fully expecting to see a gun butt similarly leveled in his direction. There was none. The figure disappeared beneath the window and David heard a muffled plea, "David, don't. It's me, Nick Medicore."

What the!

The other car's door opened slowly and the figure slid out. David verified it was Nick—outwardly unarmed. And he recognized the car as a white Buick Park Avenue.

"Stay down," David said, exiting. "Just in case." He raced to Nick's side and they both crouched between the cars. Nick pulled out a revolver from his waistband.

"You got the same call?" David asked.

"That I did," Nick said.

David raised up and peered over the top of each car. He returned to his crouch and said, "I don't think he's here at all. Looks like we've been snookered. The creep's toying with us. Whoever he is, he's toying with us."

Nick nodded.

David wondered why Nick hadn't offered the same conclusion instead of a nod and then the proclamation, "Such are the wild chases in police work."

David didn't need that and, after searching Nick's face, responded, "Well, I'm hungry and I need a drink."

"Me, too," Nick said.

David drove off without saying good-bye or bothering to ask Nick how long he had been parked there. It was unusual behavior but he had a gut feeling Nick preferred it that way, too. Ordinarily, David would have censured himself for leaving an associate so brusquely, but he held that Nick Medicore was no ordinary associate and that the last week was no ordinary time.

On the way to Kathy's mother's house, he stewed in his Mercedes, ambivalent over feelings of being duped and of becoming quasi-competitive with Nick. Dismissing any dire consequences of a different outcome, he was disappointed he hadn't found a stranger there, an out-of-towner. Not a Spritz or a Foster, and certainly not a Medicore. What the episode did was reinforce what he had thought all along. It placed the killer closer to home, roaming the spots David knew. And it compelled him to wonder about Nick's nonchalance. Somehow, he had difficulty visualizing the Chief Detective taking the same precautions he had taken in approaching the Center. But no difficulty in imagining his driving straight to the spot where his car was parked.

And another thing. Why did he blink his lights? Did he think the killer was coming down that hill? Or yours truly?

Kathy greeted David at the door with, "You got held up?"

"Not exactly," he said, removing his scarf and gloves and tossing them on the hall table. They embraced and kissed, longer than he expected.

Standing in the hall of plaster, wainscotting and high ceiling, he sketched what had transpired at the recycling center, leaving out his offense-as-a-defense maneuver.

Kathy listened and proffered her opinion: "I think both of you were nuts. Men!"

David made like he hadn't heard and said, "By the way—your boss?"

"Nick? What about him?"

"Did he come here well-recommended?"

"Very. They hated to give him up, I understand. His wife's from these parts, her parents aren't well and that kind of thing. I guess she worked on him pretty good. We had the opening, as you know, and he relocated. Why?" Kathy's eyes narrowed speculatively. "You're not insinuating … ?"

"Who's insinuating?" He took Kathy's hand and led her into the living room.

"Then why the question?"

"Curious, that's all."

But David had been aroused by more than curiosity. Perhaps our Chief Detective truly relishes my taking a lead role in the investigation for his own selfish—or devilish—purposes: to dilute professional input, maybe to screw things up. It's lame reasoning, and I'll concede he's a lame suspect, but right about now, nothing and no one's written off. He's either the killer and wants an amateur on the case—or he's not and is investigating as hard as I am.

He refused dinner and stayed but ten minutes more, engaging in a round of unfocused converation with Mrs. Dupre before he left.

For most of the trip home, a pair of bright lights filled David's rearview mirror. Their shape reminded him of a frog's eyes.

14

The next day, Wednesday, David felt the sting of January winds in the hollow of Cannon Cemetery. Specks of snow floated and disappeared into the ground, belying the morning's sun and reflections off parking lot bumpers and antennas. He considered whether snow flurries and bright sun could combine for a rainbow, deduced not, but scanned the sky anyway. Bedecked in his double-breasted funereal suit, he strode from his car along a rigid path which curled among mounds of tombstones, flowers and flags, toward a yellow and white canopy set at path level and to the right. Within its shade, most of the folding chairs were unoccupied, and he recognized those seated—perhaps thirty—as the most seasoned doctors and nurses from crosstown Bowie Hospital. Alton and Nora Foster were the only others there to represent Hollings General.

Earlier, David thought it hypocritical even to consider attending the church service for Dr. Everett Coughlin, but irreverence aside, reasoned it was necessary to check out the graveside gathering. Would the killer dare come? A surveillance mission, that's all.

He queried how the nearby burial pit had been dug

through hardened turf and noticed the front end of a hearse parked on its other side. A casket with blinding brass handles rested on a rig while a clergyman sat impassively on a front chair, flanked by four women, their sobs puncturing the silence. SOP, so far.

David took a position behind and slightly above, having calculated the best vantage point for his purpose, leaning against a tree, his foot on a neighboring stump. He perused the scene ahead, gaze askance—he had forgotten his sunglasses—avoiding the glare from the casket handles and trimmings. At first, he thought little of a linear flash of light registering in his periphery, coming at him from halfway up the mountainside on the left—like mirror signals he had seen in cowboy movies. But, weighing its location in dense underbrush, he had to confront the glare head-on, and he saw that it had changed shape—to a smaller, sharper ball of fire. David pushed off the stump, dropped to the ground and rolled behind the tree. He ended up on his back, as if for a judo stomach throw—only this time, he waved a Minx semiautomatic. Jesus Christ Almighty! A rifle! The specter of a bloody bullet wound similar to the one on the body now being prepared for interment tore through his mind. He listened for a shot. There was none. He got up and peered around the tree. The reflection had vanished. That was a rifle, goddamn it! The intended victim disappeared. So *it* disappeared.

All ahead remained serene, as serene as David was alert for flight, not away but toward the mountainside. He backed up and, intending to twirl around, clutched his knee and hopped twice on his good leg. Reconsidering, he hobbled toward the parking lot, knowing that whoever yielded the weapon, reached his nest from a road on the other side of the mountain, the same one the hearse had traveled.

David slid into his car, lifting his sore left leg with his hands. He sped off and, reaching a clump of trees at the turn to the far road, heard the poorly muffled roar of a two-stroke engine. Two strokes? He rounded the curve in time to observe a red motorcycle appear out of a swale, two hundred yards ahead. Just before a Sunoco Station, it left the road and knifed into the woods, up a trail David had often walked in earlier times. For a moment, he thought of taking the dirt road beyond the station. It was a road which led to High Rock Mountain at least a mile up its side, but he knew the parallel trail veered off half-way up and guessed the cycle had already reached that point.

Instead, David stopped at the foot of the trail, got out of the car and looked over its roof into a narrow bend, empty but for thinning fumes. When he could no longer hear the cycle, he sat in the car and puzzled over what he had just beheld. Is that our man in the first place? On a motorcycle? It looked like a Honda or a Suzuki. Or even a Harley-Davidson. Who can tell at that distance? And another thought tumbled from the depths of his brain like a coin in a pay phone. When the cycle turned into the trail, the driver's face might have looked flat. Might have.

David's watch registered noon and he couldn't re-call ever imbibing at that hour, save for celebration toasts, but as he tooled along the backroads toward 10 Oak Lane, he savored the drink he would have. That could have been curtains, back there. At home, he changed into blazer and slacks and, in the kitchen, covered a glassful of ice with

Canadian Club, leaving out the water. The liquor was gone before the ice began to melt. So was the pain in his knee. David fixed a ham and cheese and reviewed the images from Cannon Hollow. That rifle was aimed at me. If it was a rifle. But, what else would reflect up in those woods, a bird? So Buster's still trying, eh? Well, score another for the good guys.

He had no proof but instinct led him to believe it was Bernie who aimed the gun at him, and Spritz who had arranged the recycling center hoax the night before. Instinct plus a flat face and a distinctively paced falsetto voice. Once again, David made a decision not to inform Kathy—or any of the police—about his latest escapade. He told himself he couldn't run to them with a blow-by-blow account of every daily—or as it seemed, hourly—event. Alone, rather, he would face what came his way, analyze as he saw fit, and react accordingly. Keep the competitive fire a black belt is used to: just two on the mat, then hold, throw or pin. Body drops, single wings, shoulder wheels, sweeping throws.

Washing down the last of the sandwich with a swig of milk, he remained seated at the kitchen table to mull over his options. But first, a final clarification of his role as distinguished from the cops'. Nick and his pretense of noninvolvement, of hands-off. Come on, give me a break! Has anyone else been threatened? Under the gun? Maybe. But no one else is sharing. So I draw on the cops for logistic support only. Not backup. Not moral. It's the killer and me. Finis. That's my option.

For the first time since Charlie Bugles was brutalized eight days before, David felt free to maneuver, to call his own shots. Who needs approval—tacit or otherwise—for every single move? He considered his being singled out by the killer justification enough to "go it alone," irrespective of a criminal investigative unit, or even of amateur sleuthing. If there's a lunatic out there, and he's messing with you, then you do what you have to do.

Victor Spritz, Bernie Bugles and Alton Foster rattled around in his head. Other loose things, too: Sparky and his findings at the Tanarkle crime scene, Sparky and further information on the Japanese dagger, Sparky and the handwriting expert. Flowers for Robert. And, what came of those meetings among the medical staff, the Board of Trustees and the nurses' union?

David left the kitchen and headed for his computer chair off the living room, the spot he cherished for definitive moments, for clarification when he was bemused. On the way, he went to the window to pull open the drapes, walking over a heat register in the floor. He heard the furnace kick in from the basement, smelled the rush of hot air which slapped his leg, and noticed the drapes stir. As he rotated in his chair, he understood why his senses were so on the qui vive—aroused as an equivalent contrast to what he believed was another sense: thought. In other less trying times, he had poked fun at himself over a secret deduction: you know when you're thinking, because you sense it. Therefore, it is a sense. And the other senses, when stimulated, would often combine as a flashpoint for annoyance, just as now. For he had more clear thinking to do. Thus, he sat for a minute, straining to brush aside all distractions and to focus on the loose ends at hand.

David disposed of several easily: he identified the

hospital meetings as out of his control, irrelevant to the tasks ahead, and not worthy of further thought; he phoned to have flowers sent to Robert; and he had no choice but to await the outcome of the APB's on Spritz and Bernie. That left Sparky and Foster. He would check with the criminalist before awaiting the forced entry at Foster's at five-thirty. That meant contacting Musco Diller.

Musco Diller, a cabby who worked Hollings' seamy North Square District, was an old friend and world-class safecracker. David had used his services as a "freelance lock-picker," in such cases as 647 Vagrancy and 10-65 Missing Person. Never in 187 Murder, but he thought the cabby wouldn't mind. David, himself, could slip a credit card past a door latch with the best of them, but in many cases, that skill was too rudimentary.

Musco had once done time for a string of second story capers and, now having gone straight, was part owner of the most popular cab company in the city. He had also spent time on the streets, done in by muscatel, his favorite. Hence, the sobriquet.

David called the Red Checker Cab Company and, through its dispatcher, reached Musco Diller. They agreed to meet in the auxiliary doctors' parking lot at five-twenty-five.

Next, David phoned Sparky to inquire about his findings from the Tanarkle death scene and received a "Not ready, yet" response. He asked about Sparky's friend, the handwriting expert, and was told she'd be out of town for the rest of the month. Lunch? The criminalist would skip it today. He was behind in his work.

David said a quiet good-bye, but he was tempted to hurl the phone across the room; he recognized cock-and-bull answers when he heard them. It's obvious: Nick got to him. Certainly not Kathy. If the assumption is correct, then the goings-on of Chief Detective Medicore are getting stranger and stranger.

It didn't take long for David to begin rummaging through his desk drawers and closet shelves, muttering, "Okay then, I do my own forensics and I say nothing to Kathy—and that does it, pure and simple. Plus, I put Sparky's handwriting expert on hold. Or maybe get my own. Be independent but, at all costs, be civil. I don't need anyone torpedoing my licensure." He searched for gadgets and other equipment he had accumulated over the years, and gathered them on the living room sofa. Some had been given to him as gifts.

Stripped of police support, he had to institute drastic change. A given was that he could match anyone with his size and agility. Ditto, with firepower. But, not with the element of surprise. The killer has me there. It was like football's offensive and defensive lines on a rainy, slippery day: defense doesn't know the play in advance. It can only guess. Advantage: offense.

To counterbalance the killer's advantage of surprise, David decided he would surround himself with investigative and defensive tools he might or might not use. He opened Friday and added an autofocus camera with telescopic lens, an ordinary Polaroid, a pair of 7/30 Beecher Mirage binoculars, a postage stamp-sized NT-1 Scoopman digital tape recorder, a flashlight, surgical gloves, plastic sheets, various micro bugs and extra cartridges for his Blackhawk .44 Magnum.

In the course of his readings, he had come upon numerous articles dealing with "concealment capability for tight situations." Thus, behind Friday's retractable panel he stuffed a compact SIG-Sauer P226 pistol and a Gunsite folding tactical knife.

Into a Campbell's Soup carton, David packed an evidence vacuum, a small crowbar and his pride and joy—a gift from Kathy—a Kevlar-lined raincoat that could stop a 9 mm. slug. He carried the carton to the garage and, placing it in the trunk of the Mercedes, nicked his finger on a snow shovel he kept there during winter months.

As he wrapped the finger in a handkerchief, he wondered whether he'd spent the past hour expending nervous energy. He looked at the carton. Who in hell's going to use this stuff? He felt like a man dressed to the gills with no place to go.

David ran through his list of suspects. Christ, it's longer everyday and that's another disadvantage, right there. All this gadgetry? Merely a symbolic remedy for someone in a pinch. Or, just plain stupidity. And David didn't suffer fools gladly, even himself. But he left the carton in the trunk and slammed the door shut.

At five-thirty, Musco Diller beamed as David approached him, the beam he remembered Musco having whether he was down-and-out or not. He leaned his head out the window of his cab which was parked near the back fence of the auxilliary doctors' parking lot.

"Dr. David, my boy," he said. "Diller at your service. Whatcha got this time?" He was David's vintage, yet usually greeted him that way.

"Hi, old buddy, glad you could make it."

Musco was a wiry African-American who was never without his black cap with a rainbow band and shiny visor. Several tickets sprouted from the band. He seemed made out of pipe cleaners, all arms and legs, constantly in motion. David understood one of his eyes was glass but he could never guess which one. He had a small grizzled mustache and, growing in the center of his chin was a matching tuft of hair which appeared to have been overlooked in shaving.

David knew Musco's inquiry about the nature of a job was merely small talk. Way back, he had said, "Just show me what you want and give me a minute by myself. You don't ask how and I don't ask why. I don't want to know nothin'."

They took the hospital's freight elevator to the fourth floor, its highest destination beneath the administrative wing, and climbed the remaining two floors to Foster's office, encountering no one on the way. In the corridor, David put Friday down and pointed to the administrator's front door with the index finger of his left hand and in the direction of the back door with the same finger of his right hand. He preferred the back one and led Musco around to it and said, "Here it is, do your open sesame thing," snapping his finger against the large oak door before them. "I'll go check out front for a minute."

David peeked around corners as he examined the corridors surrounding Foster's suite. He returned to find Musco dusting off his hands and a door fully opened.

"What took you so long?" David asked with a wink. He added an offhand "Thanks." He had seen Musco in action many times before. What he had never seen was tools, and he had never inquired about any.

"Well, I'm off, " Musco said, "less you need more opening inside." He turned to leave.

"No, I think we're all set." David peeled the only hundred dollar bill from a wad of twenties and fives he took from his pocket. He folded it in two. "Musco," he said. The cabbie pivoted and David inserted the bill in the band of his cap.

"Thanks, my boy. You might need more opening—call—you hear?"

"I hear and I might. You can find your way out?"

"Of course," Musco answered as he disappeared around the corner.

David took the flashlight out of Friday and entered the darkened office before turning it on. He felt calm but was certain his breathing bounced off the walls. The air smelled mustier than he expected for an office closed up for only half an hour. He remembered seeing Foster's single filing cabinet on many occasions, and, keeping the flashlight angled toward the floor, tiptoed straight to it, thinking he shouldn't have dismissed Musco without first determining whether the cabinet was locked. It wasn't.

He pulled out the top drawer and flipped through its folders until he came upon a thick one labeled, "EMS Ambulance." He tucked the flashlight under his arm, freeing both hands to sift through legal documents, invoices and schedules. A stack of "Oversite Committee Minutes" was clipped to the back of the folder. The most recent set of minutes recorded the vote on Victor Spritz's renewal contract: Mr. Bugles and Drs. Coughlin and Tanarkle voted to terminate. Mr. Foster voted to renew.

Behind the stack, he found an unsealed envelope. In it was a medical discharge summary from a private psychiatric hospital in Cartagena, Colombia. David knew enough Spanish to understand the diagnosis listed: Para-

noid Schizophrenia. Discharge medication: Haloperidol.
The dates of hospitalization were February 1996 to No-
vember 1996. The patient named was Victor Spritz.

David gaped at the name and then at the diagnosis,
feeling at once engulfed by sorrow and shaken by the dread
of a psychotic on the loose. But neither engulfed nor
shaken by surprise. So the shrink wasn't far off the mark.
And that was the reason for Spritz's sabbatical.

He reread the one-page summary more slowly. It
spelled out the pathogenesis of Spritz's illness, from early
withdrawal signs, through impaired personal identity and
bouts of severe agitation, to fantasies of the annihilation
of the world. Several references were made to the patient's
"inclinacion."

His what? Inclination? A drug habit? David was un-
comfortable with his conclusion that Spritz had not been
a drug addict or else the report would have specified it,
not used the cryptic "inclinacion." But he wasn't quick to
abandon the subject. If he were on drugs, it had to be
coke. Hell, Colombia? Cocaine.

The last line of the summary read, in Spanish, "Dis-
position: Suggest patient return for follow-up appoint-
ments whenever he visits Colombia."

More cryptic writing. He visits the country often?
David returned the folder to the cabinet, turned off the
flashlight and sat at Foster's desk. Light from the corridor jaundiced the carpeting beneath the door.

Now isn't this something? They've got the goods on
each other! Foster doesn't snitch on the psychiatric background, and Spritz doesn't snitch on the love affair—if
he knows, and I assume he does. But why doesn't Mr.
Schizo kill Mr. Lover Boy? Of course, he still could, but

I suppose he's indebted to him for his support in the vote.

David fidgeted at the desk, clamping and unclamping his teeth. Minutes passed as he tried to make more sense of "inclinacion" and "whenever he visits Colombia." Finally, he arose and walked out the door, running his finger around the inside of his collar. In a feeble attempt to lighten the weight of the moment, he joked that the moisture there originated from his throat—now chalk dry.

It didn't take long for the frog's eyes to appear in David's mirror. Two nights in a row. This time, he decided to make a move. Easing out the Minx with his right hand, he used his left to swerve the Mercedes onto a soft shoulder where he came to a complete stop. David counted three heads in the darkened cabin of a black tow truck as it barreled by.

15

By the looks of Thursday morning's storm, David believed it had the potential of being the season's worst. There was nothing graceful about the snowfall—no fluff, no stillness, no feathery float of flakes so big one could distinguish their shapes. It was just straight-out sleet banging against the windows of his car, sticking there and in front, slowing the wipers and constricting their arcs. He heard the thump of an evening's accumulation bouncing off the wheels as he forged around a bend to begin the long descent to Hollings General, glancing twice at the tower clock to make out the time. He had the choice of passing a snowplow which had shot out from a side street or lagging behind, the truck providing his personal pathway. The price of the path was the gritty sound of sand pebbles ricocheting off the Mercedes. David chose to pass. He couldn't recall ever having to floor the accelerator down the hill for the rest of the way.

It was nine-forty-five. He had gotten a late start because he had slept late, his sleep an amalgam of tossing and dream shreds. The questions were piling up, the answers scarce, and David's decision scar was swollen. But he believed he had spent more than enough time in mental knots, and that perhaps there was little time to spare before more tragedy struck again. His enemy was not only a killer among a thousand suspects but also time itself. And, having discovered proof of what he and his psychiatrist colleague had believed all along—that Victor Spritz, the prime among the thousand, has some loose connections—he thought it essential to speed up the pace of his investigation. Foster's records also provided the clincher in a toss-up of whether he should force enter Spritz's house or not. He would contact Musco after lunch.

Belle had not yet arrived at the Hole and David thought it had more to do with the weather than with disturbed sleep, particularly since his was one of only four cars in the parking lot and the morning was half over. The phone rang. It was Kathy. He hadn't spoken to her for thirty-six hours, and her voice broke a thin shell of alienation which he feared since the frigid conversation with Sparky.

"You slept late," she stated, not asked. "I've been trying for an hour."

"It could have been the snow," he said.

"No way. You're good in snow."

"We never did it in snow."

"David!"

"What? We never did."

In the following silence, questions that had layered like black coral broke off and shot through his mind. Level with her about everything? About everything surmised about Nick? And Sparky? Or, just stay the course? Stay the course. He wanted nothing—not medicine, not sleuthing, not the cops—to interfere with their relationship.

"Sorry, darling," he said, "I couldn't resist. What's up?"

David felt vibrations of resignation in the phone set. "Well, I wanted you to know we picked up Bernie Bugles yesterday. Actually, he came in voluntarily. He was booked and arraigned on a charge of assault with an attempt to commit murder."

"Good. Where is he now?"

"Out on bail. On Monday, the judge is supposed to meet with the prosecutor and his attorney to plea-bargain, unless Robert withdraws charges before then. I understand he considered it for awhile."

"He still hospitalized?"

"No, he was discharged yesterday. They said there were no internal injuries."

"Any word on Spritz?"

"None."

Switching the subject without a lead-in, David said, "Kath, I miss you. How about coming over after work? We'll send out for something." Kathy agreed, adding she would pack a bag again.

"You know," David said, "we've got to stop meeting like this."

"Why?"

"All that packing. Either keep a separate wardrobe at my place or … or … "

"Or what?"

"Never mind."

"David, don't do that! Or what?"

"Move in. It's been five years."

"Plus a month. Here we go again. Why not just set the date—go ahead with it— and avoid the middle step, see?"

"That's a good point," David said with authority.

"You're cooling on me."

"How's that?"

"You usually say, 'That's a good point, darling.' "

After lunch, David called Musco and arranged to meet him outside the Red Checker Cab Company at three o'clock. This followed unanswered calls to Spritz's office and frequent ones to Spritz's home to be sure he was not around—at least for now. David also checked with Jack Ryan, Spritz's stand-in, and learned no one had heard from him since last week.

Belle, who had arrived at the Hole shortly before noon, commented that the radio indicated sleet had turned to snow and thirteen inches had fallen.

"Big deal," David said. "In the old days, we had twice as much and everybody loved it. Seemed to pull people together. Now, they all bitch." He put on his scarf and gloves.

"We're twice as old now," Belle said.

"Who? Maybe, you, but not me," David replied, bending to pick up Friday. As he straightened, he grabbed at a stabbing sensation in his knee and soured his face.

"Just me?" Belle said. Through the corner of his eye, he saw her pretend not to notice.

Outside, the snow had tapered to a near standstill and, in the parking lot, David shook his head as he peered down at the rear end of his car. From above the wheels and trunk, it was wrapped in tight slush and topped with snow.

"Goddamn it!" he said, glaring at the panel truck and plow rig which was covering other cars at the opposite end of the lot. "What's wrong with those guys?"

He wiped away the snow from the trunk and, opening it, removed the shovel, conscious of the metal strip which had ripped his finger before. Straight legged, he dug away the snow while cursing the maintenance workers, and finally got to the roof, hood and windows, clearing them with the brush end of an ice scraper. He had worked fast.

Huffing, David steadied himself against a fender. He looked up at the cardboard sky and imagined there were tiny invisible holes in it through which the snowflakes escaped. He tasted the moist air in his throat and, tilting his head back, closed his eyes and felt flakes melt on his face. He stiffened and popped his eyes open. Sometimes you'd swear you're out to lunch.

After replacing the tools in the trunk, he slid into the car and realized his feet burned from packed snow. He couldn't remember the last time he wore the boots he would have to locate at home before the drive to Victor Spritz's.

David had seldom traveled the Marblehead section of Hollings. Named after the city's most famous benefactor, there was no marble there except in the foyers and driveways of the fashionable end of its caste system of homes. To reach that end, labeled Marblehead Proper, one drove up a gentle incline, through soporific rows of World War II capes and on through the middle part, a grab bag of raised ranches, split levels, even a Georgian or two. The baby version of Levittown was named Mainline Road and the middle part, Veterans Heaven. Spritz lived with the veterans.

David had given Musco the address and followed him through the section, its roads clear and sanded. The day was also clear, the sun shining as if making up for lost time. In the distance, the hum of snow blowers spiked the air.

Musco stopped his cab across from two houses short of a house David pointed to. David pulled in behind, got out, and walked awkwardly to the cab. Besides his scarf and gloves, he wore tall black boots, tall enough to lap the knees of Mr. Average.

"That's the place," Musco said, lowering his window.

"You see anyone around?" David asked.

"I ain't seen no one."

"Let's walk over from here … but, wait, I'll be right back."

David took high steps to his car and opened the passenger side. He picked up his cellular phone which he had placed on the seat and, referring to a card he took from his pocket, called Spritz's number one last time. There was no answer.

They tramped alongside Spritz's house, heading for a back entrance. Musco led the way, a third of his tattered raincoat skimming over the surface of the snow. He pushed his legs forward; David lifted.

There had been no shoveling or plowing that David could see, and no footprints or tire tracks spoiled the meringue grounds. An elongated garage—its door shut—was attached to the two-story house, small and square, and made of red brick. He thought the length of the garage curious. For two cars in a series? The house had front dormers and vertical slots for windows, and he pictured its interior a crisscross of sunbeams.

190 JERRY LABRIOLA

At the back stoop, David opened the storm door and said, "Here we are. You want I should go build a snowman?"

"Negative. You might catch cold."

For David, a first in ten years! He watched as Musco knocked first, then produced a flexible skewer from somewhere near his heart. It was lined with miniature grooves and glistened in the sun. He inserted it into the keyhole and below it, forced in another tool which he took from his pocket. "This here's my tension wrench. Keeps tension on the pins in there while I do my rotating." He pressed on the skewer's retractable end and twisted it clockwise. Nothing happened. He pressed twice, twisted and still the door didn't budge. "This should do it," he said, as he pressed three times and twisted counterclockwise. David heard a click and the door inched open.

"Like I always say, three's a charm," Musco exclaimed. He held the four-inch device before his mouth and blew on its end like he would a smoking gun. "Homemade," he said, proudly.

"Just one question," David said, smiling. "What would you say if someone answered the door when you knocked?"

"Anyone here call for a cab? Come to think of it, I had to use it one time."

"And who would I be?"

Musco scaled David's height. "My bodyguard," he said.

David handed him five twenties which the cabby wound on a roll of bills he had taken from his pocket.

"See," Musco said, "I told you no questions—I didn't even count them." His eyes crinkled above bared gold-edged teeth.

"You're bad," David said. "Thanks, pal, I'll be in touch." Musco left.

David guided the door open and walked into a narrow laundry and utility room which stretched half-way to the front of the house. The air reeked of detergent. He placed Friday—heavier since its additions—on a washing machine, yanked off his boots, and put his scarf and gloves in his pockets. David looked into the dimly lit garage through the door window on his left and froze when he saw what he had never expected to see. He knew immediately that the car parked there belonged to Victor Spritz. Then where the hell is *he*?

Minx .22 drawn, he tested the door and, finding it unlocked, probed the garage from where he stood, then quietly closed it. He cracked open a door on the right and said softly, "Victor? Hello, Victor?"

On tiptoes, David would bump his head on any doorframe made. He ducked and skated through the doorway, then bounced on his toes into the kitchen and advanced toward the living room, raising his voice a notch. "Victor, it's me, David Brooks. Are you here?" He didn't know how he would explain his presence. If Spritz is on the lam though, who needs to explain? The silence had a sound to it because it was so intense, but then he heard the buzz of a leftover housefly which eventually dive-bombed onto a lampshade. At home, David would have attacked it with a folded newspaper.

He was surprised at the illumination in the rooms he could see, anticipating a grid but finding confluence, and finally determining the house had more slots than other houses had conventional windows. He played with the theorem that the slots concentrated the sun penetrating his face; or was it merely the flush of readiness?

He took his normal giant steps and quickly covered the first floor, looking in but not examining a small alcove off the living room. It contained a desk, chair, computer and copying machine, and he reminded himself to return to it after he had searched upstairs.

David yelled out Spritz's name again as he ascended an open staircase, pulling on a railing, bridging two steps at a time. He found the bed in the master bedroom made up, but the bed in an adjacent room was a hammock of books and magazines. Piles of rumpled clothes encumbered the floor. He peeked behind a shower curtain and prolonged a sigh after he had opened a final closet door and returned the Minx to his shoulder rig.

David backtracked, taking the shortest route to the alcove below, and after bracing his weight on the surface of the desk, sat and wiped away the palm print he made in the dust. The ceiling was low, a single slot window had no curtain and the sound of adjusting in the chair echoed off bare walls. He pawed through the desk drawers, saving the lower right—the one he thought most popular for valuables—for last. There, a composition book in a black-and-white marbleized pattern caught his attention. He sifted through it, finding page after page filled with dates, initials, units of weight and, repeatedly, the notations, "CARCAN" and "CANCAN." He studied the lettering and, in his mind, reverted to those messages he'd received before, most vividly the one taped to a stone.

He jotted down the notations in his pad, but he also retrieved Friday from the laundry room and took Polaroids of several sample pages.

In the oil stench of the garage, David held his breath while flinging open a window, then another. He switched on the lights and scrutinized all four sides of a late model Toyota, squatting at each tire to examine its treads. He placed his palm on a cold hood, bent an ear to the trunk and while inspecting the car's interior, noted the odometer reading. He slipped on a two-foot-square piece of cardboard beneath his feet and had to regain his balance against a fender. David kicked the cardboard against a wall and checked his shoe for oil stains while questioning why a Toyota with 6,200 miles would have a leaky crankcase.

His eyes lingered back on the car as he sauntered to the rear of the garage, toward a room he believed to be a storage area, one which he might give only a cursory glance. He opened the door, flipped down a wall switch, and flinched at a fireworks of light: a central cascade drenching the spacious enclosure, ensuing bursts at the periphery, a closing gallop up the walls from below. Then, the onset of a soft "Semper Fidelis."

The room was congested with glass-covered display cases of guns, guns and more guns, seven or eight tiers high and, as David sidestepped along tight aisles, he had to rise up to view them all. On three walls, American flags adorned the spaces between world maps whose shaded areas were color-coded with specific display cases, all of which were also labeled.

David felt as though he had stumbled onto a magician's secrets as he moved slowly among the rows, reading each label, studying most of the guns and rifles and rigs and spare parts and ammo. Quickly, he understood that, whereas his own collection was based on manufacturer, this one, perhaps ten times larger, was based on wars and military skirmishes. Only one case—marked "MISCELLANEOUS, 90'S"—had an assortment of more current weapons, all handguns.

The section marked "Spanish-American War" was stacked with Mauser rifles. "World War I" was divided into Germany with its Lugers, Modell revolvers and even Spandau machine guns; the Austro-Hungarian Empire with its Steyer-Hahn M.12; and Italy with its Mannlicher Carcano rifle which David recognized as having achieved notoriety in the John F. Kennedy assassination. "World War II" featured Gewehr rifles for Germany, Breda machine guns for Italy and Japan's Sniper Rifle Type 97. When David came across this representative weapon for Japan, he hardened, thunderstruck. Sniper Rifle 97? Coughlin? He remembered Sparky's description. That's the one! That's it. Or one like it.

Unattentive, he raced along the cases devoted to the Korean and Viet Nam wars and to the Warsaw Pact and hurried back to the "World War II" aisle. He had overlooked a newspaper clipping set back on its own pedestal under glass but now read the simple sentence, "Nazi Germany is overrun with racist supermen and especially raving homosexuals." It was dated September 22, 1943.

At the Japan case, David ran his hand along the lower edge of glass and discovered the seal intact. He opened Friday, removed the utility knife and pried off the case's external hinges. He unwrapped the terry cloth from his Blackhawk Magnum and, looking around at no one, gently lifted Sniper Rifle Type 97 with the cloth.

He tucked it under his arm and as he gravitated toward the door, noticed a recessed, glass encasement in the wall. It was brightly illuminated from within and con-

tained a single sheet of paper with the letterhead:
DEPARTMENT OF THE ARMY
Washington, DC

In the upper left corner was an official seal: Department of Defense, United States of America. The brief message read:

April 12, 1972
Dear Mr. Spritz:
I regret to inform you that you have been denied admission into the United States Army.
By direction,
James H.B. Simmons
Under Secretary of the Army

Scrawled in red ink across a margin was: FUCK YOU. V.S.

Open-mouthed, David stood at the door and gawked back at the hoard of guns for one last full minute. He considered himself slapped in a crisscross of emotions, uncertain what to feel and what to think. Alarm? Relief that he had discovered likely evidence? Confusion over American flags guarding the weaponry of only enemy nations? Or over the image of Spritz's limp wrists combined with a faded newspaper's reference to homosexuals and a rejection notice for military service during the Viet Nam War?

David resisted ripping away the switch as he flipped it to darken and silence the room.

Japanese rifle in tow, he drove to police headquarters after deciding—with little deliberation—to abandon any boycott of Sparky and his crime lab. He had no means of identifying firearms and, besides, he now possessed evidence of a more concrete nature, evidence that shouldn't be withheld from the authorities. Pissed off or not.

He was granted entrance to Sparky's office when he waved the rifle in the air before the receptionist and indicated its implication in a murder. It was four-fifteen.

"David, hello," Sparky said with no hint of annoyance. "I'll be right with you." It appeared as if Sparky hadn't noticed the rifle as he turned back toward a bench, extinguished a Bunsen burner and emptied a beaker of foul-smelling liquid into the sink. He wiped his hands on an apron, wheeled around and automatically latched onto the cloth-protected stock of the rifle as David thrust it toward his solar plexis.

"What's this?" the criminalist asked.

"I found it in Victor Spritz's garage. Sorry to barge in, Spark, but any chance of working on it before the day's out? It could be the Japanese model that did Coughlin in." David took off his scarf and gloves and held them in his hand.

Sparky rotated the weapon as he examined it, then placed it on the bench over two blocks of wood he had slid into place.

"I can do it right now. Hell, what's another fifteen minutes of backlog? Prints can wait—they're tough to lift from guns, anyway, but I can see if it fired the slug we have."

"Yeah, prints can wait," David said. "I suppose if it's the gun, the prints might be irrelevant."

Sparky gave him a look of benign condescension and said, "Not necessarily."

"Oh?"

"Someone else might have used it."

In his haste to have the rifle identified, David felt little embarrassment. "I can wait?" he asked.

"Uh-huh. Watch, if you want. Let me go get the slug first."

He left for a few minutes and returned with a shoebox from which he extracted a bullet with a four-by-four gauze pad cupped in his hand. "See," he said, "you guys aren't the only ones using these things."

David took two steps back and remained quiet as Sparky donned latex gloves, then worked deftly on and in the rifle, offering such mutterings as "groove and land count" and "rifling" and "direction of twist." He studied the bullet under a microscope, glanced back at the weapon and consulted a manual. He counted bullet grooves, examined cartridge casings he pulled from the box, and took photos of the rifle.

Finally, the criminalist confronted David and said, "No doubt. I don't need spectrography." He looked surprised.

"No doubt what?" David said.

"The rifle and fired bullet match."

"You're certain?" David's eyes pierced the criminalist's.

"Ninety-nine per cent, at least. I'd testify to it."

"Son-of-a-bitch! All along, I thought he was …" David looked about blankly and added, "God, I'll be … "

"Damned? Me, too. I've met him a few times and he always gave me the willies. You having him brought in?"

David knew that when his mind was sorting and collating and he was presented with a question, the crease above his nose deepened, and he felt it. "What—what's that?" he said.

"You bringing Spritz in?"

"If we can find him. Yeah, we've got to find him."

David put on one glove and paused. "One last thing— I always seem to be saying that—but, one last thing: you said your handwriting expert will be out of town for some time. Well, I really want to nail this guy and the more evidence, the better. And my guess is, the sooner the better."

"I'm not sure I can reach her, David."

"No, I don't mean that. I have a friend who does that sort of thing and I was wondering if I could borrow back a sample of the printing—you know, maybe the tape that was on the rock."

Sparky stared at David while running his tongue around the inside of his cheek. He remained silent as he searched through the box and pulled out a piece of tape that was glued to a tongue blade. He extended it to David with both hands but did not release it while he spoke. "You've asked me for several favors lately. Now, I have one to ask of you."

"By all means, shoot."

"Don't tell Nick I gave you this."

"Of course I won't." David wasn't surprised.

He snapped up the tape. Now all he had to do was come up with a friend who did that sort of thing.

David put on his other glove and was about to leave.

"Wait a minute," Sparky said. He left and in a minute

returned with the sign from the EMS office. He handed it to David and said, "You'll need this for comparison. We're assuming Victor Spritz wrote it."

16

CE LINE DO NOT CROSS POLICE LINE DO NOT CROS

David had missed teaching the karate class again—two days before—but told himself he was not to be denied his personal session with other black belts this night, Thursday.

It was one of those nights he needed right about now: rough-and-tumble on the mat, followed later by time with Kathy. A brief surcease from mounting questions. Both a decompression and a tune-up. He believed his mind had soaked up too much for one day and, although receiving the print evidence from Sparky was helpful, he sensed he was nowhere near solving the mysteries plaguing Hollings General over the past ten days.

And also plaguing David. Where were the snappy diagnoses of Medicine? The lucid paths to treatment and recovery? He had yet to make his first final diagnosis in this new world of detection.

On the climb to Bruno's studio at ten before five, he had a question for each step he took. Where is Spritz? Back in Cartagena? What about the drug connection? Has Kathy notified the Narcotics Unit?

Back to the print evidence. Who's to say the printing is Spritz's? The basis for comparison is the sign from the EMS office door. Couldn't Foster have put it there? Should printing samples be obtained from him? From Bernie? From Spritz's house? Or from Detective Chief Nick Medicore? He might want one from me! David puckered his brow as if everyone else's troubles had become his.

He reached his locker and sat with some relief, conscious of a sigh, receptive to the familiar gymnasium aroma that came down the hall like an invitation to follow where it led. He had time before the others arrived, so he made a slow ritual of changing into his *judogi* costume, then standing before the mirror attached to the end of the lockers. He adjusted and readjusted the black sash at his waist, gripped the carpet with his bare feet, and rotated his upper body from right to left several times. He stretched his head to his shoulder, a prizefighter awaiting the opening bell. He heard Bruno's tutorial voice next door.

David walked toward the main gym and, through the entrance to the beginners' room, saw a semicircle of young men standing at attention. Nine, he counted. They were clad in grey sweats. He recognized one of them, the one in the middle, the one with a swollen lip and purplish ear and wearing dark glasses: Robert Bugles.

Robert gave him a half-wave from waist level. David raised his hands in front, palms up, in a what's-going-on gesture. He had never interrupted a karate class before, but neither had Hollings General ever been racked with a string of murders, and anything or anyone connected to one of the victims could change his routine.

He waited for a natural break in Bruno's discourse

and walked through the doorway.

"Excuse me," he said.

"David, you're here," Bruno replied. "Would you like to say a few words to the group?"

"No, no, that's okay. Sorry to interrupt, but I just have a message for Robert Bugles there. Could I see you after you finish?" David knew the beginners' sessions and his own ended at six. Robert nodded yes.

"Good, I'll be at my locker. Thanks, Bruno," David said, ducking out of the room.

As David sparred with his colleagues, he had difficulty focusing on his chop and punch blocks, on counterattacks and on spin moves. To a degree, his size made up for lack of concentration, and it was not until he was clearly outmaneuvered midway in the session, that he willed himself to defer any distractions before he got hurt. He had particularly wondered about Robert's choice of a beginners' class. And also about what was in store for his brother, Bernie.

At six, David cooled down on the bench before his locker. Robert strolled in, breathing hard, glistening in sweat. He sat on an opposite bench and allowed his arms to plummet toward the floor.

"I guess I'm all right if I can do that out there," he said before taking a deep breath. He removed the dark glasses; his left eye was rimmed in black.

"I was going to say, you sure you're not pushing yourself? Hospitalized one day, a karate workout two days later?"

"Nah, just a little stiff."

David stood and slipped out of his uniform top. He mopped himself with a towel, having decided to delay a shower until after he had finished with Robert.

"Mind if I ask you a question or two?" he said.

"Nope. You want to take showers first?"

"Let's get this over with; it shouldn't take long. First, what on earth are you doing in with the beginners? I thought you were a 'brown.'"

"I am. But, see, it's been a long time. I'm going in with the intermediates tomorrow night. Bruno told me I could."

"How long has it been since you've been here? I mean, I remember seeing you back then, but it's kind of a blur. How long ago was it?"

"Two years."

David peered down at him. "You look in good shape. Which brings me to my next question. How can a brown belt like you not fend off an attack by his brother."

Robert wiped his chin with the back of his hand. "He caught me off guard with a sucker punch and I couldn't shake it off."

"And your being here doesn't mean you plan on re-taliating, does it?"

"You mean 'get even'?"

"Exactly."

"Nah. I'm just taking the advice you gave me in the hospital."

"You heard me, then."

"Yeah, I heard you. I also saw how that nurse broad looked at you." Robert shot a conspiratorial leer.

"I thought your eyes were closed."

"Sometimes yes, sometimes no. Depends."

David pretended to straighten out the shelf in his locker as he said, "Let's get back to Bernie. Have you seen him since he was released?"

"Nope. Never saw him but we talked on the phone."

"You talked? Hmm ... who called who?"

"He called me. He said he was sorry about what he did."

"Are you going to press charges?"

"Nah, he was probably right. I shouldn't of let you into dad's place."

"It would have been easy to get a search warrant, Robert."

"If that means the cops open up the place, then I wouldn't of gotten decked." His smile revealed a split in his swollen lip.

David didn't waste time on Robert's logic. "Do you know Victor Spritz?"

Robert lifted one leg to straddle the bench. "I guess so."

"You guess so?"

"I heard my brother talk about him."

"What did he say?"

"When?

"Any time."

"Oh ... that he's a nice guy and all that. He never told me much. You know, he's older than me."

All the way home, David tried to understand his discoveries of the day. It was nightfall and he drove transfixed, never using a directional signal or his horn or his rearview mirror to check for frog's eyes, crawling along as if anticipating that his arrival home might sully his mind's hard drive. He was thus in no hurry and the weather helped: a thin rain had turned the roads to black ice.

That Spritz would pick out a rifle for killing and then return it to his collection bothered David. What was the dynamic there? Just plain hiding it among other guns, or was it the twisted reasoning of a psychotic shunned by the Army but now possessing his own military hardware? And what on earth do CARCAN and CANCAN mean? Screw "staying the course." He decided he would level with Kathy when she came over later. Get her input. Share the gravity of his findings. Hell, she's wondering what's been accomplished, anyway.

As the headlights of his Mercedes fell across his driveway, David cursed Fitzpatrick Snow Removal. Half-assed job. He noticed a faint outline of tire tracks as he pressed on the remote control and entered his attached one-car garage. Probably Fitzy's truck or maybe a delivery truck making a wrong turn. He was not concerned until he reached the breezeway and spotted light shining through the window of the rear bathroom. He whipped out his Minx and streaked to the left side of the door to the den. Hugging the wall, he tried the door; it was locked. He slipped in a key and, shrinking sideways, flicked the door with his fingers and allowed it to drift open. The light thud of the door on the inside wall sounded heavy in the silence—loud enough, he thought, to rouse any intruder occupied in the back of the house.

David clutched the semiautomatic with both hands and waited a few seconds. He tried to breathe only through his nose. He recalled once reading that armed cowboys never peeked around corners from a standing position. He squatted and, ignoring the pain in his knee, eased the Minx into the doorway. His head followed close behind.

He reached around and turned on the light. The first

things that caught his eye were his desk and table drawers—every one had been pulled out. Most of them together with his considerable number of removable bookshelves lay on the floor like a pile of bricks and tiles. Scattered papers, slanted pictures, disturbed books, overturned lamps, puckered carpeting.

Infuriated, David dashed from room to room, flipping light switches, ready to shoot at anything that moved. Disarray, but not destruction, was everywhere. He found the bathroom light on. He checked his watch. It read six-forty and he deduced the visitor must have been there within the last two hours.

He ambled about—more leisurely now, but with Minx still drawn—stepping aside as he flung open closet doors. Convinced no one was in the house, he returned the gun to its rig and, circling around in the center of the living room, asked himself, "Who was looking for what?" It was a question he plucked from coals of agitation, because David was, first and foremost, inflamed over the violation of his personal space. He felt blood bubbling at his temples.

He thought of sitting but was too fired up for that. Instead, he hunched over and crossed his arms tightly on his chest like a tourniquet for the adrenaline surge he felt throughout his body. He was even annoyed over the tapping of his foot which seemed herky-jerky. Suddenly he stiffened upright. The basement!

David barreled down the stairs as he yanked out his Minx once again. Despite semidarkness, he knew exactly where to pull on the three light chains. There was no one there and his gun collection appeared intact.

Upstairs, he fixed himself a drink and considered

straightening out the mess, but decided he wanted Kathy to see it. He sat at the kitchen table, sipping while he kneaded his left knee. His glass was empty when he reassured himself the intruder had never entered the basement, a pronouncement that helped him tolerate the break-in and subjugate its relevance vis-a-vis the question he had initially asked: "Who was looking for what?"

The doorbell rang once and David, looking through the archway, saw Kathy rubbing her hand over the front doorjamb. "Did you see this?" she asked, as he approached her.

"What?" he said before spotting the splintered gauge. "Uh-huh, of course. It's been jimmied." He absorbed Kathy's inquisitive expression and said, "I stopped exploring once I found my guns were safe."

Her expression deepened. "What's *that* mean?"

David backed up and waved his hand toward the rooms. "Voilá," he said. Kathy's eyes widened. "David, my God!"

He pulled her to him and rested his chin on her head. "It looks worse than it is, Kath. Nothing's busted." He kissed her hair and said, "It'll look neat after a wine or two."

She removed her coat and threw it over a chair, then kicked off her galoshes and shoes in one piece.

"And I was complaining about the weather," she said, surveying the room. "Anything missing?"

"Not that I can tell, but I doubt it."

Kathy picked up several magazines and replaced them on the coffee table. "What do you think he was after?" she asked.

"I've got my ideas but come look around first."

Arm in arm, they sidled past strewn magazines and books and went into the kitchen where he poured drinks before leading her on a tour of the house.

Back in the living room, their sighs coalesced as they settled on the sofa, his legs in their usual position on the table, hers draped over his.

"No overturned furniture," she said, "notice?"

He didn't bother to look around. "And that's a clue of sorts," he said.

"A clue?"

"Sure," he said, already half through his second Canadian Club. "If psycho Spritz had been here, my guess is the place would have been destroyed. I'd be interested in the shrink's take on this. Besides, I just left Spritz's garage and his car is there. Not him but his car, which is another puzzle."

David put down his drink, repositioned her legs on his thighs and leaned back, hands clasped behind his head. "You know, Kath, if I smoked cigars, I'd blow a smoke ring right about now."

"I wouldn't let you smoke cigars."

David liked her catch of stubbornness. He sat forward and said, "That's not the point. What I mean is ... "

"I know what you mean, Dr. Dramatic. Let's have out with the great unveiling."

David's expression hardened. "Well", he said, "I think the culprit here is Bernie Bugles and he had something specific in mind. Something about his father's records."

Kathy drew back and asked, "What records?"

"Okay, are you ready for all this, or shall I refill your glass first?" She had taken only one sip.

"My glass is fine, and what are you talking about?"

Without warning, engine noises sprung from the direction of the driveway, now gunning, now purring amidst a series of beeps. Kathy recoiled.

In two steps, David was at the window. "No problem," he said. "Fitzy and his plow are back. He must have felt guilty."

David returned and sat next to Kathy, extending his legs over the table again, and lifting hers atop his with one hand. He drained the last of his drink and then told her of Charlie Bugles' references to possible drug shipments; of Alton Foster's surgical training and Victor Spritz's hospitalization in Cartagena, Colombia; of the circumstances surrounding Robert Bugles' beating; of what he labeled "the motorcycle caper in Cannon Cemetery"; of the CARCAN and CANCAN enigmas; and of the arsenal in Victor Spritz's garage and the Japanese rifle that matched the slug found in Bugles' head. He felt short of breath, but he thought Kathy looked worse.

The racket outside continued like a background chorus as he identified the calling card in the envelope he had handed her two days before—the adhesive strip from the elevator control room—and mentioned the paper on his windshield and, nodding toward the front of the house, the stone that had been hurled his way.

"David, my God!" she cried, as the motor noises disappeared.

"You said that before. It's okay."

"Okay? Why hadn't you told me about the calling cards?"

He crunched down on an ice cube. "I didn't want you to worry."

"I worried anyway. But now I'm ticked." Kathy reached up and, grabbing his chin, twisted his head toward her. "Listen, darling," she said, "murders, drugs, threats. You sure you don't want out?"

"Are you kidding?" David replied, "I'm just warming up. And what's this 'ticked' business?"

"I thought we'd be *sharing* evidence." Any tenderness in her voice was gone. He could tell she wanted him to elaborate on everything he had discovered at Bugles', at Foster's and at Spritz's.

"Kathy, my dear," he said, with a sarcastic firmness, "I just covered less than seventy-two hours. A big, important investigator like me can't be running to the cops every few hours."

"You're big," she fired back and looked as if she had already reloaded.

"Thanks a lot."

She pinched an ice cube from his glass to hers and said, "Let's get back to Spritz's garage. It was a gun collection?"

"That's no gun collection. It's a museum." David described the designations by wars, the flags, the music, the newspaper article, the Army rejection letter and the scrawl in the margin.

"The man's insane!" Kathy said.

David clapped his hands. "Bravo. That's why he was committed."

"He could have shot Coughlin—most likely he did—but that doesn't mean he butchered Bugles or pushed Tanarkle down the shaft." She had been running her fingers to-and-fro over the back of David's hand but then stopped. "In fact," she continued, "maybe we have two killers. Maybe Foster's the butcher. He had the training."

"Possible. But, Spritz certainly had motives, opportunities and means, even *without* insanity."

"I can think of one motive. What else?"

David counted on his fingers. "First, the obvious: not getting the EMS contract renewed. Then, I don't know, something about the report in Foster's files. Not his medical history per se, but why get hospitalized in Cartagena? I mean, I've heard of psychiatric secrecy, but why Colombia, South America, for Christ's sake? No, it's got to be related to drugs. Cocaine. And, how about a tie-in with Charlie Bugles and his Istanbul roots?" He had begun reasoning out loud.

"Sure," he continued, "heroin and Istanbul. Cocaine and Cartagena." David massaged his decision scar while Kathy finished her wine but never took her eyes off him.

"Wait a minute!" David leaped up, sending her sprawling on the sofa like a marionette. "Let me think," he said. He snapped his fingers. "That's it!"

"What?" Kathy gathered herself and stood. She tugged on his arm. "What?"

"Cartagena. The 'CAR' in 'CARCAN.'"

"Say that again."

"The 'CAR' in 'CARCAN' could be short for Cartagena. Jesus!"

He ran to the den and, on his knees, foraged in a heap of books on the floor, tossing them aside until he reached an atlas near the bottom. Kathy knelt beside him.

"That means," he said, "if there's a connection between Spritz and Charlie Bugles, and if my hunch is right that the 'CAR' refers to Cartagena, then maybe the first 'CAN' in the second word refers to a city in Turkey."

"Sorry, you lost me."

David opened the atlas to a map of Turkey and took out a pen. "See?" he said, printing "CARCAN" and "CANCAN" in the margin. "This is what we're looking for." He circled the first three letters of the second word. Without waiting for a response, he ran his finger up and down the country, confining himself to the Istanbul region.

"Kathy, *there*! Bull's-eye! Wait. And *there*. Damn, there're two of them." She strained to read the names of the two cities he had checked with his pen. They were about two-hundred miles equidistant from Istanbul: Canakkale, on the western coast, across the Sea of Marmare, and Cankin, inland and to the east.

He wrote the cities on an index card which he folded into his wallet, dog-eared the page and closed the book. "So conceivably," he said, as they arose, "the first part of each word represents a city, and the second part represents something else. But what?"

Kathy squared her body to his and said, "You're thinking 'CAR' is an abbreviation for Cartagena and the first 'CAN' an abbreviation for one of those Turkish cities?"

"Yep," David said, smugly.

"Hmm, and the second half of each word stands for something common to both? Like a code name?"

"That's one way of putting it." He stroked his mustache. "Yeah, like a code name. I like that."

They had wandered back to the living room and Kathy sat on the sofa, pulling David down beside her. "But what if CANCAN is simply shorthand for both Turkish cities?" she asked.

As the possibility sunk in, David raised one eyebrow in a questioning slant and said, "C'mon, Kath, why go and complicate things?"

17

When David awoke early Friday morning, he was cold in bed and couldn't understand why he had slept so soundly until he recalled adding sweet vermouth to another double Canadian Club the night before. There was a misty remembrance, too, of poking at some kind of goulash, and, afterward, of admonishing Kathy that she would freeze in the nude. Everything else that may or may not have transpired was a blank.

Feeling dumb that he wore only shorts, he lifted the blankets and saw Kathy curled up and still nude. He kissed her awake and neither spoke as they did what he later referred to as "The thing they did or didn't do last night." He also called it, "Filling in the blank," and received Kathy's stoneface and sharp elbow.

After breakfast, David said, "I'm behind in my computer entries and look outside because there go the tire tracks."

Kathy regarded him critically. "Now that's a sentence for posterity. I hope your mind isn't as scrambled."

"Right now? Yes. Sorry, what I meant was … you know I like to keep a diary of sorts … who knows? It might come in handy someday … and I think I'll bring it up-to-date now. Second, more snow fell, maybe two inches, so now we can forget tire impressions from yesterday."

"That's better. I know your mind's awhirl, David darling, but you have to slow down. And while you're trying to figure out how, I'm calling headquarters to change Spritz's APB to an arrest warrant."

David went to his computer and Kathy to the phone. After making his entries, he called Musco at the cab company.

"I have a strange request," David said. "Do you know of anyone who's a handwriting expert?"

"Sure. She reads everything: handwriting, palms, faces. Name's Madame Alicenova over there in Center City. We call her Madame Alice for short or sometimes just Alice."

"It sounds like she does handwriting analysis. I need handwriting identification."

"What's the difference? You'll get your money's worth."

"One's a science. The other isn't. I don't want some guess about personality traits. I want a positive identification of something."

"Believe me, David, my boy, this gal knows her potatoes. Even the FBI uses her."

Reluctantly, David took down her address and phone number and said, "Musco, thanks much for referring me to a goddamn fortuneteller."

"You wait. You'll see."

David called and scheduled an appointment for later, at four-thirty. He had expected Madame Alicenova to ask for details but she didn't. He had expected to hear an accent but there was none.

At eight-thirty, he and Kathy decided she would skip Ted Tanarkle's funeral later that morning but would attend the noon reception at Alton and Nora Foster's. He would go to both.

As he motored to St. Xavier's Roman Catholic Church, David pictured a lighted sign swinging in a cavity of his brain. It read, "CARCAN and CANCAN." He concentrated on what the last three letters of each word could possibly stand for and whether they stood for the same thing. He said them aloud—"Canada? Canvas? Canal? Candy? Candidate?"—and thought that once they hauled Spritz in, he would throttle the answer out of him.

He also thought he was becoming most proficient in two things: whipping out his Minx semiautomatic and attending funerals. Even luncheon receptions after funerals. He had not gone to Tanarkle's wake, and, flashing back to the rifle barrel on the hillside, decided to forgo the cemetery scene as well. He wanted, however, to pay his respects to an old friend and mentor at the funeral mass and, of more importance, to see who was there, a sleuthing necessity that he was sure Tanarkle would understand.

It was a summery morning in January and David found the downtown church's parking lot stuffed with cars in uneven rows and with mourners he knew: white-clad residents, nurses in uniform, department heads, an administrative contingent, and every doctor and pathology employee he had ever met. He wondered who was minding the hospital as he pulled to a stop on a crusty side street.

By the time he arrived at the church steps, the crowd

had thinned, and inside, he was given one of only two or three remaining seats in the largest and most ornate church in the city. It was a middle seat in the last row which David thought was just as well, for he would have felt embarrassed if he sat up close and blocked the view of not only the officiating priest but also the statues above the altar.

The air was thick with incense, and organ music was so loud, it drowned out its own echoes. David could see clear to the front and, as he eyed each row, was not surprised by anybody's attendance: the Tanarkle family, the Fosters, Belle, Sparky, Dr. Castleman from the E.R. But then, two rows ahead of his: Bernie Bugles and Marsha Gittings from Pathology. They sat side by side. Coincidence?

The attaché case, Friday, grew heavy on David's lap. He had discovered all he could and was tempted to leave but reasoned it was too early for the luncheon anyway. He stayed seated until the casket was rolled out past him and he had bowed his head and whispered, "Bye, old buddy. I wish you peace." He miscalculated, thinking his would be the first row to be guided out. Instead, others preceded him and it was a full ten minutes before his turn, but only ten seconds since the unlikely couple left in a hurry. As they passed by, Bernie had Marsha by the arm and had glanced back at David.

David blasted out, hoping to intercept them before they arrived in the parking lot. But it was too late. He spotted them though and gained on them, reaching the early model Ford he recognized as Marsha's. Bernie was in the driver's seat and was about to close the door when David held it back with the full length of his body.

"Hi there," David said.

"Why, Dr. Brooks, hello," Marsha said from the passenger side.

David looked at one, then the other. "I didn't realize you two knew each other."

Bernie made a feeble attempt to close the door. "May I?" he said.

David didn't answer, nor did he move. Bernie slouched and exaggerated a stare out the windshield.

Finally, Bernie turned slowly and said, "I understand you sneaked into my father's place." He pulled up the collar of a patterned windbreaker.

"I didn't sneak in. Robert let me in."

"My brother's an idiot."

"That's not my fault. At least I didn't break in. On the other hand, did my brother let you in *my* place yesterday?" David was an only child.

"I don't know what you're talking about," Bernie said, arching his back.

David glared at Bernie and had difficulty disregarding the possibility he had broken into his home. He wanted to drag him from the car and shake him into admission. Instead, he said, "Then how about this? Where do you keep your motorcycle?"

"I don't have a motorcycle, and what's with the third degree?" Bernie tried the door again.

David stood as solid as a nearby stanchion. "Okay," he said, "you don't have a motorcycle." He grinned at Marsha. "You're going to the reception, I assume?"

"Yes," she said.

"Good, I'll see you there." He released the door.

At Nora and Alton Foster's, David had left Friday in

the car and, inside, swayed from foot to foot, itching to have the man in the ascot take his scarf and gloves. Barely in the door, he had to wait in one of three lines this time, and while he waited, harked back to the reception for Charlie Bugles when he thought the music, the noise, the liquor, the ostensible merriment were more suited to a political fundraiser. Not now, he observed, casting his eyes into the living room, over still heads and touching shoulders. Wagner replaced Gershwin, it was church quiet and there was no bartender. Even the sweet cakes he sampled from the table in the foyer tasted bland.

"David," Alton Foster said solemnly, "glad you could make it." He had swum through the lines and he shook David's hand. David knew he hurt men when he shook hands, and that the only way to prevent it was to slacken his wrist. He reserved that for women. Kathy had called it a double standard.

"Hi, Alton, it's pretty grim in here."

"Yes, I know. It's a sad occasion. They don't … I mean didn't … come any finer than Ted."

"For sure."

"Let me take those, please," Foster said. One of David's gloves dropped to the floor and they both started to bend for it. "No, no," Foster said, "I'll get it." He picked up the glove and puffed, "It's a shorter distance for me, right?"

They made their way to a row of closets where Foster said, "Here, Boris, these belong to Dr. Brooks."

David didn't quite know why he found that amusing.

The administrator steered him into a side room. "David," he said, searching his eyes, "what's happening?

Has any headway been made on the killings?"

"We're still working on it." Foster was another one David wanted to extract more information from—like why he kept his surgical training a secret. He wanted to question him, not shake as in the case of Bernie Bugles, or throttle as in the case of Victor Spritz. Just start questioning right now. But, once again, he congratulated himself for not allowing Foster's guard to be raised any higher than he thought it might be.

Foster pointed in the direction of the living room fireplace. "That Detective … Med–i–core, is it? Kathy's new boss. He's here, you know."

"He's here?"

"Yes. He's questioning people like there's no tomorrow, and I sort of resent it. It's an inappropriate time and place, really. Some of them have come up to me and complained. He hasn't gotten to me yet—I sure hope I can stay civil."

There we have it. Nick's no passive observer. Or is it a sham?

Foster went on. "I received a letter from the bunch at the Joint Commission on Accreditation office. They want a full accounting of … how'd they put it? … 'the murder spree at your hospital.' Murder spree. What a shit-eating way to put it. They asked how we're coming along with our in-service educational efforts. Can you believe it? An in-service on how to outguess a murderer. And, do you know what? Our census is the lowest in our history. The bottom's fallen out. How can a backlash happen so fast?"

David was still assessing Nick's conduct but suspected he had heard the correct question and said, "Pardon me for saying so, but what do you expect? We've had four high profile murders, the killer's still at large, and there could be more."

"More?"

"Think about it. Don't just think about the census."

"But it's ruining us!"

David wondered why Foster's body language didn't match his emotion. "Look, Alton, patients are concerned, the Joint Commission's concerned, the police are concerned and, frankly, I'm concerned. Now, we can talk more later, but I must chat with some people before they leave." He wanted to range about and, eventually, to corner Bernie again. Besides, lately he felt listening to Foster was like moving a refrigerator and then having to strip floors.

"Yes, yes, of course. Go right ahead. I'll see you later. Oh, there's my wife. Go say hello."

They had edged back toward the foyer which was drained of early arrivals. David saw Nora Foster by a planter near the step to the living room and heard the click of fingernails. He moseyed over and caught the sweet fragrance of flowers he couldn't identify and had never seen in the winter except at funerals. She nipped at dead petals and placed them in the pocket of her striped bouffant skirt.

"Hello, Nora. Nipping in the bud—I mean after the bud?"

"Oh, Dr. Brooks. Welcome again. This is getting to be a habit."

Her husband, now at their side, retorted, "Getting to be? I can't take her to a flower show. We'd get thrown out."

She countered, icily, "Alton, dearest, I was referring to funeral receptions, not blossom cleansing."

She deposited a fistful of petals into a plastic sandwich bag and, shaking a finger at David, said, "Now don't
forget the blood drive tomorrow. It's the staff's chance to
do its duty. Remember, you missed in July."

"Yes, ma'am," he replied, in the manner of a school-
boy caught playing hooky. *That's all she's got to think
about at a time like this?*

David excused himself when he spotted Betty
Tanarkle sagging on a window seat at the far end of the
living room. Several guests appeared to be offering her
their condolences. He walked over, waited his turn and
said, "Betty, I'm terribly sorry and I suppose it's no com-
fort to say he lived a full life." He took her hands and
leaned over to kiss her.

"Thank you, David. Ted was one in a million," she
said, her voice, wooden.

David thought it odd that whereas he remembered
she had worn black at Bugles' funeral, now she was in
emerald green. *At least she yielded on her neckline this
time,* he mused.

He moved on to allow others their expressions of
sympathy. Just then, he detected the scent of his favorite
perfume and felt a gentle tap on his shoulder from behind. Without turning, he said softly, "Darling, I've been
waiting for you."

Kathy walked around to face him and said, "It's a
good thing it's me."

"Hmm, excellent point. Listen, before I forget, how
come Nick's here?"

"He told me he called Foster and asked if he could
come."

"Well I'll bet Foster's sorry he said 'yes.' Appar-

ently Nick's forcing himself on people. Think you ought
to call him off?"

"Hey, I couldn't do what he's doing. Here, I mean.
If he picks up anything, so much the better."

"Just thought I'd raise the question," David said with
resignation. "By the way, you look nice."

"You mean uncop-like?" Kathy was dressed in navy
blue: turtleneck blouse, opened fanny sweater, snug skirt
and stiletto shoes that elevated her to the level of David's
bowtie. She added, "You noticed. Thanks. I left the badge
off, though."

"You look naked without it."

"I always look naked to you."

"Complaining?"

"No." She quickly shifted to a different gear.
"David!" she said, "This is a funeral reception."

"So? Life goes on."

"Well, I hope it does around these parts. At the rate
it's going ..."

David shifted to his own gear. "Wait here," he said,
"I think they're getting ready to leave." He made himself
thinner as he sidestepped through a dense wall of guests
toward Bernie Bugles and Marsha Gittings.

He reached down to lift up Bernie's limp hand, and
shook it with all the force he would have liked to use on
his narrow shoulders.

When David released the hand, Bernie looked at it
as he might a fallen sparrow and, addressing Marsha, said,
"What are we doing here?" He poured a contemptuous
look around. "Let's go."

"Wait," David said. "May I ask you a few questions?"

"You already did," Bernie snapped.

David plowed ahead. "You know Victor Spritz?"

Bernie hesitated, then answered, "The ambulance guy? Sure, why?"

"Do you know where he is?"

"No, where is he?"

"That's what I'm asking." David knew he had framed the question wrong and his own response was the best he could do. He decided to press on.

"Are you still living in Manhattan?"

"That's none of your business."

"Bernard!" Marsha shrieked. Heads turned their way. "Yes, he is, Dr. Brooks."

"Thanks," David said, not so much to be polite as to distinguish her answers from Bernie's. "And, oh, before you leave, Marsh, let me ask you something. Who's stepped into Ted's position? Jake?"

"Yes, and I'd guess Dr. Reed has the inside track to become Chief. He's been with us for more than fifteen years. Came just after I did."

While David and Marsha spoke, Bernie gravitated toward the foyer and waved for her to follow.

"One last question, and you don't have to answer," David said. "How long have you known that guy?"

"Who, Jake Reed?"

"No, Bernie, over there."

Marsha nodded yes to Bernie and then, addressing David, said, "I met him at a party his father had many years ago. What? Twelve, thirteen years?"

David decided to take a chance on something he realized was out of bounds. "You and he serious?"

"I'm not sure what you'd call it. I have to go now. Good luck, Dr. Brooks."

He watched as she and Bernie stole off. What a strange answer! Didn't deny a relationship. "Good luck?" Murders on her mind.

As David looked around for Kathy, he noticed Nick in a cluster of long faces, notepad in hand. David thought there was nothing to be gained by speaking to him so he headed off in the opposite direction, finally locating Kathy finishing a cup of coffee.

"How did that go?" she asked.

"You learn some things, you don't learn some things. I'll explain later. We're out of here. You going to headquarters?"

"I have to run home first." She spread her arms. "These aren't my work clothes."

"Tonight?" David said.

"Tonight, except let's make it at my place."

"Like in 'your place or mine'?"

Nostrils flaring, Kathy responded, "Please, I hate that expression."

"Why?"

"Because of the insinuation."

"Okay, I understand. Then shall we insinuate at your place or mine?"

"You're incorrigible!" Kathy growled. "Bye."

She began to strut off when David took three steps to catch up to her, and, following her ear, whispered, "Don't forget to say hello to Betty Tanarkle."

Without breaking stride, Kathy swerved off at a right angle as if she had thought of the courtesy herself.

From one o'clock on, two thoughts nagged David's subconscious like an inflamed toe: the Bernie/Marsha alliance and the CARCAN/CANCAN conundrum. Beyond those, he was determined to tackle several loose ends among many; the pearl-handled dagger and past flights to Istanbul, Cartagena and Tokyo headed the list.

He settled in at the Hole, informed Belle he didn't want to be disturbed except for an urgent message—"like from someone claiming he committed all four murders"— and started calling pawnshops other than Razbit's, museums, historical societies, Army-Navy stores and any other place that might sell, collect, trade or otherwise deal in daggers. In an hour, he knew no more than he did when he first sat down. So much for Operation Dagger Hunt, he grumbled.

Next, after consulting with a travel agent friend, he contacted every airline that had planes flying into Turkey, Colombia and Japan. The response was uniform: they could not release past flight manifests except to a bona-fide law enforcement agency. Sometimes, as in a disaster, to the media.

David sat ruminating as he tossed a paper wad of phone numbers from hand to hand. Belle slid a cup of coffee on his desk, startling him.

"I thought I said no disturbances," he said.

"Oh, right," she said, cowering. "Well, let's say this was brewed by someone claiming he committed all four murders." He threw the wad of paper at her.

Cuddling the cup, he took a sip, then another, and cleared his mind as if to make room for ideas to germinate. Travel ideas. Commercial flying ideas.

There was a case he had six years ago when he first started sleuthing. It dealt with an embezzler trying to flee the country, and he vaguely recollected the criminal may also have done drugs. It conjured up a litany of federal agencies he had to deal with: the Immigration and Naturalization Service, the Drug Enforcement Agency, the U.S. Customs Service. He remembered how sympathetic they were to the plight of amateur detectives but also how slowly the answers filtered back.

Finally, bingo! *Kathy*. Legitimate, legal, authentic. Professional police detectives have the full resources of the local, state and federal law enforcement communities. Have her find out. He contacted her.

It was two-thirty. By four, he had his information. Kathy phoned to say that over the past five years, Victor Spritz had flown to Colombia twelve times; Charlie Bugles had traveled to Turkey ten times; and his son, Bernie, had landed in Tokyo twenty-one times. She added that she couldn't wait to discuss the implications at her place later that night. Neither could David.

At precisely four-thirty, he pulled into the driveway of a yellow Victorian house set back slightly from a thoroughfare of fast-food restaurants, chain stores and discount houses. Out front, an ice-crusted sign with faded green letters spanned two posts stuck in the ground. The letters spelled: READINGS.

David thought the house looked as if it had been wheeled to a sliver of land left over from commercial development. And he was certain it violated side lot zoning regulations.

He obeyed the WALK-IN command on an index card thumbtacked to the doorjamb. The far end of a foyer as expansive as the four rooms at 10 Oak Lane contained a ponderous glass door trimmed in carved oak figurines. He followed the instructions there to RING BELL AND

ENTER. Inside, there was an echo to his steps in a room with no carpeting and circumscribed by chairs and tables of all sizes, shapes and hardwoods. Its floor dimensions were double those of the foyer and its ceiling was higher than either dimension. He sank into an easy chair that elevated his kneecaps to eye level and picked up a tattered copy of *Life* magazine from an end table. He remembered being told once that mirrors tend to enlarge a room and he wondered whether they were wasted on all four walls.

In ten seconds, a door directly opposite David opened and a tall women swanned into the room. She had symmetrical facial wrinkles and titian hair. She subdued the billow of her floral-print skirt with one hand and offered the other to David, but he didn't have a chance to shake it as she reached for the convexity of her black silk blouse and withdrew a card from a pocket.

"I believe you are Dr. Brooks. So nice to meet you," she said. Her voice was firm, resonant and coordinated with the style of the house.

"Yes, Musco sent me. You know, from the Red Checker Cab Company."

"Ah, yes. Mr. Diller. I've spoken to both of you about your request. Do you have something for me?" She descended into a chair next to David and moved a table lamp to the side.

"Yes, one's a piece of tape; the other's a sign. Can you tell me if the writing was done by the same person?" He opened Friday, pulled out the tape and cardboard sign, and placed them on the table.

At the same time, Madame Alice brandished a round magnifying glass the size of a coffee saucer. David assumed she took it from the table drawer but he never saw or heard it open.

"Yes ... hmm ... yes ... nice," she said, examining the articles with her naked eye. "I don't need this." She put down the magnifying glass. "I can tell you, straight away, that they match. Whoever wrote the sign also wrote on the tape."

David tossed her a how-do-you-know look.

"See here," she said, "notice the spacing between letters, and the same buckle on these letters over here, and especially how short the upper loop is on the 'S' in both specimens. I have no doubt, Dr. Brooks."

But David did. Or at least he wasn't convinced her comments were not boilerplate.

Madame Alice leaned back and, searching the air for words, lapsed into a monologue that included historical data on manuscript writing, cursive writing, calligraphy, Gothic writing, hieroglyphics, Spencerian writing, and what she called, English Round Hand.

David was now convinced. He thanked the lady, forked over a fifty-dollar bill, and considered asking her the cost of a palm reading or, better still, of naming Victor Spritz's whereabouts.

Halfway to Kathy's, he glanced at the persistent lights in his mirror. Well, if it isn't Kermit. Where's he been? He missed a night.

18

Kathy's condominium complex—Hollings Hollow—was only a few blocks from police headquarters but insulated from noise and neon by beige baffling on three sides. The fourth side was an elongated cluster of shade trees. One time, David jested that if he had been awarded the contract for the baffles, he could have opened a plush Medical and Detective Bureau somewhere and never drawn a salary for life. "Baffle money" would suffice.

Her corner unit comprised one of the smallest there: kitchen, living/dining room combination, single bedroom with bath. It opened directly on an interior roadway and, to the side and rear, a one-car garage, wooden deck and intervening slice of yard occupied more space than the rooms inside. She and David liked to barbecue year-round on the deck which, attached to the kitchen, bedroom and garage, formed a secluded horseshoe. A rock ledge, half as high as the unit, ran along the driveway and garage, defining her property line on the right. More than once, he had said, "This deck right here is the Hollow, not the whole damned place." They would position chairs and a small table not an arm's length from the gas-fired grill and edge even closer in freezing weather.

That evening, he sipped on a second drink and flipped steaks while she shuttled dishes, silverware and seasonings between kitchen and table. A pie plate thermometer on the garage's cedarwood registered thirty-six degrees, and the air smelled fresh as if everything could start over. They chose not to turn on the mushroom lamps, preferring the glow of the fire and slender threads of moonlight.

David wore a burgundy flannel shirt, tan sleeveless sweater, corduroys and his black stocking cap. He forgot the scarf. Kathy was in stirrup pants and a ginger duffle coat whose fleece lining showed at the collar. They flexed and unflexed their fingers as if trying to unfuse them.

He was about to begin discussions of the Bernie/Marsha alliance and the excursions of Victor Spritz and both Bugles when Kathy sat down and, gripping her hands together, said, "Nick wants you off the case."

He put down a spatula and said calmly, "He what?" David believed she was joshing for she, too, had consumed a generous drink, yet he looked at her as if sizing up an abstract painting and added, "Now run that by me again."

"He wants you to withdraw from the investigation."

David now felt his pulse pounding in his ears but stood there, mute, waiting to hear more.

"I asked him why and he said, 'What's he getting done? Nothing.'"

" 'That's not fair,' I said. 'Neither are we when you come right down to it. He's working full-time on the murders.'" Kathy's face turned placatory.

"Then he seemed to lose it. I was at my desk and he stomped around the office, mumbling to himself. So I just expressed what I believe: 'Well, we can't stop him.' And David, he gave me such a keep-your-mouth-shut stare that I was frightened for a second."

"Oh, he did, did he? Then what happened?" David kept his lips pursed with suppressed but building fury.

"He said ... said? ... he almost shouted ... 'We can't? Well, let me tell you something: for starters, we can sure stop helping him.' Then he leaned over my desk and said, 'And I can sure charge him with interfering with a criminal investigation. Do you know what that means? It means obstruction of justice. Plus, he's making us look bad.' That's when I lost it a little myself. I said something like, 'And how will that make us look?' Then, he stormed out."

David pulled a chair next to hers, resisting the urge to drive his knuckles into the table. "That son-of-a-bitching carpetbagger! It wouldn't surprise me if he had something to do with the killings."

Kathy dipped her head as if peering over reading glasses. "You're kidding, of course."

David stiffened. "Kathleen, what do you definitely know about him?" He had a million questions about Nick on his mind but waited for an answer.

"Only what came through official channels. He applied for the job. They said he had good recommendations. We checked with San Diego—that I know."

"Ever see him at one of your conventions?"

"No."

"He ever talk about any of his cases?"

The questioning seemed to settle David down. He

rose and checked the steaks with a knife and fork, returned to his seat and covered both Kathy's hands with one of his. "Level with me, Kath, don't you think he acts ... well ... weird at times? Like now?"

"I can't disagree, but I think you're jumping to conclusions."

"Then, you know, he's friggin' stupid. What's he gain by alienating me? There could be times where he might need me more than I need him."

"There's no doubt about it. And no matter what he says, don't ever think of taking yourself off the case. He'll never file a complaint because it wouldn't stand up. You're too well-liked by the rest of the department and he knows it. The only reason I mentioned his ranting and raving is because you should know where you stand with him."

David pulled his hand back. "Another thing," he said. "How come you and he get along so well?"

"That's hardly the case, believe me."

"Well, you're always defending him ... "

"Oh, we've had our battles."

"Like over what?"

"You name it." Kathy got up, circled around David and put her hands on his shoulders. "It seems they always end the same way, too. I say, 'Whose side are you on, anyway'?"

"What's he say?"

" 'And whose side are you on'?"

"What a jerk." David twisted in his chair and, facing Kathy, said, "And, come to think about it, I can do without Sparky, if that's the help he's talking about."

"Why do without Sparky? Who says you have to deal directly with him? I'm eventually privy to anything he comes up with. And sooner if you need it."

Kathy's revelation had reinforced David's distrust, if not suspicion, of Chief Detective Nick Medicore. For the rest of the cookout, he tried to put a tolerable spin on a stressful development, but deep down he felt like one possessed because Nick had dared to act up at a time when his own head was still churning over other problems. Once again, he ran the words CARCAN and CANCAN slowly through his mind, trying to pin down a meaning for all four syllables. The last three letters in each word are short for something, right? Maybe not. Maybe they're complete words that start a phrase. Like, for example, "Can do."

Eventually, he brought Kathy current on discoveries that had continued to baffle him.

David had eaten his steak, but never tasted it. He had watched a TV movie with Kathy, but never saw it. Later, sleep came in spells.

At six in the morning, he sprung up in bed. "That's it!" he cried.

He felt Kathy's hand on his forearm. "What's the matter?" she said. "David, what's wrong?"

"The dictionary! Of course. Where the hell have I been? Where is it, Kath?"

"In the bookcase, but can't it wait till later? What's in the dictionary, for heaven's sake?"

He stumbled into the living room, turned on a desk lamp and leafed through a Webster's New Collegiate Edition until he got to "C." A few pages along, he ran his fingers down eight columns of words starting with "can." Nothing caught his attention so he began the process again, this time more slowly. At the midway point, he passed a word, then returned to it as if he had overshot the mark: the finger equivalent of a double take. He slammed the dictionary shut and pumped his fist. The word was "canister." The silver canisters. "Yes!" he exclaimed aloud.

His mind's eye focused on Victor Spritz's equipment room, his "Ambulance Without Wheels," with its spare parts and shelf of silver canisters. Six in all, and identical to the ones that had held gauze and cotton in a Navy treatment room years ago. He mouthed words and word fragments and suddenly realized he had forgotten the names of the two "Can" cities in Turkey. He returned to the bedroom, smiled at Kathy's deep breathing and, in the dark, groped for his pants.

Back in the living room, he removed the index card from his wallet and now had all the pieces of the mosaic, he thought. He took one word at a time. "CAR" is "Cartagena," so we have "Cartagena Canister." "CAN" is either—he looked at the card—"Canakkale" or "Cankin." So it's either "Canakkale Canister," or "Cankin Canister." And who care's, it's over there in Turkey. David rubbed his decision scar before editorializing. Where they grow the old opium poppy, and process it into heroin, and smuggle it all over the place, like in the old U.S. of A., to fry human brains. And the same for Cartagena, only we're not talking Colombian coffee here, we're talking cocaine, Big C, lady, nose candy. Candy to fry the same human brains.

He wanted to leave immediately for Spritz's office but, at the same time, wanted to digest the events of the past day. And of the days before that. It was Saturday so he let Kathy sleep. Over coffee, he sat at her desk, took his notepad out from Friday and began to make notes which he would later polish to enter into his computer. He wrote about shipment dates, coded containers, drugs, murder suspects, loss of forensic support, excursions to known drug producing countries—estimating relevance, drawing lame conclusions, offering actions to consider. And he didn't know what to make of the Bernie/Marsha alliance, but since he had cast everyone he had come across lately as a killer, he characterized them temporarily as Bonnie and Clyde desperadoes.

At eight-fifteen, he left for the hospital, charged with questions and few answers, determined to enter Spritz's office even if it meant breaking down the door. He had forgotten the Red Cross blood drive next door in Pathology. While working there two years ago, David was instrumental in expanding the drive to three mornings at a stretch and in having the doors open at eight.

He walked into the Pathology wing and at the entrance to its large conference room, stopped to view donors lying on tables—two rows of four each—like live bodies in a morgue, their arms restrained and guarded by nurses in grey uniforms. The room's fluorescence was more than it could handle. David leaned against the archway, picking up the smell of alcohol sponges and smarting from the sting of needle insertions, while pink-smocked ladies tended to plastic pouches bearing the Red Cross logo or to intravenous tubing and refrigerated white boxes. Men and women sat beside desks for screening interviews and blood pressure recordings; others waited in line.

He winked at Marsha who looked up while interviewing the psychiatrist, Dr. Sam Corliss, but David didn't bother to address Nora Foster as she scurried from table to table and desk to desk, straightening tubing, whispering to volunteers. Nora had been the director of Hollings' blood drives for as long as David could remember.

He watched the cool precision of bloodletting for only a minute because he had other matters on his mind. Deciding to take a shortcut to Spritz's office, he bypassed the labyrinth of laboratories and zigzagged through empty suites off a parallel corridor. The Saturday morning silence of the department's administrative rooms bothered him.

In the last room before the hall to the EMS office, he came upon John Bartholomew, the hospital's chief microbiologist and a confidant during David's four years of Pathology there. Although Bartholomew was not an M.D., he was considered an expert in the clinical findings of infectious diseases as well as one of the area's top bacteriologists. He sat at a desk, pressing the telephone receiver down against his shoulder. David had often asked the veteran, skin-creased researcher how it felt to witness the laying of Hollings General's cornerstone in the century before.

"Hey there, John, you're not whistling, what's up?"

Startled, Bartholomew dropped the phone on the desk before replacing it in its cradle. His hands shook.

"Oh, David, it's you. Sorry, I'm a bit jumpy."

David narrowed his eyes. "Can I help?"

The microbiologist appeared to welcome the question and said, "Can you keep a secret? I've been bottling it up too goddamned long."

"Of course. You know better than to ask that."

Bartholomew relaxed his shoulders. "Alton Foster

just hung up on me. I called him at home. He still refuses to notify the County Health Department about something I think is an emergency— and I don't want to be a part of it any longer."

David sat on the corner of the desk. "What emergency?"

"You remember the botulism study we started just before you left here?"

David nodded.

"Well, it was expanded. We got a grant from CDC to see if we could find a way to improve the trivalent botulinum antitoxin."

"And?"

"As you know, you need clostridium bacilli to generate the toxin."

"You're beating around the bush, John. What happened, you ran out of clostridium?"

"Worse," Bartholomew said, swallowing audibly. "We kept it in a tube of thioglycolate broth, and it's gone."

"What do you mean, gone?"

"Disappeared. I can't find it."

"Since when?"

"Thursday."

David pulled at his ear until it hurt. Jesus Christ, now what, germ terrorism? He pushed himself away from the desk and paced. "Anybody else know about this?"

"Just Foster. I called him immediately."

"No one in the department knows?"

"No. Remember, it was my baby, so nobody else paid much attention to it."

"Hmm," David said, "and what's with Foster?"

"He says I probably spilled it down the sink—which

is ludicrous—and that the Health Department would only create panic if they heard about it. That they'd go to the press, ask a lot of questions around here. And he went on and on about the census of the hospital. He said the murders were more than enough to overcome—if we ever did—and we shouldn't scare people about something that probably didn't happen. David, it did happen. Someone stole the tube. I would have remembered spilling it. And there'd be an empty tube lying around."

"The whole tube couldn't have been discarded accidentally somewhere, like in the trash can?"

"I doubt it." After a burst of eye blinks, the microbiologist repeated the phrase.

David was well aware that botulism food poisoning was on the list of biological weapons reportedly stockpiled by international terrorist groups, along with anthrax, brucellosis and plague.

"Look," he said, "don't do anything on your own quite yet. Let me speak to Foster—he sounds completely off base on this."

"Tell him if he doesn't, I'm reporting the theft myself."

"Hold off, John, I'll call him. You working today?

"I'll be here till noon."

"Good, I'll try to get back to you. If not, later. Now, don't do anything rash."

David took his leave, walking more slowly now, as if uphill. A vial of poison had been added to a consciousness already scrambled with people, places and other things, including the silver canisters he hoped to examine momentarily.

He had anticipated calling Security for a key to Victor Spritz's office, but he found the door unlocked, the overhead lights on. The status of the outer room was the same as when he looked in from the corridor ten days before: mostly empty and in general disarray. In the center was a table burdened by days of unopened mail. He danced around the litter on the floor.

In the past, he had entered the back room on only a few occasions but now, approaching it, he clearly pictured the six canisters that had caught his attention each time. It was a large room, perhaps twenty-five feet square, and after he walked in and looked toward the shelf on the right wall, he arched back as if he had been shot. The canisters were not there.

David put his hands on his hips and retreated in order to improve his view of the entire room. Like stalking prey, his eyes darted to all four corners, across and under tables, from cabinet tops to carton tops, and up along the ceiling, for good measure. Where are they?

He tossed splints aside, looked behind aspirators, and moved stretchers stacked like furniture in storage. The more supplies and equipment he encountered, the more careless he became; oxygen tanks clanked against each other like bowling pins, metal drawers thwacked pulley weights, I.V. poles toppled over and bounced off his toes. He felt no pain, an obsessed hunter looking for round silver containers.

Pillows and blankets were piled in a corner while, nearby, one blanket lay crumpled on a folding cot. Under a bench, he uncovered a leather trunk covered by a blue tarpaulin. The canisters are in there? Why? He yanked out the trunk, threw off its covering and opened it. Stuck into a clutter of books and manuals were a pair of bloody latex gloves, a roll of yellow tape and a woman's black wig.

Their discovery was enough to jog him away from his silver search, like releasing him from a cobra hypnosis and, for the first time, he realized the room was cold and drafty, and what had been missed before, he now spotted at the far wall. The back door was half-open, its edge caught on a table. David took soft half-steps in that direction, inspecting the floor in line with the opening. There was no snow. He moved to the wall left of the door and stood motionless for a few seconds before switching Friday to his left hand and pulling out his Beretta Minx with his right. He felt uneasy packing heat in a hospital.

The unlocked front door. The partially open back door. David knew his batting average with a sixth sense would never be exalted, yet he could swear he would find something unexpected in the parking area beyond the door. So he hesitated for fear he might be right.

He came to a full crouch and—still nearly as tall as, say, Kathy—led with the barrel of his gun, sliding his head sideways until one eye had cleared the doorjamb. He saw nothing unusual.

The parking area was a space large enough to accommodate no more than three or four vehicles, and it was separated from the main doctors' parking lot by a cement wall smothered by vines. David suspected the private spaces had been created for the administrative hierarchy when their offices were on the first floor before renovation three decades before.

There was a single vehicle there, not forty feet away. Box-like and white, it was Spritz's defibrillator van and sported black lettering on its sides and back:

Hollings
Cardiac Defibrillator
Vehicle

It was a combination of curiosity, basic detection procedure and that sixth sense that drew him out into the crisp morning. He steadied his Minx against his chest and Friday against his thigh as he advanced toward the van.

It was unlocked. He lifted one foot up to the floor before stopping short, barely able to maintain his balance. He felt his heart hammer on his chest wall and, swaying forward, caught the stench of gunpowder, blood and death. He tried breathing through his mouth but that only distilled the smell on his tongue. He settled on short expiratory grunts until adaptation kicked in.

To the left, a male body lay doubled over, wedged between a folded stretcher and the floor, while lining an adjacent glass cabinet were the objects of his hunt minutes before, the objects he momentarily felt were anticlimactic. Except David knew better. Six silver canisters shone in the light that beamed over his shoulder.

The body's face was obscured. David stooped and climbed into the van, tossing Friday toward the driver's seat to the right and sliding his Minx behind it. He didn't bother checking for a pulse because the exposed surfaces of the body felt cold, clammy and stiff. He righted the head with difficulty and flinched at the agonal face of Victor Spritz.

David eased upright and for a split second—until his head tapped the ceiling of the van—he felt lifeless, detached, as if he were disembodied, suspended in some other location, but certainly not there, cramped in quarters too small for even average size men. In his day, he had treated many patients who had had acute anxiety attacks but he had never had one himself, and in a moment of self-diagnosis, reckoned that if he were disposed to having one, this discovery would have triggered it by now. He bent forward, probing the full extent of the body. Spritz was completely clothed and wore a blue windbreaker which David unzipped. Underneath, a tight sweater in bright yellow contrasted with streaks of desiccated blood. He palpated the chest, abdomen and all four extremities, and then pulled up the sweater and a shirt to inspect Spritz's exposed flanks and to press on his skin.

There was a circular bullet entrance wound on the left side of his forehead with no surrounding gunpowder traces. A single bead of caked blood ran from the wound to the angle of his jaw like a crimson termite tunnel. David counted five other round entrance wounds through the sweater, two in the vicinity of the heart, two at the level of the navel and one at the right clavicular area. The one nearest the left heart border appeared to have sucked in threads of yellow fabric. He detected no soot smudges and estimated the shots came from a distance greater than fifteen to eighteen inches. Several pools of dark blood lay clotted on the floor and on the lap of the body.

David braced himself against a side wall and calculated: full rigor mortis, fixed lividity, van temperature about thirty-five to forty degrees. Dead twelve to fourteen hours.

He massaged his knee and, feeling the strain on both legs from maneuvering in a crouch, backed up to allow one leg to extend out the door, his foot to be planted on the snow-filmed macadam. His body spanned the length of steps in the van as he supported his weight on his hands and searched for other details before he would return inside for a closer look. He noted five spent shells to the right of the body and, tilting his head sharply to the side, identified a sixth one partially hidden by the wheel of a red metal crash cart. David reminded himself to refer to the shells as "empty brass" in talking with the police later. He combed the van like a robin looking for worms but found no gun.

An electronic defibrillator which he knew was ordinarily stationed on the cart lay askew on the floor. The cart itself was tipped on its side, all five drawers exposed and emptied of drug bottles, vials and ampules; of scalpels, tape, airways and catheters; of syringes, suture materials and tourniquets. They were scattered about, some items intact but most crushed or bent out of shape.

David returned his attention to Spritz's body. When he had forcibly lifted the head minutes earlier, it remained frozen in that position and now he had a better view of its neck. At Zone I, between the collarbone and the Adam's Apple, there was a straight-line bruise around the circumference. The bruise was broad and irregular in spots, wider in others. He noted several satellite markings above the line and some egg-shaped discolorations over the face and forehead. There were blotches on the backs of Spritz's hands which David interpreted as defense wounds.

Strangled and shot. Shot? Riddled! He had heard about the difference between "stranger" murders with their trim format, and crimes of passion with their telltale evidence of anger and rage, of the repeated stabbings or shootings, of the usual conclusion that such a killer had a strong relationship with his or her victim. He wondered why the multiple shots hadn't been heard. No doubt a suppressor. Another baby nipple?

In a matter of minutes, David had observed and acted swiftly, not permitting himself time to react emotionally to his discovery. Quite aside from the violence of the murder, he grappled with the question of its relationship to the others in and about Hollings General. And his expectation of soon nabbing a killer had been dashed, as in the case of an athlete with a supposed insurmountable lead who then sees certain victory evaporate.

19

David knew that within minutes of notifying others of Spritz's death, the area around the cardiac defibrillator van would be swarming with humanity, so he decided first to complete his snooping and then to place calls to Security, Foster and Kathy.

He snapped on a pair of surgical gloves he took from Friday and went straight for the silver canisters. He picked one up and before opening it, looked at its undersurface. A strip of tape read, "CAR." The bottoms of two others were similarly labeled while those of the remaining three read, "CAN."

In removing the lids, David treated each canister like a jack-in-the-box. All were stuffed with sealed glassine bags filled with white powder. The "CAR" powder appeared fine in texture; its bags, about four inches square, were unmarked. The "CAN" powder felt denser, more crystalline; its bags, tiny by comparison, measured no more than an inch by a half-inch and were stamped with the word "HORNET" above a small lightning bolt. Spritz's trademark for the street, he thought. He hadn't gotten to the fine stuff yet. He opened representative bags and sniffed; the powders were odorless. He reminded himself that narcs never sample drugs, that the finger test was a creation for TV actors.

His moves had been rapid, his reaction to the discovery matter-of-fact. After all the deliberations that had ultimately led him there, he never doubted drugs would be found somewhere along the way and that the fine powder was cocaine smuggled from Cartagena and the crystalline was heroin from Turkey. Yet, until now, he hadn't realized how small a cache of six canisters would be. If Victor Spritz was a trafficker, he told himself, there had to be a bigger supply around. Elementary, David. Any illusions of a supersleuth dissipated, however, for when he glanced back at the body—at the one who was once his key suspect—he felt as stymied as he was proud of the drug find. Plus not yet totally convinced all the murders were drug-related.

But, the given was that Spritz was a narcotics dealer—perhaps mid-level—possibly below a bigger and more powerful supplier. Was it Charlie Bugles? Or someone still living? Is it the correct assumption in the first place? If so, did Spritz renege on a payment? Or is the assumption wrong and is this brutality the work of a simple junkie? No, the drugs hadn't been touched. Spritz's pockets hadn't been turned out.

Another likely given was that Spritz wasn't your usual street peddler whose supply was limited at any one time, who maintained enough for, say, a few days' distribution and no more. On the other hand, a mid-level dealer would "connect" with such a person to dole out specified quantities, to monitor use, to retrieve cash payments, to exert control. No doubt, then: Spritz was either a mid-leveler or someone higher in the hierarchy—perhaps part of a far-reaching operation run by Bugles. Hell, they could have been on equal footing. After all: Colombia and Turkey.

David rotated in the van like a hawk in a canary cage, and was about to exit when he spied three oxygen cylinders on a shelf behind him. Below, an open bin contained three additional cylinders piled in a pyramid. He turned, yanked open the bin on the opposite side and found three more. Nine green cylinders, each the length of his lower leg and about as wide as his calf.

He stared at the shelf until he finally understood what had seemed so odd: the top portion of one cylinder had been unscrewed and several rows of threads were visible. He picked it up. In his medical career, he had often requested oxygen for patients but he had never handled a cylinder before. It felt cold against his palm and heavier than he had expected. David unscrewed and removed the top. The cylinder was packed with four-by-four bags similar to those in the silver canisters, so packed that none fell out as he tipped it over. He ran his finger over a film of white powder that coated the inside rim of the cylinder, but, again, he chose not to taste it. But why beat around the bush? Cocaine. Hurriedly, he checked the other cylinders, and discovered they contained either four-by-fours or "HORNET" heroin bags.

Six canisters full and nine cylinders full. All in all, a respectable supply for a mid-leveler undoubtedly receiving regular replenishments from Mr. Big. Or Dr. Big. A mid-leveler dealing from a medical emergency vehicle, one that David realized only Victor Spritz drove because all the other ambulances had their own crash carts and cardiac defibrillators. He also realized that way back when—early in private practice, or even early in low-level sleuthing—he could never have predicted that on a Saturday morning in January, he'd be pretzeled in a van once dedicated to restoring hearts to normal beats but now converted to a stage for illegal drug transactions and grisly murder.

And he reconciled himself to the fact that given the new circumstances, the official investigative team would be expanded to include the Narcotics Task Force.

David scrambled out to give the exterior surroundings a once-over before making his phone calls. But he returned to retrieve the Minx which he inserted into its shoulder rig, and his attaché case which he placed on a step and opened. He removed the Polaroid and took four shots of the van's interior and one of its exterior after he had circled to face it from the exit to the main parking lot. The grey sky conveyed its dullness to the last photo.

He was about to phone Security and request them to notify Alton Foster before they came to investigate. Then he would call Kathy at his home. It was only eight forty-five. As he raised his cellular, he glanced behind the dividing wall and his attention was drawn to the corner marking the end of the main lot. A red motorcycle stood out against a shallow bed of snow. It was parked obliquely and David estimated two inches of white crust covered its uppermost parts.

He sauntered over as he drew up a three-day-old image of the motorcycle—off in the distance, fleeing Cannon Cemetery. At the cycle, he copied down the designation CB750 which was part of the Honda logo on the fuel tank. He kicked snow away from the rear tire to measure its accumulation and uncovered a splotch of thick black oil. David made a mental note that the oil was beneath the snow, not mixed with it. Another image: the scene was Spritz's garage. And he thus eliminated the Toyota automobile as the source of the oil spot there.

He took a rear view Polaroid of the cycle before racing back to the interior of the van to search Spritz's pockets for keys. There were none.

Within minutes of his calls, hospital security personnel, uniformed police, plainclothes officers and administrative types arrived, followed closely by a contingent from the medical examiner's office. And within minutes of that, the usual Major Crime Scene Unit of Nick, Kathy and Sparky. Foster was the last to arrive and immediately took turns with the others, voicing dismay, proclaiming the curse of Saturday mornings, or getting David's "take" on the killing. By nine-twenty, conversations strained above pandemonium as scores of additional people flooded the area. Screaming news reporters and neighborhood gawkers pressed against yellow cordoning tape. A light snow was turning the grey sky to silver.

David leaned back against the dividing wall, watching individuals scurrying in and out of Spritz's back room and around and about the van. Flashbulbs flashed, walkie-talkees talked, television cameras televised, and radio reporters reported. Several writers from the *Hollings Herald* wrote in their notepads, prompting David to ask himself whatever happened to his own note taking? He would catch up later. He doubted that an action movie set of actors, directors and crew looked as confusing as this one.

Kathy and Sparky entered the van, replacing the

medical examiner and his associates who had been inside, David estimated, a mere thirty seconds. Not much difficulty pronouncing Spritz dead. At the wall, he found himself hemmed in by Nick, Foster, a man he recognized from the Narcotics Task Force, and a young woman he had never seen before. She had a plain face, plain clothes and wore a badge on a beige hooded pullover.

"Why so brutal?" Foster asked. He posed the question as if the brutality mattered more than the death itself, as if he had become hardened to expect murders on hospital grounds.

"It looks like the perp had more than a simple score to settle," Nick said, not giving David a chance to respond. "Dr. David Brooks," he added, "meet Sally Schmidt. She's assisting in Narcotics for the time being." Sally smiled and nodded.

"Nice to meet you," David said nonchalantly. He turned to Nick and asked, "Who's heading up the Task Force?"

"I am," Nick responded.

David's head jerked back. "You?" he said. "That's some division of labor you've got down there."

Nick's eyes skimmed over David's. "Well," he said, "when you're shorthanded, you take shortcuts."

David chuckled internally over the malapropos remark but had to give him credit for trying to be cute. He wondered, though, what Nick knew about narcotics investigations. Or—now—about narcotics in general.

Nick signaled to his assistants that they should head toward the van, then said to David, "I should ask you what you found in more detail, but I'll check myself. Nothing's been disturbed?"

"Nothing's been disturbed. Aside from the body, you'll find a horde of drugs in there."

Nick turned to leave, stopped, and added, "I assume you have all the details down?"

David didn't like the comment nor the answer he was about to give, but he gave it anyway. "You assume right, as usual."

Nick stormed away with his two assistants and entered the van just as Kathy emerged. She walked over to David and pulled out a handkerchief from the pocket of her fleece-lined jacket.

"Not at all pleasant in there," she said. She blew her nose without regard to daintiness.

David bent over and kissed her on the lips. "Happy birthday," he whispered.

"What? Oh, that? Isn't this a nice way to spend it?"

"We still have tonight. Dinner out, okay? Olivio's? Let's not break the string." They had celebrated their birthdays in elegant style for the past five years.

"Of course, where else? Pick me up at six." She pointed to the EMS entrance. "That's where Spritz hung out, you say?"

"That's the place."

"You hanging around or what?"

"No, I'd better scram before your boss and I tangle out loud. I'll interrogate some people later." He lowered his voice as if he were speaking decisions. "Like Foster … and Bernie … and Robert. Maybe even Dr. Corliss."

"Corless, the psychiatrist? You suspect the psychiatrist?"

"At this point, I don't know who to suspect." He rubbed his decision scar. "And even whether Spritz killed the others. And, if you want to know the truth, whether those stupid drugs in there have anything to do with them."

Kathy appeared disappointed. "Really?" she said. "Let's talk about it tonight."

"On your birthday!" David said in disgust, not as a question.

"David, my beloved, if I were you about to phrase this, I'd say, 'Bleep my birthday, we've got trouble, big trouble, and I don't mean in River City.'"

Kathy barely enunciated the last word before David shot back, "I don't say 'bleep.'"

"You know what I mean."

"I'll still sing you *Happy Birthday.*"

Kathy teased out a smirk.

"Incidentally," David said, "what's Nick know about narcotics?"

"Sparky said he worked in the San Diego Unit for a while."

"Sparky? How'd *he* know?"

"They go back. That's why Sparky recommended him ."

David did little to hold back a scowl. "You never told me that." He gave each word equal emphasis. "And what do you mean 'they go back'?"

"I heard they met at some national law enforcement convention and they've kept in touch."

David ironed out his face. "I see," he said. "How long ago?"

"Twenty years. I think that's what I heard."

David knew Kathy sensed his bad vibes.

"What's wrong?" she said. "You worried about something?"

"No. Curious, that's all."

After this latest murder—now five in all—David felt like a fledgling engineer on a runaway locomotive. What to do? First, take a shower.

Before leaving the scene, he had reluctantly approached Nick to inform him of the gloves, tape and wig in the EMS room. Without hesitation, Nick theorized that maybe they had been planted, something David thought strange, yet conceivable. The gloves, the tape? Maybe. But who would know a wig might be important except maybe old man Razbit, the pawnbroker? David would have congratulated anyone else for proposing the theory but, in this case, he ignored it and asked how long it would be before the body could be released for autopsy.

Nick responded, "Released? I'd say by noon. Autopsy? That's up to what's-his-name. Tanarkle's replacement."

At 10 Oak Lane, David took a longer shower than usual, shampooing his hair over and over again. Another one of his "things" was that odors had a special affinity for hair, which accounted for nostril hairs perpetuating the sensation of a smell. Both in and out of the shower, he blew his nose nonstop.

He contacted Dr. Jake Reed at his home and learned the postmortem was scheduled for three p.m.

At three-ten, David walked into the autopsy room with the single purpose of obtaining the findings in the region of Spritz's neck. Especially the condition of the hyoid bone whose fracture would most likely indicate strangulation. No light filtered through the elevated windows as was the case during Charlie Bugles' autopsy, and the corpse looked less waxy overall. David observed pur-plish lividity confined to the lower body and the head and neck above its straight-line bruise were dark red.

Dr. Reed was decked in surgical cap, gown, gloves, but no mask. He greeted David warmly and turned off the power supply to the microphone attached to the gown.

"Good to have company, David. Lots of bullet wounds here. I counted six—all entries in front, exits in back. And since three slugs were found in the floor either beneath or behind the body, I'd say he was shot after he hit the floor."

The Acting Director of the Department was consid-ered a superb forensic pathologist in his own right. He appeared in his early thirties and, up on his toes, would rival David in height, but he was as thin as his name. He had the gravelly voice of a smoker and David often as-serted he should know better, inquiring of Reed when he would flatten his chest, a reference to the rectangular-shaped breast pocket where he kept his Marlboros.

"Dead about twelve hours, Jake?"

"Yes, I'd say about that time." Reed was preparing the neck dissection and had not yet gotten to the "Big Y," as David called it.

"And strangled first?"

"Strangled first. Not by a cord or anything like that though. The linear bruise there, the satellites? Bare hands. The satellites indicate quite a struggle and I'll wager there's plenty of internal damage. But that's usually the case—they use more force than is necessary to kill the victim." He spread open Spritz's eyelids. "And here are the hemorrhages."

David informed the pathologist that he would stay

only until the neck dissection was completed. During the procedure, Reed pointed to the extensive deep bruising which he had predicted.

"And here's the hyoid, David. Fractured, see it?" Reed extended the exposure downward in the neck. "And also the thyroid cartilage. Plenty of force—there's the evidence." He cut deeper and ran two fingers up and down the cervical spine. "Feels aligned. It's a wonder he didn't snap the vertebrae apart, though."

David thanked the pathologist and hurried home to take another shower.

For four days, David had not uploaded any summaries into his computer; nor had he used his notepad. He had an hour to kill before leaving to pick up Kathy and sat alternately thinking and typing as he brought his entries current:

Saturday, January 24

MURDERS, continued—

Victor Spritz—strangled and shot in his own defib. van. Drugs all over the place.
Wild-goose chase to Recycling Center. Nick there: got same call or did he do the calling?
Sniper at cemetery.
Spritz: Spent time at psych. hosp. Has 4+ gun collection. CARCAN and CANCAN.
House vandalized.
Botulism vial missing.

He added some narrative summaries in contrast to past entries, a symptom, he thought, of a brain bathed in shreds of detail and speculation, too fluid to compress. He typed one item—"I found Spritz both strangled and shot in his cardiac van. There goes our murderer."— with the frustration of a child who had just lost a coin down a drain.

This time, he decided to include comments on suspects from the standpoint of motive, opportunity and means, but his inclusions presupposed Spritz had murdered the others before he himself was killed. "Yet," he wrote, "it's entirely possible this was not the case, that we have a single cunning killer on the loose and he set Spritz up, for whatever reason."

David recorded that every suspect's possible entanglement with the illicit drug trade would satisfy the "motive" criterion, but that only Charlie Bugles and Spritz appeared to have had that connection. And they were both dead. He also believed each had the "means" but made no references to it. That left "opportunity," and he felt grossly remiss in not having considered it for each person, at least as it applied to Spritz's murder. He resolved that, beginning the following morning, he would press each suspect on his whereabouts early the morning before; it was time to pull out all stops in his interrogations.

Thus he entered Foster, Bernie, Robert, Nick and Dr. Corliss, and he dubbed them "Suspect-5." Then, he made a printout of his last summary and placed it atop a birthday package for Kathy.

Before preparing to leave for dinner, he scanned his four-page summaries of the murders and the events surrounding them. He double-checked the pages on the computer screen several times, and, arching his back, spoke aloud as if it would ratify what he had discovered: a pattern. Bugles had been killed on a Tuesday. Coughlin on Saturday. Tanarkle on Tuesday. Spritz on Saturday. Tuesday was little more than two days away.

20

Olivio's was a turn-of-the-century restaurant with elegant atmosphere, elegant meals and elegant prices. Set in the industrial valley near the junction with Center City, it was secreted within a sagging stockade fence overwhelmed by ivy, euonymus and other assorted vines. The building was ash faced and stucco framed, reminiscent of those in ancient Florentine villas, and it was not without design that the restaurant's menu derived from the tastes of Tuscany, even as its name reflected one of the dominant crops of that region.

The stucco had been continued inside, wrapping around and suffusing into ceilings slung low above Old World furnishings. There, generations of soft and russet candlelight had transformed the grimmest patrons into temporary romantics.

After helping remove Kathy's overcoat, David escorted her into the basil aroma of Italian cuisine, imagining the ceiling growing two feet lower as he snaked among the tables, grumbling about pricey restaurants unable to pay electric bills. He touched the shoulders of some people he knew and addressed them by name. There were only two empty tables in the main dining room and the maitre d' sat them at the recessed corner one, David's favorite which he had phoned ahead to reserve. Mellow Sinatra oozed from a speaker directly overhead, clouding the hum of diners in their designer clothes and the chitchat of fawning waiters. It would be the best spot to discuss the summary after dinner.

Kathy evened out her burnt almond sheath dress before sitting. "And don't tell me I tore my dress in the back," she said.

"I hadn't noticed," he retorted, sitting alongside her and sliding the birthday package under the table onto the next chair.

"Why do we hide it," she said, "when this is the ninth gift in a row we've exchanged here?"

David gazed around the room and said, "What gift?" He unbuttoned his blue blazer and tugged down the only turtleneck he owned. He felt it snap back up.

"Can I open it now?" she asked, tightening an earring.

He placed the book-size package before her and said, "Happy birthday. Hope you like it. By the way, where's your gun tonight?"

"What? What's that got to do with anything?"

"I don't see any bulges."

"It's in my purse." She eyed him suspiciously. "Don't tell me you bought another holster. You did that three years ago."

He remained silent while she admired the red bow up close and put it aside next to her purse before removing the outer wrapper. She separated the tissue inside, frowned, peered up at David and back at the box.

"This looks magnificent, but why?"

He leaned over to view a Beretta Cougar F semiautomatic as if he had never seen it before. A card attached to its grip read, ".45 cal. firepower with Cam-Loc System."

Kathy ran her fingertips along its muzzle and then replaced the tissue. "David, I love you dearly but I hate guns. Plus, I have one already. Thank God, I've never had to use it."

"But this is state of the art. It puts that ridiculous government issue to shame," he said. "And the 'Cam-Loc'? That means there's less recoil."

"But I hate guns."

"So do I."

"David, come off it," she said with a sardonic grin. "Then why the big deal with *this*?"

"I already said it. It's state of the art. You've got to keep pace with criminals."

"How can you hate guns when you have that ludicrous collection taking up half the house?"

"You know the answer. We've been through this before. I inherited it."

"Then sell it."

"I can be talked into that." David was surprised at his own firmness.

Kathy's eyes crinkled at the corners, thinning the shadow she seldom wore. "Will you give me that promise as another present?"

"Will you keep the Beretta and throw out the other one?"

"Yes."

David said, "It's a deal," and held out his hand.

She studied the hand for a moment and said, "I want more than a handshake."

"Not here," he said, looking around.

"Oh, for crying out loud," she responded and lifted up to kiss him on the lips. He pulled back.

"Wait," he said. "Let's clarify this. If the house goes when we get married, the guns go, too."

"Now there you go again." Kathy rearranged the silverware. "Why do you always have to rethink things?"

"Because I'm wrong so many times." David thought his response was clever and his face showed it. "Let's put it this way," he continued, "the house and the collection go together. We'll treat them as one."

Kathy paused, her features shifting as if she were reaching for the marrow of a complex solution. "David, let's face it. You're nearly forty and still living in a pad."

David signaled for the waiter and said, "Sure, and that's why we'll probably sell it."

"And the guns?"

"And the guns."

David had been going through the motions. Kathy's fortuitous birthday, talk of guns and the future of 10 Oak Lane, his studied repartee—they all combined to inhibit, however feebly, the angst of a punishing day and of yesterday and of the days before that. And he shrunk from thoughts that the days were running out before more violence erupted, before more friends were taken, or clues were lost or the hospital became buried in terminal scandal.

He felt pinched in and, try as he might, failed to develop into a temporary romantic even after two rounds of drinks. He knew Kathy shared the emotion but it was an unequal sharing because the killings had occurred on his turf, some of the victims were his friends and, after all, she was the professional. But they both agreed to forgo a champagne toast this time.

After pledging they would refrain from "detective talk" during dinner—prime rib for each—they ate in near silence. Finally, over coffee, David sensed his features turning to steel as he said, "Okay, now down to business. First, about Nick back there in the parking lot. I thought you said he wanted me off the cases. He was his usual frothy self but other than that ..."

Kathy blurted, "I spoke to him."

"Saying what?"

"That you're of more value in the investigation than out of it. Simple."

"He agreed?"

"It sure looks like it."

"Okay, end of that." He pulled out the summary print-out from his breast pocket. "Next, here's a nutshell of what's transpired lately, plus what I think are possibilities and who I think the suspects are. Look at the last line—no big surprises, you agree?"

Kathy read the list of suspects and replied, "I agree except for Nick." She shook her head. "Hey, it's your list. And I still have doubts about the psychiatrist, but tell me again, why's he included?"

"He wanted the Chief of Staff job pretty badly and ... just a vague hunch, I guess."

"But David, before we go any further, when you say suspects, you mean in the Spritz killing or what?"

"Ah, one of the two sixty-four dollar questions. Did Spritz kill all the others or are there two murderers? The other is, how do the drugs tie in, if at all?"

They discussed the trilogy of motive, opportunity and means and debated the merits of the physical evidence to date. They had engaged in "detective talk" for over an hour—it was now nine o'clock—before deciding in favor of David's confrontation with each of the suspects as the next priority.

David paid the bill in plastic and they rose to leave. He bent down, kissed her forehead and said, "Happy birthday, again. You're sleeping at my pad as you call it, right."

"I'll suffer through it."

"No more detective talk there?"

"No talk at all."

As he led Kathy to the exit, they approached the other table that was empty when they had arrived. Three of the four chairs were now occupied. Kathy crashed into David as he stopped in his tracks. Seated were Nick, Sparky and a matronly woman David had never seen before. They were drinking wine.

The two men scraped their chairs back along the wooden floor and stood, baring their teeth in broad smiles. David's ears felt like molten rocks and he was sure they noticed but decided he didn't care.

"Please sit," he said. They returned to their chairs.

"David, I'd like you to met my wife, Gretchen," Nick said. "Dear, this is Dr. Brooks."

She extended her hand and David reached down and shook her fingers. "Hello," he said, evenly.

"Nicholas speaks of you often, Dr. Brooks."

"And I speak of him often," David said, too quickly. He put his arm around Kathy to guide her to his side. He noticed her saying shut up silently.

"And of course you know Kathy Dupre," Nick said.

"Yes, hi there again," Gretchen said. She was an industrial size woman with a puffy face, a shade shorter than her husband. In silhouette from the shoulders down, she resembled a question mark. Her smoky hair was coifed high on her head and she wore a black granny dress without ruffles. David wondered whether her pearl necklace was real.

"What brings you here?" David asked, looking at Nick. What he actually had in mind was, what brought him and Sparky there?

"Just a night out," Nick said. "And you're here to celebrate Kathy's birthday, I take it?" He wore a dark business suit and appeared to be on his best behavior.

"I didn't know you two were social friends," David said, bowing first at Sparky, then back at Nick.

"Oh, but we are," Nick replied. "Cross-country for years. I guess that's not really social but it's good to celebrate *any* friendship at last."

David had to work at a smile. Is that all they're celebrating? He faced the unmarried criminalist whom he had seen eating out many times before, usually alone. Sparky looked out of place in a blue pinstripe.

"Spark, as long as I've run into you, can I ask two 'shop' questions? It'll save a phone call."

Sparky gave an annoyed nod before glancing at Nick.

"Prints and slugs," David said, not waiting for a reply.

"You mean at the Spritz scene?"

"Uh … yes." Where else, pal?

"I couldn't lift any prints except his own on some of the equipment."

"Not even mine?" David knew he had his winter gloves on when he entered the van and latex when he probed it.

"Not even yours."

David noticed Nick's etched smile and Gretchen buttering bread as if shoptalk had been her way of life.

"And the slugs?"

"There were six of them. I only examined the three we pried out of the floor some distance behind the body. Incidentally, I think he was in a sitting position when the perp pumped him. I'll get the other slugs from the medical examiner tomorrow but I'm sure they're the same. Anyway, they check out as .45's. I can't be a hundred per cent sure but they could have been fired from one of the new Kimber ACP's. We just got some information on them. They come in a series."

"Hmm," David said. A bit too much information, or is he trying to impress Gretchen? Even David felt he was over reading the criminalist. He took Kathy by the hand.

"Thanks, Sparky," he said, leading her away. He looked back. "Good to see you folks. Enjoy your meal. Nice meeting you, Gretchen."

"Good night, everybody," Kathy said, bracing her legs. "See you two tomorrow."

Verdi had replaced Sinatra as they edged their way among the tables. Only Kathy acknowledged well-wishers.

Seated in the Mercedes, the ignition off, David said, "Well, what do you think?"

"I think you never let me ask a question in there—or say anything for that matter."

"You see them everyday."

"Exactly. Aha, exactly. So do Nick and Sparky—see each other everyday, I mean. So what's the fuss about their eating out together?"

"What fuss?"

Kathy snuggled against him, reached up and grabbed his chin as she always did to make a point. "Darling, you've already pegged them as the killers because they had dinner at the same table."

He snatched her wrists, circled them to her back and, elevating her to his size, gave her a brief but hefty kiss on the lips. He pulled back an inch and said, "Wrong," even as he informed her he'd changed his list to "Suspect-6."

"Suspects, not killers," he added. Then he replanted his lips and released her arms which she wrapped around his neck.

As Kathy dozed on the drive home, David dwelled on questions they hadn't addressed, and the one that kept recurring was: why didn't Spritz dispose of evidence better? Its corollary: was the evidence planted? The answer to the last question would shape the entire character of the future investigation. In one scenario, he reasoned, Spritz killed the other four and someone then killed him. In the other scenario, a serial killer was still on the loose. David's inclination was that Victor Spritz murdered the others for very clear-cut reasons, but David questioned how long he could rationalize away Spritz's sloppiness in disposing of the evidence by means of his psychiatric history. Therefore, unless and until additional findings tilted the scales in that direction, he would assume a single evil-doer was responsible for all five slayings.

David swerved into the driveway at 10 Oak Lane and Kathy flinched awake. He thought the night, though clear, seemed darker, the trees brooding, the silence thicker. In the garage, he noticed the slit to Kathy's eyes and, once in the den, he said, "You go on up. I'm clear on something and I want to upload it. I'll be up soon."

She opened the closet door and in attempting to hang up her coat, dropped the hanger twice. Exasperated, she said, "I give up," and flung the coat over the back of the sofa before climbing the stairs.

David, following her actions, said, "See you in the morning."

He sat at the computer and typed:

Five Point Tactical Plan:
1— Interrogate 4 of the 6 suspects: Foster, Bernie, Robert, Corliss
2— Visit or revisit homes. May need Musco: Bernie, Spritz, Robert
3— Visit murder site: Coughlin at parking gate
4— North End for druggie belchers. Definitely need Musco
5— Special situation with Nick and Sparky: SUR- VEILLANCE

He turned off the computer, picked up Kathy's coat and dropped the hanger once himself before securing it in the closet. Upstairs he found her in bed, approaching full sleep. He was not far behind.

21

David heard rain pounding against the window, his first cognitive process in a dreamless sleep he had not anticipated nine hours ago. For if children had visions of sugarplums dancing in their heads, he had expected sour balls.

It was seven o'clock Sunday morning and he marveled at the clarity of church bells penetrating the dense showers outside, calling it Archimedes' Law. Or Bernoulli's. No, neither. It's the law of reflection: "As sound reflects off tiny moist barriers, the sound intensifies." David had made that up and chuckled as he poured orange juice. Getting ditsy, he told himself. Or just trying to cover up the anxiety already congealing for the day. Once again, he questioned his presence in the suction of escalating and violent unknowns. Too premature for a beginner detective at this level? Too emotive a baptism for a medical man trained to keep his cool, to call the shots?

It mattered not that it was Sunday or that the weather he checked through the kitchen window appeared dug in. And it mattered not his mood or his uncertainties; he had to make the most of Time. He heard the bathroom shower running and, slipping off his robe, joined Kathy there, then in bed, learning what mattered for the moment and what had jump-started his day.

After they smiled through a light breakfast, David drove her to her condo. They sat in the car while, for the first time, he explained his general course of action as outlined in his Tactical Plan. She offered to accompany him after church but he declined, announcing his greater-maneuverability-when-solo to a raised eyebrow. They would touch base later in the afternoon.

It was eight-thirty, the rain had eased and warmed, but the air smelled sassy. He hadn't until then determined his agenda for the day as he streaked along a byway toward the main parking lot of Hollings General. It would be an ideal time to reconnoiter the site of Everett Coughlin's shooting: doctors made their rounds later on Sundays, surgeons performed only emergency procedures on weekends, and the overall vehicular flow was minimal. David preferred not to tip his hand in any way to any person.

He ran his entry card across the automated machine at the gate and parked his car in the center of the lot between two cars of the only half-dozen there. He had never understood his acceptance of a raincoat for rain, yet his aversion to an overcoat for cold. He unbuttoned two buttons of a London Fog for easy access to the shoulder rig and— Friday in one hand and a Tote umbrella in the other—walked back to the gate, stopped, and looked up at the knoll where the killer had been positioned eight days before. David realized that back then he had not fully appreciated how isolated the spot was, shielded in front by thick bushes and at the rear by the construction site for the new psychiatric facility.

Out in the open, on a morning when the lot was not jammed with doctors' cars and the construction site was free from workers, he would have felt sufficiently secure with the hardware attached to his shoulder and ankle. But he strutted around the gate two or three times, swinging Friday for the benefit of anyone who might glance out windows, not to convey to him or her a message of added firepower—because no one knew its contents—but to announce he was officially sleuthing. He was aware that most hospital personnel had come around to recognize the attaché case as a special badge, distinct from the hospital-issued floppy one he refused to clip to his jacket and, as such, Friday conveyed an aura of legitimacy.

Of all the murder sites—here, the O.R. suite, the locker room, the elevator shaft, the van—this was the one he believed he had given short shrift to. Although he had recovered a spent shell and baby nipple, he recalled the ice on the incline, the distraction of the Major Crime Unit below, and his failure, at the time, to explore the construction site by motoring to a higher level and approaching it from the rear.

He tipped the umbrella and gave it a smart shake, but no drops dislodged. He tucked Friday under one arm, held out his other and felt no moisture on his hand. Convinced the rain had stopped, he looked toward the hospital windows, collapsed the umbrella, squeegeed it with his fingers and inserted it in the attaché case.

The ground sounded moist but not soggy beneath David's shoes as he climbed the incline. He passed by several bushes, paying no heed to the point where he had located evidence on his prior inspection there because, now of a single purpose, he headed toward the partially erected building, the cobalt blue of its cinder blocks more striking than he had remembered, its contour honey-combed with window and door holes like a child's drawing of a house. David was one of many who had voiced their disapproval to the building committee of the structure's facade color, but then again he was not fond of its contemporary architectural design, either. In the face of entreaties by Alton Foster and Dr. Sam Corliss, however, who was David Brooks to complain?

And now, perhaps the color was a divine selection because the mortar's hue was unmistakable and potentially incriminating. David had reasoned that particles of masonry might have stuck to the killer's shoes, particles that might have been tracked by workers to the ground around piles of sand and gravel, between strewn empty soda cans, around the backhoe and generator and steam shovel, now silent. In all likelihood, David thought, the perp had arrived at his vantage point by way of the road on the upper level and, therefore, around the roughly assembled shell or through jambs on which doors had not yet been hung. He conceded to himself that the ice of two Saturdays before might have hardened any particles but counterpointed that the shortest route from the road to the top of the knoll was through and not around the shell.

The brusque remark of Nick Medicore that evidence could have been planted to ensnare Spritz had layered David's subconscious only to surface as he stooped over to examine dust and particulate matter on the floor of the shell. The remark had been too offhanded to suit David at the time but, nonetheless, he was in a position now to invalidate it: who would ever think of planting blue particles? But then again, who could ever have carried off all five murders? He stared briefly at a stack of cinder blocks and considered knocking off the corner of one of them and then pulverizing it, but he wanted to simulate in the aggregate *all* material that might have been picked up by a shoe.

He took out several small plastic bags from Friday and brushed in samples from random locations in the building, coughing from the smell of masonry, smacking his lips together as dust powder settled on his tongue. Kathy always told him he didn't keep his mouth closed long or often enough.

He held up one of the bags against the sunlight beginning to elbow through a window hole. His jaw tensed but could not hold back a compact smile. That son-of-a-bitch is blue—definitely blue.

He packed the plastic bags in Friday and stole away, like the winner in a game of marbles thirty years ago.

It took David ten minutes to make the fifteen-minute drive to Marblehead. Nor did he waste any time removing a crowbar from the trunk of his car and jimmying the back door of Victor Spritz's house. There had been no need to summon Musco, no need to fool a dead man.

David's visit had a dual purpose, and if his hunches were correct, he hoped that the issue of Spritz's having been set up would finally be put to rest.

Passing through the laundry room, he noticed a pair of black leather gloves, palms down on the washing machine. They reminded him to squeeze into latex gloves which he removed from Friday, along with a flashlight. He flexed and unflexed his fingers like a pianist about to embark on a concerto and, picking up the gloves, reflected on the meaning of grey powdery smudges on the inner aspect of its fingers and palms. He concluded the markings lacked even a suggestion of a bluish cast before placing the gloves in his case, palm surfaces together.

David opened the garage door with less stealth than before, cleared his throat of hydrocarbon and approached the Toyota's tires. Although he had turned on the lights, he shined the flashlight over the treads of all four tires: they were clean. He didn't know whether to wring his hands or clap them. But he did have an alternative idea.

He hurried to the carton of equipment he had packed in the trunk of the Mercedes and brought back his evidence vacuum. He vacuumed a thin layer of gritty material off the floor of the Toyota on the driver's side, bagged it and held it up to the overhead light bulb. Blue? Maybe, maybe not. But he was happy to have the material for analysis and would confer with Kathy about who the analyst should be.

Through the corner of an eye blurred by the bare bulb above, the oil-stained cardboard came into focus. He folded it in a plastic sheet and, along with the bag of vacuumed matter, compressed it atop the gloves in Friday. He then knelt and, beaming the light on the floor below the car's crankcase, saw no oil droppings.

David's sweat felt heavy at his neck and along his spine. And he hadn't yet entered the room he was anxious to enter. He unbuttoned his raincoat and opened the rear door to Spritz's gun collection and war memorabilia. The splash of lights and martial music startled him even though he knew what to expect. He marched straight for the case marked "MISCELLANEOUS—90's." Its middle shelf contained a tray of pistols labeled, "KIMBER .45 ACP's."

Within the tray, four guns lay spread out in a row. Corresponding cards beneath them read, "CUSTOM"—"TARGET"—"POLYMER"—"COMPACT." In the center, a fifth card was labeled, "GOLD MATCH STAINLESS." The space above the card was empty. Hallelujah! Sparky's words about the Kimber series thundered in his ears. One more thing to do, but not here. He changed his mind, entered the house itself and checked the front door and all the downstairs windows. On the way out, he examined the back door closely, blocking out the damage he had created to the jamb minutes before. Other than his own, there had been no forced entry into the Spritz house.

David had fulfilled his twin objectives: to collect particulate evidence that might be there, and to determine if another evidentiary item might or might not be there. Two bonuses were the powder-stained gloves he happened upon and the oily cardboard he had kicked against the garage wall forty-eight hours before.

On the ride back to the hospital grounds, he decided not to fine-tune the meaning of his discoveries until Kathy returned from church. Some pieces were beginning to fit, but he wanted her input.

The overnight rain and rising temperatures had melted the snow into dirty water on and around the red Honda. David's single purpose in returning to the parking lot was to compare the black oil stains beneath the cycle with the ones on the piece of cardboard. They matched. Another hallelujah. He rubbed his decision scar. But wait, isn't an oil stain an oil stain? Sure, but one's color could have been golden. For good measure, he checked the footrests and found no particulate matter stuck to them.

At eleven-thirty he arrived at Kathy's condo.

22

David asked Kathy why raincoats are hot and winters don't stay cold and how does anybody know what to wear? He ripped off his dark blue London Fog, a lighter blue sweater and, exhaling a full morning's breath, spread out stiffly in an easy chair like a dental patient awaiting root canal surgery.

Kathy ignored the questions and said, "You want coffee, or some lunch?" She had just returned to her condo from church and wore a pink cowlneck sweater and black pants. He got up and followed her into the kitchen.

"Just coffee. I'm not hungry." He wiped his brow with a handkerchief, sat at the small table before a bay window, and placed Friday in front of him.

The kitchen was airy with pastel-colored appliances. Scant white curtains hung over double windows facing the driveway and on the bay window of the opposite wall.

"So what did you start with?" she asked, flicking on the coffeemaker and joining David at the table.

"Come again?"

"The plan. Your strategic plan."

"Tactical."

"All right, tactical," she said, derisively.

"The Coughlin site."

"And?"

David was not being unattentive but realized that once he got started, the findings of the day—and his interpretation of them—could flow nonstop. He evened the attaché case with the near edge of the table as he arranged his thoughts.

"David, are you sharing with me or not?"

"Of course. I just don't know where to start." He snapped Friday open, removed one of the bags of bluish particles and the bag of vacuumed material from Spritz's car, and laid them aside. "Okay, let's do it this way. First off, I think the evidence is overwhelming that Spritz wasn't set up and that he murdered the others. His was the rifle used to kill Coughlin, the writing samples match, he had the opportunities and plenty of motive and besides … "

"Wait now," Kathy said, "motive for which killing?"

"All of them." He counted on his fingers, "Tanarkle—Coughlin—Foster—Bugles. They were the EMS committee that turned him down. Remember, we're dealing with a paranoid schiz here. So he kills the first two, lets Foster go because he was a supporter, and as far as Bugles goes, that was a special case. And forget Dr. Cortez—he had to be eliminated in order for Spritz to get to Bugles."

"Why's Bugles a special case—except for the brutality?"

"Precisely." David underscored the word by slamming two fingers against the table. "The brutality. There had to be something more to kill like that, and it's obvious: the drug connection. Something went sour between

Bugles and Spritz, and Spritz handled it his way. His psychopathic way. He'd been around hospitals for years and undoubtedly understood some anatomy and had observed O.R. procedures, and he had the balls to pull off ... as we say ... the brutality."

Kathy looked as though she didn't want to get up to get the coffee, but did. "Hold up a minute," she said. She poured two cups and cut two squares from an apple Danish. David would never have guessed his charged moment might allow an appreciation of coffee aroma. He took a long swallow, felt the burn on his palate, and followed with two cautious sips.

He held up for not much more than her requested minute, then raised the bags to the light and, after describing their origin, received Kathy's concurrence that a match was indefinite to the naked eye.

"Is Sparky any good in forensic geology?" he asked.

"I thought he was a suspect," she responded, biting into the pastry.

"He is." David twisted his mouth. "Hmm—yes, of course. Anyone else around?"

"Sure. Joe Bangor. He's a geology professor over at the university. We've used him in the past. Good with the microscope."

"If I leave these specimens with you, can you arrange for him to examine them?"

"It'll be done tomorrow."

"Good." He eyed her suspiciously. "Is it okay if I dip a corner of this?" he asked, dangling the Danish over his coffee.

She skewed her lips and said, "Yes, certainly. Anyone who lives in a pad is entitled to dip a Danish."

"Hey, that's clever," he said, buoyed by the way his evaluation was proceeding. "Now then, there's the matter of these gloves." He pointed to the pair in Friday. "I found them in Spritz's laundry room. I don't feel like putting on latex when I'm having coffee so take my word for it—on their undersurface, there's a powder which I'm quite sure is fireclay."

"Fireclay, like in safes?"

"Like from the lining in safes. I learned all about that from Musco. I'll wrap them in plastic before I leave. Can you give them to your professor friend?"

"Yes."

"See if he agrees it's fireclay. And don't bother asking me— I have no idea yet where it fits in. All I know is these gloves weren't at Spritz's when I was there on Thursday."

"Do you think they belong to Spritz?"

"Absolutely—if we've ruled out evidence planting ... ."

"And we haven't."

"Kath, let's just say we have. I can't imagine someone sprinkling blue mortar powder around the floor of a car. But, regardless ..." He let the sentence trail because he was anxious to speak of the missing pistol and the Spritz murder.

"Now, moving on," he said, "I think I have a reasonable explanation of the events leading up to Spritz's death. Sparky said the murder weapon was probably a handgun from the Kimber series, right?"

"Right. You found it?"

"No. Spritz had the series in his collection and one of them is gone. I would have noticed it was missing Thursday—I'm sure of it—and there was no forced entry to the house."

"Maybe the perp has a Musco pal, too."

"C'mon, next thing you'll be saying Musco did it." David finished his coffee and Danish before continuing.

"Here's what I believe happened. The motorcycle you saw in the parking lot belonged to Spritz. He drove to his EMS place armed with the pistol, and either invited the killer there under some pretext—therefore, they knew each other—or was surprised by the killer. No doubt the murder was drug-related. They had some kind of struggle, and Spritz was disarmed and done in by his own gun. The murderer fled, taking the gun with him. Which, by the way, could possibly eliminate organized crime. It's not a hard and fast rule, but they usually drop the gun before they scram." David noticed Kathy's half-smile. "I'm sure I'm not telling you anything on that score," he added.

"They'd have their own gun or guns anyway," she cut in.

"Exactly."

"There's one other possibility, David." She licked her middle finger of frosting.

"Go ahead, I'm listening." He was beginning to wrap the gloves in a plastic sheet he took from Friday.

"Maybe the cancellation of the EMS contract had nothing to do with it and Spritz didn't act alone in the killings."

David elevated his eyes. "Are you saying two people collaborated for the same drug motive?"

"Why not? It's possible."

"Because I can't see Tanarkle or Coughlin involved in a drug operation."

"Not involved per se, but maybe they stumbled

onto it."

David turned his head aside and looked at Kathy with one eye. "You really think that could have happened? Or did happen?"

She shrugged and answered, "Could have? Yes. Did? No."

"Well, let me say this: the most common things occur most commonly and I think there was just one killer for the first murders, and he was Spritz. In any event, the Spritz saga is over and now we have a brand new ball game." He made the last statement with the assurance of an umpire's call.

Kathy responded timidly, "We'll see. Which reminds me—you should know that Nick's stepping up the investigation."

"I thought you were short-handed."

"We are. He's asked for state assistance. And he made the point of saying he's glad you're still involved."

"That's a switch. Did he hope to butter me up because he's worried about being a suspect?"

"David, for heaven's sake! A suspect for all those murders?"

"No. For Spritz's."

"But why?"

"Some drug business? I don't know."

Kathy got up and paced, something he had never seen her do. She turned and said, "Besides the whole premise being ludicrous, think about it. Nick carries his own gun, so if you can say the Mafia has its own hardware and therefore can be ruled out, why can't you apply the same reasoning to Nick?"

David came close to stepping on her last words. "Because I'm not ruling anything out. Or in for that matter. If I had done that in medicine, I'd have been run out of town years ago. So let's just see what the final diagnosis is."

Kathy gave him a comprehensive look and finally said, "Yes, doctor."

David closed the attaché case, leaving the bags and protected gloves on the table. "I'm curious," he said, rising. "Who claimed Spritz's body? Do you know?"

"No, I don't know about 'claimed,' but I understand Bernie Bugles is making burial arrangements."

Squares of dull light had brightened and crossed the table to the foot of the twin windows. David was about to kiss Kathy before leaving when, with the suddenness of a crack of lightning, a percussive shot and simultaneous shattering of glass reverberated behind them.

"Down!" David screamed, pouncing on Kathy and rolling with her on the floor. Instinctively, his eyes swept over her and what he could see of himself. He was looking for blood and detected none. His breathing felt unimpeded but deep and rapid, as deep and rapid as hers sounded and, as he pushed her against the wall beneath the windows, he blurted, "You okay?"

"I'm—I'm okay. Are you?" she said, her voice constricted.

"Yeah, now stay where you are," he said as he withdrew the Smith and Wesson snubby from his ankle rig. He crawled to the side of the left sash, avoiding several slivers of glass on the floor and, glancing up at the windowpane, noticed a stellate hole immediately above a cracked mullion and twisted lock. He looked over his shoulder at the bay window on the other side of the kitchen and saw a smooth-edged hole in its left lateral border.

Alternating a studied gaze between windows, he detected no movement through either one.

"That lock up there probably saved our lives," David said. "I'm sure it diverted the bullet. It went clear out the other side. See, over there." He spoke breathlessly.

Kathy nodded as she rolled her neck. David swung his head around and peered out the near window at an elevated rock ledge beyond the driveway. The ledge separated her property from her neighbor's, some forty feet away. "That's where he pulled the trigger, the son-of-a-bitch. No doubt a pistol; that's what it sounded like, anyway. If he'd used a rifle, we'd have been goners. Even without a telescopic sight." He began easing to a standing position.

"David, careful," Kathy said, appearing ready to elaborate.

But David clamped his hand on her shoulder and said, "Shh … wait … listen." He cocked his head toward the front of the condo unit, toward a repetitive blast and final roar. He knew it had come from a two-stroke, internal combustion engine, and he jerked himself up and scampered out the kitchen, through the living room, out the front door and onto the lawn. He stood straight, feet spread, arms hanging, snubby pointed toward the ground. Through barren trees lining the road parallel to Kathy's, he followed the blur of a red motorcycle.

He returned the pistol to its rig as Kathy arrived, and, with an edge of impatience creeping into his voice, he said, "What the hell's going on, anyway?"

"What? What was it?"

"A motorcycle. A red one." David felt the lines of his face grow pensive. "Didn't your men confiscate the

Honda?"

"I'm not sure. You think this is that one?"

"Unless there are two floating around, which would be a helluva stretch."

He put his arm around her waist and pulled her toward his hip as they walked back in. For the first time, he didn't like how fragile his detective felt in his grasp.

"Do you pack your gun when you're home?" he said.

"Not usually."

"Pack it."

They returned to the kitchen and, after a superficial inspection, David said, "I'll be right back. There's got to be a shell casing out there."

He hurried out the front door as if the casing might soon evaporate, and, reaching the forward extent of rock near the beginning of the driveway, climbed the slope back toward the unit, to a point above and opposite the kitchen windows. He shuddered as he looked through the shattered one, able to distinguish almost everything inside.

David scoured the area and, finding no casing, guessed it had disappeared down one of many deep crevices in the rock surface. Or else it wasn't a semiautomatic. The ledge was filthy and damp but he didn't care; he sat on it, legs over the side, fingers wrapped around the edge, unaware of the moisture he'd normally feel.

He asked himself whether the biker was the killer. The potshot here was not target practice.

He ran through his list of suspects, wondering who among them would—or even could—ride a motorcycle. Bernie—Robert—even Nick? Possibly. But Foster, Sparky, the psychiatrist? One more stretch.

And while we're on the subject, pal—if you can be

so far off on who owned the red cycle, how far off are
you on everything else? He thought of calling it a day but
convinced himself it was much too early. Does the killer
quit plotting his dirty deeds this early?

Before rejoining Kathy, he examined the opposite
side of the unit—a courtyard of underbrush and trees adjacent to the kitchen's bay window—and he recovered no
bullet.

David checked his watch. Only twelve minutes had
passed since the gunfire and, back inside, he and Kathy
took turns trying to locate the suspects, she on her home
phone, he on his cellular. No contacts were made but Nora
Foster believed her husband would return from a round
of errands in a half-hour— one o'clock—and was certain
he wouldn't mind talking with David at that time.

"You'll be all right?" David asked.

"I'll be all right," Kathy replied.

"Remember, pack the gun, and I mean it."

On the way to Alton and Nora Foster's, David de-
toured to the hospital's parking lot, making a simple U-
turn before heading back out. The area behind the vine-
covered wall was cordoned off and a uniformed police
officer waved as he drove by. The red motorcycle was
not there. He would later check on whether the police
had confiscated it, secretly hoping that if there had indeed been a foul-up, it was Nick's.

David took the usual hilly route to the Foster estate,
the Mercedes barely qualifying for DRIVE, its top up and
tapes quiet. He felt like a circus aerialist who yesterday
had a new routine down pat and today woke up as the
clown.

"David, welcome," Nora said in the foyer. "No scarf or gloves today?"

Where's she been? It's like summer out. "No, it's too mild—for a change."

"Alton should be here any minute. Come in. Have a seat. Let me take you to his study." Her shoulders were still speckled with dandruff. "Awful stuff yesterday, wasn't it? Did you read the morning paper? Now there are narcotics in the picture. What a mess."

They walked two abreast down a long hall. Six could have fit. He was struck by the echo of their voices, undampened by the crowded receptions of previous days. Nor were there now any perfumes or food spreads to mask the fusty smell of the Tudor's interior.

They sat opposite each other in rococo chairs more appropriate in a nineteenth century parlor than in a private study. The room had blue papered walls, oak trim, and cluttered surfaces. Two patterned nine-by-twelve rugs covered the floor, corner to corner.

David wasted no time. "Nora, while we have a minute, all right to ask you a question or two?"

"Why, yes. But shouldn't we wait for Alton?"

"With all due respect, I'd rather speak to him alone. Would that be okay?" David purposefully wanted separate interviews to see if their stories jibed.

"Well … he's much closer to everything, but I'll try to be helpful."

"Good. Does Alton own a motorcycle?"

Nora hesitated and then laughed uncontrollably.

She hadn't finished when David said, "Does he?"

She dabbed at the corner of her eye with a tissue she pulled from the sleeve of her housecoat. Then, clearing her throat, she said, "But whatever in heaven's name for?"

"Then he doesn't?"

"No, of course not. Why do you ask?"

"Curious, that's all."

He was about to inquire about their whereabouts Thursday night when Foster appeared at the door. "I saw your car out there," he said, fixing David with a level stare. "Is anything wrong?"

"No," David said, standing. An earlier adrenaline rush had begun to wane and he felt a stitch in his knee. "Nothing new."

"I'll leave you two alone," Nora said, looking relieved. The study door squeaked as she closed it behind her.

Foster did not replace her in the rococo chair, instead choosing his desk swivel chair, a piece among the mishmash that represented four centuries of furniture. Foster signaled him to sit.

"Alton, I won't take much of your time but there are some questions and … "

"Don't be silly, fire away. Take all the time you need but first—any leads?"

"On yesterday?"

"On any of them. Christ, will it ever end?"

"No, nothing definite yet."

"They're shutting down the hospital, you know."

"They're what?"

"Starting tomorrow. I suspected it would happen, even without Spritz's killing. We'll have to discharge the electives home and ship the emergents across town. The accreditors said once they feel the hospital's safe, they'll allow us to reopen." Foster ran his fingers through his hair. "Would you like a drink?"

"No thanks, too early."

"Mind if I have one."

"No, not at all."

Foster reached into the cabinet behind him and produced a glass and a bottle of *Chivas Regal.* He downed half a glass—no water, no ice—in less time than it took to pour it.

"Okay, let me start," David said, "and if a 'yes' or 'no' answer will do in your opinion—that's fine. You don't have to expand unless you want to."

"Got it," Foster said with a silly grin.

"Do you have a motorcycle you're keeping under wraps?" David took out his pad.

"Do I have a what that I'm what?"

"A motorcycle. A red one."

Foster eyed the Scotch bottle and replied, "No, I'm afraid not. But if I did, I'd hightail it off into never-never land right about now."

David looked at a blank page without writing a note. "Do you own any guns?"

"No."

David checked off an imaginary question. "Did you know Victor Spritz was involved in drugs?"

"No, not as a dealer which it appeared like he was. As a user? That wouldn't have shocked me."

David curled his finger under his mouth. "Can you tell me, Alton, where you were Friday night?"

Foster didn't hesitate. "Right here. I had a headache after the funeral reception and I went to bed early."

"What time was that?"

"Eight-thirty ... nine."

"And Nora?"

"She had some club meeting to go to. I think it was the Garden Club."

"When did she get home?"

"I have no idea," Foster snapped. "I was asleep."

David pretended to write meaningful notes on two pages of his pad to allow time for Foster to decompress. "Okay, that's that," David said. "Next, the missing botulism vial ..."

"I was going to call you about that misunderstanding, David, but it makes no difference now. We're being closed anyway, so I'll notify the Health Department. I know John Bartholomew thinks someone made off with the vial, but I really think it must have been accidentally discarded. He's slipping, you know."

"That much?"

"That much."

David regarded the hospital administrator with cold speculation. "We'll see," he said. "Now you won't like this, I'm sure, but about your surgical training."

Foster probed David's face. "How did you find out about that?" he asked, without emotion. "I haven't advertised it."

"I can't say at the moment, Alton, but can you tell me why P.G.H. let you go?" How can he be so calm? The liquor?

"That's a no-brainer." Foster stuck his chin out, defiantly. "They didn't like the quality of my work."

"And it took two years for them to come to that conclusion?"

Foster, who had been swiveling in his chair as he answered questions, stopped abruptly and gave David a blistering look. "That's it!" he cried, his voice rising an octave. "End of conversation." He leaped from his chair, threw open the door and stormed down the hall like a duck with sore feet. David remained seated but watched him gradually slow his pace and, reaching the end of the hall, turn and waddle back.

Foster ignored David as he passed him. He eased into his chair awkwardly, poured himself another drink, took a long slug, then another. He slammed his fist into an open hand and said, "Jesus, I hate it when I get like that. Sorry, David—nerves, I guess." He finished the drink and continued, "Look, I understand your position and that you're helping out the police and all that. But given that they're closing us down and that—let's not beat around the bush—that I'm a suspect ..." He heaved a breath. "Why, for Christ's sake, I have no idea. It's *my* goddamn hospital!"

David thought Foster, eyes like pinwheels, might run out the door again.

"So, David, let me say—I'd better stick to answering just the cops' questions. Kathy's, that Nick guy, whoever. It's more official that way, and I hope you understand."

David was not sure he did, but he nodded his approval. One question short of completing his planned list—he had intended to ask Foster about his affair with Betty Tanarkle—he thanked him for his time.

At the front entrance, David said, "I hope we can get to the bottom of all this—for the sake of justice, and for the hospital." Foster's expression had turned opaque.

The ride home was as fitful as an insomniac's sleep. In thinking about the brazen attempt on his life and possibly on Kathy's, he was certain if the perp had seen him fall, he would have turned the gun on her. And since he botched the first shot, he panicked and ran. But David lingered on his error in assuming the red motorcycle belonged to Spritz. And what of the oily cardboard? A week ago, he might have become stalled in questions of his analytical skills—but not now; there was too much at stake, and, he sensed, too little time. Although he considered it a giant leap in deduction, the error also warned him against prioritizing his suspect list. It leveled its membership.

At 10 Oak Lane, as David crossed sheets of light that had dispersed from his oaks onto the driveway, he thanked the window lock for saving two lives. And he felt a greater resolve shaped by self-admonitions: keep digging, assume nothing, and work fast.

He noticed his storm door was not fully shut. He swung it open and stepped back to pick up a number 10 envelope which fell at his feet. It was addressed to INSPECTOR BROOKS. David scowled as he opened the envelope and unfolded a single sheet of paper. His scowl deepened as he read the uppercase typing:

INSPECTOR: NO DOUBT YOU KNOW OF GIFFORD'S AUTO WRECKING IN TOWN. EVER WATCH THEM CRUSH A CAR? ENDS UP NICE AND THIN LIKE A DIME. EVERYTHING IN IT, TOO. DON'T BECOME SCRAP METAL. GET OFF THE CASE NOW !!!!

David slapped the paper with the back of his hand and put it into his pocket.

23

CE LINE DO NOT CROSS POLICE LINE DO NOT CROS

In the days before he had become embroiled in investigations of this intensity, David would have settled in for a Sunday afternoon football game before his television set. Instead, he sat in front of his computer, wolfing down a ham sandwich and uploading the events of the past twenty hours and some carefully thought-out embellishments to his tactical plan. It took only twenty minutes.

He contacted the hospital lab, obtained Marsha's home number and called her.

"Have you seen Bernie Bugles lately?" he asked.

"Sure, but he just left."

"He was there?"

"He's been staying with me for a couple days, and he's thinking about giving up his Manhattan apartment."

"How come? Doesn't he like Manhattan?"

"I'm not sure, but that's nothing new—he's pretty closemouthed about everything."

"I see." David tried not to make much of the information. Besides, he was more interested in the past few hours. "But today, how about this morning and over the noon hour?"

"He was gone when I woke up."

"When was that?"

"Ah—do I have to say? Ten o'clock. But it's Sunday, Dr. Brooks."

David felt intrusive. "And I'm sorry to bother you on a Sunday."

"That's okay."

"You don't mind the questions, then?"

"Don't be silly. I know you're doing your job. And I've got to tell you, Dr. Brooks, not many people liked Victor Spritz but he didn't deserve getting killed that way."

David reminded himself of the "keep digging" admonition. "And so Bernie came back there and left again?"

"Yes, he stayed only a few minutes."

"Where had he been?"

"I have no idea."

"And where did he go? Did he say?"

"Yes. To Boston. He'll be there for two days of meetings with some delegations from the Far East. He wanted to arrive today so he'd be fresh at eight in the morning."

David tingled with the sensation of becoming airborne. So he's occupied tomorrow. Hello, Manhattan! "What exactly does he do, anyway?" he asked, gazing at a list of phone numbers he kept nearby.

"He's a medical equipment consultant."

Still that, eh? "One last thing, Marsh. He said before that he didn't own a motorcycle. Have you ever seen him riding one?"

He couldn't interpret the momentary silence. "No, I can't say that I have," she said, "but he'd look real neat on one if he did."

"By the way," David said, "Do you remember where the two of you were the night before last—that's Friday." "Me? Sure, right here. I was waiting for Bernie. He didn't show up till after eleven."

"How did he seem?"

"Funny you should ask, Dr. Brooks—you must be psychic. He was agitated. Very agitated."

"Do you know why?"

"No, and I didn't ask. He always screams at me if I 'meddle in his affairs,' as he calls it."

After praising Marsha's cooperation, David hung up the phone and punched in Musco Diller's number in one swift motion.

"Musco, old buddy! Listen, Monday mornings are probably busy for you but any chance of your getting away for a few hours tomorrow?"

Musco's response was not immediate and David had a fleeting inclination to curse to himself. Finally, he heard, "Ain't no job takes me that long."

"It does if it's in New York City." They agreed to meet outside the Red Checker Cab Company at nine and after hanging up, David resolved the call to Kathy would be the last one of the day. "Are you okay?" he began.

"Yes, I'm fine. Where are you?"

"Home." He capsulized his encounter with the Fosters and his conversation with Marsha as if they were a mere preamble to his next question. "Are you packing hardware?"

"David," she said, "that wouldn't have helped at all if the perp were a better shot. About as helpful, I'd say, as wearing a badge around the condo. But, yes, I'm okay, and yes, I'll wear the gun. At least until Mr. Wackado's caught."

"Good. And when you arrange to have the windows fixed—call Carl's Carpentry, they'll do it—arrange for some curtains that you can't see through and that cover the whole window."

"Oh, sure, why not just board them up real tight?"

This time, it was David who initiated a phone silence. He broke it with, "I should have hugged you, Kath."

"What? What are you talking about?"

"Back at the kitchen. That bullet whizzed by our ears. He could have killed us both, you know. When he didn't, I should have hugged you."

In the course of informing her about Musco's willingness to accompany him to Manhattan in the morning, he interrupted himself. "Damn!" he said, snapping his fingers.

"What's the matter?"

"I should have made it for today. I could have asked Musco to go with me now. Why not? Bernie's not around."

"David, wait till tomorrow."

"But this is a perfect opportunity … "

"So's tomorrow. It can wait till then."

"I don't think so. I'm calling him back."

"Will you do me a favor? Don't do anything for ten minutes."

"What do you mean, don't do anything for ten minutes?"

"I'm coming over."

Kathy didn't remove her light clutch before taking David's hands in hers. "Look, darling," she said, "I think you're trying to do too much too soon. Rest up. Collect yourself. I really think you've gotten a little ... well ... frankly ... emotional."

"Collect myself? Emotional? For Christ's sake, we've got bodies dropping like flies. You and I could have been two more, and you say I'm emotional?" Kathy took a step back. "Listen to yourself," she said.

David's silent concurrence dominated the next two hours along with the blare of a football game he had trouble processing. But, after drinks and hamburgers on the barbeque, he and Kathy mixed business and pleasure talk, and he realized he couldn't remember the last time he had heard the roar of his own belly laugh.

At one point, Kathy phoned Nick to get exact directions to Bernie's New York apartment. And David leveled with her that he always believed Nick's one-day stakeout there had been a new Chief of Detectives' effort to impress his superior as a hands-on guy.

Later in bed, he hugged her for most of the night.

The top was down on the speeding Mercedes, a toy beneath its towering driver and a slouching passenger. The Merritt Parkway at nine-thirty was cleared of its earlier morning traffic rush and the weather, deceptive in January, rendered use of a heater redundant.

"Someday, I'll get me one of these Benzos," Musco said, patting the dashboard.

"Uh-huh," David replied.

It was their only conversation for the initial fifty-mile stretch as David sifted through a logjam of thoughts and the cabby mostly dozed, his cap pulled down over his eyes. David felt the manufactured wind leveling his hair and watering his nose, and he knew it would be a day when he was alert for any contingency and ready to take on any question—one of which was why in hell he was making the trip in the first place.

He wasn't sure what he'd find at Bernie's apartment on Manhattan's Upper West Side nor what he was even looking for. But if he's on "Suspect-6," and if the discoveries at Bugles', Foster's and Spritz's are any measure, then Bernie's place is worthy of inspection, and a drive there, especially without snow or ice, is a fair price of admission.

He believed Bernie was the most enigmatic on the list. Were there shady ties—drug ties—to the Far East? Was "medical equipment consultant" simply a cover? Did he have similar ties to his departed stepfather and to the departed Spritz? They clearly had territories. Did Bernie? Or Robert? Was his half brother thought capable of maintaining a territory, or had he been cut out of a deadly family affair? And what of the hospital connection on the list: Foster or Corliss, the psychiatrist? And the police connection: Nick or Sparky? Drugs? *Other* motives?

Often, even in diagnostic quagmires, the more David tried to purify its waters, the more darkened they became, but he was used to that, familiar with the feeling of wading through distractions and red herrings. So he still felt alert and ready as he drove along the Hudson River, beyond the George Washington Bridge with its double-decker ant procession, and, on the left, Riverside Church, its spire saluting the heavens.

Deep in its canyons, David realized he had forgotten the smell of New York City—not altogether unpleasant but distinctive. He hadn't forgotten its vehicular frenzy though, the cagey maneuvering and charging and honking,

MURDERS AT HOLLINGS GENERAL

the competition of taxicabs and delivery trucks and cars darting around one another, eager to secure yet another advantage.

He was acquainted with the area, having spent some time training at St. Luke's Hospital back in the mid-eighties, yet he gave Nick Medicore a mental bow for providing expert directions. As David idled before the designated brownstone off Cathedral Parkway, he saw an Avis Parking Garage diagonally across the street.

In its cramped waiting area, he remained in the car and said to an attendant, "Tell you what. I'll double your fee if you let me park my own car." The man agreed and pointed to an empty spot just inside a tunnel.

The door to Bernie's ninth floor apartment was fifty or sixty of David's paces down from a glass and gold-plated elevator. Musco, following close behind, made it in one hundred. They passed no other doors on the way. Monet and Renoir replicas lined both walls of the carpeted hallway, ornately framed paintings David thought might have been reserved for the apartments themselves. It was a thought related to the incongruity of a building with outward elegance but without a security guard or elevator operator.

At the door, ten feet from a fire escape, David shielded a crouching Musco who gave the usual knock, then performed his skewer routine with silence and speed. He cracked the door open an inch and whispered, "I'll wait out on the landing here. Do a good job, whatever it is."

"You can come in this time, you know," David whispered back.

"What, and go around with my eyes closed? Dr.

David, like I told you, I don't want to know nothin'."

David walked through the entrance and into a narrow antechamber with a large window on his right and, to his left, double doors as high as the ceiling, as wide as the span of his arms. He yanked out his Beretta Minx and used Friday to nudge open the doors, all the while calling out Bernie's name.

The apartment was enormous, extending as far back as the elevator, and laterally a similar distance. It was a "Master Quarters" space he had read about but had never seen during his study of Japanese culture through the years. In the center there was one main room containing a raised platform covered by a mat and pillows and surrounded by panels of antique lace and netting. Sitting and storage rooms encircled the apparent bedroom. A kitchen and dining area were located in a far corner and what appeared to be a study was adorned—or unadorned—with simple furniture pieces of lacquered wood: small desk, cabinets with grapevine designs, two straight chairs with single vertical splats forming their backs. There were no interior walls per se: the rooms were divided by hanging bamboo screens, sliding paper screens or draperies. Scattered about were bronze mirrors, wind chimes, ewers and goblets of hammered gold and silver and dishes made of porcelain and blown glass. The dominant colors of the quarters and its contents were those that David recognized as the colors of the finest jade: white, pale blue and green.

Stalking from room to room to ensure he was alone, he cleared his throat of a smell he finally pinpointed as an admixture of cooking oil and spices. He banged his head on a wind chime as he gravitated toward the platform bed and stood looking down at it, puzzled over something that seemed strange, or out of place—something inconsistent with what he had learned about Japanese furnishings. He walked around the bed before tensing to a halt. It was too high! It should be a simple slab on the floor, not raised on two-foot sideboards. He pushed aside the netting as he would cobwebs and lifted a white skirt at the foot of the platform. The slab was attached to the footboard with hinges.

He circled to the head of the bed and, swatting the pillows to the floor, lifted the skirt and raised the slab. David gaped in disbelief at a king-size compartment stuffed with batches of four-by-four bags at one end, and at the other end, tiny glassine bags with "HORNET" stamps. All bulged with white powder.

David took several Polaroids of the cache and lowered the slab, having documented what he had suspected all along: first, there was papa Bugles; then, Victor Spritz; and now, we discover, Bernie Bugles, U.S. citizen but devotee of Japan and probable narcotics operative there.

He took stock of the rest of the apartment and photographed each room. In the study, he ran his hand along the over-lacquered desktop and, instead of searching each drawer, followed his usual hunch and pulled open the one on the bottom right. Inside was a metal box containing a ledger book. He riffled through its pages; it was the exact ledger he had seen and photographed at Charlie Bugles' condo.

David made several entries in his notepad as he sauntered out of the study and toward a side stationary wall dotted sparingly with colored photographs. He focused on three; they were captioned in Japanese characters, some of which David identified. One photo depicted The National Stadium of Tokyo. Another was a much smaller version of the stadium, though still immense. It sat on a lush hillside beyond a stone driveway that snaked to an unattached garage. Bernie's Nipponese hangout? The third, an interior shot, was a facsimile of Manhattan's "Master Quarters," but with one exception. The elevated platform was longer, wider and higher.

He snapped pictures of the photographs and, feeling like a gourmet who had overindulged, packed his camera in Friday and headed for the entrance. Pulling back one of the double doors which he had left open, his knees quaked at the sight before him. Twin leather sheaths hung from the wall. One was empty. The other contained a pearl-handled dagger.

24

On the drive back to Connecticut shortly after noon, Musco closed his eyes and David wrestled with the idea of rounding up Bernie in Boston because he had found the twin dagger in his apartment. Why go any further? Call a halt to the investigation. Wrap this up.

But, hold on, pal. Wasn't it concluded that Spritz murdered the others, and wasn't it he, therefore, who must have plunged the dagger into Cortez? Therefore, also, what's its twin got to do with the Spritz killing? In fact, what's it doing down there in New York City?

He reminded himself of the lessons he had learned in the instance of the red motorcycle: don't rush to conclusions; don't succumb to surface evidence. No, there were other members of "Suspect-6" to query, other components of the Tactical Plan. Carry on.

One of the components—number four—was to comb Hollings' North End for druggie belchers who might rat on their sources. He visualized seedy characters nodding yes to a newspaper photo of Spritz, or pointing to Bernie in the photo he'd swiped at Charlie Bugles' place. But he already had the goods on Spritz and Bernie. What about

Robert and Foster and Corliss and Sparky, though? And Nick? If any one of them could be brought into the drugs equation, would that strengthen the likelihood he was the killer? Were they known in the North End? He needed their pictures. Robert's was no problem; his was in the one with Bernie. David would have Kathy supply Nick's and Sparky's, and Belle would supply Foster's and Corliss'.

And he needed one other thing for his foray into the seamy end of the city where he hoped to rub elbows with hookers, pimps, winos and other denizens of a local subculture whose infrastructure was a steady stream of illicit drugs. Once again, he needed Musco's assistance.

"You awake, Musc?" he said.

"Your thoughts are keeping me awake. I can almost hear them."

"Mind if I ask you a personal question?"

"Don't ask, I don't have one."

"One what?"

"A sex life."

David had a ready supply for the opening he'd been given but he was too preoccupied even to fake a smile. "I realize you never stopped hacking even though you own the business. What do you normally take in on a busy Monday when you handle some fares yourself?"

Musco arched up and replied, "You mean in money?"

"Yes, and you don't have to answer if you don't want to. I could probably figure it out myself."

"Oh … maybe two hundred clams, give or take a few."

"I'll double that if you can help me a couple more hours—say till about four."

"Doing what?"

"I want you to show me around the North End."

"Double? You're in a doubling mood today, but I gotta say no."

David felt the start of a facial contortion when Musco added, "That's too much dough to shell out."

David relaxed his face, "Okay, then, you buy lunch when we're halfway home."

"Forget what I said," Musco retorted, joining David in a raucous laugh.

David had two phone calls to make. He was not concerned about Musco's listening in and, moreover, he knew no questions would be asked. Besides, the talk of narcotics would save explaining about their upcoming visit to the North End.

He called Kathy at police headquarters and informed her of the drug find and dagger sheaths. After expressing an emotion of equal parts of shock and joy, she said, "Do you think we should go ahead and nab him?"

"No, not yet." David never conceived of advising her on police procedural matters. He referred to the Tactical Plan and elaborated on getting burnt on the red motorcycle issue.

"Speaking of motorcycles," he said, "did you ever ask Nick whether it had been confiscated?"

"Yes, and you were right—no one ever did. He said it just disappeared."

"*He* didn't take it, did he?"

"David, let's not go into that again."

He hadn't totally dismissed Nick as a suspect. "Okay, I won't just now, but I'll tell you one thing. Whoever has that red cycle is our killer. I'd swear to it."

"I'd go along with that," Kathy said, unconvincingly. David sensed she didn't want to spar.

"Next question, Kath. What's with your geologist friend?"

"I was waiting for you to finish before I told you. He called and you were right again—and on both counts. The stuff you vacuumed from the car matched the material from the construction site, and the powder on the gloves is definitely fireclay."

"Figured." David was less satisfied with the news from a forensic point of view as he was from deducing it as another reason why Kathy sounded so deferential. He had had no doubt about the match but had hoped the powder didn't prove to be fireclay. *Great, that means Spritz was tinkering with someone's safe. Whose, and why?*

"Now back to Bernie's apartment before I forget," he said. "He's in Boston, remember, and is due back late tomorrow. Can you have his Manhattan place staked out beginning—let's see—say about two tomorrow? And give your man ... sorry ... person ... my cellular number and have him ... that person ... call me soon as Bernie arrives."

"Got it. That's outside our jurisdiction but I can arrange for one of our off-duty people to run down. And, darling ..."

"What?"

"Oh, never mind."

No sparring, more deference. David then requested photos of Nick and Sparky from the department's administrative files. He explained why he needed them and held his breath.

Without editorializing, she agreed to provide them,

and also added, "But how strange. Nick said he's going up there, too. He asked for directions to Townsey Street. Said he might mosey around after work today."

David didn't comment vocally. Strange, indeed! But why announce it, if there were something clandestine going on?

Kathy continued. "You be careful, David. There's more crime up there than you can shake a stick at. And that includes drive-by shootings."

"And drugs."

"Of course, and drugs."

"And," David said, "I think, more than ever now, that drugs—drug trafficking on a big scale—were behind all the killings. Know what I'm saying? Not an illicit love affair, or not having a contract terminated, or not getting a Chief of Staff position. They could have figured in, depending on who we're talking about. But it's the goddamned drugs. That's why I'm checking out the North End—I've got to exhaust every possible drug angle."

"Is Musco going with you?"

"Yes."

"That'll help. But still watch your flanks."

"You bet. And if I'm not back in a week, send out a search posse." There was no response, so he tried again. "But don't worry. When I stop by there to pick up the photos, I'll bid you my last farewell."

"Very funny," Kathy said.

David hung up the phone and Musco leaped to say, "You know, I couldn't help hearing what you said."

"No kidding."

"Yeah, about drugs. I don't care about them other things like the red bike, but drugs kill people, or people kill for drugs. Either way, it's bad business. Real bad. That's why I thank my god I was never zonked out or hooked. And I was never a connection. Even after all the time I spent up on Townsey Street and King Street. Booze was my thing. But man, I saw *plenty* up there."

David had placed a call to Belle at the Hole as Musco wound down his commentary. He learned that the hospital was phasing out services except for the Emergency Room and a skeleton crew in Radiology and the lab. And that Victor Spritz's funeral was scheduled for Wednesday morning. Belle stated she would arrange for Foster's and Corliss' photos to be delivered to police headquarters in time for his arrival there.

Hollings' North End was a twelve-square block enclave of junkies, hookers, pimps, alcoholics, vagrants and other assorted skid row types—a kernel of humanity the crime busters couldn't bust. The area's only stability centered around mom-and-pop businesses whose native proprietors felt they could survive nowhere else, much like over-institutionalized criminals or patients. Its destructive social dynamics had been on autopilot for as long as David could remember.

The late afternoon was hazy, the kind of day normally reserved for springtime when it was about to rain and you could see the air. And smell everything that hung in it.

David and Musco drove past an old African-American woman on a corner. She was arranging red and white flowers in burlap bags which were tied together and slung over a bicycle.

"She's still around," David said. He knew that "Rose

Lady" marked the beginning of the North End district. "She'll always be around," Musco said. "She was around when I was growing up in these here parts. Taught me a lot, too."

"Like what?" David drove slowly, leaning forward on the wheel, taking in both sides of the street. The Mercedes' top was up.

"Like stay out of other people's business. You live longer—especially up here."

At Musco's suggestion, they veered up a hill past, in turn, a medical clinic, a bar, a soup kitchen and shelter, a bar, a cheap-looking hotel and another bar. David glanced down side alleys strewn with faceless bodies already bedded down beneath newspapers or ragged blankets. He shook his head, touched by the realization that each lay alone with his pneumonia, too weak to cough effectively, destined before winter's end to be replaced by others on the way down. Musco pointed to a graffiti-wrapped warehouse where he had often slept, describing with sober disgust its empty rooms with rotted floorboards.

They reached the leveling-off point of the district, the center park, the hub from which all cracked, ice-heaved roads radiated. It was a container for broken benches, bottles and cement walkways submerged in dirt and yellow grass, compressed weeds that no one had bothered trimming. Peeling tenement houses with open stairwells cluttered the corners and back edges beyond a ring of storefronts, half of them vacant. David saw few people, fewer cars and no patrol cops.

"Where *is* everybody?" he asked, pulling over to a curb and turning off the ignition.

"They're around. In the bars. In their rooms—sleeping, or shooting up or turning tricks. And the street dealers are here, too. I don't know who they are any more but you can bet they're here, crawling the back alleys, counting their bread. So are their suppliers. Little higher up, but they're here, more out in the open though—maybe running the butcher shop or the cleaners, or something like that."

"Shouldn't they be the ones we show the pictures to?" David knew enough about drug hierarchies to understand that the individuals of "Suspect-6" wouldn't deal directly with lowlifes or street peddlers, but with the mid-levelers.

"We could do it that way, but my buddy over at that first bar we passed? He's the guy who'd be just as good as all of 'em put together. Get my drift?"

"How reliable is he?"

"Meaning?"

David reached around to the back seat for Friday. He removed an envelope of photos he had picked up at Kathy's office: Foster, Corliss, Sparky, Nick. He shuffled through them. "If we ask him if he's seen any of these people and he says 'no,' how valid is that answer on a scale of one-to-ten?"

"Minus one."

David crossed his arms and looked down at Musco. "Then what are we doing here?"

"Hey, it's your show, not mine." Musco paused. "But you didn't say it the other way around."

"You lost me," David said, bewildered.

"What if he says 'yes'?"

"Okay, what if he does say 'yes'? How valid is that?"

"Eleven."

David doubted a bartender or anyone else in the depraved North End would embrace the truth, but he had to plow on, to run the gamut.

"So you'd expect your friend to cooperate?" David asked.

Musco waved his hand to start up the car and proceed, "Let's try and see," he said. "Willie used to be my closest friend when I was down and out in these parts. And you know how I know? I don't remember much from those days—but he refused to serve me drinks. That I do remember. Probably saved my life."

They retraced their route to the Blue Rock Cafe where Willie Daniels, its proprietor/bouncer, struck a black Bunyanesque pose behind the bar. David thought Willie's plastic bow tie was an insult to Bow-tiers International but he wasn't in a North End barroom—wearing his floppy hand-tied version—to make a fashion statement.

"Well, look what the wind blew in," Willie said, "the man who made Red Checker famous." He put down the glass he was shining. Musco's hand disappeared in Willie's.

"Willie Daniels, this here's Dr. David Brooks from over at Hollings General—you know—where they been having all those … ah … accidents." The room smelled of beer and vulcanized rubber. Chitchat dwindled.

David and Willie shook hands, a standoff.

"Pleasure to meet you," David said. "You know you've got a lifetime friend and admirer here?" He grabbed Musco's shoulder and pleated his upper body against his own flank. Musco struggled to cough.

"No way a friend if I have to pay full fares in his hack," Willie said, winking.

"Shit, man, I should charge you double for the over-weight," Musco cracked.

The Blue Rock was a favorite watering hole for the after work crowd from the region's rubber factory. The bar was lined with men caught between ardent discussion and a game of "Chicago." Several drained their beers and left, leering back at David as they headed for the door.

"Two *Buds*," he said, nodding to Willie.

"No, no, none for me. I'll stay pat," Musco said.

They drifted to the end of the bar, near the cash register. David remained standing and Musco climbed onto a stool. Willie joined them after sliding down a tall glass of beer, its foamy head intact. David snatched it off the bar as if they had rehearsed the maneuver.

"So, Dr. Brooks, I hear you're helping the cops on those murders. How's it going?"

David knew that Willie knew he wasn't paying Blue Rock a visit simply to down a few suds. "We're making progress," he answered. "And that's why we're here. Wonder if you could help us?"

"Sure, if I can. Always glad to oblige the law." Willie looked at Musco and mocked, "But I don't know about that millionaire cabby you dragged in with you." Musco, his mouth crammed with peanuts, delivered a scathing salvo with his eyes.

David removed the photos from the envelope and handed them to Willie, along with the picture of the Bugles brothers. "Do you remember seeing any of those six men—either in here or in the area?"

Willie inspected the front and back of each photo separately while David zeroed in on his expression. He learned nothing.

Willie handed them back. "Can't say that I have … no, I'm afraid not. The killer's one of them?"

"We don't know yet." It was the response David had anticipated. He exaggerated neatness in returning the photos to the envelope while he thought of his next move. "Well, thanks anyway," he said, his voice as even as Willie's. He turned and gazed about the sparsely occupied tables and then out the front plateglass window, into the darkening and empty tangle of streets. He turned back to Willie.

"Awfully quiet around here," he said. "No yelling, no sirens. What's your best guess? Crime down? Drug dealing down?"

"Neither, but I have no inside information, know what I mean?" He scratched his stubbly chin. "The crime won't pick up for a few days. Second or third of the month. It's like clockwork. That's when the state checks come in."

David finished the beer, dropped a twenty on the bar and handed Willie his card, asking to be notified if he came across any useful information.

"About what I expected," David said as they walked to the Mercedes. "A minus one."

In the car, he felt his cellular phone's vibration and checked his watch. It was five-ten.

"He just left," Kathy said, her voice a shade above a whisper.

"Who just left?"

"Nick. He said again he's going up to the North End. Are you still there?"

"We were about to leave, but not now. A white Park Avenue, right?"

"Right."

"Is he alone?"

"He left here alone. Did you find out anything?"

"Nothing more than I could have by phone. At least so far."

David drove up and down several dimly lit side streets, settling on the darkest one. He parked the car in shadows, a vantage point allowing full view of the moonlit Blue Rock and, if he leaned forward, the two other bars as well.

"Wake me if there's any action," Musco said, yawning.

David used the time to evaluate the encounter with Willie Daniels and the up-front behavior of Nick Medicore. Despite a minus-one answer and the blank face, big guy Willie knows more than he lets on. His face was too blank. And Nick? Why wouldn't professional police procedure dictate being up-front with a colleague? But if his intentions are other than professional, then the announcement to Kathy was pretty clever: eliminate any suspicion over his presence in the North End.

In an hour's worth of ten minutes, a white Buick angled into a parking space in front of the Blue Rock. David checked his watch; it was five-thirty. He decided to hold off waking Musco and arched back in his seat. Nick emerged from the car and walked around to the sidewalk. Under a lamplight, he tugged on the brim of his fedora, flicked a cigarette into the gutter and looked up and down the street. He took two steps back toward the curb and checked the crude and faded signs above the row of establishments.

David watched as Nick went into the bar to the left

of the Blue Rock. He came out in three minutes. Nick repeated the procedure with the bar to the right before finally entering the Rock, staying three minutes, getting into his car and driving off.

David had a choice of tailing the Buick or questioning Willie. "C'mon, let's go," he said, shaking Musco. They reentered the cafe.

"Would you mind telling me what the fellow who just left wanted—or is it too personal?" David asked, after motioning Willie to the end of the bar.

"No problem. He flashed a badge and did what you did. He showed me two pictures and asked if I'd seen them in my place. I told him 'no.'"

David took out the photos. "Any of these?"

"Yeah, them two." He pointed to Foster and Corliss. "And this is the guy who came in," he added, pointing to Nick.

David left another twenty on the bar.

At the front of the Red Checker Cab Company, he thanked Musco and waved four one-hundred-dollar bills before him.

Musco snapped them up and said, "Ain't this getting expensive for you?"

"Yeah, but it's worth it. And there's more."

"More?"

"You're going to kill me for this, but I need you one last time, I think."

Musco folded the bills and slowly pinched their corners together. "You think you need me, or you think it's the last time?"

"I think it's the last time. I sure as hell hope so."

"When?"

"Tomorrow. Can I call you in the morning with the exact time? First I have to be sure someone's where he's supposed to be."

Musco stared at the bills and smoothed out the corners. "I'll do it," he said, "but there's a hitch."

"Which is?"

"That I toss it in with today's work which you already paid me for."

David began the drive home with several burning thoughts surfacing from a conflagration of others. If it's not Nick, then most likely Sparky's not involved. But there's that Tokyo connection. And Bernie's no surprise. But what does Nick know about Sam Corliss?

Three blocks away, David stopped at a traffic light ten yards before the entrance to a railroad underpass. The area was desolate. The light seemed interminably red. He was momentarily more concerned with a temptation to run the light than with the silhouette of a tow truck parked near the cement embankment to his left. By the time the light had turned green, the truck lumbered from the shadows and faced the Mercedes head on. David recognized the Kermit eyes, and he felt a pulse flutter in his neck.

The truck inched closer. There was insufficient room to charge around and forward, and David gave only passing consideration to backing up because he was certain the truck would ram him in an instant. Instead, he would wait for the driver or drivers to confront him. *But be ready.* He pulled in his elbow from the balmy night wind and was thankful he hadn't chosen to drive with the top down this time. He reached for his shoulder rig, quickly changed his mind in favor of greater firepower and leaned to his right, toward Friday and its Blackhawk .44 Magnum.

Before he could open the case, however, he ducked at the sound of two gun blasts and shattering glass near the front of the Mercedes. David elevated himself slowly, his eyes barely eclipsing the dashboard, and saw only darkness around the frog's eyes. The headlights! They shot out my headlights! Sons of bitches! David breathed in sucking swallows, and, despite an urge to charge out and retaliate in some fashion, he reasoned it would be the worst of his limited options. Should he fire a shot out the window to show he, too, was armed?

There was no time to exercise any option for as David lifted his left shoulder to free up its rig, he heard a popping sound and he winced from a stabbing pain beneath his collarbone—not unlike the sting of a wasp. He grabbed at the spot and felt the smooth contour of what he thought was a thin writing pen projecting from his shoulder, and, ripping it out, sank in his seat from the searing sensation of skin unwilling to let go. Then, instinctively, he locked the door and raised the window.

David thought his eyes were crossing as he twisted the "pen" in his hand. It was a dart needle. Television shows managed to flash through his clouding mind: *Wild Kingdom, National Geographic Specials*. Shows of lions and bisons stunned by tranquilizer guns for scientific study. In his progressive daze, he wondered whether his ear would be tagged.

David's head pounded and he tasted the dryness in his mouth as he smacked his lips, and he couldn't tell whether the car was spinning around him or he was spinning in it. His arms were both heavy and weak and he let them stay limp at his side. He smelled a lime cologne at the window but his head was too wobbly to turn. He wanted desperately to see not so much those who had incapacitated him as those who had shot out his headlights. He knew what was happening and he didn't know what was happening. Yet, he clung to one flimsy thought: that he had yanked out the needle almost on contact— before, he prayed, total damage had been done.

The pounding had ceased but David knew his eyelids contracted and some breaths had been skipped. He was aware of his heartbeat, however, and although it was steady and forceful, he had no doubt he would soon slip into a coma. Or, he prayed again, into a light and temporary sleep.

But before that, one last stab at looking out the window. He tried to force his eyes to rotate left but they were frozen forward. He then released what little positional strength he had to keep his body upright, and as he fell to his right, he was able to maneuver his head in the opposite direction for one fleeting glance. He saw three men leaning over, peering at him. They were dressed in solid black and medallions dangled from their necks. They were big, smiling and Asian. One looked in like a child at a candy store, his forehead and hands pressed against the glass. Above his right eyebrow was a small tattoo of a sword. Three of his finger tips were missing.

When David awoke, he found himself in a sitting position but tilted at a forty-five-degree angle backward in the front seat of the Mercedes. He rubbed at his eyes with the back of his hands which were rope bound at the wrists. He could lift his arms! The moon was full and he could see the dirty steel hook before him through the windshield and felt the back bumper hit bottom as his car was towed up familiar terrain. His watch read six-thirty-five and he calculated he had been in the light sleep he had preferred over coma for forty minutes. He knew it was light because he could hear Asian chatter and grating, scratching sounds, penetrating even in sleep.

He could turn his body freely and tried to pull apart his hands as well as his feet which were also tied at the ankles. David had never been tranquilized as such before, although he remembered coming out of Pentothal anesthesia for a minor surgical procedure while in the Navy. His nearly total lucidity at that moment was similar to what he experienced now, and he was convinced his quickness in removing the dart had something to do with it.

David would deal with the significance of the outside landscape later, although he already had a terrifying inkling of his captives' intentions. But first he jerked around to view what he instantly grasped as the origin of the scratching sounds: the windshield, both side windows, and the back windows were covered with barbed wire. Encaged in barbed wire?

He wedged his head into the seam of the roof and the left window and fairly determined that wide strips of wire extended down under the car's chassis. David began to breathe the breaths of a claustrophobic wrapped on all sides. He felt for his Beretta Minx and his snubby; they were gone. His cellular phone as well. Friday lay open on the passenger seat, all its contents except the .44 Magnum strewn about the floor. That gun had also disappeared.

Outside, it was more light grey than dark, and even on a hardened dirt road and through grimy closed windows pecked at by sharp barbs, he could see dust rising. And a petroleum smell was asphyxiating as the truck ground up High Rock Mountain Road.

David had spent many hours playing in and around High Rock during his early school days. He still knew each bend of the road and could picture its dead-end offshoots to rugged forestland and the footpath that ended halfway up, at a rock as high as the tallest evergreen engulfing it. And he recalled never having told his parents of the mountaintop itself and walking fearlessly at its edge, a stunt he would never try today. If he ever had a chance! There was little guesswork about where his Asian friends were taking him. And what they had in mind.

Not far from the rock, David was gripped by a sense of urgency so intense that its deadliness, though understood, was of minor consequence. Lowering the top was not an alternative, so secure was the wire cage. He had to escape and he had to escape fast. He pounded his shoulder against the door but there was little give.

He looked left and right, and up and back and, deliberating, felt his taut expression soften. Maybe! Just maybe! At the back rim of both doors, he had noticed an inch-wide column uncovered by wire. Could it extend back toward the trunk? Frenzied, he tore the visor from its attachment and lowered the window. Using the visor as a shield, he forced his head against the barbed wire and narrowly out the window. But it was enough to confirm his hope, and he estimated the column to be at least a foot wide. Now it *must* extend across the roof, right?

Awkwardly, David pushed himself forward in the angled car and searched among the dispersed items on the floor. He snapped up his flashlight. Next, he pulled back Friday's retractable panel: the secreted items were undisturbed! He fumbled among them and, after retrieving the Sauer pistol, twisted from side to side and managed to slip it into his pant's pocket. Then he unfolded the tactical knife and cut through the ropes at his ankles with ease, using both hands as one. His wrists took longer. The chatter ahead continued.

David felt sweat spilling over his shoulder blades and rubbed his palms across his wrinkled blazer. He turned around and, kneeling, attempted to climb through the space between the seats, but it was too narrow. With a combination of bulk and adrenalized strength, however, he mangled the passenger seat like a stuffed toy and crawled into the back. His head was compressed against the roof as he ripped through the canvas with his knife, creating an opening between the last two iron struts. He suppressed the urge to laugh convulsively when he rose above the opening and realized his shoulders would clear it, too.

David dropped back down into the car and, checking his exact whereabouts, knew the rock was nearby, that the road bifurcated around it and that the truck would have to slow up. The Mercedes was so pitched that the back end of its roof was a mere three feet from the ground. In a crouch and poised to blast off, he waited for the slowdown, but then he went limp when the truck came to a complete stop! Dive out now or wait?

He squeezed himself into a ball. The cabin window ahead was in darkness and David assumed he was, as well. Suddenly, the truck started up again and before it could gather any speed, he plunged headfirst out the opening and, glancing off the trunk, hit the ground in a fetal but relaxed position. He rotated to the side and stretched out in one speedy motion, whereupon the steep incline took him in a roll toward dense underbrush. David scrambled to his feet and, clutching his knee, ran into the woods and found the path he knew by heart. He doubted the men were aware of losing their cargo. In any event, he never looked back and never needed the flashlight or pistol.

In the Sunoco Station at the bottom of the mountain, he phoned Kathy at home and sketched out his ordeal. She asked no questions, but amidst her sobs, indicated she would be there immediately.

At 10 Oak Lane, Kathy sat on the sofa staring at the floor as David approached. He had taken a shower and, now robed, was dabbing at superficial barb wounds on his forearm. She bolted up and resumed her earlier embrace.

"They were headed for the cliff?" she asked.

"Of course."

She shuddered and pulled him to the sofa. "Not that it matters, darling," she said, "but what about the car?"

He smirked and replied, "Sure as hell, it's in the ravine—and, sure as hell, they got pissed when they unhooked it. Probably pushed it over harder when they saw I wasn't around."

David pictured the descent in his mind and wondered why he didn't feel agitated. Still numb? He kissed Kathy's lips gently. "We can check on it sometime later."

They pressed their bodies together in a protracted silence. Finally, David broke away and said, "Christ, we forgot something."

"Oh?"

"Yeah, drinks."

After moving to the kitchen table where David gulped and Kathy sipped, she said, "You know, I'm confused. If they wanted to—God help us—kill you … "

"Believe me," David interrupted, "they wanted to kill me."

"But my point is, why like that? Why not just shoot you?"

David didn't hesitate, as if he had reached the answer before. "I'm quite sure they were Japanese and, who knows, it may have to do with the psyche of Japanese hit men. Maybe they're latter-day samurai warriors." He put down his drink and snapped his fingers. "Come to think of it," he said, "let's look it up."

He went to his computer corner in the den and Kathy followed. He sat and flipped through the pages of a reference book as Kathy leaned over, her hands on his shoulders.

"Here—here it is," he said.

They read about organized crime elements in Japan—the *Yakuza*—and their loyalty rituals such as self-mutilation and tattooing.

"Look at this," David said with disgust as he tapped on a sentence. He turned to Kathy and summarized, "Some of these goons cut off their own fingers to show respect."

David had not told Kathy about what he had seen through his window.

She crossed her arms and, heaving a breath, said, "It gives me shivers."

David stared down at her. "Why so? You're a cop."

Kathy stepped into his body and, pulling his arms around her, said, "I'm a cop, all right. A cop whose future husband was nearly tossed off a mountain by a bunch of

Yacamos—or whatever they're called."

David wiped at her eye with his hand.

Kathy pulled back. "Who do you think ordered the hit—Bernie?"

"Maybe so," David answered. "Pretty hard to discount his Japanese connection, wouldn't you say?" He knew his expression was taut again. "I can just feel myself throttling him to find out."

"The reason being?"

"The reason being he suspected I was on to his drug involvement, or soon would be."

Bernie felt his face become a boil as he listened to Junzo.

"So what did you do?" Bernie screamed into the phone.

"We pushed it over the cliff. At least we got rid of the car." Each of Junzo's words was crisp.

Bernie's were not. He ran them together, blurting, "You got rid of the car? What good is that? What fuckin' good is that?" He rubbed saliva from his lips. "You and your 'enlightened methods.' I can still hear you: 'We'll make him suffer first. We'll make him watch his ride down … down … down.' Sure you did!"

"You want us to do it another way, Mr. Bugles?"

"Are you kiddin'? No thanks. That's it with you guys. I should have used Baranelli in the first place. You guys stick to your pushing. That's all you can fuckin' handle. Dopes pushing dope."

Bernie hurled the phone and its cradle across the room. He ran his hands through his black hair, then ran them down his black shirt. He paced aimlessly around his apartment, cursing, grunting threats, knocking over furniture.

Finally, he retrieved the phone, stroked his chin thoughtfully and pressed New Jersey numbers he didn't have to look up. "Hello, Tony?" he said evenly. "I need a favor. You there for awhile? Good, don't leave, I'll be right over."

That night, sleep came hard as David relived his brush with an aerial and craggy death. He felt strangely distanced from most negative emotions, although he ran several through his mind. Fear was not among them; there was no time for that. Retribution? Against whom? Relief had replaced anger. Earlier, he had been furious over the loss of headlights but now cared little about the loss of his car—and guns and cellular phone and equipment. And Friday. He felt lucky to be alive. Resolve had replaced uncertainty. He was unfamiliar with the code of conduct that bound members of the underworld and their "clients." If hit men fail to execute a contract, are they expected to try again, or are they given up as failures? No matter—he had to solve the mysteries plaguing Hollings General as swiftly as he had escaped from the car.

25

When he arrived home the night before, there had been a message on David's telephone answering machine to drop by Dr. Corliss' office at the Center for Behavioral Health in the morning. But now, there was the matter of transportation.

The Mercedes dealership began business at eight a.m. and Kathy deposited him there as the doors swung open. Within the hour, David had test-driven and leased a late model convertible not unlike the one he was certain had been pancaked halfway down the western slope of High Rock. He wanted to drive up to its cliffs but there were other more pressing things to do. His day had been mapped out. Perhaps tomorrow. A few streets away, he stopped to buy a new cellular phone for his hip, but he couldn't bear to replace Friday yet.

During the ride to the hospital, he focused not only on Bernie but also on Hollings' chief psychiatrist and psychiatrists in general. The field of medicine that produces the most suicides. What about murderers? And what's the call about? Something to do with "the best defense is a good offense"?

He was also concerned about time. He remembered his computer summaries. Bugles: Tuesday. Coughlin: Saturday. Tanarkle: Tuesday. Spritz: Saturday. It was nine o'clock Tuesday morning.

David didn't expect the sadness he felt when he came upon a virtually vacant doctors' parking lot where, at that hour, they normally jockeyed for spaces. From the outside, there was no doubt that the shutdown at Hollings General was underway, if not complete.

The inside looked like a school during summer vacation. He encountered no corridor greetings, heard no overhead paging, appreciated no medicinal smells. He marched directly to Sam Corliss' office, crossing the ramp to Rosen Hall.

"You got my message, David. Thank you for dropping by." As before, David sat on the edge of the recliner, the psychiatrist behind his desk, beneath Freud and Menninger. The psychiatrist's expression was one David couldn't be sure about. Strained? "I decided to speak to you after grappling with my conscience for two days now," Corliss said.

A confession? It should *be* so easy. I could go back to house calls.

"Remember my high-and-mighty talk about ethical canons?"

"Yes." Not a confession.

"Well, I want to admit to a touch of deception. I told you Victor Spritz's record was not in my file cabinet, indicating to you that I hadn't seen him professionally."

"Correct, I remember that."

"Well, there's the deception. His record wasn't in the cabinet. It was sitting on my desk." Corliss picked up a swollen folder. "Look at this—it's the thickest file I have."

David wasn't as fazed by the "deception" as he was curious about what would follow.

"I was really protecting my patient's confidentiality at the time, but it was a juvenile way of doing it. To relieve my anxiety over the impulse to show you the record, I repressed it with reaction-formation, a common psychological mechanism. And now that Victor's dead and has no relatives that I know of, I feel I can say, yes, he was a patient of mine."

A bit much? There's got to be more.

"And my description about the person with diffuse rage? That was Spritz to a tee. I wanted you to know that. Also, one other thing. A Nick Medicore, the chief of detectives downtown—he came in yesterday. He wanted to know if Charlie Bugles' son, Bernie, was ever a patient of mine."

"Was he?"

"No."

"No file in your cabinet, or on your desk. Or in your garage?"

David smirked but the psychiatrist laughed nervously, then said, "You're angry with me."

"No, I understand completely—just forcing a little levity before what will undoubtedly be another day loaded with my own brand of anxiety. Have you got any leftover reaction formations?" David's laugh was legitimate and he sensed Corliss' was, too.

"Incidentally, did the detective ask any more questions?"

"No, not really. He saw that I was between patients."

"Not even about Spritz?"

"No, it was pretty short and sweet."

David took out his pad. "Now then, Sam, fluke of all flukes, you called me, but I was about to call you. I have some questions to ask—more or less official. Is that okay?"

"Sure." The psychiatrist thrust up his hands, mimicking surrender. "But I didn't do it. I swear I didn't."

David was not amused but covered it with, "I don't think you did it ... or them ... either, but I've got to go through the motions with most everyone but the butler. And I'd have to include him, too, if hospitals had them." Corliss did appear amused.

"Do you own a motorcycle?"

Corliss hid a smile with his hand. "You're serious?"

"I'm afraid so."

"Then, a question first and the answer second. What would an old man like me be doing with a motorcycle? And, no, I don't and never did."

"Do you own any guns?"

"No."

"Good." David made a check on a blank page. "Next, and this might be harder because it was over three days ago, but can you recall what you were doing last Friday night?"

"Of course—not hard at all. I remember because that was the night our son and his wife and two children arrived from Cleveland. They're staying for a week."

"When did they arrive?"

"Oh, about suppertime."

"And you were home with them all night."

"Yes, we had lots of catching up to do."

David scratched behind his ear with one finger but kept his eyes fastened on Corliss' for a moment. "That's really all I have, Sam, thanks."

"And thanks to you for coming. I feel better."

"So do I."

David did his assessment thing on the walk to the Hole. Alibi seems sound. But all that gibberish about a guilty conscience? I don't know. He's either one terrific actor who's pulling out all the stops, or else he's terribly innocent. Terribly.

26

At the Hole, David was pleased to find his small base of operation had not been included in the shutdown. He hemmed and hawed as he offered Belle a stack of reasons why he shouldn't call Russ Selby, president of the Reliable Box Factory.

"Look, David honey," Belle said, frenzied, "people do it all the time. Sometimes, workers have to be called away. Phone the guy and ask if Robert can be spared for five minutes, for heaven's sake."

"But I don't want to jeopardize his job. Selby will think he's either very sick or in trouble with the law."

"No, he won't. First, Selby's your good friend, your classmate. Second and third, he knows Robert's father was hacked to death, and he knows five minutes of an employee's time is a drop in the bucket. Fourth, this is no big deal, really, so why are we discussing it?"

"I'm glad we came to an obvious conclusion," David said, pumping his fist in the air. "Get him on the phone."

Belle drew in her breath, then let it out slowly.

If ever there were a commercial building shaped like the products it housed, the Reliable Box Factory was it. And if ever David had felt bathed in the strangest of odors—of a mixture of glue and ink and new paper, and of machinery oil and grease thrown in—this was it. The place was teeming with its work force and whirling noises as he was ushered into a small reception room by a female secretary who, five years ago, he would have engaged in conversation.

Within minutes, the door opened and he flipped a tattered *Popular Mechanics* back onto a table. Robert strolled in and gave him a puny handshake.

"Sorry to take you away from your work, Robert." They sat facing each other, on red wooden boxes with simple backrests.

"Are you kidding?"

"I like your shirt," David said. It was red and long-sleeved, and above its breast pocket was a black and white imprint of a box containing the letters "RBF."

"Thanks. See these letters? I tell everybody they stand for 'Robert Bugles Factory.'"

"Why not? It's funny but it makes sense." David's words were lost in Robert's burst of laughter.

"Rob—ert," David said in his most conciliatory voice, "I haven't seen you since … when? … I suppose it was last Thursday at Bruno's. Remember, in the locker room? You were kind enough then to answer some questions. Well, as I'm sure you know, Victor Spritz has been murdered since then, and we have reason to believe all the murders at the hospital are somehow tied together." David leaned forward as if to share a secret. "Anyway," he continued, "I thought I'd drop by to ask you a few more questions—the same ones I'm asking anybody connected with the victims: family, friends, co-workers and so-forth. Is that okay?"

"Sure, that's okay." Robert looked at the clock on the wall. "It won't take too long, will it?"

"Not at all. Just a minute or two." David launched into his interrogation as if he expected Robert to reconsider cooperating. "What kind of car do you drive?"

"A van. It's a Dodge Caravan. Ninety-three."

"Do you own a motorcycle?"

"No, sure wish I did. Maybe I will someday."

"How about a gun? Do you own one?"

"No." It was Robert's turn to lean forward. "But my dad had both of them—a long time ago when I was a young kid."

"Both of them?"

"Yeah, a motorcycle and a gun. I saw the gun in the closet."

"How long ago was that?"

"Way back. I was a kid. Mom was still alive. She used to yell at him about having a gun."

"I see." David produced his notepad. "And just for the record, do you remember the color of the motorcycle?"

"Sure. Black. It was a big black one." David printed "BLACK" in the pad. He saw Robert glance at the clock.

"Just one more thing and we'll be through," David said. "Friday night. Can you tell me where you were?"

Robert cocked his head in apparent thought. "That's when who-do-you-call-it got killed, right?"

"Right. I'm not implying anything at all, Robert. It's the same question I have to ask everyone."

"I'm not worried about nothin'. I went over to

Bruno's again."

"That was at the usual time—five?"

"Yeah, five … five to … around seven."

"And after that?"

"I went home."

"And you did what?"

"Watched the shows."

"What shows?"

"Whatever's on the TV— you know— on Fridays."

David consulted the blank pages of his pad. "That's all, my friend. You've been very helpful. Thanks a lot." They stood and, in lieu of a handshake, David briefly put his arm around the shorter man's shoulders. "You put in a long day here?" he asked, feigning small talk.

"Eight hours. That's the morning shift."

"You start real early?" David opened the door.

"Seven. Then we go to three-thirty. They give us a half-hour for lunch."

In the Mercedes, David contacted Musco. "Be out front at your place at one o'clock."

The Chestnut Apartment Complex, a red brick structure of eight units, was an uphill five-minute walk from the hospital, on a street otherwise reserved for physicians' and dentists' offices. Word had it that once Charlie Bugles had assumed the Board chairmanship years ago, he finagled a shady deal for his complex to be built by the same construction company retained by the hospital for future expansion projects.

David had made house calls there and was familiar with its interior layout: two floors of four units each, their entrances approached from a center stairwell. He recalled the opposing doors on each landing, the knockers instead of bell buttons, the name cards askew in their metal frames. From Red Checker to Chestnut Street, he thought of his Tactical Plan and "Suspect-6" list, particularly in the context of Robert's involvement or noninvolvement in murder, of his operative role or nonoperative role in the drug ring. Almost reverently, David had stuck to the Plan and satisfied all but one of its items. This, the inspection of Robert's apartment, was the last, and he didn't expect it to reveal much. Because if his suspicion that the entire batch of killings was drug-related and that Robert was incapable of managing a territory, the upcoming inspection became academic.

The weekend warm rains had melted the snow and two days of sun had dried its waters. David drove into the building's rear parking area, its glossy black asphalt patterned in yellow lines that ran parallel to one another like the teeth of an immense comb. Musco followed in his cab. A solitary car was parked in an end space.

David bent an ear to faint music and dog whimpers coming from within the building as they walked into the main back door. He examined the nameplates on the first level where the music disappeared but the whimpers changed to nasty growls. He assumed Musco would knock somewhere on the second floor shortly, and hoped they wouldn't be as loud. Upstairs, they found Robert's door. David asked Musco to dispense with the knock, indicating its combination with the utterances of an aroused dog would attract further attention. The cabby did his thing and took his leave.

Inside, David rushed through the three-room apartment in a span of time commensurate with his expectation of discovering any worthwhile evidence. The apartment was simply furnished and neat. Neater than he had anticipated—except for the hall closet he passed as he prepared to leave.

Its bivalve doors were partially open, wedged by a rectangular object which came to his knees and was draped by a bedsheet. A clothes hamper? He lifted up a corner and ran his hand over a cold black surface underneath.

David yanked off the sheet and arched at the sight of a metal safe. Stupified, he crossed his arms and attempted to fathom its meaning. He kneeled down to try the door. Its dial was gone and in its place was a round hole rimmed in variable shades of grey and blue. Blowtorched! He thought he smelled burnt metal but wasn't certain that burnt metal had an odor. He swung the door open without effort. Except for the scorched dial that lay on a shelf, the safe was empty.

27

After a brooding lunch at home, David concentrated on the meaning of the invaded steel safe. He had no doubt it was Victor Spritz who had removed the dial with an acetylene blowtorch. The gloves in his laundry room. The fireclay. David hadn't thought it necessary to rub off a sample from the lining of the safe to prove a definite match. He was satisfied.

But what did it mean? How did it fit? Would it fit? Should he dare contact Robert and attempt to bait him into providing some answers without giving away his trespassing? Later, maybe. No, better still—he checked his watch—martial arts at five. He'll probably be there.

David had a time gap to fill. He called Kathy to inform her of the revelation at Robert's and to get her take on it. She expressed the same bewilderment he felt. He verified she had dispatched a person to stake out Bernie's place—a Detective Paul Johnson.

David uploaded new material into his computer, not only to stay current but also—typing slowly, hopping back and forth to previous entries—attempting to hit upon a magic solution to the puzzle of murder and drugs. Again, he saw the pattern of Tuesday/Saturday in print, but he wove no magic.

He picked up a stack of Polaroids by the side of the computer and flipped through them. The bottom one was the rear shot of the red Honda motorcycle in the hospital parking lot. He had looked at the picture before but only in passing. He now thought its tire was too narrow for a chunky tread design, and that its overall appearance was that of an early model, perhaps one of the earliest. There was no fender, no saddlebags or backrest or luggage rack. But he noticed a blue Connecticut license plate and some words on plastic strips above and below it. He reached into his desk drawer for a small magnifying glass. The words read, "One Day At A Time."

It had always been one of David's favorite sayings— trite but good, he believed—and often therapeutic for his patients. One day at a time. But somehow he hated to see the expression on the back end of a motorcycle that was quite likely connected to murder.

Bruno Bateman's martial arts studio was never over-crowded fifteen minutes prior to the beginning of evening classes.

David found him sitting at his desk off the main gym. His was more of a cage than an office, its walls composed of wire mesh, corkboard and posters of men and women acting out various judo moves.

"Hi Bruno, what's happening?"

"Hey there, glad you came tonight. You need some time off, I'll bet. Rid your system of bad energy and all the … " David had heard the sermons on the balance between good and bad energies many times before, and he would have interrupted even if he weren't prone to stepping on people's words.

"Will Robert Bugles be here, do you know?"

"No, I don't. But as long as you asked, I think I'd better mention something. He came to me last week and wanted to brush up on karate-chops and the old two-knuckler. That's fine, I thought. But when he asked about *atemiwaza*, I got concerned. Self-defense? Okay. But striking to kill? That's different. I don't know if he plans to use it, but I thought you should be aware of it."

Once again, David still-framed in his mind. This time the scene was that of Victor Spritz—an overkilled Victor Spritz riddled by bullets and bruised about the neck.

His voice quivered when he thanked the Grand Master and, striding to the locker room, he quickened his pace in anticipation of finding Robert there. Suddenly the matter of the burned safe was not a burning issue.

But he didn't find him there, nor had Robert arrived at five-fifteen when David decided to validate his suspicion in a different way. He reached for the cellular phone at his hip when he felt its ring.

"Yes?"

"Dr. Brooks?"

"Yes."

"This is Detective Paul Johnson. Kathy Dupre asked me to ... "

"Yes, I know. Thanks for your assistance, Paul."

"He just arrived."

"Bernie?"

"He just now walked in. Kathy gave me a photo of him. He didn't spot me, of course. You want me to remain here?"

"Yes, yes, by all means. He may be our murderer, Paul. I'm leaving shortly and should arrive there at—" He pointed at the numbers on his watch and calculated— "at eight, eight-thirty. Keep me posted." David punched the "Off" button and reclipped the phone to his belt.

He felt momentarily cemented to the floor, now torn between following up on Bruno's disclosure or dashing to New York City again. He chose to check out Robert first.

He ripped the cellular from his belt and obtained the home phone number of Hollings' acting chief pathologist from the hospital operator.

"Hello, Jake? Sorry to bother you at home, but where's the body?"

"Whose body?"

"Victor Spritz, who else?"

David arranged to have a portable x-ray machine rolled into Albright's Funeral Home at five-forty-five. The technician was to take front and lateral views of Spritz's cervical spine.

Thirty minutes later, David and Dr. Jake Reed waited in the hospital's Radiology viewing room for the films to develop.

"More than once, I've seen severe injuries with complete dislocations and cord compression," Jake said, "and death or quadraplegia—delivered by so-called karate experts who miscalculated. In this particular case, the satellite bruises above the linear one looked like the result of a karate-chop but I couldn't say for sure. And as you probably remember, the bony column felt in line when I palpated it."

"Maybe we should have taken a picture of it then and there."

Jake continued as if deaf to David's aside. "I can tell you one thing, though. If there was a bona-fide karate-chop, one of those cervical vertebrae is partially dislocated on the other. And, if not, then the bruising was a result of thumb compression or some such thing. Certainly not a chop."

The technician burst into the room with four films. David snapped them onto the viewing box. He read them as negative: no karate-chop.

28

Back at the Hole, David called Kathy. "I don't have time to elaborate right now, Kath, but Robert is clean and our man is Bernie Bugles. I'm leaving for New York in a few minutes to bring him back."

"Not so fast, now," Kathy said. "Think of the legalities. What about your authority to bring him back? Have you thought about that?"

"I have, and I've got it."

"You've got it?"

"Yeah, I'm bigger than he is." David left no room for comment. "What I'll do is haul him in and you make the arrest."

"Forget it, we'll issue an arrest warrant. That's simpler."

"Kath, I've come this far and I want to bring him in myself. Play it my way, okay? If he eludes me, God forbid, issue the warrant."

"Then I'm going with you. No—we're going with you. I'm calling Nick."

"I can handle it."

"David, I'll only worry about you. We're coming

along," she said, sternly.

He weighed the pros and cons of Kathy's decision. "Okay, you're the law," he groused, like a man complaining that rain was wet. "I'm here at the hospital. How long will it take for you to get here?"

"I'll ring Nick right now—hope he's home. Half an hour?"

"I'll be out front."

In the interim, David sat at his desk, reflecting on Robert's request of Bruno, odd under the circumstances, he thought. Buttressed, however, by Dr. Jake Reed's opinion that no karate-chop had been levied against Spritz, he eventually interpreted the request as Robert's way of asking for a total self-defense package, not realizing how deadly *atemiwaza* could be.

David was tempted to call Robert not only to inform him he was picking up his brother on suspicion of murder but also because, in so doing, he would be absolving him of culpability. Deep down, David felt a strange sense of relief that final arrows pointed away from Robert. For some time, he believed the box company shipping clerk was the odd man out in a global narcotics enterprise and deserved to be left alone, not subjected to the same scrutiny as Bernie or Spritz.

Yet, he reasoned, the blood of a half brother is still thicker than water. David fretted that Robert would tip off Bernie about his departure. So the dilemma was how to inform him and, at the same time, prevent him from warning Bernie. Solution? Ask him along.

After consulting the phone directory, he called his home. "I have some news for you, Robert. It's not about you personally, I assure you, but it's the kind of thing best handled in person. Any chance of our getting together, say, in your parking lot out back?"

"Right now?"

"Right now. It's that important. I can be there in ten minutes."

David filled the silence with a flash forward of either Kathy's or Nick's car trailing his to Manhattan. They'd better keep up, but I'm not about to help.

Finally, Robert cleared his throat and said, "Sure, Dr. Brooks, if you say so. I'll be out there."

Seven minutes later, on the shiny asphalt, David popped out of his Mercedes and draped one arm over its top as he shook hands with Robert. Familiar barking seemed shriller in the thin night air. David chose his words carefully after stumbling on the first few, "I think … I believe … I owe it to you to inform you I'm leaving for New York to pick up your brother on suspicion of murdering Victor Spritz, and I was wondering whether you'd like to accompany me?"

The sky was black, the lighting economical, and David couldn't read Robert's reaction.

"Bernie?" he said softly, a cigarette caught on his lips, his head shrouded in clouds. He looked around. "Bernie wouldn't hurt a fly. You sure?"

"Yes, Robert, the evidence is overwhelming."

"And you want me to go with you? Why?"

Now, the giant leap. "Because I want to avoid any violence, and having you along will give the situation some stability. You can talk him into cooperating, if it comes to that."

Head bowed, Robert silently moved a pebble around with his foot, and David quickly added, "Plus you probably know the directions better—you know some karate—all those things." Hurry up, man, I don't have all night.

Robert stomped the cigarette into the asphalt and zipped up his tight Flying Tiger jacket. "Yep, I'll go," he said. "But you got the wrong man there, Dr. Brooks."

As he swung back to the hospital, David felt fortunate that Robert hadn't asked why a gun wouldn't be trained on his brother and, therefore, why his assistance was needed. Because David had no answer.

Conversation on the Merritt Parkway was meager as David was caught up in a farrago of loose ends. He tracked the lights of Nick's Buick in his mirror and gave hollow responses to Robert's recurrent but mild rejection of Bernie's guilt. He kept the top up despite the reading of forty-four on the dashboard's digital thermometer.

On the Henry Hudson Parkway in New York City, David twitched at the pulsation of his cellular phone.

"Yes."

"It's me, Paul Johnson. The lights just went out in his apartment. He could be leaving. Shall I tail him if he does?"

"You have a car phone?"

"Yes."

"Tail him—but, wait. Call me back to let me know definitely." David spoke as if he were conversing over a piece of string from tin can to tin can. He clicked off and, after turning on the audible ring, placed the phone on the seat between his legs.

"Tail him?" Robert said. "You mean Bernie?"

"Yes." For most of the trip, David had included Robert in his glances to check right-hand lanes. And for most of the trip, he saw a wake-me-when-it's-over expression. But the phone call had changed things.

David crushed the accelerator pedal. Nick's lights kept pace.

The phone rang.

"Yes."

"He left all right. Heading north on Amsterdam. I'm right behind him."

"Good. I just pulled into 125th. Now if he comes this far, we're golden. I'll wait at the corner—where Amsterdam comes in. What are you driving?"

"A grey Ford Taurus."

"What's he driving?"

"Looks like a Lincoln. Black. Man, he's got three antennas on the thing! One's as long as the car. Bends in the wind."

"Stay on the line."

"You bet. We're almost there. And—in fact—yes—I can see you. Black Mercedes convertible?"

"That's me. And I see him coming. Slow up at the corner and let me sneak in ahead of you."

"Will do. By the way, did you know there's a white sedan parked right behind you?"

"Yeah, local gendarmes."

"Local?"

"I mean Connecticut. They begged me to come along. Try to wedge in before them and then keep close to my tail. That'll bust their you-know-what."

"As long as I don't have to answer to anyone back home."

"I'll accept full responsibility. I'm signing off now … and, Paul?"

"Yes?"

"Great job. Many thanks."

The four-car motorcade streaked over cracked cobblestone and tar, beneath outrageous neon, past pushcarts and inconsiderate buses trying to horn in. David took down the license number of the lead Lincoln. After rounding the back side of a fruit and vegetable wholesaler's, it swerved up a ramp and spurted onto Riverside Drive. It sliced its way to the far left and, gathering speed, weaved among lanes, with David and the others in its wake. Within seconds, ten to twelve cars separated Bernie's from the rest. But, within minutes, the gap had narrowed to five as David intensified the pursuit north, focusing on the bobbing antenna. At 178th Street, the Lincoln veered to the right. The Mercedes followed, climbing a series of narrow bends, along graffiti-sprinkled walls, in the direction of the George Washington Bridge.

29

At a virtual standstill, David drummed on the steering wheel as he inched along the lower deck of the bridge spanning the Hudson, four bumpers behind Bernie. Their starts and stops did little to change their position between George Washington's two massive towers, and for as far as David could see, the line ahead was a packed one. And also for as far as he could see, he counted three closed-down lanes, leaving three open for passage. He hated exhaust fumes at tollbooths, and this was worse.

Robert, whose periodic glances back at the others had fast annoyed David, said, triumphantly, "I think we lost them."

"We're not trying to lose them, Robert, we're trying to gain on the son-of-a-bitch ... sorry, I mean, Bernie ... ahead of us." David's comment was reflexive because he was lost in a debate over whether or not to abandon his car and rush Bernie on foot. The risk that traffic might unsnarl settled the issue, and David stayed put. He wondered whether Bernie knew he was being followed.

He checked the time. They had been stalled within the towers for twelve minutes. He pretended to scratch his ankle but nudged the snubby there, and then tucked his elbow into the Beretta Minx. He thought about chewing gum. And with time on his hands, he harked back sheepishly to his reference to Robert's brother and, though he felt Bernie was guilty of murder, still he hadn't yet been convicted. David would atone for an insensitive remark.

"It must be tough on you, Robert. First, your father is killed in an awful way. A terrible way. And now your brother's being hunted for murder."

Robert shifted his weight. "Yeah, I know," he said and paused. "One day at a time."

In the honking that began to crescendo, David wasn't sure he caught the last phrase. Still, he felt his body grow taut. He turned and glared at Robert. "What did you just say?" he asked.

Robert hesitated, then answered, "You mean 'I know?' I said, 'Yeah, I know' because you said ..."

"No, no, not that. What did you say following that?"

"One day at a time?"

Oh, my God! *Him*, after all? I'm chasing the wrong man and the killer's along for the ride? David gripped and regripped the wheel as fear welled up and gagged him. Couldn't this have been avoided?

In the silent vacuum that followed, he felt Robert's eyes on him and he struggled with the urge to confront his passenger. About the phrase he used, about his relationship with Victor Spritz, about where he really was Friday night. And, about the red motorcycle with the saying attached to its license plate.

But he looked straight ahead. If Robert had tipped a losing hand—a killer's hand—the middle of a traffic jam

on the George Washington Bridge was no place to ac-
knowledge you'd seen it.

David felt the charged circuitry of his mind, coiled
lights as bright as those strung along the cables above.
Motive. Opportunity. Means. Past conversations. Options.
Is Robert armed? But most pressing: Did he get it? Does
he realize his giveaway? David wished he could vitiate
the suspense once and for all.

He convinced himself, however, not to question further, not to draw his Minx, not to call out to the police
officers roaming among the congestion of cars and angry
drivers hanging out their windows and doors. It was a
combustible situation: there might be gunfire. Get off the
bridge first.

Whistles blew. Lanes moved. Officers waved their
arms. Finally, on the New Jersey side of the bridge, at the
edge of Fort Lee, cars fanned out and resumed the speed
of the highway.

"Pull over, Dr. Brooks," Robert said, baring his ca-
nines.

In the rush of traffic, David caught only a glimpse of
Robert, but it was sufficient to behold a pistol aimed at
his head. David's eyes darted about wildly as he tried to
maintain the wheel. He felt his foot tremble when he eased
up on the accelerator and, changing to the far right lane,
his eyes met the glinting pistol head-on. Even in semidarkness, he recognized the gold grip and stainless steel
barrel of a Kimber .45, the same model missing from
Spritz's collection and the same model used in his murder.

"Hurry it up," Robert said, menacingly.

"Put the gun away, Robert," David said, galvanizing

the same composure he'd shown in medical emergencies. "Just do like I say, Dr. Brooks."

David slowed further and spotted a boarded up factory set back from the highway, two-hundred yards ahead. He decided he must act swiftly and knew that the maneuver he had in mind hinged on a precise synchrony of reflexes, on certain movements he hoped were engraved in his muscles. The factory's sprawling vacant lot was exactly what was required to execute it.

He coasted into the lot, floored the accelerator for a count of two and slammed on the brakes. Quick as a spark, before Robert's whiplash sequence was completed, David unleashed a karate-chop to his wrist. The pistol squirted to the floor. Robert clutched the wrist, groaning and writhing in his seat.

"You broke my arm!" he screamed.

David's intention had been to stun, not to shatter, and the trick was to deliver the blow with the speed of a chop but without its force. "I didn't break it, Robert, but believe me, if I'd wanted to, I could have."

David used his Minx to wave Robert out of the car and to lean over the hood. As he frisked him, two cars screeched in beside the Mercedes. Nick and Kathy piled out of one, Detective Johnson out of the other.

"Forget Bernie," David said with finality. "Here's your killer."

During the return to Connecticut, David decided to drive with the top down. Robert sat handcuffed in the passenger seat, Kathy in back with her new Beratta Cougar at her side. The others followed close behind.

At the factory lot, David had capsulized what had

happened, and Kathy had phoned back to headquarters to have Bernie seized on suspicion of major narcotics trafficking. In a brief verbal exchange out of earshot of Robert, Nick joined her in claiming that jurisdiction of the suspect belonged to the state of New Jersey. But David argued that if there were no arrest and Robert agreed, they simply had embarked on a joyride and could then turn around and head home. Robert agreed, and at the border in Greenwich, Connecticut, Kathy arrested him.

Midway on the Merritt, Robert continued to massage his wrist and, for the first time since he'd complained Nick resorted to police brutality in appling handcuffs, he spoke. "Dad would have been proud of me," he said, mawkishly. "I got the guy who cut him up." Neither David nor Kathy responded.

"He was a good dad. He gave me the motorcycle, you know. He was the boss and he was tough, but that was no reason to kill him like that. He was a sick man, too. That there pancreas. Those bastards—they were doin' good but Spritzy wanted more."

David wished he had a tape recorder turned on.

"Bernie!" Robert shouted, "that son-of-bitch, he hated my father."

David had not anticipated such an effusive suspect and decided to milk the opportunity. He began gently.

"Robert, you said your father—who incidentally was a friend of mine at the hospital—you said he gave you the motorcycle. Is that the red one?"

"Yep. It's a 1969 Honda. Only two more like it all over the world. His friend in Japan gave it to him four years ago and Dad gave it to me on my birthday." Robert brushed an eye with his cuffed hands. "He told me not to drive it where people could see me because Japan wouldn't like it. So I only used it out in the country, except when I went back to get Spritzy. He wanted to kill me, you know, but I took care of him."

"So that was you with the rifle at the cemetery?"

"Yep."

"Where did you get it?"

"Spritzy gave it to me. He told me to shoot you with it, but you were looking at me."

"I see. And where did you keep the motorcycle?"

"In my Dodge Caravan." He spoke like a child.

David reached further. "And you say that Victor Spritz killed your father. How do you know that?"

"Bernie told me. And Spritzy killed those doctors, too."

"Do you remember that one of the doctors was killed with a dagger?"

"Yep."

"Where did the dagger come from? Do you know?"

"That was Bernie's. Well, not really. It was Spritzy's. He had two of 'em and gave one to Bernie."

David was sure of the answer to the next question. "I suppose that was you who fired the shot at Detective Dupre and me?"

"I'm sorry I did, Dr. Brooks. I'm sorry now."

30

The air had chilled during the night. In the morning, David noticed the single birch outside police headquarters was not as white as the thin snow cover.

He ambled into Kathy's barren office. It was nine-fifteen. She stood near a makeshift serving table, fixing coffee.

"You want some?" she said, her voice husky. He nodded.

"Who wrote up the report last night?" he asked.

"I did. Robert would still be talking if I hadn't started turning my lights out."

"When was that?"

"Oh, about three."

"When did you get here this morning?"

"Seven-thirty. I overslept. And when I arrived, the parking lot was crawling with media. Nick went out and had a nice little press conference right on the front steps. He gave you all the credit."

He looked at her solemnly. "How many coffees have you had?"

"Three. Did you know that Robert once helped co-ordinate drug shipments to Florida?"

"Robert?"

"Yes. And I'd have to say, David—the longer he talked, the more I realized he's no dummy. His father knew that."

"What do you mean?"

"Read the report." Kathy carried two coffees to her desk, sat and pulled a folder from the top drawer. She handed it to David who leafed through several of its pages.

"Here," she said, getting up, "park yourself here, and take your time. I just remembered. I'll be in Nick's office checking on what's happening with Bernie in New Jersey." She gulped down her coffee, waited for David to sit, kissed his forehead and left.

He scanned the report and was impressed with its question and answer layout, an easy read. His sleep had been shallow and, despite his closeness to the case, he would have been in no mood yet to suffer through the usual soporific narrative. He parodied an archetypical beginning: "The alleged perpetrator took a swing at the alleged victim—blah—blah—blah—blah."

David read that Charlie Bugles was the kingpin of an international narcotics ring with cohorts in Istanbul, Tokyo and Cartagena. Spritz and Bernie were lesser but equal cogs in the operation and shuttled between the United States and foreign drug territories in South America, Europe and the Far East. But Spritz had become "too damn greedy" and "Dad wanted to cut him out and have me take his place. He changed his sources in Istanbul and gave me the list. So Spritzy cracks my safe and steals the names."

David spilled a drop of his coffee, whisking aside the report as if it were the Magna Carta. He skipped ahead.

"Question: Why did you kill Victor Spritz?"

"Answer: Because he butchered my Dad. Because he stole the secrets in my safe. Because he called me stupid."

"Question: What exactly took place Friday night, January 23rd?"

"Answer: Spritzy called me and said he wanted to show me some new drugs at his office. He wanted to kill me, you know. But I wanted to kill him, too. With karate. I drove my motorcycle there because I didn't want anybody to see my Dodge. I got there early, I guess. He wasn't there and the back door was open. I looked outside and saw the light in the ambulance. I went in and Spritzy pulls a gun, but I was too fast for him and I choked his neck. Then I picked up the gun and shot him good."

"Question: Then what did you do?"

"Answer: I got scared and ran home. I took the gun with me and sneaked back for my Honda later on."

Kathy came into the room and David closed the folder and swept it to the side.

"Well?" she said. She perched on the corner of the desk.

"Well, I'm glad it's over," he replied, grunting as he rose from the chair. "My knee's sore, my back's sore, and my brain's sore." He moved stiffly to the service table to return his coffee cup.

"You'll be happy to hear," Kathy said, "the hospital's gearing up again."

"How do you know?"

"Just before you got here, Foster called to congratulate us. So did Dr. Corliss. Foster said he might throw a celebration party at his home."

"Oh, wonderful," David said, yawning. "And what's with Bernie?"

"They located him in Teaneck. He didn't resist. In fact, he waived extradition and should be here before the morning's over. We'll charge him as an accessory because of the dagger. Then we'll turn him over to the feds on the drug thing. Are you going to Spritz's funeral?"

David gave her a frosty look. "No way," he said.

"Good, hang around for Bernie. We'll see what he says."

"Nah, that's a no-brainer. He'll deny everything: the lovely scrap metal letter, the Asian goons with their stupid barbed wire, ransacking my place last week." David massaged his decision scar before adding in a softer tone, "Even that he believed I was onto his drug operation."

He walked over to Kathy, lifted her to her feet and folded her hands in his. "But will you do me a favor," he said. His voice was firmer.

"What's that?"

"Tell him thanks for not breaking any of my stuff."

"Amen. And what are you doing today with nothing more to chase?"

"That's easy. First, I call Belle to see if she can whip together some house calls for this afternoon. Then, I go home and put my guns to bed. Maybe even myself for an hour or two. Care to join me?"